Granville County Library System

D0007672

ST. DALE

SHARYN McCRUMB

 WHEELER PUBLISHING

Copyright © 2005 by Sharyn McCrumb

All rights reserved.

Published in 2005 by arrangement with Kensington Books, an imprint of Kensington Publishing Corp.

Wheeler Large Print Hardcover.

The text of this Large Print edition is unabridged.
Other aspects of the book may vary from the original edition.

Set in 16 pt. Plantin.

Printed in the United States on permanent paper.

Library of Congress Cataloging-in-Publication Data

McCrumb, Sharyn, 1948–
    St. Dale / by Sharyn McCrumb.
        p. cm.
    ISBN 1-58724-909-X (lg. print : hc : alk. paper)
    1. Earnhardt, Dale, 1951– — Influence — Fiction.
2. Tour guides (Persons) — Fiction.   3. Automobile
racing — Fiction.   4. Southern States — Fiction.   5. Fans
(Persons) — Fiction.   6. Travelers — Fiction.   I. Title:
Saint Dale.   II. Title.
PS3563.C3527S7 2005
    813′.54—dc22   2005000392

*Also by Sharyn McCrumb
in Large Print:*

Ghost Riders

This Large Print Book carries the
Seal of Approval of N.A.V.H.

ST. DALE

ST. DALE

SHARYN McCRUMB

WHEELER PUBLISHING

Copyright © 2005 by Sharyn McCrumb

All rights reserved.

Published in 2005 by arrangement with Kensington Books, an imprint of Kensington Publishing Corp.

Wheeler Large Print Hardcover.

The text of this Large Print edition is unabridged.
Other aspects of the book may vary from the original edition.

Set in 16 pt. Plantin.

Printed in the United States on permanent paper.

Library of Congress Cataloging-in-Publication Data

McCrumb, Sharyn, 1948–
    St. Dale / by Sharyn McCrumb.
      p. cm.
    ISBN 1-58724-909-X (lg. print : hc : alk. paper)
    1. Earnhardt, Dale, 1951– — Influence — Fiction.
2. Tour guides (Persons) — Fiction. 3. Automobile
racing — Fiction. 4. Southern States — Fiction. 5. Fans
(Persons) — Fiction. 6. Travelers — Fiction. I. Title:
Saint Dale. II. Title.
PS3563.C3527S7 2005
813′.54—dc22   2005000392

To Jane Hicks — the voice in my headset

National Association for Visually Handicapped
---------------------- *serving the partially seeing*

As the Founder/CEO of NAVH, the only national health agency solely devoted to those who, although not totally blind, have an eye disease which could lead to serious visual impairment, I am pleased to recognize Thorndike Press★ as one of the leading publishers in the large print field.

Founded in 1954 in San Francisco to prepare large print textbooks for partially seeing children, NAVH became the pioneer and standard setting agency in the preparation of large type.

Today, those publishers who meet our standards carry the prestigious "Seal of Approval" indicating high quality large print. We are delighted that Thorndike Press is one of the publishers whose titles meet these standards. We are also pleased to recognize the significant contribution Thorndike Press is making in this important and growing field.

Lorraine H. Marchi, L.H.D.
Founder/CEO
NAVH

★ Thorndike Press encompasses the following imprints: Thorndike, Wheeler, Walker and Large Print Press

There are only three real sports: mountain climbing, bullfighting, and automobile racing.

— Ernest Hemingway

CHAPTER 1

Midnight in Mooresville

It was not the end of the world, but you could see it from there.

She was an educated woman with a career and a social position to think of, so she lived in fear that people would somehow hear about what had happened to her in April, 2002, on the road to Mooresville. A supermarket tabloid might shanghai her into the role of prophetess of a new religious cult, and people she didn't even know would point and stare at her, and think she was a fool. The thought made her shudder. So she only told a few friends about the peculiar incident, and those to whom she did mention it heard it in the guise of a funny story, open to some logical explanation. Of course, Justine had accepted it without batting an eye. Had been *expecting* it, she said. But then Justine's vision of reality was pretty much at right angles to everybody else's anyhow. She herself had stopped trying to make sense out of it, because she had the terrible feeling that Justine was right, and that what really happened was . . . what really happened.

"It was not the road to Damascus," she would say, invoking Biblical precedent, "because I had just come from there. Damascus. Virginia, that is, a little town on the Tennessee line, a couple of hours north of where I ended up that night, broken down on the side of a country road en route to Charlotte."

It was not the end of the world, but you could see it from there. She had pulled over to the side of the road and flipped on the visor light to look at the map. Now the engine wouldn't start, her cell phone had no signal, and the dark road was deserted. She hadn't seen a house for miles. In this landscape of pine woods and barbed-wired pastures, streetlights were nonexistent, which was part of the problem. She must have missed a road sign somewhere back there when she got off I-77.

She was pretty sure she was somewhere north of the city, maybe in Iredell County, which wasn't where she was supposed to be at all. By now she ought to be closer to the city limits of Charlotte, but the sky was dark — no bleed-in of artificial light from the sprawling city — so that was past praying for. It was her own fault, though. What kind of an idiot would have taken Justine's advice about a shortcut in the middle of the night? *Justine*, for heaven's sake, who could get lost in a revolving door. Now here she was, trying to follow a set of directions that were vague at best. *("Turn left after the yellow house, only I think they painted it.")* Oh, why had she listened? There wasn't much traffic on I-77 in the middle of the night, for heaven's sake. If she'd stayed on the Interstate, she'd be home by now.

Well, at least Justine had been right about that Oriental rug outlet in Virginia. It had been a great place, cheaper than any place she'd found in Charlotte. Of course, that was exactly the sort of thing that Justine invariably was right about. They called Justine *"The Shopping Fairy,"* because if you wanted designer purses, Italian tile for your bathroom, or an 18th-century American candle stand, Justine could tell you three places to find it and which one was the best deal. Just don't ask her about more mundane matters, like how much to tip the waitress, the name of the Speaker of the House, or how to find Charlotte when it's too dark to read road signs.

Granville County Library System
11 P.O. Box 339
Oxford, NC 27565

She ought to turn off the radio to save the battery, but Garth Brooks was singing "The Dance," and she couldn't bear to cut it short. Another two minutes wouldn't matter. Later, Justine would tell her the significance of that song, marveling that she didn't know it already, but she didn't. That intersection of those two roads of pop culture was simply not on her radar screen. She had not been thinking about *him*. She was sure of that.

She had not been afraid, because she'd always considered country roads, even dark ones, infinitely safer than cities, and also because she didn't see herself as the sort of person who was likely to be attacked by a crazed killer lurching out of the woods. Unfortunately, she was exactly the sort of person whose car broke down just when she became good and lost. She didn't suppose Justine could be blamed for that. Now it looked as though she could either spend a long night in the car or ruin her Ferragamos hiking up a country road.

She had cast her eyes up to the closed sunroof of her Chevy and said to no one in particular, "Please get me out of this."

She did not remember hearing the other car drive up. She had been too busy seething and working out the withering remarks about shortcuts that she would make to Justine the next time she saw her, while in the back of her mind she was trying to decide whether to walk or wait in the car until sunup.

The tap on her driver's side window startled her so much that she dropped the useless phone. In the rearview mirror she saw a black car parked close behind her bumper, its headlights illuminating the scene so that she could see the shadow of the man at her car door. She lowered the fogged-up window, half expecting to see a baby-faced highway patrolman — certainly not expecting to see that eerily familiar face: mustache, sunglasses and all, *(sunglasses?)* beneath the red and black "Number 3" Goodwrench cap.

She was so startled that she said the first thing that popped into her head, which was, "I thought y'all's headlights were just decals."

He nodded. "Yep. Sure are."

She glanced out the back windshield into the glare of headlights bright enough to illuminate the road. "But —"

"Your car died?" he asked.

She stared up at him, so detached from the experience that she found herself thinking, *You're one to talk.*

13

He nodded, no trace of a smile. "Okay, then. Flip the hood latch and I'll take a look."

"Are you —"

But he ambled around to the front of the car without giving her time to finish and raised the hood while she peered out through the windshield, thinking that it was a good thing she was driving a Chevrolet. He probably *would* know how to fix it.

As he poked around in the engine, she sat there, her mind full of so many simultaneous thoughts that she forgot to get out of the car to actually voice any of them: *I don't think it's the battery, because the power windows still work . . . Excuse me, sir, are you who I think you are? . . . Justine, it was him. Hat, white firesuit, everything. Of course, I'm sure! I saw his face plain as day in the headlights . . . Listen, I have half a tank of gas, so it's not that . . . The Reverend Billy Graham, Dear Sir: Can dead people come back from heaven or wherever and fix cars? . . . Hey, I was a big fan of yours . . . well, my friend was anyhow . . . and I just wanted to say how sorry I am . . .*

The roar of the engine interrupted the flow of her thoughts.

He slammed the hood and walked back,

dusting off his hands, one against the other. "It ought to get you home," he said.

"What was wrong with it?" she called out above the noise.

He gave her a look that said *Do you know anything about cars?* and shook his head. "It runs fine now. Wanna race? I'll spot you a quarter mile."

She shook her head. "I don't think so . . . sir. Besides, I'm lost."

"Oh. Well, the Interstate's ahead a few miles. Keep on going. You're on Route 136 in Iredell County."

"Oh. Okay. But I think it's Route 3 now. They renamed it."

A smile flickered across his face, and she thought, *He hadn't heard about that,* which emboldened her to say, "Well, thank you. Um — Thanks for your help. And — Look, before I go — do you have any messages for — well, for anybody?"

Again the smile. "Yeah," he had said after a moment's consideration. "For Mike Waltrip." As he walked away, the man in the white firesuit said, "Tell him: next February, pray for rain."

CHAPTER II

The Also-Ran

Harley Claymore

"You didn't say nothing about having to wear this cap." The scruffy man in front of Harry Bailey's desk held up the black baseball cap with the white number 3 sewn above the bill. The script "3" had cartoon angels wings on either side and a halo encircling the top. "Now, I don't mind staying sober for ten days. Well, I *can,* anyhow, but you didn't say nothing about this fool cap."

"Perhaps it was an oversight on our part." Mr. Bailey consulted the folder on his desk more for effect than for information. Then he looked at the dribbles of rain sliding down his office window, obscuring the view of the Dumpster outside and the one tree in the parking lot, still leafless in early April. Finally he looked up at the scowling man in the damp leather jacket, who was leaving a puddle of rainwater on his tile floor. It was an odd jacket — it had black and white checkered patches from

16

shoulder to elbow and red trim on the pockets. The perfect costume for the tour, Mr. Bailey thought; though perhaps he ought not to put it like that to this proud little man who apparently wore such out-landish garb in the street. And he was objecting to the cap? He repressed a shudder. At least it would have kept the fellow's head dry.

"An oversight," he said again, forcing a smile. "On the other hand, Mr. Claymore, *you* claimed to have won the Daytona 500 in 1992."

The fellow had the grace to blush. "Well, I won a race *at* Daytona in 1992, anyhow. Same track, just not the hyped-up race. They have other events there during the year, you know."

Mr. Bailey nodded. "We looked it up on the Internet. We here at Bailey Travel may not know much about stock car racing, Mr. Claymore, but I assure you that we do know how to Google. It says here that a driver named Davey Allison won the Daytona 500 in 1992. Perhaps we ought to see about hiring him for this job instead."

Harley Claymore snorted. "Hell, mister, don't you know *anything?* If Davey Allison was still on this earth, I reckon things would be so different that you could have

17

hired Earnhardt himself for this damn bus tour, 'cause Davey could have driven rings around —"

"I thought you wanted this job, Mr. Claymore. I thought you needed some ready cash." He was watching the scruffy little man, noting the signs of strain about the eyes and the tinge of sweat on the upper lip. He would take the job, all right. He just wanted to save face by protesting his reluctance. That was all right. Mr. Bailey had allotted three minutes for that.

"Well, that's the God's truth," Claymore said, running a hand through his broom-straw hair and shrugging. "You think Brooke Gordon was a rottweiler, you should meet *my* ex."

Mr. Bailey nodded sympathetically, wondering who Brooke Gordon was. "We pay a thousand a week plus expenses," he said. "The tour begins in August at the Bristol Speedway. It will get you to the tracks should you wish to make contact with some of your former associates about future employment."

"Well, you said you needed a NASCAR expert for a guide, and I sure qualify as that —"

Mr. Bailey glanced at his notes. "Although, in fact, you are not the third-generation NASCAR driver you claimed to be? Your father did not win the race at Talladega in 1968?"

Harley Claymore smiled and shifted his weight to the other foot. "Well, he didn't lose it, either. Bill France didn't build that track until '69."

Mr. Bailey continued to give him the unblinking stare of a monitor lizard. Harley blinked first. "Well, okay," he said. "My dad drove dirt track in the Fifties. Wilkesboro and Hickory, and all, before the sport got so jumped-up. He raced against Lee Petty and Ralph Earnhardt — none of 'em made enough to live on back then. And my grandaddy — he did his driving with a second gas tank full of moonshine on U.S. 421, and that ought to count for something 'cause Junior Johnson got started that way too. Only, Junior made it to the pros and my people didn't. Until me."

"Yes. You did drive in the Winston Cup circuit — until you lost your sponsor. A drinking problem."

"Naw, I can hold my liquor pretty well. I think it was food poisoning that day. But, you know, when you throw up all over a Make-A-Wish kid, the sponsor finds it tough to forgive and forget. Uh — I won't

19

be driving the bus, will I?"

Mr. Bailey closed his eyes. "Mercifully, no."

"Anyhow, I do know racing front to back. Stats, cars, trivia. All of it. Like . . . let's see . . . like: Junior Johnson used to run races with a chicken riding shotgun with him in the car. Did you know that?"

"Indeed, no. Does it happen to be true?"

"It does. Google away, Mr. Bailey. But, see, about this trip — I thought you were just taking racing fans on a tour of Southern speedways."

"That, incidentally, yes." Mr. Bailey paused, choosing his words carefully, "But actually the trip is being advertised as an Earnhardt Memorial Tour."

"Oh, sweet Nelly," Claymore groped for the plastic chair and sank down in it. "You're shitting me, right?"

"I assure you we are perfectly serious," said Mr. Bailey, who had decided that sarcasm would be wasted on Harley Claymore. "Unlike you, Dale Earnhardt did win the Daytona 500, you know."

"Well, *finally*. He lost it about twenty times, too. He and that soap opera lady who always lost at the Daytime Emmys ought to have got together."

"Dale Earnhardt is a legend," said Mr.

20

Bailey. "Did you know him while you were on the circuit?"

Harley shrugged. "Seeing a black Monte Carlo in my rearview mirror still gives me the shakes." He waited a moment for Bailey to correct him, but there was no response. Back when Harley was still racing they had been driving Luminas, not Monte Carlos but, in deference to Mr. Bailey's ignorance of the finer points of racing, he had mentioned the model that was now synonymous with the Intimidator.

"I mean, do you have any personal anecdotes about yourself and Dale Earnhardt?"

"Nothing out of the ordinary. He put me in a headlock once in a drivers' meeting. Snuck up on me from behind, like he always did. And he gave me the finger a time or two when he went past me in a race."

Bailey closed his eyes. "Perhaps we should forget about personal anecdotes. I'm sure we can provide you with some more heartwarming stories about Dale Earnhardt."

"What the hell for?"

"Because he is a legend, Mr. Claymore. — Is that your real name, by the way?"

"Sort of. It was Harley Clay Moore. My dad was into cars, and he named me for Harley Earl and Willie Clay Call." He

21

could see that the names meant nothing to Mr. Bailey to whom the world of motor sports was a never-opened book. "Anyhow, I changed it when I was eighteen and needed a classy name for the pros. See, claymores are . . ."

"Scottish swords. I know."

"Well, I was going to say antipersonnel mines in Nam. I thought it sounded cool."

Mr. Bailey's face was impassive. "No doubt," he said. "We were discussing this job. Bailey Travel has been inundated with requests for a tour in honor of Dale Earnhardt. More than a year since his death, people are still grieving. They are putting the number three in Christmas lights on their houses and I'm told that they raise three fingers during the third lap of every race as a tribute to him." He paused, shaking his head wonderingly at the improbability of such a thing. "We have received considerable correspondence and even e-mails from articulate and re-spectable people —" *People with valid credit cards,* he thought, "— who tell us that they want such a tour, a gesture of mourning if you will, in honor of the late Mr. Earnhardt. People want to say good-bye. The speedways where he drove are now shrines. People want to pay homage at his racing shop in Mooresville. They long to lay a memorial wreath on the track at Daytona."

Harley Claymore shook his head. "I never would have believed it."

"Well, he died on camera in the biggest race of the sport, so that was a factor. Our firm offers a Graceland Tour as well, so we are familiar with the mindset of the devoted fan and the fact that people need closure. They feel that they know these celebrities. It is a personal loss. I grant you that we here at Bailey Travel did not expect to find this phenomenon in a NASCAR milieu. But there it is."

"But he was just a regular guy who had a knack for driving," said Harley. "He was good at it, but so was Neil Bonnett. So was Tim Richmond. And nobody's painting their numbers on billboards."

Mr. Bailey shrugged. "Why Elvis and not John Lennon?" he said. "Who can explain these things? Still, Mr. Claymore, the demand is there and we have devised this tour accordingly. To celebrate the life and sport of NASCAR's most illustrious driver. And now we need someone — a name, if you will, to host it."

"Well, I guess I ought to be flattered that y'all picked me instead of Geoff Bodine."

"Mr. Bodine was unavailable. So do we have a deal?"

Harley Claymore looked at the Winged Three on his cap and sighed. "Eleven hundred plus expenses?"

"And you are to be sober and reliable. And you will wear that jacket and the number 3 cap."

"Deal." Claymore spit in his palm and held out his hand.

Harry Bailey pointedly ignored the gesture. "We will write down some suggestions for the commentary you will be making on the tour. For instance, you might begin by explaining why Dale Earnhardt is associated with the number three."

"Why?" said Harley.

"Well, because that was the number painted on the top of his race car."

"No," said Harley. "I meant *why should I explain that?* Will there be people from other planets coming along on this tour?"

"Ah-hah. Most amusing," said Mr. Bailey. "And one last thing — for the duration of the tour you must say and think that Dale Earnhardt was the greatest driver who ever lived."

"Oh, sweet Nelly."

So Harley Clay Moore had taken the job.

What choice did he have, really? What choice would any of them have had? Dale Earnhardt with his ninth-grade education had worked in the mills in the lean years and back in Alabama Neil Bonnett had been a pipe fitter. Their educations mostly took place out of school, hanging out in local garages or watching their fathers tinker with stock cars. Cars were what mattered; everything else was a distraction.

He sat on the sagging bed in the cheapest motel room he could find and watched the SPEED channel on the television, but it was showing drag racing. Nobody he knew. The brown polyester bedspread was patterned with stains and cigarette burns. He'd lived better than this once, but those days were getting more distant all the time and now he was used to rundown places like this. Why spend good beer money on fancy digs?

All Harley had ever wanted to do was race. The new face of NASCAR — the sponsors, the autographs, the hat and tee shirt sales were all necessary evils — the cost of the ride. Money buys speed, and the only way to get enough money to race these days was to cozy up to the national sponsors. Forget swearing, or chewing, or fighting off-track. Hell, you even had to knock the corners off your accent these days, because NASCAR was national now, and vanilla was the flavor of the month — every month.

He had mugged it up in Bailey's office because showing your desperation never gets you anywhere, but he couldn't fool himself. He had to find a way back in.

CHAPTER III

Tri-Cities

"Wake up, Bekasu! We're coming into Tri-Cities, and Stewardess Barbie wants your tray table put back before we land."

Rebekah Sue Holifield squinted one eye long enough to close the tray table, and then resumed *her* former upright and locked position.

From the window seat Cayle said, "She's not asleep, Justine. She's just being passive-aggressive again."

"Being a spoilsport is what it is," said Justine. "A deal's a deal. Last year she made us go to Toronto and sit through a whole week of operas that sounded like they were neutering the pigs, and this year was my turn to choose." She lunged across her sister's lap to peer out the window. "*Wake up*, Bekasu! You're going to miss seeing where Alan Kulwicki's plane went down!"

Cayle stopped scanning the fast-approaching ground, shut her eyes, and turned away from the window.

"Who?" Bekasu's sigh meant she didn't much care.

"You remember Alan Kulwicki," said Cayle, carefully not looking. "First Winston Cup champion from up north? Wisconsin. Degree in chemical engineering?"

"Okay. — *Get off me, Justine!* — Unless the crash was yesterday, I'm sure there's nothing to see down there now."

"Just a field," said Cayle. "Same as it was back in 1993. He was the reigning champion, flying in for the Bristol race one cold, wet night. April the first, it was. Anyhow, his private plane was right ahead of Earnhardt's, on the descent, maybe two minutes out when it went down in a field a few miles out on approach."

"Yeah," said Justine, "and about a minute later, Earnhardt's plane touched down at the airport. You know, I always figured Dale traded paint with him, trying to land first."

Cayle shivered. "Dale wasn't even flying his own plane, Justine. Of course he wasn't. You know that. She's putting you on, Bekasu."

Bekasu closed her eyes again. "Justine,

you know that I would rather participate in a reenactment of the Bataan Death March than go on a NASCAR tour, so would you please not make it any worse with your tasteless commentary?"

"Oh, don't be a pill, Bekasu. If I'd wanted to vacation with a killjoy, I'd a brought an ex-husband. Now hand me my carry-on, will you? I want to put on my Dale hat before we land."

"We could be on St. Lucia right now," said Bekasu. "In that mountaintop hotel where one wall of your suite is just a wide open space facing the Caribbean, but no . . ."

"Well, I'm sorry that we're not having a vacation you can brag about to all your friends down at the courthouse, Your Honor, but I need to say good-bye to Dale."

"Justine, you never said hello to Dale."

"I did *so.* One time at Talladega when that guy who owned a Chevy dealership took me on to pit road, we went right up to Dale and shook his hand, and I wished him luck in the race."

"Which he lost."

"Yes, but that's not the point. The point is that I have been a Dale Earnhardt fan through five presidents and two husbands, and this tour is part of my grief process,

29

and I think as my sister you ought to respect that. Not to mention Cayle. After what happened to her, how can you even argue?"

Cayle winced. They'd promised they wouldn't talk about it.

"I'm here, aren't I?" said Bekasu. "But I am not going to wear that stupid black tee shirt with the Winged Three. And another thing, Justine: if your luggage takes up so much room on the bus that they have to get rid of a passenger, I will be the first volunteer to stay behind."

"Can you finish this argument in the terminal?" said Cayle. "I think they want us to get off now so they can clean the plane."

"Okay, let me just ask them if they have any extra little bottles of Jack Daniels, in case the bus doesn't stop near any liquor stores. Y'all want some of those pretzel things, too?"

Bekasu rolled her eyes at Cayle. "I still say we should have drugged her and carried her on to the flight to St. Lucia."

Near the baggage carousel, a lanky dark-haired man in a leather jacket with checkered sleeves stood holding a Winged-Three placard. As people retrieved their suitcases, they began to congregate around him.

"Do you recognize him?" Cayle whispered to Justine. It was no use asking Bekasu. "They said a real race driver was going to host the tour. Is he one of the Bodines?"

Justine narrowed her eyes, sizing him up. "Well, I can't recognize all the young ones, but he's not one of them. I don't think he's a Bodine, but we'll find out when he opens his mouth. They're from New York, so if this guy sounds normal, he's not one."

"Welcome to the Tri-Cities Airport, folks," said Harley Claymore.

Justine and Cayle looked at each other and shook their heads.

Harley Claymore found that he was more nervous about meeting this group of tourists than he had ever been about driving 180 miles per hour with Bill Elliott on his bumper and Earnhardt closing fast.

Glad-handing people was not one of his more conspicuous talents. He was not afraid of coming up against a question he couldn't answer. He was more nervous about the prospect of facing a question he had heard so many times that a rude retort would escape his lips before he could stop himself. Candor was his besetting sin.

He remembered an unfortunate encounter with a lady reporter during his racing days. She hadn't been a sports reporter, he knew that. Maybe she had been down to collect recipes from the wives or some such meringue assignment, but he had encountered her at one of the pre-race appearances that sponsors liked to host in hopes of getting their driver more publicity.

The woman in black, swizzle-stick thin and improbably blonde, had tottered up to him on stiletto heels and announced that she was a writer. She named a magazine he'd never heard of, but he nodded and smiled as if she'd said *Newsweek*. Then she wanted to know if he was a driver. Harley said that he was, and asked politely if she followed the sport.

The woman had attempted to wrinkle her botoxed forehead, and then — with the air of someone making a startlingly original observation — she smirked and said, "But it isn't really a sport, is it? Just a bunch of cars going around in a circle for three hours."

"Yes," said Harley. "Yes, it is." He tapped her little green notebook. "And writing isn't very hard, either, is it? Just juggling those same old twenty-six letters over and over again in various combinations?"

In retrospect, he conceded that the remark had not been designed to convert the lady to an appreciation of NASCAR. She had stalked off in a huff, with the word "redneck" hovering on her lips, which Harley didn't mind, because if people are going to think it, they might as well say it, and then you know where you are. He'd ended up going home alone. Maybe the reporter had found someone more willing to humor her. Thinking it over later, Harley supposed that he could have found a more diplomatic answer to the woman's tiresome display of ignorance. Maybe for future reference he should have asked Alan Kulwicki, who had an engineering degree, what technical explanation you ought to give to people who didn't realize that the "simplicity" of the sport was merely their own incomprehension, just as — to the uninitiated — opera was noise and modern art a paint spill. The difference was that people felt embarrassed about not understanding music or art, but they seemed almost smug about being ignorant on the subject of motor sports. Stupidity as a status symbol. He never did understand it, but it had long ago ceased to surprise him.

What did surprise him was that people seemed to think of NASCAR as a

Southern sport, despite ample evidence of "continental drift" in recent years. Jeff Gordon was from California; Kurt Busch from Vegas; Ryan Newman had an engineering degree from Purdue; and Ricky Craven was from Maine. There were races now in Phoenix, Vegas, and all over California; one in Texas, one out in Michigan, another in New England, one at the Brickyard in Indy where the Indianapolis 500 was run — and still undernourished women thought it was a redneck pastime that couldn't really be called a sport. Fortunately, Harley believed that ignorance was a constitutional right, so he did not feel called upon to show people the error of their ways.

What worried him was the idea that NASCAR might not be Southern *enough* anymore. Harley thought of all those clean-cut college-educated guys with their flat broadcast accents, and he felt like a unicorn watching the Ark set sail. Was driving no longer enough? The thought of speech lessons and plastic surgery made him shudder. Such things hadn't been an issue when Dale started driving in '79, but times had changed. It cost a quarter of a million dollars to field a stock car — and the car was good for only one race. Then you needed another quarter of a million to compete the next Sunday somewhere else. That's why an advertisement in the form of a small decal pasted on the hood of the race car could cost that sponsor $80,000 *per race*. The days of the independent owner-driver — as the Bodine and the Elliott teams had been — were past praying for. Now you needed a principal sponsor with deep pockets. A beer company. A detergent manufacturer. A cereal maker. And in return for millions of dollars to fund your racing team, the sponsor would feature you in their TV commercials, and put life-size cardboard cutouts of you in the aisles of grocery stores all over the country. So you'd better be good-looking and you'd better be good at glad-handing with the corporate types, and you'd better be a pussycat with the press and the fans. Because winning races was nice, but public relations was *everything*.

Harley figured that the ten-day tour would be good practice for his affability.

On the appointed day for the tour to begin, he had arranged to meet the bus driver in the airport parking lot so that the two of them could compare notes before the arrival of the tour group. Harley had flown into Tri-Cities on the last flight the night before, and planned to spend the night in the Sleep Inn a mile from the airport, but since Bailey Travel had neglected to make a reservation for him many months in advance, no accommodations were available for that night, so he had spent the night sleeping in a chair in the airport waiting room. He'd shaved and changed in the men's room an hour before the passengers' flight was due in from Charlotte.

To prepare himself to guide the tour, Harley had driven part of the route on his own that week, traveling from Martinsville to Darlington, covering all the tour stops north of Georgia, anyhow. Since the tour would end after the Southern 500 in Darlington the following Saturday, Harley had ended his practice journey there, leaving his car at the speedway, so that he could just drive away at the end of the tour — hopefully with a new job in racing to go to.

At least it was going to be a small tour. Only thirteen people instead of the fifty or so that Mr. Bailey said they usually tried to book. "How come it's so few people?" Harley had asked. "I'd have thought people would be falling all over themselves to do an Earnhardt tour."

"Well, they were," Mr. Bailey admitted. "We were inundated with applications. But since we have never driven this route before and since you're an inexperienced guide, we thought we'd make this a test run."

Harley thought about it. "This tour includes race tickets," he said. "And you didn't plan far enough ahead to get enough tickets for Bristol, did you?"

Harry Bailey reddened. "We could only get fourteen," he said. "We thought three months in advance was a gracious plenty."

Harley smirked. "Try three years."

The tour bus was easy to spot: a full-size silver cruiser with the Winged Three emblazoned on the side and the slogan "The Number Three Pilgrimage." Harley shook his head at the sight of it, wondering if the driver would be expected to knock cars off the road while trying to pass them. He didn't plan to suggest it.

He rapped on the glass of the passenger door, and waited while the driver cranked it open.

"Harley Claymore," he said, shoving his leather duffel bag into an overhead bin. "I'm the NASCAR guide."

The man behind the wheel was red-faced and barrel-shaped. Not a former racer judging by the look of him. *Good thing this bus has a door,* Harley thought, picturing the fellow trying to get in and out of a stock car through the window as drivers always did since race car doors are welded shut for safety.

"Ratty Laine," said the driver, making no attempt to stir from his seat. "Bailey Travel. Here to drive this bus and help you out with the touring bits any way I can."

"Are you connected to racing?"

Ratty Laine rubbed his chin while he considered this. "I can be," he said at last. "Cousin of the Pettys, maybe, or a former member of somebody's whatchacallit — pit crew, maybe?"

Harley blinked. "What do you mean 'I can be'? Don't you know?"

"Well, it's up to you, really. If you think this tour group will have a more rewarding experience thinking that I'm an old racing guy, then that's what we'll tell them."

"But *are* you really?"

"Oh, *really.* I never talk about *really.* That's why they call it private life, you know. 'Cos it's private. Like I said, I'll drive the bus and get you where you want to go, but the way I see it back story is your job. Just tell me who you want me to be." He stretched and yawned. "Sorry. Long drive in this morning."

"Where from?" asked Harley.

"Home," said the driver.

"Where's that?"

"Where do you want it to be?"

"Can't you just be yourself?" asked Harley.

The driver shrugged. "No percentage in that. Well, you think it over. You've got an hour or so before the plane lands. My schedule says they all met up in Charlotte and took the same connecting flight up here."

"But what am I supposed to tell them about you?"

"Look," said Ratty Laine, "I've been driving for Bailey Travel for umpteen years now. When we go to Opryland, I'm the ex-mandolin player for the Del McCoury Band; on Civil War tours, my great-great-grandaddy fought at Gettysburg — which side he was on depends on the home states of the people on the tour; at Disney World, I was the voice of Goofy or a talking teapot in the latest movie, or something; then at —"

"Okay. I get it." Harley shook his head. "Look, I really was a race car driver, so why don't we forget the fake identity for you this time, and tell the folks you're the

39

bus driver, all right?"

Ratty shrugged. "Whatever. But I could say that I was the guy who changed Richard Petty's mufflers."

Harley sank down in the front seat next to the driver. It was going to be a long trip. "Stock cars don't have mufflers, Ratty," he said. "Now, where can I put this?" Harley held up a bulky canvas bag. "Won't fit in the overhead. I won't be needing it very often."

"What is it?"

"My firesuit. Driving boots. Helmet."

The driver raised his eyebrows and looked from the canvas sack to Harley's face, now tinged pink with embarrassment. "What and where will you be driving?" he asked.

"Well," said Harley. "I just thought I'd come prepared. You know, in case somebody gets food poisoning or something and they need a replacement driver *toot sweet*. Drivers carry their own gear. It's like jockeys with saddles, I guess."

"You mean you brought gear to drive a stock car? On the off chance?"

"Well, yeah. I mean, just in case. You never know."

Ratty gave him a look that mixed pity with scorn, but he made no comment except to haul himself out of the driver's seat and amble down the steps to the pavement. "Help me open the hold," he said, tugging at the door to the outside luggage compartment. "It ought to fit in there. Way toward the back." *'Cause you won't be needing it.* The unspoken words hung in the air.

"Thanks," said Harley, shoving the bag into the hold. He never went anywhere without it.

Ratty slammed the door to the luggage compartment, and wiped his hands on his khaki trousers. "You sure you don't want me to have a racing connection?"

Harley shook his head. All they needed was to get caught in a lie and lose the trust of the tour group. Mr. Bailey would probably dock their pay back to lunch money. "Look, Ratty," he said. "I'll handle all the NASCAR patter. You just worry about getting these folks from one place to the next, and feeding them, and scheduling pit stops."

"What?"

"You know — trips to the toilet."

"Oh, sure. No problem. And, you know, that reminds me, if race car drivers go for three straight hours without ever getting out of the car, how do they — ?"

41

Harley sighed. Sooner or later everybody asked that question. "It's hot in a stock car," he said. "If you sweat enough, you don't have to pee."

The airborne contingent of the tour, eleven people as diverse as any other group of airline passengers, wore expressions that ranged from barely contained excitement to a polite wariness that might have been shyness. The exception was one well-dressed woman who looked as if she had been brought there at gunpoint.

Justine elbowed her sister in the ribs. "Stop looking like a duchess at a cock-fight!" she whispered. "There's some perfectly nice people here. I told you there would be. Check out that hot young guy in the yellow Brooks Brothers sport shirt with the little dead sheep emblem — bet you ten bucks he's Ivy League. And look at that distinguished fellow in the clerical collar. Oh, isn't that sweet? He has a little boy with him. Oh, Lord, I hope they're not on their honeymoon!"

"*Shut up,* Justine," Bekasu hissed back, edging away.

Spotting their fellow tour members had been easy. Along with the tour itineraries the Bailey Tour Company had sent

Winged Three caps to match the one worn by the guide and the driver. Several of the travelers had dutifully worn the headgear on the flight, in addition to various other items of Dale-bilia currently displayed about their persons: Intimidator tee shirts, sew-on patches featuring a replica of Earnhardt's signature, and, in the case of one enterprising matron, a hip-length cotton vest featuring a montage of black Monte Carlos, made of the special Dale Earnhardt fabric sold at Wal-Mart.

There were more women than one might expect to find on a NASCAR-themed tour. At least on a tour that wasn't dedicated to Jeff Gordon. Funny that so many women liked Earnhardt, Harley Claymore was thinking. You'd think he'd remind them of their ex-husbands. You'd think women would see Earnhardt as the weasely redneck version of the Type-A executive: the man who puts his career first, his hobbies and his buddies second, and his family a distant third. Except for all that money and fame, Earnhardt seemed to Harley an unlikely sex symbol. Wonder if he'd even managed to snag a date for the high school prom. Ah, no. Scratch that. Dale had dropped out in junior high, before the social pressures of adolescence became much of an issue. The glad-handing imperatives of his future success must have come as an unpleasant surprise for him, but he had made the transition as gracefully as he took the turns on the track. If he hadn't, he'd have been left in the dust years ago.

Harley would like to have mused on the whole charisma aspect of the Earnhardt mystique in a group discussion on the bus, but he half suspected that the driver was under orders to report any heresies to Bailey Travel, so if he wanted his paycheck, he had better not get caught letting in daylight on the magic.

Most of the men looked like normal sports fans in a spectrum of ages, except for the preppy and the minister, who were both dutifully wearing their Winged Three caps, but with the air of generals in camouflage. And he hadn't expected the little boy. The kid was the color of chalk, and he didn't seem to have any eyelashes, but he seemed chipper enough. The man with him wore a priest's collar — so probably not the boy's father. He wondered what the story was. Harley held out his hand to the boy. "Hello, Sport," he said. "I'm your guide. You a big Dale fan?"

The boy glanced up at his companion and received an encouraging nod. "Yep."

Well, there was a precedent for that, thought Harley. He wondered if the sick kid was hoping for a miracle from Dale. As he recalled it had been the other way around. "How old are you, Sport?"

The kid gave him an owlish look. "Name's Matthew. I was born the year Sterling Marlin won the Daytona 500," he said.

Harley let out a sigh of mock exasperation. "Well, that's no help. Sterling won in both '94 and '95, so I still don't know your age."

The kid grinned. "Okay. The first time. So, who won Daytona the year *you* were born?"

"Ben Hur," said Harley. He wondered how long it would take him to match names and faces. He glanced again at his tour notes, raising a hand to indicate that a speech was forthcoming.

The tour members clustered around him and the chattering subsided.

"Tri-Cities," he said, savoring the word. "Now you know we didn't choose this airport just because it has a *three* in its name." He'd had four months to work on his NASCAR patter for the tour and to bone up on Earnhardt connections to any place they might visit. Now he thought he could

45

recite Earnhardt trivia without clenching his teeth. If he didn't run out of nicotine patches, he might even survive the tour.

"Of course, this is the closest airport to the Bristol Speedway, our first stop. It was at the Bristol Motor Speedway that the young Dale Earnhardt won his first ever Winston Cup race. April 1, 1979, to be exact. Bobby Allison came in second in that race. This evening we'll be attending the Sharpie 500 there." To identify the race's sponsor, Harley waved the Sharpie fine point permanent marker with which he had been taking roll. "Dale Earnhardt himself used to fly into this very airport for the race."

For a moment everyone paused, picturing an Earnhardt wraith walking past the baggage carousel, but Harley, who had been warned not to let the tour turn into a death march, changed the subject. "Did everybody's luggage make it? Okay, good. Then let's get started. This is the very first Dale Earnhardt Memorial tour, and my first tour of any kind, so there ought to be a yellow stripe painted on the bumper of the bus. Just go easy on us, folks. Over there hauling your suitcases onto the baggage cart is our bus driver, Mr. Ratty Laine. I'm your guide — Harley Claymore, NASCAR driver . . ."

A hand waved in the air. "Do you do those hair growth commercials on television?"

"Hair growth?" Harley caught the reference. "Ah, no. That would be Derrike Cope. The way you can tell us apart is: Derrike sort of accidentally won the Daytona 500 in 1990, and I didn't lose my hair. Hard to say which of us got the better deal." He looked down at his notes. "Okay, speaking of Derrike, let me do a head count. We'll get acquainted later. Right now the bus is waiting for us in the parking lot, and we have a wedding to get to."

Justine waved her sunglasses. "I thought we were going to the Bristol Speedway."

"Yes, ma'am, we are. The race is this evening. The Sharpie 500. *After* the weddings. Didn't they put that in the brochure?"

"Heck, no. If they'd told us about a wedding, I would have brought somebody besides my sister."

"I don't think they're taking volunteers, ma'am. We're just going to watch. Oh, but two members of our party are getting married there by pre-arrangement. You'll meet them shortly."

"Well, if you need somebody to marry them, my sister's a judge. Hey, Bekasu, can you marry people in Tennessee?"

While Justine scanned the crowd for her,

47

Bekasu edged her way toward the silver-haired minister. She wanted to make allies before people figured out that she was with Justine. "Hello," she said with an after-church smile. "I'm Rebekah Sue Holifield, and I am a hostage on this tour. How are you . . . Father . . . ?"

"Just Bill," he said quickly. "Bill Knight. I'm Episcopalian, but not that High Church." He put his hand on the boy's shoulder. "And this young fellow is Matthew Hinshaw, who is the real racing fan. He's promised to help me along, because I'm new to all this."

"Well, how do you do, Matthew," said Bekasu, shaking his small hand. "You may have to help me along, too. I came with my sister, who is the real fan, and our cousin Cayle, who had a most extraordinary experience. She — well, never mind. Anyhow, I'm the novice in our party. To me, stock car racing looks like rush hour in Charlotte."

"Except they're going 180 miles an hour," said Matthew solemnly. "And sometimes they hit each other on purpose."

"Matthew, why did our guide say there ought to be a yellow stripe painted on the bumper of the bus?"

The boy grinned. "That's easy! In NASCAR rookie drivers have a yellow stripe so that people will know to cut them some slack. Hey, Bill, do you mind if I get a drink before we leave the airport? It's time for the white pill."

Bill Knight fished a dollar out of his pocket. "Need any help, Matthew?"

The boy shook his head and ambled away.

"Your . . . nephew?" asked Bekasu.

"No. Matthew lives in the children's home affiliated with the parish. This is what he wanted to do more than anything else in the world. He's . . . ill."

Bekasu watched the little boy saunter away clutching his dollar. "Yes, I thought he must be," she said. "I'm so sorry. Is this one of those wish tours for him?"

"Yes. He's such a great little guy. He's had a rough year. He lost his parents in a wreck, and a few months after that he was diagnosed with his illness. I suppose a tour is hardly enough compensation for all that tragedy, but it's all we could do. I'm accompanying him, because the tour coincided with my vacation — not because I share his passion for NASCAR. He's a bright little fellow, though. His doctors assure me that he'll be all right for the duration. I worry, of course."

"It's an interesting choice," said Bekasu.

49

"He did choose this tour himself, I suppose?"

Bill Knight sighed. "Oh, yes. I think everybody was a little surprised about that, but he was adamant."

"I'd have thought that most children would have picked Disney World," said Bekasu.

"Matthew is an unusual boy. Very — focused. It occurred to me that perhaps an intense interest in one subject keeps him from thinking about all the things in his life that he can't control, which is nearly everything. And I suspect that his parents were race fans, but he's never really said. I can't say I'd have preferred Disney World over this, but I wish I could have got him interested in my hobbyhorse, which is the medieval pilgrimages of the Church. Santiago de Compostela . . . Canterbury . . . But, I suppose a trip abroad would have been too risky for his condition. And perhaps too expensive. Anyhow, young Matthew preferred *this* pilgrimage. Insisted on it, in fact."

"I didn't know what to expect on this tour. Most tour passengers are middle-aged married couples, but I was afraid that a NASCAR tour might be a busload of drunken good old boys. This one seems to be neither."

"Did your husband not want to come along?"

Bekasu hesitated. It was still hard to say it casually. "He died a few years ago. A few months after that Cayle got divorced, and that's when we decided that the three of us would make a tradition of vacationing together."

"That sounds like fun."

"It has its moments. But I didn't bargain for a racing tour. What about you? Are you from —" Bekasu cast about for a city associated with racing. "Umm — Indianapolis?"

"Rural New Hampshire. Our town is just north of Concord, about eight miles from the New Hampshire International Speedway. It's called Canterbury, so you can imagine my delight when I was posted there, but, much to my chagrin, I have since discovered that Thomas Becket takes a backseat to Ricky Craven there. I keep trying, though. Slide shows, lectures at church functions. To no avail — racing fever is rampant. Still, the drivers are very good about coming to the Children's Home and signing photos for the kids. One of them played Santa Claus for us a few years ago, they tell me. I'm new to the parish, so I'm still getting used to all this. I didn't really know much about Earnhardt until the day he died."

"I think we're being rounded up," said Bekasu, glancing back at the cluster of travelers. "And here comes Matthew with his drink."

Cayle appeared beside them. "You'd better come on, Bekasu. Justine is asking whether they have a P.A. system on the bus, and I'm pretty sure she's going to try to sing *Matthew, Mark, Luke, and Earnhardt . . .*"

Bill Knight laughed. "Must be a Southern hymn," he said. "Not in our hymnal in New Hampshire."

"Excuse me while I go and rain on my sister's parade," said Bekasu.

CHAPTER IV

The Knight's Tale

February 18, 2001

Some time that week, he could not remember exactly when, Bill Knight had seen a shooting star flame out against New England's winter sky. He recalled thinking, as he always did at such a time, *The heavens themselves blaze forth the death of princes.* You could hardly call it a premonition. Still, he never quite forgot it.

That Sunday morning several big-screen TV owners in his congregation had invited him to Daytona Parties, the Super Bowl of NASCAR they called it, but he had begged off, saying he had paperwork to do. Instead, he promised them that he would watch the race by himself while he worked. An easy promise to keep, since he usually did turn the television on for noise while he wrote.

He was looking forward to a relaxing evening alone with his slides and lecture notes: pilgrimages in the medieval Church, an erudite and obscure pursuit that had long afforded him a retreat from all things modern and confusing, like church sound systems and word processing software. He hoped to work up a lecture on the pilgrimage of Santiago de Compostela, and so he told himself that the bookish evening might indeed be considered "work" or at least the preparation for work. He would skip the Daytona parties with a clear conscience but, in deference to local customs, he knew that he must not skip the race itself. It was a restrictor plate race — whatever that meant.

The culture of stock car racing took some getting used to for someone who had heretofore believed that any major sport must end in the word "ball." When Knight had first arrived, so many people asked him to remember 19-year-old Adam Petty in his prayers that he had looked up the name in the church directory to see which of the boy's relatives belonged to his congregation. Finally, someone explained to him that Adam Petty had been a novice driver, NASCAR royalty — the grandson of Richard Petty himself — who had been killed in a wreck at New Hampshire International Speedway that summer. People grieved for this famous stranger, killed in race practice in their vicinity, much as they would have mourned a local high school quarterback killed on I-93. For Bill Knight, it was a mindset that he was still trying to master.

With barely a glance at the race already well under way, he had settled in behind his desk with an NHIS coffee mug (a legacy from the parsonage cupboard) and a stack of note cards and photographs. He thought about muting the sound of the race so that he could concentrate on his work without distraction, but he decided that this would not be quite in keeping with his promise to watch the event, so he left it on. Later, he came to think of this decision — or indecision — as a sign that some higher authority than his parishioners had meant for him to watch this race, but he never shared this pious thought with anyone. His flock of New Hampshire Protestants might believe in messages from heaven as a general principle, but they frowned upon modern-day citizens — particularly their own clergymen — claiming to receive them. As befitted their Puritan ancestry, his congregation preferred a faith of austere simplicity, one in which visions and prophecies were as suspect as incense.

A native of western Maryland, Bill

Knight was still charmed by the Christmas-card prettiness of the countryside, and of Canterbury itself with its colonial homes, its village green, and the Shaker Museum, all a few miles north of Concord, off I-93, and — as if in apposition to all this colonial simplicity — one exit away from the New Hampshire International Speedway. Loudon, as the track was usually called for the sake of brevity, after the town closest to it, was a major regional attraction, bringing in tourist dollars and turning traffic into a nightmare one weekend each July and September. Then 50,000 people converged on the area for the NASCAR Winston Cup races. He soon realized that the sport would affect him whether he followed it or not, just as residents of Wimbledon or St. Andrews cannot be indifferent to tennis or golf.

On the whole, he was pleased with the area and with the cadence of life in New England. Less than a hundred miles from the amenities of Boston, but well out of the city sprawl and traffic — he had the best of both worlds. No one had objected to a divorced pastor, and none of the unattached women in the congregation had made any strenuous efforts to change his marital status. He found the people kindhearted, but a bit shy with newcomers, and he was still finding his footing with the local customs. When people asked if he found New Hampshire to be very different from Maryland, he would smile and say, "Colder, but I'll get used to that." He resolved to learn how to ski, for his own pleasure and for winter exercise, and to take an interest in stock car racing as a gesture of goodwill toward his congregation.

For the next hour or so, he sifted through photographs of churches in southern France and Spain. He kept encountering himself in various seasons and outfits, standing, hands in pockets, trying to look earnest as he posed squinting in the sunshine in Ardilliers or holding up a souvenir of St. Martin in Tours. There were well-composed photos of church architecture in which he stood in the foreground for perspective, but he was still tempted to remove those shots from the collection. He kept staring at the image of his old self, knowing that he had been looking at Emely. There were no photographs of her in the pilgrimage program. He had been careful to remove them, so that he would not come across them unprepared and be blindsided by the memory. Emely was gone, and he had gotten over it.

He worked on his notes, scarcely glancing at the television screen as the rainbow of race cars streaked past. He paid little heed to them beyond thinking that the sight of a balmy day in Florida made a pleasant contrast to the New England winter evening fading to black outside his window.

As he wrote, with half an ear tuned in to the rhythmic voices of the announcers, newly-familiar names like "Waltrip," "Labonte," and "Bodine" slid past. And Ricky Craven, of course. Craven, who was from Maine, was a favorite son on the New Hampshire track. Occasionally Bill Knight glanced at the screen, but the blur of cars told him nothing about the progress of the race. With the cars racing in an oval, you couldn't tell who was winning by which car seemed ahead of the rest: it might be on a different lap from the others, and the race consisted of 200 laps. Hours and hours of going round in circles. Much like a church council meeting, he thought to himself.

It was the change in the tenor of the voices that made him look up. The race was nearly over — twenty-six laps to go, according to the posting on the screen — but the proceedings had been halted because of a wreck. Some driver had ventured too close to the next vehicle in the throng of cars, jockeying for position at 180 miles per hour. That contact between bumpers had caused a chain reaction. Cars collided with others, blocking the passage of the approaching vehicles, so that they, too, skidded and spun.

Seconds later, an orange car, emblazoned with the number 20, left the track and sailed upside down above the crush of cars, spiraling over and over like a football until it landed in the grassy oval at the center of the speedway, joining a dozen other cars also taken out in the crash.

Bill Knight found himself staring at the screen, even as he reproved himself for watching the violent spectacle. He felt reproached by St. Augustine, who had been so enthralled by the games in the Coliseum that he had been forced to exile himself from Rome to overcome his obsession. Even in his desert refuge, the saint's sleep had been troubled by dreams of chariot races and gladiatorial combat.

As the television replayed the crash over and over from different angles, the race itself was stopped so that the wrecked cars and injured drivers could be tended to. "Surely that man is dead," Knight thought, watching for perhaps the fifth time as the orange car went flying above the rest.

Apparently not, though. The announcer kept insisting that the driver was not badly hurt, and that he was only complaining of a pain in his shoulder. *I should think he would,* thought Knight. The trip to the hospital appeared to be little more than a formality for the driver of the orange car: Tony Stewart, according to the announcer. The other drivers were equally unscathed, but their cars were out of commission. Presently, with the dozen drivers sidelined by mechanical problems and minor injuries, the track was cleared of debris and the race resumed.

Knight supposed that the excitement for the day was over, and that with fewer cars to contend with the final twenty-six laps would play out peacefully, but he did wonder if that Stewart fellow could really have escaped with so little injury.

According to the commentators, the big drama of the race now centered on whether the winner would turn out to be the brother of the television announcer, himself a retired stock car driver. He kept hearing the excitement in the broadcaster's voice, anticipation mounting with each lap as the younger brother maintained the lead, on his way to winning his first

Daytona 500. *How pleasant for the television network,* thought Knight, *a happy occasion to focus on, rather than a tragic death.* The after-race interview was sure to be unique, because for once the television personality was really part of the story. The human interest angle of the two brothers would no doubt increase the news value of an otherwise routine sports story, and it would make it easy for him to find something pleasant to say about the event. He still wondered, though, about the spectacular wreck on lap 26 that had shut the race down for so many minutes. That car had sailed through the air, flipping over the other contenders. Could it really be as inconsequential as they said it was?

The lap numbers went down every minute or so, until at last the remaining cars were on the homestretch, or the last lap, or whatever they called it, and sure enough the yellow car, number 15, driven by the announcer's brother, kept its lead. The announcer was shouting excitedly into his microphone as if his brother, and not 20 million viewers could hear him: "You got him, Mikey! Come on, man! Oh, my! Get him in the fold!"

Bill Knight wondered what that phrase meant. *Get him in the fold.* To his ministerial ear it sounded like a phrase from a revival. As he was making a mental note to ask about this term, the lead car crossed the finish line, followed by great jubilation over the airwaves. Seconds later, though, Darrell Waltrip in the skybox mentioned that another wreck had taken place a hundred yards or so down the track from the finish line only seconds before the end of the race. A footnote to the race, it seemed: this incident was not as spectacular as the previous pileup.

Knight looked up again as the network showed an instant replay of the latest collision. A black Monte Carlo with a white number 3 painted on its side — that was Dale Earnhardt, he knew — had collided with a yellow Pontiac emblazoned with the number 36 and a logo for M&M's. The black Chevy had been ahead of a knot of close-packed cars, when it seemed to lose control, veering sideways into the path of the oncoming cars. It was hit broadside by the approaching M&M car, slammed into the wall, bounced back, and then both the Chevrolet and the Pontiac slid across the track and came to rest on the grassy oval infield. As before, there were no flames. Both cars were right side up, parked peacefully on the grass, as the race went on without them to end eleven seconds later. The television cameras kept cutting back to the crash site and the voice-overs said several times that Dale Earnhardt was one of the drivers involved, but the focus now was on the ecstatic young driver who had won his first Daytona victory.

"I just hope Dale's okay," the television announcer remarked as he looked out the window of the sky box.

Dale. Oh, well, that was all right, Bill Knight thought. Today's little mishap would have been all in a day's work to him. Indeed, after a few more replays, the coverage went back to the winning driver, whose car, it turned out, had been owned by Dale Earnhardt's company. An ecstatic Mike Waltrip was thanking everybody and marveling at his victory. The race was over. Credits rolled up the screen.

Earnhardt. People either loved him or hated him. The men seemed to root for him; most women thought he was too rough, but like him or not, they all knew him. He was big. His face looked down at you from the walls of half the restaurants in the area. On race weekends, there was a waitress in a local diner who wore an Earnhardt cap, and she would count out your change, "One, two, *Dale,* four, five . . ." Probably

63

doubled her tips doing that.

Dale Earnhardt.

Bill Knight kept staring at the television, waiting for news that the drivers were all right or that the Stewart fellow in the previous wreck was out of the hospital, but the broadcast ended without further comment on any of the other drivers. On the back of an old envelope, Bill Knight scribbled the words "Mike Waltrip won Daytona 500. Announcer's brother" as a reminder to himself in case anyone of his acquaintance should try to talk about racing in the week ahead, then he turned off the television and went to the kitchen to make more coffee.

When the doorbell rang, Knight had forgotten the race and was debating whether to have leftover take-out or a microwave meal for his supper. He walked to the door, hoping that just this once some kind soul had brought him a dish of beef stew and homemade biscuits, but as he never expected miracles any more than his congregation did, he was not surprised to see his neighbor Bob Henderson, empty-handed.

"Come in, Bob," he said, and the man's stricken expression made him add, "Is anything wrong?"

Henderson stamped his boots on the

64

mat outside, and unwound the red-and-black scarf that had covered his mouth and chin, revealing an expression of barely contained grief. His eyes were red and he looked like someone teetering on the edge of shock.

"Has there been a wreck?" asked Knight, saying the first thing that came into his head. The Interstate was so near.

Tears rolled down the man's cheeks. "Oh, yes," he said. "There's been a wreck."

"I'll get my coat, Bob. Are they still on the highway or are we going to the hospital?"

Henderson shook his head. "The hospital is in Florida," he said. "But I thought I'd ask if you had any prayers for the dead or Bible verses. Something like that."

Bob Henderson followed him into the study and perched on the edge of the leather sofa wiping his eyes with the back of his hand. He nodded toward the dark screen of the television. "Didn't you see the race?"

"I did," said Knight. He remembered that he had turned off the set when he went to fix his supper. "The Daytona 500, you mean?" Realization dawned. "I'm sorry to hear it, Bob," he said. "Truly sorry. Though I can't say I'm surprised. When I saw that car go sailing into the air,

I thought, That poor fellow will be lucky to survive that. I'm so sorry to hear that he didn't."

Henderson took a gulp of air and stared at him with a puzzled frown. "Sailing through . . . Through the *air?* . . . Are you talking about Tony Stewart on lap 26?" he asked.

"Was that the Home Depot car? Yes. A terrible wreck. Such a pity."

Henderson shook his head. "Tony Stewart is fine, Bill. It's *Dale* that got killed."

"Dale — *Earnhardt?* — but — wasn't he in that little wreck in the last few seconds of the race? Are you sure?"

By now, Henderson had the box of tissues in his lap. He was taking deep breaths and dabbing his eyes. "A crowd of us were over at the sports bar watching the race on the big screen. They just announced it over the TV," he said. "But I knew in my heart already. Knew it was bad."

"But that first wreck?" Knight was still trying to follow the thread of the conversation. Surely that first multicar pileup . . .

Henderson managed a damp smile. "I forgot that you were new to racing," he said. "Flying through the air looks scary, but the force is being dissipated by the rolls before the car lands or hits anything. So Stewart was fine. But Dale went straight at the wall at 180 miles an hour — more maybe, because there was another car pushing him forward as well. I knew it was bad. He didn't get out, and then I caught sight of a blue tarp being spread over the car, and I knew."

"I'm so sorry," Knight said again. "Er — You weren't a relative of his?"

"No," said Henderson. "But he was family, all the same."

"Well, is there anything I can do?" Knight was surprised to see that a driver who wasn't from here and hadn't died here had elicited such a powerful response in the otherwise steady and sensible lawyer. He wondered if many people locally would react so strongly — and what was he to do to help them through their pain?

"That sports bar, where I was watching the race," said Henderson. "Two guys were in there — I didn't know them. Truckers, maybe. They'd had a few beers too many and they were arguing about something over by the pool table, getting louder and louder. It looked like they were about ten seconds away from a real brawl and I was about to call the police on my cell phone. Just then, though, the special bulletin came on the television announcing that Dale was dead and those two burly guys just froze in mid fight. They stood there for a minute staring at the screen like a couple of pole-axed steers, neither one moving a muscle. Then they started sniffling and finally they just came over and sat down in front of the screen, side by side. One of them kept patting the other's shoulder and saying, 'I know, man. I know.' "

Knight stared at him in silence, turning it over in his mind. "I see," he said. People in the area would be grieving. All those people with number threes on the back windows of their cars. The waitress in the Earnhardt cap. This was the Speedway's parish as much as it was his. "I guess we'd better go, then," he said. "Can you show me the quickest way out there?" God knew what he was going to say when he got there. At least Bill hoped He did.

Nearly eight o'clock on a cold Sunday night, and the residential streets of tiny Canterbury were all but deserted. The Interstate would have its usual tide of southbound weekend traffic, but they weren't headed that way. "I know a shortcut," Bob Henderson had told him. They drove through dark streets in silence for a few blocks, following the road that skirted the lake. He shivered, wondering how long it would take the heater turned up full blast to warm the interior of the car.

As he drove, Bill wondered if this intense grief over the passing of strangers was a phenomenon of modern times. Did people mourn the death of, say, a Lincoln or a Mozart with such passionate intensity, or did the immediacy of television coverage magnify people's emotions these days? It is one thing to hear weeks later of the death of some beloved figure, but to see it happen, to follow the events as they unfolded hour by hour, surely this heightened the feelings for many. He had been at his last church, back in Maryland, when Princess Diana died, and he had been surprised at the number of women who reacted as if they had lost a close relative. Of course, he had also seen people who *had* lost a close relative and hardly batted an eye over the loss. It was hard to tell these days who was close to whom.

But what was it about some people — no more beautiful or talented than a hundred others — that touched a chord in humanity that elevated one person's death to the level of tragedy? Some quality of glamor or drama that made strangers weep for them. The death of Princess Diana had set off a spontaneous wave of worldwide grief, while a few weeks later the death of Mother Teresa in India had elicited little more than a collective shrug. Which proved, he supposed, that goodness had nothing to do with it. Why Elvis and not John Lennon? He would have said that Lennon was the more spiritual, the more universal, figure. But it was Elvis who had received the secular canonization. Why after a quarter of a century did weeping strangers still flock to Graceland to mourn the passing of a man they never knew? And now — Dale Earnhardt? His nickname had been the Intimidator. Could there be a more unlikely angel?

Knight felt that he had been given an opportunity to watch something unfold and he hoped that he would be given the wisdom to make sense of it.

"I didn't know you were a racing fan, Bob." As soon as he said it, Knight realized that this was an unworthy thought. Just because Bob Henderson was a lawyer, he had assumed him to be somehow above the thrall of stock car racing, but he ought to know by now that you couldn't pigeonhole people by your own biases.

"Because I don't drive a pick-up truck with decals on the back window, you mean?"

"I'm new to all this," said Knight by way of apology.

"Well, you're a couple of decades behind the times with that image, but, yeah, I was as big a fan of Earnhardt as anybody. He was one of a kind. I have a signed picture of him in my office. You'd be surprised what an icebreaker that is with clients sometimes. Gives us something in common."

"But why Earnhardt in particular?"

"Because he didn't take any crap from anybody. It was his way or no way. I think he would have made a hell of a lawyer. I think he could have gotten the devil himself off with a reprimand."

In spite of the seriousness of the man's tone, Bill Knight smiled. "I thought that was Daniel Webster," he said.

"I see you've been reading up on New England's folklore," said Henderson. "It's hard to explain the attraction of Dale Earnhardt. You don't follow racing, so you wouldn't get it. When I said he'd have made a hell of a lawyer, I didn't mean that Earnhardt was a silver-tongued orator. He wasn't. But without looks or pedigree or education, he managed to make himself a celebrity and a multimillionaire — in a profession that the opinion-makers sneer at. That's quite an achievement. He just wouldn't give up. It was that certainty that he was right and that nobody else's opinion was worth a damn. I've always thought saints must be like that."

Knight thought about it. "I suppose some of them were," he said. "That's why I've never wanted to meet one."

On a Sunday evening in winter the Speedway parking lot should have been empty, but as they pulled in, he saw dozens of cars and even a couple of eighteen-wheelers already in the lot.

"Trucks?" he said.

"Interstate," said Henderson. "They'll have heard the news on the radio. Makes sense for them to come here, I guess. Dale was here last summer, racing, you know. He was here when Adam died."

Knight nodded. "Adam Petty. I know about that. I wasn't here then, though."

Consecrated ground.

They parked next to a red pick-up, and began to walk toward the main gates, where a crowd was already gathered.

Taped — or perhaps tied — to the fence was a square of white poster board bearing only the number 3 outlined in black-and-red marker. On the ground beneath it light flickered from red glass candle holders that might have been taken from the table of a restaurant. Above the wind, he heard the muffled tones of a radio that someone had thought to bring, but the crowd was quiet. No one sang or wept or talked except in low murmurs. They were just waiting. Or coming together, perhaps, to pool their grief. The odd thing was that many people had felt the need to bring something. He understood the custom of bringing food to a bereaved family or flowers to a grave site to honor a departed friend, but what instinct made these strangers bring tokens to a place so far from the death scene, so far from the man's family or final resting place, to someone they had never met? He supposed that the offerings were grief made visible.

On the ground beside the candles he saw potted plants and bundles of convenience store roses, left over from Valentine's Day, now offered up to the memory of a man killed two thousand miles away. In this cold, he thought, they would not last the night, but at least the gesture had been made.

As Knight stood taking in the scene and wondering what he ought to do, a big man in a plaid jacket edged past him. He was carrying a plastic pine Christmas wreath, which he set down against the wall. A black toy car dangled from the red satin bow of the wreath. The man knelt down, propping the wreath so that it would not fall, and making sure that the die-cast car faced outward, the white number 3 visible on its tiny door. As he straightened up, he saw Knight looking down at the wreath, and tried to smile, a bit shamefaced at this uncharacteristic display of emotion.

"I felt like I had to bring something," he said.

Knight nodded. "People do," he said.

"I didn't watch the race," the man said. "I was all set to, but I'm a plumber. Had an emergency call — frozen pipes at a mobile home. Anyhow, I left my wife home watching the race, and as I went out, I said to her, 'Dale knows I'll be pulling for him.' Well, my wife can't stand Dale Earnhardt. She says he's a bully on wheels. Likes that California surfer boy, that Jeff Gordon. Anyhow, I'm going out the door, she yells after me, 'I hope your old Dale gets run into the damn wall!' And I was coming back home, hoping to catch the end of the race when I heard the news on the radio. I went on into the house, and Judy was sitting there white as a sheet. 'I didn't mean it,' she says to me, but I didn't even look at her. I just went on up into the attic and got the Christmas wreath. 'I'm going out to the track,' I told her, and she asked did I want her to come with me, and I said no. I didn't want her. She isn't hurting for Dale. But I am."

"I'm sorry," said Knight. That seemed to be all there was to say.

Nearby a woman in a red ski parka was crying. She held a candle that she was trying to light with a cigarette lighter, but the wind kept extinguishing the flame, making her cry all the more. "The flame has gone out," she said. Finally, she put the unlit candle down against the wall with the wilting flowers and walked away without looking back.

"I'll bet the Shaker Museum has a run on candles tomorrow," said Henderson.

Bill Knight nodded.

"You know, when Princess Diana died, my wife got up at some ungodly hour before dawn to watch the funeral and I laughed at her for being so upset about it. But, by God, now I know how she felt, I guess. You feel like you knew them. It hurts."

"And Dale never won a race here at New

Hampshire," said a heavyset older woman in the crowd. She was wearing a black-and-red Earnhardt jacket, but shivering anyhow. "He never did. Every year I'd go to the race, hoping this time would break the charm, but now it's never going to happen." Quietly, she began to cry.

A man in a black leather jacket and work boots stopped to look at the toy car on the Christmas wreath. He did not smile. "I wish I'd thought to bring something," he said. "All I had in the truck was a can of beer, and that just didn't seem right." He pointed to one of the big rigs in the parking lot. "I got a load of Texas onions on their way to Maine," he said. "Couple of tons of Texas sweets. And, you know what? They ain't getting there. 'Cause I'm turning around. I can pick up I-95 outside of Boston and take it to Washington — twelve, fourteen hours. Take 66 west out of DC over to I-81 down the spine of the Blue Ridge. At Wytheville, Virginia, go south on I-77, and from there it's a two-hour straight shot into Charlotte."

"Charlotte?" the wreath man said.

"Charlotte." The trucker nodded. "The funeral will be there. Bound to be."

That made sense. Everybody knew Earnhardt was from a little town just north of there. "Do you suppose they'll let ordinary people in?"

"Doubt it. But I can be there. Stand outside. I can say good-bye."

"I don't know about going to the funeral," the wreath man said. "Drivers didn't go to funerals. Too close to home, I guess. Knowing that the next race might be their turn."

"Well, I'm going. The chance will never come again."

A white Chevy pick-up truck pulled into the parking lot and the driver emerged carrying a poster portrait mounted on cardboard: Earnhardt in black-and-white coveralls leaning against his number 3 car. A gaggle of mourners helped the newcomer attach the poster to the fence above the pile of freezing flowers but some of them seemed more interested in the man who brought it than in the poster of the fallen hero.

"Vince! I thought I recognized your truck," said one. "Are you going on to the store tonight?"

Vince shook his head. "No. I think tonight ought to be a time of mourning, that's all." His voice was hoarse. "I can't open tonight."

"But your shop is closed on Mondays."

"No, I'll open in the morning. I already

drove over there and put a sign on the door. Nine a.m. — not a minute before."

"You won't mark up the Earnhardt stuff, will you, Vince?"

The man sighed and wiped his face with his hand. "No. That wouldn't be right. Just give me time to get in and get the lights on and open the register, that's all. Nine o'clock tomorrow. All right?"

Bill Knight, who had been listening to this exchange, said, "NASCAR souvenirs?"

Vince nodded. "It's going to be a nightmare tomorrow. I've never seen people act like this. Not even when Adam died here. While I was putting the sign on the door, a couple of cars pulled into the parking lot and four guys rushed to the door, but I told them to come back tomorrow. Then a police cruiser drove up, so I went over to explain to them that I was the owner, and that it wasn't a burglary or anything." He sighed. "Turned out *they* wanted to buy Earnhardt stuff."

Bill Knight shivered as a gust of wind bit through his overcoat. It was too cold for people to stay out here very long, he thought. He wondered where they would go, and what would become of their grief.

"I'm a minister," he said to the shop owner. "I could open the church."

"Most of these people wouldn't go, sir.

78

They need to be where Dale has been and, besides, people keep showing up all the time, and if everybody here left, there'd be no one for them to talk to, I guess. It's better here."

Bill Knight found himself wondering if people had gone to the cathedral on that winter day in 1170 when news of Thomas Becket's death had reached them, and if so what had been done to comfort them.

A man in a well-cut black overcoat set a red-and-black Earnhardt hat in the pile with the other tributes. He saw the minister watching him, and gave an embarrassed shrug. "I just wanted to say goodbye," he said.

A short man in a *Rescue Squad* ski parka hurried over. "Thought I recognized you, Doc!" he said to the man in the overcoat. "I'm glad you're here. A couple of the guys have been arguing over this, and you'll know — do you think a good trauma team could have saved him after the wreck?"

The doctor shook his head. "No. He was dead before they got him out of the car. A hundred and eighty miles an hour. We're all just bags of water, you know. People. Just bags of water."

As he turned to walk away, the short man crossed himself. "Well, he's in heaven, anyhow," he said. "I know that."

The doctor watched him go. "In heaven," he said. "You know, I was thinking about that on the way over here. Here's a guy with a ninth-grade education and an average face, and by driving a Chevrolet, he gets to be the fortieth-richest person in America and hang out with movie stars — and I wondered: just what kind of a heaven would there have to be to top that?"

Knight knew that some ministers would have taken that remark as an invitation to expound upon the joys of being in the presence of God, but he couldn't bring himself to do it. He would have felt like a salesman. Perhaps, after all, it was better to let people speak their minds, without trying to rationalize away their grief. Faith was for later.

For the next hour, until the cold wind numbed his face and forced him to leave, Bill Knight mingled with the Speedway mourners, going from person to person, saying little. Just listening to the grief and the memories.

A year later, when the Children's Home needed someone to chaperone young Matthew on his Last Wish trip, Bill Knight volunteered, thinking that perhaps he could understand the boy's feelings as well as anyone. Besides, he might finally learn exactly what a restrictor plate was.

CHAPTER V

Richard Petty in Heaven

The Volunteer Parkway

After the luggage had been stowed, a process accompanied by prolonged debates about who got carsick and who would sit where, the Number Three Pilgrims, as Harley now thought of them, allowed themselves to be herded into the bus to take their seats.

The buxom ex-beauty-queen type, whose gray hair was silvered blond, stopped in the aisle beside the driver and called out, "Lord, I hope nobody's taped a Bible verse to our steering wheel!"

"Shut up, Justine!" said her traveling companions in unison.

The minister, who was next to board, looked up at Harley with a puzzled frown. "Bible verse?" he said.

Harley sighed. It was starting already. Unauthorized trivia. He leaned in close and whispered, "I think she's referring to the fact that at the 2001 Daytona Darrell Waltrip's wife taped a Bible verse to

Earnhardt's steering wheel. It's a Christian tradition in NASCAR."

"Oh, yes," Bill Knight nodded. "The race in which he died. A Bible verse to his steering wheel." He considered this fundamentalist tradition for a moment. "I wonder which verse it was."

Harley shrugged. "Somebody here is bound to know." He consulted his clipboard, trying to match names and faces. He knew the minister and Matthew, the two newlyweds were joining them at Bristol . . . He looked up from the list, as one name gave him pause.

"Cayle Warrenby," he said. *"Cayle?"*

The baby-faced blonde in black jeans raised her hand. "I get that a lot," she said. "My mother wanted to name me Gail, but my dad was a big racing fan."

"Well, I knew you weren't named after the vegetable," said Harley.

"No. My dad even called our dog Old Yeller, after that Chevy Laguna Cale was driving when he won Daytona in '77."

Harley smiled. "I guess you're lucky they didn't name you that, you being a blonde and all." He sighed. "Cale Yarborough. Used to drive for Junior Johnson at one time. And I'll bet old Cale was the Winston Cup champion the year you were born, right?"

She nodded. "Yes, but since he won it three years in a row, that gives me a little fudging room on my age."

"So, where you from and all that?" asked Harley. He had written himself a note to ask that. It didn't come naturally to him.

Cayle gestured to include her two companions. "Little towns around Charlotte, all of us," she said. "I'm an environmental engineer, Bekasu here is a judge, and Justine is — well, she — um . . . this is Justine."

A hand shot up in the air, and the tinkling of silver charm bracelets punctuated a cry of "Here I am, y'all!"

"Welcome aboard," said Harley, who knew the type. With very little encouragement Justine would take over the bus and talk nineteen-to-the-dozen from here to Florida. She would bear watching. He glanced down the roll. "Cayle Warrenby, Justine, Rebekah Sue Holifield —"

"Hostage," said the stern women in the white linen suit, raising her hand.

Harley wasn't going there, either. He gave her a wary smile and said, "Okay then, who's next? Reverend William M. Knight —"

"Bill!" said the silver-haired man who looked like he ought to be doing boomer-

83

oriented commercials, for vitamins or mutual funds, maybe.

"And that's young Matthew with you. Welcome aboard, guys. Mr. and Mrs. Shane McKee . . . Oh, no, they're meeting us at the Speedway. I'll tell you about them in a minute. Mr. Reeve? Mr. Franklin?"

A scowling older man in a black cowboy hat and a dark sport coat raised his hand. "Ray Reeve," he said. "Norfolk, Nebraska. We're not traveling together. We're just sitting together."

"So what do you do back there in Nebraska?" asked Harley, wishing he'd thought to take out a pen to record the answers he wouldn't otherwise remember.

"Agro-business." Mr. Reeve leaned back in his seat, arms folded, to indicate that the interview was over.

"Jesse Franklin," said his pink-cheeked seatmate with a nervous smile. "Michigan. I guess you'd say I'm a native, but my folks were from down here, so I'm sure I'll feel right at home."

"We can provide an interpreter if you need one," said Harley with a straight face. "And what do you do when Brooklyn, Michigan turns back into a cow pasture?"

"In non-race weeks, you mean? Ah. I guess you'd say I'm a bureaucrat. I'm the county auditor. Caught the racing bug from my uncles, though, when I was a kid. Nice to meet all you folks."

"Welcome aboard," said Harley. "Who's next here . . . Mrs. Richard Nash?"

Midway toward the back of the bus a slender tanned arm went up, and a woman said, "Here."

Harley looked up. That's all she said. "Here." She was a fine-featured woman who might have been anywhere in age between fifty and seventy, depending on whether that well-preserved handsomeness owed more to good genes or to an expensive plastic surgeon. She wasn't wearing much jewelry or makeup, and her clothes and hair were simple enough — but Harley knew the instant he saw her that this woman had more money than God. One thing about being on the NASCAR circuit, even if you didn't make a ton of money yourself, the social aspect of the job certainly put you in the path of people who did and, without even intending to, Harley had developed a radar for spotting power people, and this was one. How odd to find her on a down-market bus tour. He hoped she wouldn't be the type to demand imported tea bags and linen sheets.

"Terence Palmer?" That had turned out

to be the fellow beside Mrs. Nash. Her son, maybe? He looked expensive, too, but not with that patina of power that radiated from his companion. If you could bottle that air of assurance and entitlement, he thought, it would be worth more than four new tires in a five-second pit stop.

"Where are you folks from?"

The two human greyhounds looked at each other and shrugged. Sarah Nash leaned forward in her seat, but Harley was already walking down the aisle to spare her the inconvenience of shouting. "I'm from Wilkesboro, and Terence lives in Manhattan."

"Wilkesboro!" said Harley, eyes shining. The name conjured up the good old days when NASCAR races were run in the shabby old Speedway there, the days when stock cars really were stock cars with working headlights and tires with tread. When the daddies of Dale Earnhardt and Richard Petty drove their cars *to* the track as well as *on* it. Harley wished things could have stayed that way. He'd have a better shot if they had.

"Wilkesboro," he said again. "So do you know him?"

He didn't have to say who. There was another famous "Junior" in NASCAR now,

86

but in Wilkesboro, the name meant only one person, the man who invented drafting, the "Last American Hero" himself: Junior Johnson.

Sarah Nash smiled. "Yes, of course. He sends his regards."

Harley wished they could make a detour to Wilkesboro on the tour, but even he could see that ten days to get from Bristol to Daytona and back to Darlington would be a stretch as it was without trying to improvise extra stops along the way. With a sigh of resignation, he turned back to the clipboard, to the next set of names.

"Jim and Arlene Powell?"

A white-haired older man near the back of the bus waved his hand. The woman with him was the one wearing the Earnhardt patterned vest. She did not look up at the sound of her name. *Uh-oh,* thought Harley. He should have paid more attention to the notes about the passengers. He hadn't bargained on sick kids and out-of-it seniors, but at least they were race fans, so he reckoned they'd be easier to deal with than a bus full of New York media types.

"Justine . . ."

In the second row from the front, the platinum-haired woman with the huge

87

dark eyes and her weight in jewelry (definitely real), waved her hand. "He-ey, Harley! Can I tell a story to get us started?"

Harley nodded for the bus driver to pull out, while he tried to think of some reason not to let her. The takeover was beginning already. She was an Earnhardt fan, all right. If you ever saw a woman at the track who looked like she ought to be following Patton into Belgium in a pastel pink tank with a rhinestone-collared poodle on the gun turret, you could bet the rent she'd be an Earnhardt fan.

"Well, let me start you off with a trivia question first," he said, playing for time. "In fact, ma'am, you brought it up. The reverend here —"

"Bill," said Bill Knight hastily.

"*Bill* wants to know if anybody knows which Bible verse it was that Mrs. Stevie Waltrip taped onto Earnhardt's steering column on that fateful day."

In the silence that followed, people looked around to see if anyone was going to volunteer the information. Finally, Sarah Nash, the regal older woman sitting next to the preppy said, "It was from Proverbs. Chapter eighteen, verse ten. *The name of the Lord is a strong tower: the righteous runneth into it —*"

"And is safe," said Bill, nodding. "Ah. That one."

Justine tossed her head. "Well, what kind of *idiot* would tape a verse like that onto the steering wheel of somebody who was about to run the Daytona 500?" she demanded. "Talking about running into a wall —"

"A tower."

"*Whatever.* That's exactly what he did, though. Ran into something. Just like it said in the verse." Her voice dropped to a shocked whisper. "Do y'all think she hexed him?"

"Shut up, Justine," came two voices in unison.

"No, *think* about it, y'all. Who put the verse on there? *Mrs. Waltrip.* Okay. And who won the race that day? Mike *Waltrip.*"

Harley resisted the urge to put his head in his hands. Why hadn't he thought to bring a hip flask? Or a stun gun. "The driver who won wasn't her husband, ma'am," he said in the firm but soothing tone one uses for people who line their hats with tin foil. "The lady is Mrs. *Darrell* Waltrip, ma'am. The winner of the race, Mike, is her brother-in-law."

Justine nodded. "Even so. I ask you." She looked around for affirmation from

89

her fellow passengers.

"Why don't you tell your story, now?" said Harley. *Before word of this gets out and the Waltrips sue us for slander,* Harley was thinking. *Or tape Bible verses to our steering wheel.* He pictured himself pilloried in a medieval stocks on the lawn outside DEI while NASCAR officials and Waltrip fans pelted him with ripe fruit. Stories like that wouldn't make him any friends on the circuit, that's for sure, and he was going to need all the friends he could get if he was going to find a way back in.

"Okay, then." Justine tottered up to the front of the bus, her good humor restored. She waved a wrist full of bracelets at her fellow passengers. "Hey, folks!" she said. "I'm Justine, and those two over there trying to cover up their heads with their jackets are my sister Bekasu and our friend Cayle. Now, speaking of Bible verses, I'm going to get this party going with a little story about heaven. Can I use the microphone, Harley? How do you work it?"

Wordless with dread, he adjusted the mike for her.

"Okay, here goes," she crooned into the bus P.A. system. "It's about Richard Petty going to heaven. Oh, don't roll your eyes, Bekasu. It's a *cute* story. Besides, it's clean.

90

Okay, so the story is . . . this is a long time in the future, of course — I hope! — but Richard Petty finally dies." She scanned the audience until she spotted young Matthew. "He may have been a little before your time, hon, but you know who Richard Petty is, right?"

Solemnly, the little boy nodded. "The King," he said. "Like Elvis, only NASCAR."

"That's him. He wears a big black cowboy hat like Mr. Reeve back there. Okay, so Mr. Petty dies, and he goes up to heaven. God meets him at the pearly gates and starts showing him around. Finally, after they've toured the streets of gold and seen the heavenly choir and all, God takes Richard Petty out to a country road that looks just like the piedmont, North Carolina — you know, red clay and pine trees — and there at the foot of a hill, God points to a little white frame house with a big front porch, and roses on the picket fence, and chickens in the yard. Richard notices a faded number 43 flag on a pole beside the front steps.

"So God says, 'Richard, this is your house. You've earned it, and I know you'll be happy here. Welcome to heaven.'

"So Mr. Petty, he starts up the steps to

the front door, when suddenly off in the distance on a hill overlooking the forest of pine trees, he notices a big old palace. It looks like the Disneyland castle, only it's made of shining black rock with a black sidewalk, and a big old black-and-white Number 3 banner flying from the tallest tower. Sure enough, there's a big old *'D-E-I'* logo painted on the drawbridge.

"Well, all of a sudden Richard's little white frame house didn't look so good to him anymore. He walked back down the sidewalk to the gate where God was standing, and he said, 'Lord, I don't want to seem ungrateful for your gift house here, but something is troubling me. You know, I was a legend in NASCAR. I won seven championships, too, Lord. And I won the Daytona 500 seven times. *He* only won it once!'

" 'What do you mean, Richard?' asked God.

" *'Earnhardt!'* he said, pointing to the shining black castle. 'I want to know why Dale Earnhardt got a better house up here than I did.'

"So God chuckled and then he said, 'Shoot, Richard, that's not *Earnhardt's* house. It's mine.' "

The other passengers laughed the polite

chuckles of people already familiar with the punch line, but Reverend Knight called out, "Mr. Petty should have known that."

"Known what?" said Justine, handing the microphone back to Harley.

"That the big black castle was God's house. You said it had 'Dei' painted on the drawbridge. *Domus Dei — House of God*. So *I* knew."

Justine just looked at him and shook her head sadly.

Cayle leaned across the aisle. "*D-E-I* stands for Dale Earnhardt, Incorporated," she whispered.

"Oh." He pulled out a small leather notebook and made an entry. "Dale Earnhardt Incorporated . . . DEI. Hmmm . . ."

"Do people in heaven have houses?" Matthew wanted to know.

"Well . . ." Bill Knight hesitated, trying to scale his answer to his audience. "I think this particular story was metaphorical, although in the Bible, Jesus does say, 'In my father's house there are many mansions . . .' So I guess you can take it either way, Matthew."

The boy had gone back to his Game Boy, so perhaps he was satisfied with the ambiguous answer.

"How's the game going?" Bill asked him, hoping to change the subject.

Matthew shrugged. "It's okay. Kind'a lame, though. I'd rather have a racing game, but this was all they had. This one is about this knight who has a mechanical horse, and a magic mirror that can tell if people are lying to him, and a ring, of course. There's always a ring."

"What does it do?"

"Lets you talk to animals."

"Well, that could be handy." Bill smiled. "If I'd owned that ring I wouldn't have had to buy a new living room rug. So what does the knight do with all this gear?"

Matthew sighed. "Fights monsters. Same as every other game. I'd rather have the racing one."

"Well, maybe we can find you one." Bill thought that a game championing fast driving might be marginally more healthy than one encouraging players to violence. He tried to remember what games he had played at that age, in his pre-electronic childhood, the era when a house had only one television, a black-and-white set in the middle of the living room. He could remember sandlot baseball and bike riding with the other guys, every dog in the neighborhood trailing after them like a canine convoy. He remembered his childhood in mirror fragments: sunshine streaming through pine needles; a litter of

94

newborn hamsters, like tiny pink thumbs, nestled in an old chiffon scarf; long night drives to his grandparents' house, his parents in the front seat singing Hit Parade tunes because the radio wouldn't pick up any stations; his grandfather's chair with its comforting smell of old leather, tobacco, and cough drops. What would Matthew remember, he wondered.

They were approaching the Speedway by the time Harley remembered that he had not given all the Number Three Pilgrims a chance to say much about themselves. Now there were too many distractions and not enough time to get to everybody. Better save it for the dinner hour. He glanced at his clipboard, and skipped to the next spiel.

"The Bristol Motor Speedway, folks," he said into the microphone. "At point-five-three-three miles, it's one of the smallest tracks in NASCAR, but don't think it's easy on account of that. One lap on that track takes fifteen *seconds*. It's an oval with 36-degree banked turns. With those steep sides, driving there at 100 miles per hour is like trying to fly an F-14 around a clothes dryer. Anybody ever been to a race here?"

No hands went up.

"Yeah, I didn't think so," said Harley. "Bristol races sell out *years* in advance. It's almost easier to get a sponsor than it is to get a seat. And the hotels are probably booked into the next millennium. That's why we'll be staying at a bed-and-breakfast tonight. Possum Holler — it's a real nice place they tell me. Got lots of rooms. And they specialize in racing weekends. I hear there's a sign in the front hall that says *Terry Labonte Fans Welcome. Other Racing Fans Tolerated.* We're heading for the Speedway first, though. Bristol Motor Speedway — one of the hardest tickets to come by in all of sports. Oh, Cayle, your buddy Mr. Yarborough made history here at this track in 1973 by leading in every single lap of a 500-lap race."

"Did you ever drive here?" asked Matthew.

"Sure did, Sport. Last time was in '95. Terry Labonte was leading the pack and Earnhardt was trying to get past him, so on turn 4 of the final lap — headed right for the finish line — Earnhardt gave Labonte a little tap on his bumper that should have spun him out across the in-field, leaving the way clear for Dale to finish first. But it didn't work like that. Somehow Terry Labonte managed to keep enough control over that car to stay on the track, and he went over the finish line in first place — but *backwards*. Tail end first."

"Did it count?" asked Matthew.

"Sure did. First is first."

"And where did *you* finish?"

"Well, you could say that I finished before Terry did. My engine went out on lap 34, and put me out of competition in a cloud of black smoke. I got to see the finish from pit road, though. It was almost worth it."

They were silent for a couple of minutes, in deference to Harley and the loss of his engine. Then Justine brightened and called out, "So tell us about this speedway wedding. I might want one someday."

Harley was ready for this one. "The folks at Bailey Travel figured you'd want to know about that. How are we fixed for time, Mr. Laine?"

At the steering wheel, Ratty Laine gave a grunt of disgust and said out of the corner of his mouth, "Take all the time you want. This road is a parking lot. Volunteer Parkway traffic's flowing like molasses in January."

Harley nodded. "I'll bet the locals know a shortcut or two. Wish I'd thought to ask about one at the airport."

"But you've driven here," said Matthew.

"Inside the Speedway, not out here," said Harley, repressing a shudder. "Took a helicopter right to the Speedway parking lot. Wish we could do that today. Anyhow, as I told you before, our first event of the tour is a wedding to be held smack-dab in the middle of the Bristol Motor Speedway. Now you might not think BMS is a romantic kind of place, but as a matter of fact Mike Waltrip proposed to his wife Buffy in Victory Lane after he won the Busch Grand National event here in 1993, so I guess that sets a precedent."

"I saw that race," said Jim Powell. "It was two days after Alan Kulwicki died here — the reigning champion he was — and people were still in shock after the plane crash. So when Mike took the checkered flag in the Busch race, he turned that car around and did a Polish victory lap in honor of Alan. And then in Victory Lane, there was Benny Parsons trying to interview him, and Mike went and popped the question to his young lady right on the air. It was quite a moment. Happy and sad all at once. I swear Arlene must have cried for two days after that. Didn't you, hon?"

His wife gave him a vacant smile and he patted her hand.

Harley noticed that Justine's face had

clouded over at hearing the name Waltrip again, so he hurried to change the subject. "While we're crawling through this traffic, we have a little something to pass the time here on the bus." He held up a cassette tape. "One of the couples getting married today is taking their honeymoon with us on this tour, and, as part of their deal with the company, the bride-to-be agreed to send us a homemade tape, talking about how they came to do this. I'm going to play it for you now, so that when the newlyweds come on board, you'll feel like you're already acquainted with them. Here goes . . ."

CHAPTER VI

The Bride's Tale

"Honky Tonk Truth"

"Tap . . . tap . . . Testing . . . I wonder if this thing is working. — Oh, I guess it is . . .

"Hello. My name is Karen . . . um . . . Well, it'll be McKee by the time you play this, I guess. Or almost . . . Anyhow . . . um . . . I just wanted to say that we're getting married at the Bristol Speedway, me and Shane . . .

"Well, of course it wasn't my idea. People keep asking me that — like they think I'd planned it that way back when I was a little girl, staging those under-the-porch weddings with Malibu Barbie and Dream Date Ken (Kleenex veil and clover flower bouquet).

Oh, sure. Me in a white organdy dress and a straw picture hat, carrying a bouquet of wild multiflora roses, tripping toward the minister in the infield of the Bristol Motor Speedway, wedding march on the P.A. system, 50,000 total strangers looking on, and a passel of media types smirking like possums every which way I looked. Not to mention Dale Earnhardt serving as best man, even though he would have been dead for sixteen months by then.

The wedding of my girlish dreams? Not hardly.

I just wanted to marry Shane McKee, that's all. The rest of it was *his* idea.

When I told Shane's wedding plans to the wait staff on my shift at the Wolf Laurel Inn, they said I ought to be glad that my fiancé was taking any interest in the ceremony at all. They said most men get about as involved in weddings as a convict does in an execution: just dreading it while everybody else makes the arrangements.

Mama's friends took a different view, of course. They pride themselves on it. After she and Daddy called it quits when I was twelve, Mama joined the local Wiccan Friends of the Goddess and Book Discussion Group, which is sort of a Junior League for the counterculture around here. The members of the coven are mostly divorcées over forty or unmarried college professors, and so they are all prime candidates for a religion that puts men in the back pew instead of in the

101

pulpit. I'm not a member — Mama says it will take another fifteen years and a few stretch marks to make me see the point — but of course I have to attend the gatherings that are family events, which means the vegetarian picnics and the Winter Solstice party, which is just like a Christmas party, except that the presents are given out by a lady in white robes instead of by Santa Claus. At the Solstice party once I asked Mom if she believed in the virgin birth, and she said it wouldn't surprise her one bit, because she had yet to see any man lift one finger to help with any of the Christmas preparations, so she figured that must be the precedent for it.

The Wiccan Friends of the Goddess position on marriage is that it is a submission to the patriarchal oppressor — well, in theory anyhow; some of the members are married or have been — although they try to be supportive of any member who is dating somebody, which gives them both the appearance of being broad-minded and the opportunity to say I-told-you-so when the relationship crashes and burns. But despite their misgivings about the male of the species, they did throw me a bridal shower. I was worried about that when they told me about it, because Wiccans are sup-

102

posed to perform their rituals *sky-clad,* which is goddess-speak for naked, and the thought of spending an afternoon playing toilet paper bride with a roomful of naked ladies just made my head hurt. Mrs. Tickle, the librarian and coven leader, told me not to worry about that, though. "We will all wear long loose robes," she told me, "because if you're over 45 and sky-clad, the sky had better be overcast."

Of course after they found out about Shane's idea for the ceremony, the Wiccans said that a NASCAR wedding was just the sort of tomfool thing a man would dream up. But since I had been hearing them go on about their ideas for a traditional pagan ceremony for weeks by then, I began to get relieved that all I had to worry about was motor oil puddles and the Associated Press, instead of a Cherokee-Druid priestess from Knoxville and a wedding night in the neighbor's corn field.

Shane was all fired up about the wedding, I'll give him that. I think he always figured on marrying me, but he'd never given a second thought to the ceremony itself until February 18 — you know, *when it happened.*

Shane hasn't been the same since.

We had been dating since seventh grade,

so the idea of us getting married wasn't really a surprise. It was more inevitable, like getting the license when your learner's permit is about to expire. We were juniors that year, fixing to graduate the next June. Next year, I was figuring on applying to the local college, which is all we could afford, and Shane was hoping to switch over to full time at Williams' Body Shop and get a place of his own, so the subject of marriage was coming up more and more. Shane was driving dirt track on the weekends, and last summer he'd done some work on an ARCA car for a guy over near Charlotte. I'd go to the race track to watch him, and he'd ask me if I was ready to be a driver's wife. "You have to be a size 8 or smaller," he'd say, and I'd laugh, but even if he was kidding, he was right about that.

We'd kid about it as we waited in line for movie tickets or sat on the couch in the basement, him in his red-and-black number 3 hat watching NASCAR on TV and me looking through old copies of *Modern Bride* that I had bought from the Goodwill for a quarter apiece.

"Hon, what do you think of this dress?" I'd said, shoving the magazine under his nose during a commercial.

Shane glanced at it for maybe two seconds, and then he said like, "Fine, if I can wear my white Earnhardt Goodwrench coveralls."

And he'd grinned when he said it, so I laughed and went back to turning pages.

'Cause I thought he was kidding. Well, maybe he was. I had already looked into tuxedo rentals at the mall, and Shane was okay with that. The Goodwrench overalls remark was just something he'd said to try to get a rise out of me that Sunday afternoon before the race started. The Daytona 500. February 18, 2001.

Well, you know how that ended, I guess. The whole world must know that, I reckon. But nobody could'a been hit any harder by it than Shane McKee. He was tore up worse than that black Monte Carlo. In fact, it wasn't hardly torn up at all, which was why I had such trouble believing it at first.

I'd never seen Shane cry before — not even that time in eighth grade when Bo got hit by a Kenworth. He loved that dog — still keeps a picture of him in his wallet to this day — but when Dale Earnhardt hit that wall in the last little bit of the 2001 Daytona 500, I thought we'd have to call the rescue squad for Shane.

He had been looking forward to the

Daytona 500 since Christmas, and I can't say that I had, but I was determined to be a good sport and watch it with him. I know it's the Super Bowl of auto racing and all, but I didn't exactly find it riveting, just watching a bunch of cars with numbers painted on the side, going around in a circle, turning left for three solid hours. Not at first anyhow, but after spending years with Shane McKee, I did begin to get the hang of it. I didn't know all the drivers by number and sponsor the way he did, but I could recognize most of the important ones, though I tended to get all the Bodines mixed up. Mostly I spent the afternoon paging through my fashion magazines, and glancing at the screen every now and again, especially when Shane yelled at somebody. By the last lap, he was about yelled out, and he was sitting on the edge of the sofa cushion, saying, "Come on Mike," as if his voice was going straight into Mike Waltrip's headset. Then he just froze and stopped making any sound altogether, and that's when I looked up to see what the matter was, and saw the replay.

"It's not that bad," I said when we first saw the black car up against the wall, within hollering distance of the finish line. "He's always doing stuff like that."

Shane didn't even look away from the television screen. He started shaking his head.

Then trying to cheer him up, I said, "It was an unusual wreck, though, wasn't it? Not a Bodine in sight."

Shane never took his eyes off the screen. "It's bad, Karen," he said, real quiet, like he was talking to himself.

"No. They're just playing it up for the suspense," I said. "He can't be hurt. They wear helmets and harnesses and all kinds of safety equipment. And the car's not stove in too much and it's not on fire. They'll cut him out or something and he'll be fine. Look, Mike Waltrip won the race and Dale Junior, came in second, both of them driving for DEI. He'll be drinking champagne out of the trophy with 'em in the winner's circle by the next commercial."

"Blue tarp," said Shane, like he didn't even hear me. He slid off the couch and sat shivering there on the rug about a foot from the television, like he wanted to crawl through the screen and look in the car for himself.

I tried to talk him into going out for pizza — my treat, I said, the race is over — but nothing would budge him. "My whole life," he said. "I've been pulling for Dale my whole life."

"I know," I said. The first Christmas present Shane ever gave me was a little gold number 3 to wear around my neck. It matched his.

I always thought that Shane had elected Dale Earnhardt to be his substitute dad, because his real dad wasn't good for much, and in fact Shane hadn't seen him in quite a few years. There's some of Earnhardt's kids who could have said the same once, I think, but Shane wasn't interested in the personal details of his hero's private life. Men mostly aren't. I think he just looked up to Dale Earnhardt so much that he didn't care a bit what the man was really like. As far as Shane was concerned, Big Dale was a knight in a shining Chevy, a place to channel all those feelings you're supposed to have for your dad, and somebody you'd be proud to be kin to, whereas his own dad wasn't much to brag about, by all accounts. Believing in Dale got Shane through childhood anyhow, but when it all ended on February 18, 2001, he wasn't ready to let go.

So we never did eat dinner that night. I don't remember what came on after the race, because we weren't really watching the show. We were just waiting for the program to be interrupted with more news about the wreck, which finally came about seven, and then Shane started to cry, and I was crying because it scared me so bad to see him like that. I didn't know what to say to somebody in that much grief. I haven't had much experience with people dying. Mostly it's friends of our grandparents who pass away, and they're usually so sick or senile that people go around talking about what a blessed release it is, though I've always suspected that they mean for the family instead of for the dead person.

Now Dale Earnhardt was pushing fifty, not exactly young by high school standards, but no way was he some broken-down senior citizen ready to kick the bucket for want of anything better to do.

"It's not fair," said Shane.

Well, it kinda was, I thought, but I didn't say so. Dale Earnhardt was known as the Intimidator, because his trademark was to tap some other car with his bumper when he wanted them to get out of his way in a race. In 1987 at Pocono, Dale won by bumping his way past Alan Kulwicki just half a lap from the finish line. And in the first Winston Shootout in Charlotte, he crashed into Bill Elliott and Geoff Bodine, and then went on to win the race, and Old Awesome Bill from Dawsonville and Bodine got so mad at Dale that they

109

crashed into him during the cool-down lap *after* the race. So I know for a fact that Dale had caused a bunch of wrecks his own self, not that he ever got anybody hurt bad that I know of, unlike poor Ricky Rudd who once ran over a pit crew guy coming off the track too fast, which is why they have speed limits now in the pits.

Still, the way that wreck happened at Daytona, it looked like somebody had tapped Dale's bumper, giving him a taste of his own medicine, maybe, only things went terribly wrong after that. It was fair, I guess, but that wasn't going to make it right to all the Earnhardt folks who were out there brokenhearted that night, especially not to the one I was trying to comfort.

"Shane, look at it this way," I said. "What if some angel had appeared to Dale this morning before the race and had said to him, 'Mr. Earnhardt, you can either live thirty more years and die old and bypassed in some Charlotte hospital, or you can go out today in a blaze of glory on the last lap of the Daytona 500 with two of your own DEI drivers coming in first and second, and be a legend forever after . . .' Well, what do you think he would have said?"

Shane clenched his jaw. "He had a little girl," he said.

There was a smart comeback to that about how much time his older kids had seen him while they were growing up, but I let it go. "But what do you think he would have said, Shane?"

He wouldn't look at me, but finally he said, "I guess he'd have picked to go today."

"Well, all right then."

Shane sat there for a while rubbing his chin, and mulling over what I said about the angel, which I know for a fact he believes in because he was raised Baptist and he reads Billy Graham's column, too, since our paper puts it on the comics page right under "Dear Abby."

"Maybe he was even living on borrowed time as it was," I said. "Remember 1990?"

Shane finally took his eyes off the screen and stared at me. Slowly, he nodded.

"It was right about there, wasn't it? Dale was the favorite to win the Daytona 500 that year. Didn't Rusty Wallace say that the only way for Dale to lose that time would be if somebody shot out his tires?"

"Wasn't Rusty. Somebody on his crew said it, I think."

"Whatever. The back stretch of the last lap, and he's way out in front, and he runs over a bell housing that fell off somebody's car on the lap before, and blows a tire. And Derrike Cope shoots past him to win, probably wondering if he had two more wishes coming. *Last lap of the Daytona 500, Shane.*"

"Borrowed time," muttered Shane, and he kind of shivered.

"And don't forget about Neil," I said. Neil Bonnett was just about Dale Earnhardt's best friend in the world, and he was killed at Daytona in a practice race just a few yards up the track from where Dale himself got killed seven years later. It's spooky when you think about it: like Neil might have been waiting to walk him through to eternity. "Maybe Neil was there for him."

Shane nodded. "Okay," he said at last. "If that's the way it was — God's will and all that, then I want God to show me a sign. Show me that Dale wanted to go and that he's okay with how it all went down."

"I don't think God does signs anymore," I said.

Well, okay, maybe He does.

A whole year went by, and we graduated. On the top of his black mortarboard, Shane put a number 3 in adhesive tape, and he made sure to bow his head when he got his diploma so that the people in the audience could see it. They started cheering and hollering, and Mr. Watkins looked out across the footlights, completely bewildered by the crowd's enthusiasm for a mediocre student like Shane. He must have figured that Shane had a slew of relatives packing the house, but all the cheering was for Dale, because nobody was there for Shane except his mom, like always. Later Shane said he hoped Dale Earnhardt had been there in spirit to see it happen, and I smiled and hugged him, but I didn't say anything back. I was thinking that Dale hadn't even gone to Junior's high school graduation, so why would he bother with some stranger's, and besides, he was probably busy in the Hereafter.

Racing on tracks of gold, if you believe that country song by David Alan Coe, which personally I don't. But Shane found it very comforting.

That summer Shane started working full time at the garage, which means he sometimes gets to work on a Busch-circuit car for a local guy. Shane is hoping that the garage work will lead to a job on somebody's pit crew someday. He got his own place, too, which looks like a shrine to Dale Earnhardt, with the posters, the black

113

number 3 couch throw, the Dale Earnhardt calendar, the race car lamp, the shelf of die-cast cars representing every ride Earnhardt had ever driven in NASCAR, even the pink one, and so on. I told Shane I hoped he didn't think that this decor was going to carry over into our married life, and he just smiled and wiggled his eyebrows at me. He was still mourning for Dale, but he didn't talk about it much after the first couple of weeks.

I had asked him at the time did he want to go to Charlotte and stand outside the church for the funeral, but he said no. Race people didn't hold with funerals, he said. So I suggested sending flowers, but he didn't even dignify that with an answer. I guess Shane thought it over by himself for a couple of weeks, because one day he announced that he couldn't go to the mall with me on Saturday morning because he was taking some senior citizens grocery shopping. I almost dropped the phone. It turned out that Shane had thought up a volunteer program for his church. "Driving for Dale" he called it. People who had cars would volunteer to take old folks or handicapped people to doctor's appointments or shopping, wherever they needed to go —

as a sort of way to honor the memory of Dale Earnhardt. The way Shane explained it: the best way to honor a driver was — to drive. I don't know if Dale would have been proud of Shane, but I was. A reporter from the local newspaper even did a story about the "Driving For Dale" project, and he told Shane that somebody ought to send a letter to Dale Junior, at DEI telling him about the program. "I'll bet you'd get a thank-you note," the reporter said, but Shane just shook his head, and said he wasn't doing it to impress Junior, that this was between him and the Intimidator.

For Christmas that year, I gave Shane a quilt that I pieced together myself, with a patchwork silhouette of Dale standing beside his black Monte Carlo on a white background, and a big number 3 with wings and a halo for a center medallion. Across the top of it, I embroidered a line I found in *The Oxford Book of Verse*: "Smart lad to slip betimes away . . ." which is from "To an Athlete Dying Young," by Mr. A. E. Houseman, and I figured Shane needed to be reminded of that sentiment. He liked it, anyhow. He even asked to see the whole poem, and when he saw that the first line was "The time you won your town the race," he thought it had been written espe-

115

cially for Dale, so I didn't tell him any different. He said we ought to put the whole poem on the web site of memorial verses for Dale, at 3peacesalute.com, but I don't think he ever got around to it. He put the quilt on his bed and said it was a comforter in more ways than one.

He was pretty much back to normal by that time, although he would still choke up when he heard a Brooks and Dunn song on the radio. Kix Brooks and Dale Earnhardt were friends, and Earnhardt even did a cameo in one of their music videos, "Honky Tonk Truth."

The first time you see that video on CMT, you might not notice anything out of the ordinary — just Brooks and Dunn singing together as usual, but if you watch real closely you'll realize that about twenty-five percent of the time they'd switched an identically dressed Dale Earnhardt for Kix Brooks. I must have seen it half a dozen times now, and once you know the gimmick, you can easily tell them apart. Kix Brooks looks like Dale Earnhardt-on-his-best-day, after a week at a spa, with a good hairdresser and makeup artist, and an acting coach. But there are some nice touches, like when Brooks (or possibly Earnhardt himself . . . no, I think

116

it is Brooks . . .) nudges Dunn off the set with his butt, just like Dale used to do to other drivers with the bumper of his Monte Carlo. The joke of the song is that in the chorus, he says it isn't him. The honky tonk truth means it's a lie. The lyrics are supposed to be a guy telling the girl who dumped him that he doesn't miss her, and that the pitiful fellow hanging out in the bar all day, drinking and crying, isn't really him. So they're singing that it isn't him and it isn't. Isn't Brooks, I mean. It's Earnhardt. They say that Brooks used to get mistaken for Dale when he went to NASCAR events, too. We thought the music video was a hoot, but now anytime it comes on the television, Shane finds an excuse to leave the room.

Then, more than a year after it happened — the wreck at the Daytona 500, I mean — Shane got his sign.

He called me up while I was on my shift at the Wolf Laurel Inn, which they get very testy about, so I knew it had to be important for him to risk getting me lectured at for receiving personal calls.

"You won't believe this!" he said, practically shouting into the phone.

"What's wrong, Shane?" I said, motioning for Tamara to take the iced tea pitcher to my tables.

"I got the sign, Karen! Just like I asked for."

"What sign?" I was picturing something tacky like an Earnhardt signature in red neon, and I figured the Logan's Steak House in town must have had a yard sale, because they are the only ones with more NASCAR stuff on the wall than Shane's got.

"Listen, Karen, I just heard about this, and you won't believe it: a goat was born in *Florida.*"

"It happens," I said.

"Yes, but listen to this: the goat has a number three in white hair on its side! A number *three.*"

"Okay."

"Don't you get it? It's got Dale's racing number and it was born in Florida — which is where he died."

"Shane, you're not buying a goat on eBay, are you?"

"Don't you get it? A *goat!* Now what are goats always doing?"

Well, to humor him I thought about it. Goats . . . Dale Earnhardt . . . Goats . . . "Butting!" I said. "Dale Earnhardt used to butt other cars with his front bumper just like billy goats ram people's backsides with their horns."

"Exactly," said Shane. "And that's my sign."

Well, it sort of is. Shane *is* a Capricorn, but if he thought that nanny goat was a sign from NASCAR heaven, then he was getting weirder than the Wiccans, and I was pretty sure that Billy Graham would agree with me.

"I want to see that goat," said Shane.

"Yeah, but it's in Florida."

"Well, I have to get there somehow. Maybe we could honeymoon in Florida."

So that's what set him off, I think. Our perfectly ordinary plan to go to Myrtle Beach for three days after the wedding, which is what people from here mostly do, got sidelined, and all of a sudden Shane was on the Internet scheming for ways to get to Florida.

"It's not just the goat," he said. "I want to see Daytona, too. Pay my respects."

"Sure. And maybe I could lay my bridal wreath on the Speedway," I said.

Never use sarcasm when you are dealing with a devout fool, because they will take you up on it in a heartbeat.

He found this bus tour advertised: "The

Number Three Pilgrimage, a 10-day tour of East Coast Winston Cup Speedways," starting near us, in Bristol and going down through the Carolinas and Georgia, scooting over to Talladega, and ending up at Daytona, with a wreath left in honor of Dale at every speedway.

Shane figured that was a sign, too, because the time the tour was being offered coincided exactly with when he had signed up for his two weeks off from work so that we could get married. Without even talking it over with me, Shane called the number in the ad, and told the travel agent how he was just about the biggest Earnhardt fan in the whole world, and how we wanted to take the Memorial Bus tour for our honeymoon. Well, to hear him tell it, the organizers got so excited about having newlyweds on the tour, for the publicity of the thing, that they offered him a two-for-the-price-of-one deal to sign up for the tour, which just put it within our budget. The condition, though, was that they wanted us to get married at the start of the tour, right there at the Bristol Speedway before the start of the Sharpie 500 Race, which is the first stop on the bus tour. Well, Shane was so excited about the prospect of getting to go on the Dale tour that he agreed to the whole thing right there on the phone, even gave them his Visa card number, though the deposit just about maxed out the credit limit.

Then he had to break the news to the other half of the bus ticket, which was me. He bought a rose at the Speedy Mart, and took me out to dinner that night. He told me the whole thing over steak kabobs at Logan's, with Dale Earnhardt glowering down on us from his shrine on the pine-paneled wall. Shane knew that this was a radical departure from our previous wedding plans and he was scared that I was going to start crying right there in the booth, but he kept bouncing in his seat, too, like he wanted to get up and shout out the good news to everybody in the restaurant. After that, I didn't have the heart to say no, and like I said, the alternative wasn't Westminster Abbey anyhow, or even the First Methodist Church, which would have been just as good to me. No — the alternative was Mama's Wiccan fellowship with their vegetarian whatevers and their Cherokee-Druid priestess from Knoxville, so I figured that whatever the Bristol Speedway came up with couldn't be much worse than that.

And that's the Brooks and Dunn truth.

CHAPTER VII

An F-14 in a Clothes Dryer

Bristol Motor Speedway

Like a flying saucer on scaffolding, it loomed on a hill across an expanse of grass near the four-lane Volunteer Parkway. Harley Claymore wasn't used to seeing the outside of the Bristol Motor Speedway from that perspective — that is, from the ground. On race day, most NASCAR drivers traveled to the track by helicopter, ferried over from the nearby Tri-Cities Airport, where drivers flew in for the Saturday evening race.

Some of the prominent drivers owned helicopters which met them at each airport on the racing circuit and transported them trackside in style, but Harley had never been a member of that exalted circle. Once, when he'd had a couple of good finishes in a row and it looked like he might be somebody someday, he'd been given a ride to BMS in Bill Elliott's private bird. Harley remembered sailing over green Tennessee hillsides, spiraling in on the cordoned-off patch of blacktop that was the fenced-in drivers' area of the vast parking lot. He had stepped out onto the Speedway helipad, still feeling like he was walking on air from the honor of being flown to the track by Awesome Bill himself. But that high ride had been only one fleeting moment in Harley's lackluster career. His customary arrival for race day was glamorous only when compared to the world of the average fan: his racing team simply shelled out the $75 for the helicopter shuttle service from Tri-Cities, just as any skybox tycoon could do, but, hey, it was better than crawling along the Volunteer Parkway at five miles per hour with the rest of middle America.

From the bus window, he looked down on the snails' procession of Fords and Chevys, and even a few non-Detroit models driven by those who did not put their money where their hearts were. Becalmed in this tide of spectators, Harley was surprised by the cold hollow in his chest that told him he cared more than he realized about his fall from glory. It had taken all his life to break into that charmed circle of famous drivers, but only a season or two to be eased out again. It had happened so fast that he'd hardly realized it.

Out in a heartbeat. But he was wiser now. He had grown up a lot in these lean years: he was going to find a way back in, and when he did, the only way they'd get him out again would be under the blue tarp.

It was a sweltering, cloudless mid-morning in east Tennessee. Race time was set for 7:30 p.m., but — knowing that the county's roads were not equal to a one-day influx of 160,000 people all heading for the same place — the crowd had already begun to arrive. The roads to the Speedway were jammed with a succession of cars and pick-up trucks, whose back windows and bumpers proclaimed allegiance to a chosen driver. Some of the more alert Number Three Pilgrims pressed their noses to the bus windows to enjoy the first moments of the spectacle. Terence Palmer, his Winged Three cap pulled over his eyes, was making up for the sleep he'd lost on the red-eye flight from LaGuardia, while beside him, Sarah Nash read his rumpled *New York Times*.

"Look! A mixed marriage!" Justine called out, pointing to an old white Bonneville with two circular decals at opposite corners of the back windshield. The driver's side of the window sported a white number 8 in a red circle, offset on the op-

124

posite side by a yellow 24.

"So the family favors two different drivers?" asked Bill Knight, leaning over Matthew to see the car in question.

"That's not it," said Justine. "It means the couple doesn't agree on who to root for. See, that 8 on the driver's side means *he's* a Dale Earnhardt, Jr. fan, while over on the passenger side, *she* likes cute little Jeff Gordon, number 24, who looks like he ought to be on *Dawson's Creek* instead of driving a stock car."

"Ah, factions." Knight nodded, reaching for his notebook. "The Romans would have felt right at home here. In ancient times, the chariot races in the Circus Maximus were divided into teams: The Reds. Green. White. Blue. And their followers wore flowers or scarves sporting the colors of the faction. Some people based their whole identity on their team affiliation. Even had it carved on their tombstones: 'Marcus Flavius, beloved father and lifelong supporter of the Greens.' "

"Did they paint their faces?" asked Cayle.

"No," said Bekasu, looking up from her magazine. "That would be the *other* supporters of the Green: Packers fans."

"You should see the camping area." The

125

older man, whose companion was decked out in the Earnhardt fabric vest, leaned forward to join in the discussion. His name tag said "Jim." "Arlene and I used to camp there back when we were going regularly to the races. It's like a big party down there in the Earhart Campground."

Matthew perked up. "Earnhardt had a campground?"

"Not *Earnhardt,* son. *Earhart.* Like Amelia. It's the name of the family that owns the land."

"I'll bet they're sick of explaining that," said Cayle.

"That campground," said Jim with a reminiscent smile. "Oh, my, that's where it's really happening. People bring kegs and guitars and tape players. Some folks set up tables and sell the racing-related crafts they spend the winter making. You can buy tee shirts, bumper stickers. Home-made CD's. Keychains. Lots cheaper than the official stuff, too, but just as good. 'Course the track might frown on that, 'cause they don't make anything off it. And the drivers don't get their cut, either, but I reckon they're rich enough."

"Some are," said Harley, thinking about Bill Elliott's helicopter. "Some are."

"Well, Arlene and me, we loved it at the

campground. It's just one big festival from camper to camper. So many nice people. All the picnics and the things to buy."

"Who looks after their belongings when they go over to the Speedway for the race?" asked Bekasu, who saw a lot of burglary cases in her court room.

The old man smiled. "Well, the fact is, don't half of 'em even go to the race. Can't afford to. Tickets are around eighty-five bucks apiece these days, if you can even get one."

Bill Knight shook his head. "You mean, people drive all the way here in RVs and then don't even attend the *race?*"

"Oh, well, sure they watch it," said Jim. "A lot of folks bring televisions hooked up with big old extension cords and set them out on picnic tables outside the campers. Then a whole crowd can bring their own lawn chairs, gather around the TV, and watch the race for nothing. From the campground, you can hear the crowd cheering and the roar of the engines from the race track over the way, so it just makes it much more exciting than sitting home in your den watching it."

"I bet you get a better view off the television than you would in the grandstands," said Justine. "Close-ups and replays and all."

127

Jim nodded happily. "It's the best of both worlds. Living room reception and lots of folks to celebrate with."

Arlene turned back from the window with a vacant smile. "Jim, that looks like Bristol out there!" she said.

Her husband patted her hand. "Sure is, baby," he said. To the others he added, "This trip is our forty-seventh anniversary celebration."

"Forty-seventh?" said Cayle. Then she looked again at Arlene's blank eyes and her tentative smile. "Why, I think that's wonderful," she said.

"Well, Arlene thought the world of old Dale."

"Dale!" Arlene brightened at the sound of the name. "Is Dale racing today?"

Jim smiled and patted her hand again, but no one else seemed to have heard her.

Ratty Laine maneuvered the bus into the designated parking area in the shadow of the towering coliseum that was the Bristol Motor Speedway, with the word "Bristol" spelled out in giant red letters on a vertical stack of blocks down the side of the grandstand supports. The bus turned into the Speedway road and into the parking lot adjoining the grandstand, where a billboard-size visage of Dale Earnhardt scowled down at them from the wall near the entrance. The boldly colored silhouette painted on the upper wall of the massive structure proclaimed the location of the "Earnhardt Tower," the newly constructed upper tier of seating built to accompany the existing grandstand sections named in honor of other legendary drivers: the Allisons, David Pearson, Darrell Waltrip, Junior Johnson, Cale Yarborough, Richard Petty, and Alan Kulwicki. The Earnhardt image was a familiar one: the black cap, wire-rimmed sunglasses, the bushy moustache, and the steely stare that made you want to step aside even if he wasn't headed in your direction.

Harley stared up at the image, sure that he could detect a smirk on those painted features. *Lost your ride, boy,* the Earnhardt totem seemed to sneer at him. He pointed out the windshield toward the scowling face. "There he is, folks," he said into the microphone. "The one and only Dale Earnhardt, haunting the place in death just the way he did in life."

"I'll bet he'd be right pleased to be remembered," said Jim.

"I'll bet he's pissed that Darrell Waltrip's section is bigger than his," said Harley.

Ratty Laine pulled the bus into one of the grassy parking areas behind the Speedway. "Are y'all going to lay the wreath now?" he asked.

Harley was already on his way out the door of the bus when the question caught him in mid stride. "Say what?"

"The wreath. Mr. Bailey at the travel company told me that the folks on this tour were going to lay a wreath at every Speedway we stopped at. In memory of Mr. Earnhardt. I got 'em all stacked in cardboard boxes in the luggage hold, but I put the one for today up in the overhead luggage rack." He nodded at a white box above Harley's seat. "You all gonna do that now?"

The phrase "might as well get it over with" was hovering on Harley's lips, but then he remembered the stern face of Harry Bailey, so he composed his features into an expression of earnest solemnity. "Certainly," he said. "It's only fitting that we should pay our respects to Dale first." He went back up the steps and pulled down the box from the luggage rack. "We're going to lay this tribute wreath now," he called out to the Number Three Pilgrims. "Photo opportunity. Bring 'em if you got 'em." To Ratty Laine he murmured, "Where the heck are we supposed to put this thing?"

The pilgrims stood on the pavement beside the bus in a respectful silence while Harley slit open the box. The wreath of silk flowers mixed white carnations and red rose buds in a design shaped to resemble a wheel. The black ribbon stretched across the face of it bore the message: *Dale Earnhardt: Victory Lane in Heaven.*"

"Oh, dear," murmured Bekasu.

Bill Knight gave her an understanding nod. "Grief does strange things to people," he said. "You see it at funerals. Whatever we say we believe in times of sweet reason, grief strips all that away and the pain reveals what we really do feel, deep down. Many people think of heaven as a place where they can do what made them happiest." He thought of tombstones. In recent years, the angels and lambs of Victorian times had given way to an almost Ancient Egyptian preoccupation with the survival of the self. He had seen tombstones depicting skiers in midjump; leaping bass adorning the monument to a fisherman; and more than one set of checkered flags, signaling the arrival of a racing fan into the Hereafter. Nothing surprised him anymore.

"They're every one of 'em different," Ratty Laine announced to no one in particular. "I peeked in all the boxes."

"I think we ought to take turns carrying the wreath," said Cayle. "A different person at each Speedway. That is, if you don't mind, Harley?"

He blinked at her in astonishment. Surely they didn't expect *him* to parade through the Bristol Motor Speedway crowds carrying a gaudy funeral wreath in memory of Dale Earnhardt, did they? He looked at their solemn faces. Apparently, they did. Harley summoned a wan smile. "Why, I couldn't deprive you folks of this chance to pay your respects," he said. "Anyhow, I believe Dale would rather have a pretty lady bringing him flowers than a beat-up old racer. You notice they never have guys handing out the trophies after a race." He presented the wreath to Cayle Warrenby.

She held the tribute out straight-armed, and looked back at her fellow travelers. "But where shall I put it?"

How about on the top of Kevin Harvick's car? thought Harley. They took care not to publicize the fact, but Harvick had taken Dale's ride at Richard Childress Racing,

132

and the cars he had driven last season — repainted of course, and with a different, less sacred number, would have been Earnhardt's Monte Carlos, if he had lived to finish the season.

"On the drivers' message wall," said Jim Powell. "Bristol always has a wall where fans can leave messages to their driver of choice. I don't know if they'll have a section for Dale, since he's not racing today, but we could check. I reckon a wreath could go right against the wall where the messages go."

Yeah, thought Harley. *Dale will be sure to check there for his messages.*

Cayle turned to him. "Would that be all right?"

Harley shrugged. He hadn't noticed any Earnhardt tributes on display as they drove by, but that didn't mean there wasn't still a shrine somewhere around. Or ten. Earnhardt had been dead a year and a half, but there were still thousands of mourners who'd fly the flag at half-staff for him if they could. In the camping area, there were probably a dozen makeshift memorials to the Intimidator. If there wasn't a formal shrine — and why would there be? He hadn't died here — then the BMS official message wall would be as good a place as any to leave the wreath. "The message wall it is, then," he said, leading the way.

They marched up the hill from the parking area, with Cayle proudly holding up the wreath, leading the others along in a way that made Harley want to hum "Onward, Christian Soldiers." People passing by stopped to look at the procession and a couple of Earnhardt fans took a picture of the wreath. One burly, bearded man with a leather vest over his black tee shirt stared for a few seconds at the tribute wreath and fell into step beside Harley. "Y'all mind if I come, too?" he said in hushed tones that suggested he was crashing a funeral. "Never really got to tell him good-bye."

Harley shrugged. "Sure. Come ahead." He was beginning to feel like the Pied Piper — lead all the Earnhardt fans out of the Speedway and into the creek . . . Then it occurred to him that he should have reminded them about sunblock, because the August sun beat down in unclouded intensity, so that they were sweaty and breathless by the time they reached the graffiti wall. They were also a bigger crowd now, since the procession had been picking up strays all the way up the hill. Harley kept turning around to make sure that all of his charges were still in the pack. Ray Reeve, squinting in the blazing sun, was bringing up the rear, but he didn't seem to be in difficulty — just walking at his own pace. There's always one, thought Harley.

A small weaselly man had hurried up to accompany his friend, the big guy who had first joined them.

"Say, what is this here march?" the scrawny fellow said, double-timing to keep pace with Harley's longer strides. "I didn't see no official announcement about this."

"It's part of a special Speedway tour," said Harley, wishing the man would go away. "Earnhardt Memorial Tour."

The man brightened. "Yeah? My buddy there was about the biggest Earnhardt fan there ever was."

In size, certainly, thought Harley, stealing a glance at the weasel's burly friend. The two of them looked like a Saint Bernard and a Chihuahua who had decided to go into partnership.

"Yessir," the weasel said, leaning close to Harley to exude his garlic-fumed confidences. "My buddy Cannon just thought the world of Dale. He almost quit the business after the 2001 Daytona."

"The business?" said Harley, suddenly interested. "What is he, pit crew?"

The little man smirked. "Naw. Even better. You know when they have wrecks

135

out on the track? Well, ol' Cannon skulks around afterward and picks up the debris. Or else he talks the pit crew into letting him have it. Or slips 'em a few bucks. Old hoods, bell housings, whatever. And he collects discarded lug nuts, racing slicks — any old thing they're fixing to throw away. Then he sells 'em to race fans. Sometimes he makes them into little plaques or lamp bases or something. Lug nut key chains. It's like turning scrap metal into gold, the prices folks'll pay for Speedway trash. My buddy Cannon is a master at it."

"He must be in hog heaven at Bristol, then," said Harley. The Bristol short track was a series of wrecks punctuated by laps.

The weasel grinned at the thought of a fresh haul of car parts in the wake of the Sharpie 500. "So where's this tribute tour going after this, then, huh, mister?"

Harley didn't want to tell him, though he couldn't quite pinpoint the cause of his reluctance. The tour itinerary was not only public record, it was common sense. Where would anybody go to pay their respects to Earnhardt? Bristol, Martinsville, DEI in Mooresville, Rockingham. Duh. Finally, because he was beginning to feel petty about snubbing the eager little man, Harley said, "The Southern

speedways. Here to Daytona."

"Yeah?" The guy nodded eagerly. "So from here to Martinsville, right? Then, what? Richmond?"

"Not Richmond. Too far east and out of the way. We've only got ten days. Martinsville down to DEI and then to the Rock, Charlotte, so on."

"Yeah? You gonna leave one of them wreaths everywhere you go?"

Harley, gritting his teeth, managed to nod. *Please don't let this runt be a* USA Today *reporter,* he thought.

"Well, that's great," said the weasel. "A little late, maybe, 'cause he's been dead over a year, but my buddy Cannon will love it. He took it hard when it happened. He had a whole stack of used parts from the black number 3, and it's all he can do to part with one of them. He gets offered top dollar, too. Just kills him to sell one. Hey, maybe we'll meet up with you again down the road."

"Whatever," said Harley, who couldn't summon the energy to argue the matter. He mopped the sweat off his brow with a slightly used tissue.

"Say, buddy, who's leading this tour anyhow?"

Harley sighed. There was nothing for it. "I guess I am," he muttered.

"Yeah? No kiddin'. How'd you get that job?" The weasel peered up into Harley's red face. "Did you used to be somebody?"

"I was a NASCAR driver. Yes."

"Hot damn!" cried the weasel. "Hey, Cannon, guess what? This guy here used to be somebody!"

That's right, thought Harley. *I used to be somebody.*

On race day, Bristol Motor Speedway provided a specially papered white wall on which fans were encouraged to write a few words of praise or encouragement to their favorite driver. The number of each car entered in the day's race was painted in numerical order on the top of the wall, with each number allotted a space about six feet high and three feet wide for messages. Number 6 was Mark Martin; number 9, Bill Elliott; and so on. If you knew your driver's number (and who didn't?) you could leave him a message or inscribe your support on his section of wall. Presumably, after the race, the message papers would be given to each driver. Some numbers still had more white space than writing, and Harley felt a pang of sympathetic kinship for the slighted ones. He felt like writing *Hang in there, buddy!* on Todd or Brett

Bodine's wall, and he didn't even particularly like the Bodines. Jeff Gordon and Dale Junior, though, might want to set aside a couple of hours to decipher all their fan messages.

When the little procession of mourners reached the graffiti wall, they found that no message space had been allotted for the number 3, since of course no car of that number was racing today. Harley willed himself not to roll his eyes as he met the looks of outrage and tearful disappointment on the faces of the assembled pilgrims.

"Well, he's not driving today," he said. "And Richard Childress, who owns the number 3, isn't about to put anybody else out there in it." They nodded in agreement that this would be blasphemy.

Jesse Franklin spoke up. "Well, actually, Happy Havewreck, er — Kevin Harvick that is —" He gave them a twinkling smile to show that the slip had been deliberate. "He took Earnhardt's spot on the Childress team and, for the rest of the 2001 season, he was driving cars that were made for Dale. Of course, they gave him a different paint job, and his number is 29."

"I know," said Harley. "My heart goes out to him. Chance of a lifetime, maybe, but a hard act to follow." A black Monte Carlo

with "Goodwrench" written on the side —
he'd seen people cry at the sight of it.

With no number 3 car entered in the
Sharpie 500, the numbers jumped from 2 to
4. However, just after number 2 (hello,
Rusty Wallace), the wall curved at a pillar
where the number 3 ought to have gone, so
that there was a section perpendicular to the
rest of the wall that was left blank. But since
the blank wall was positioned between "2"
and "4," the fans were quick to notice this
opportunity (a little miracle, really, a blank
space just where a thousand people desper-
ately wanted one), and to appropriate that
side wall for an impromptu memorial. Earlier in the day, some still-grieving Earnhardt
supporter had drawn a big "3" at the top of
the wall with a black Sharpie, and now the
side of the pillar unofficially dedicated to the
late Dale Earnhardt had more messages
than the sections for drivers actually running
in the day's race.

What was the purpose of those messages,
Harley wondered. You couldn't wish him
luck in a race he wouldn't run, or wish him
well in general. He supposed people's messages to the Intimidator meant simply that
they missed him, and that they still needed
to express their undying devotion. It didn't
matter if Dale was somewhere reading

them in spirit or not; it was enough to his supporters that they could make the gesture. Would the Speedway officials who set up the graffiti wall continue to leave a place for the missing man? And would the messages someday evolve into secular prayers, requests for help with health problems, or money troubles, or for lost loves? Harley tried to picture Dale Earnhardt in some celestial cubicle next to St. Anthony (lost objects) and St. Martin (reformed drunks), listening to prayers of the faithful through earphones attached to his halo. Naw. That dog wouldn't hunt. Harley had *known* Earnhardt. The man didn't belong on top of a Christmas tree, whatever these Hallmark-happy mourners might think. Take it to ol' Dale in prayer, and he'd probably just give you that possum grin of his and tell you to "suck it up." Dale had come up the hard way, same as Harley had, and he probably felt the same way about being beholden to anybody.

Given the Speedway's relaxed attitude toward the impromptu wailing wall, Harley didn't suppose that the management would object to the tour group's presentation of a heartfelt floral tribute to Earnhardt, as long as the ceremony didn't disrupt the race day festivities. He was

141

more worried about stray journalists capturing the scene on film, especially if any photogenic kneeling, or weeping, or hymn-singing accompanied the wreath-laying. That wasn't the kind of publicity that would put him back on pit road.

Cayle held the wreath above her head for a moment, as if she were showing it to the heavens, before she bent over and placed the floral tribute against the side wall. No one spoke or moved while she positioned it and smoothed the ribbon so that its letters were readable.

After an awkward silence Cayle turned to Harley. "Er — are you going to say anything?"

He shook his head. "I wouldn't know where to start." He faced the group, careful to keep his back turned to the wall, half afraid that if he turned around he would see a sneering grin spread across the features of a transparent Intimidator. Flowers for Earnhardt — how the man in black would have laughed. Why, Earnhardt hadn't even gone to Neil Bonnett's funeral — practically his best friend in the world, and yet he had stayed away. Drivers didn't like to be reminded of death. They were too close to it, most of the time. What would Earnhardt make of this little gathering of adoring strangers, and the thousand or so ceremonies like it that had taken place all over America when he died?

Bill Knight raised his hand. "I guess I could say a few words," he said. "I mean, I've had a lot of practice at memorial services." He gave them a nervous smile. "I come to praise Caesar, not bury him."

"No." The voice of quiet authority belonged to Sarah Nash. She stepped up to the wreath. "You're new to all this, Mr. Knight. I've always thought that eulogies ought to be delivered by people who knew the deceased."

The others gave a little gasp. "Did *you* know him?" asked Ray Reeve, with a scowl that dared her to lie about it.

She sighed. "Well, I met him just once — at one of those wine-and-cheese parties in Charlotte that corporate types like to host. He wore a dark suit, and he shook hands and spoke courteously to everybody who wanted to meet him, and if he was as bored as I was, he didn't show it, either. But I wouldn't claim acquaintance on the strength of that. When I said someone who knew him, I didn't mean that. I meant that all of us who watched him in the races *knew* him. Even if you never got within a hundred yards of him, you were his friend

143

if you cheered for him. And that's who ought to speak up for him now. My friend Tom Palmer was supposed to come on this trip, and if partisanship counts, he'd have been a friend of Dale. So, I guess on behalf of Tom Palmer, I'll start." She took a deep breath and spoke toward the graffiti-covered wall.

"Well, good-bye, Dale. I'll miss you out there on the track, because it was never a dull race while you were in it. You and I both started out poor and countrified in the North Carolina piedmont, and we both came into prosperity after we grew up, ending up at parties with people who had more money than sense, so I always felt a sneaking sense of pride in the fact that you handled your wealth and fame with such grace. You didn't kowtow to rich folks, but you didn't run from them, either. You always knew you were as good as anybody — and I think your fans needed somebody to assure them that this was so. This wreath is just a reminder that we haven't forgotten you, and maybe it's a thank-you from all the people who watched you win races and watched you climb to the top of society, and who never felt like you left them behind in either place. If they end up making a spun-sugar angel out of your memory, I reckon you'll have the grace not to laugh too much about it, wherever you are.

"You knew the power of believing in something, and it took you a long way. So now the believing is on the other foot. People want to think you're still there for them — somewhere. Still the people's champion. I hope you're happy with the way things turned out. A lot of people wish you hadn't left, but they wouldn't begrudge you a state of grace and eternal peace. So . . ." She looked up at Bill Knight and smiled. *"Ave atque vale,* Mr. Earnhardt."

Somebody in the back of the crowd said "Amen," and a handkerchief was surreptitiously passed to the big man in leather who had tagged along to pay his respects. Justine fumbled in her purse for Kleenex.

Bill Knight shook Mrs. Nash's hand and whispered, "Well done!" in tones of professional admiration.

When Sarah Nash stepped away from the wreath, Terence Palmer stepped up close enough to murmur in her ear, "Thanks for doing that. It would have meant a lot to my father, I'm sure. But I thought you said you weren't a fan of Earnhardt."

She shrugged. "Never knew the worth of him until he died."

CHAPTER VIII

Racing With the Angels

Terence Palmer had never seen a decal on a coffin before. There it was, though, pasted to the gunmetal lid of his father's casket: a black number 3 encircled by a halo and buttressed on either side by cartoon angel's wings.

Odd to see that symbol on the top of a casket. He had seen it often enough on the back windows of cars, though. He was glad to see something at this funeral that made sense to him. That one little symbol told him as much about his father as he had ever known. He smiled at the image, wondering if the funeral home people had known its significance. Would they have thought it some sort of religious emblem (which perhaps it was, in a way)? He saw the Winged Three as a badge of allegiance, a reference to the Trinity, and even a kind of Honk-If-You-Love-Jesus bumper sticker for the trip to the Hereafter.

Throughout the graveside service he stared at it, wondering if his father had requested it and who had put it there, but he knew there was no one he could ask. Everyone here was a stranger — or, more precisely, it was he who was the stranger in the little burying ground above the farm. The rest of the mourners all knew each other, but he knew no one — not even the man they were burying.

"I saw you staring at that decal, son. Tom meant that as a joke." The rangy older man in the Air Force bomber jacket had come up beside him. He had been one of the pallbearers. Terence finally remembered his name: Vance Howard. But that was all he knew about him.

Now Howard was nodding toward the Winged Three, and smiling. "Well, it was mostly a joke. Although if there's anybody old Tom would have wanted to be there to open the pearly gates for him, that's who it would have been."

Terence hesitated, wondering what to say to such a remark. He was the only blood relative present, so perhaps he should remain solemn despite this man's invitation to share the joke. How would his father have wanted him to behave, this man who had them put racing decals on his coffin? Truly, Terence felt he was among strangers. Not just people he didn't know. *Strangers.*

In Terence's experience, funerals were sedate occasions that marked the passing of his parents' friends: the lawyers, bankers, and diplomats who would be buried in leafy memorial gardens outside Washington, or — rarely — back on some family estate in New England or Virginia. These services were usually held in a local Episcopal or Catholic church, sometimes in a synagogue, with all the mourners suitably attired in black, and everything from flowers to eulogy quietly understated, as if the deceased had made reservations with some celestial maître d' and could now be whisked into heaven without attracting undue attention. Individuality was not stressed at these upscale funerals, perhaps because belonging had been the whole point of the deceased's life, and for the mourners as well. Not that anybody did mourn, at least publicly.

Terence could not remember hearing or seeing any displays of emotion at the funerals he had attended before this one. Even here, the reaction of the mostly male attendees was subdued. They all looked over fifty, members of the generation who did not show their feelings lightly, but they were certainly not conformists. The outfits of the mourners around the casket ranged from black dress suits to western attire that he had heretofore thought restricted to working cowboys and country singers. All right, he had expected people at this funeral to be dressed less formally than the people he knew, but even among his mother's social set, the dress codes were relaxing these days.

He supposed it was the displays of flowers that marked the main departure from the funerals he was accustomed to. Rows of wreaths were lined up on either side of the coffin, each one bearing a satin sash across it, like the chest of a beauty pageant contestant, and the sentiments spelled out in gold press-on letters were in keeping with the artwork on the coffin: Tell Dale and Neil and Alan Hello . . . Tom's Victory Lap . . . Racing With the Angels . . .

Terence had expected more conventional slogans: "In Memoriam," perhaps, or simply "Rest in Peace." He wondered what other peculiar customs might be in store for him at the reception that would surely follow the service. A slender woman in her sixties, silvery blonde, with a Hermès scarf at the neck of her camel-hair coat, had introduced herself as "Mrs. Richard Nash, one of Tom's neighbors." When she shook his hand, the rings on her knobby fingers bit into his palm and he winced, finding no consolation in the fact that her weapon of choice was a three-carat diamond.

Terence remembered seeing stone pillars flanking a long driveway just up the road and he thought this must be where she lived. If his mother had come to the funeral with him, Mrs. Nash would have been the person she would talk to. His mother's radar could spot *one of us* in half a second. After a lifetime with her, so could he, but he tried to ignore the signals, uncomfortable with the taint of elitism.

After Mrs. Nash offered her condolences, she had made a point of telling him that the neighbors had brought food to the house so that he could receive visitors afterward. The custom was common enough at home, but in these unfamiliar circumstances he found the idea disturbing. He hoped that he wasn't in for a marathon of soggy reminiscences or a drunken party, and then he scolded himself for that unworthy thought — his mother's DNA again, swamping his every impulse toward humanity . . .

Well, he would accept the occasion with grace, whatever it was. Before he left New York Terence had resolved that no matter what happened at this funeral or its aftermath, he would not tell his mother about any of it.

"He asked that a checkered flag be draped over the coffin," Vance Howard, the elderly pallbearer was saying, "but we couldn't find one big enough on short notice. I did find a casket advertised on the Internet that had a painting of a stock car on the side and blue sky and clouds on the lid. I bet Tom would have loved that. He wanted to treat the whole thing as a joke. Dying, I mean. To show he wasn't afraid."

"I see," said Terence, who didn't see at all. He was wondering: *To show whom?* It seemed to him that death always had the last laugh, anyway.

"We spent many an hour coming up with outlandish funeral arrangements. Before he found out that the cancer had returned, of course. For the longest time, Tom didn't tell me how ill he was. He just kept on making a running joke out of the idea of dying, that's how brave he was. Or stubborn. I thought he'd be around for another twenty years."

Terence nodded. So had he. He had always meant to look up his father, to see if they had anything in common. One of these days. It was always going to be *one of these days.* But he never got around to it. He supposed he had put it off partly out of embarrassment, or fear of being rebuffed, and partly from a desire to be successful beyond reproach when he did seek out his father. Now that he had seen the cozy hill farm his father called home, Terence wondered if such distinctions would have mattered to the old man, and if he would ever get over the uneasy feeling that he had missed something.

"He joked about it right to the end," Vance Howard was saying. "Tom once said he wanted the hearse to do a donut as it pulled into the pasture, and you know I actually tried to talk them into it, but Elton Grier — the fellow that runs the funeral home — he said that Lincoln was a brand-new vehicle, and he wouldn't hear of it."

Terence tried to picture a low-slung, gray Lincoln hearse skidding around a rolling cow pasture making ruts in the grass. It would have been something to see, all right, but he supposed it was just as well that the funeral director had erred on the side of caution. After all, his father wasn't here to watch anyhow.

"You a racing fan yourself, then?"

Terence smiled, hearing his mother's voice in his head. *Racing,* she would have said in a voice like maple syrup. *Do you mean the Preakness?* Any races involving automobiles were considered by her to be a sport of philistines, right down there with bowling and pro wrestling. *It's just driving around in circles,* she would say. When he was an adolescent, it had been fun to argue with her, to say that if race car drivers weren't athletes then what about jockeys, but now he avoided the subject with her altogether, in order to escape the inevitable comments on his obviously defective paternal DNA. It was odd, though, because he had known nothing about his father's interests.

"Your daddy would have been pleased that you came," said Vance Howard. "You are his only family, you know, and I can see the resemblance. I know you never got to meet one another, but he never forgot you. Used to talk about you every now and again. I remember when you got accepted into Yale a few years back. He was real proud of that. He'd want you to know that. Your name's Terry, isn't it? I think he said he named you after Terry Sanford. That was always Tom's favorite governor."

"I'm Terence," he said, offering his hand. Nobody had ever called him Terry. Ever since he could remember, his mother had treated him as a little adult and insisted on formality; and since prep school boys devise rude nicknames for their associates, his was not one he would ever want to share with anyone outside his own generation.

"I was your dad's best friend, I guess. We were in Vietnam together, and we kept in touch over the years. We've been neighbors since I retired and moved out here. How's your mother?"

"Oh, you know her?" Terence could not keep the surprise out of his voice.

"I remember her well," Howard said. Neither his expression nor his tone of voice gave any indication as to how he felt about the former Mrs. Palmer.

"I'll go with you if you like," his mother had said when she phoned with the news, and he'd announced his intention of attending the funeral.

If I *like,* thought Terence. *You were married to him, weren't you?* But that question would have used up a year's worth of plainspokenness in his family, so he let it pass. He could picture his mother sitting at her desk in the morning room in her at-home uniform of cashmere twinset and pearls. There would be a vase of fresh-cut tulips in front of her, and perhaps her cup of morning tea. Right now she was probably leafing through her monster address book to see if they knew anybody who mattered near Wilkesboro, North Carolina. Her view of life seemed quite feudal to him sometimes, especially her conviction that if you went to an unfamiliar place, you must always present yourself to the most influential family you could connect with in the area. He used to joke about it. Mother in heaven: "Is Saint John the Divine anywhere about? I attend a church named after him."

Surely, though, rural Wilkesboro would be beyond the reach of her Rolodex. At the other end of the telephone, Terence had sat at his own desk looking at this week's page on his Papini leather desk diary. *Would it be convenient for you to attend the funeral of your biological father?* he asked himself. He sighed and drew an X through all the appointments for the next two days. He cradled the receiver between his jaw and shoulder as he wrote. His mother was still rattling on about how she had come to be notified about the funeral. From the law firm who had represented the deceased, apparently. Terence, who was consulting his planner, hadn't been paying close attention.

"Will you know anybody there, Mother?" he asked when she finally paused for breath.

Terence heard a gasp and then silence, a sound which he recognized as his mother's moment of deliberation before saying something cruel in the gentlest possible way. *Pas devant les domestiques* might be her motto. Or *devant le monde,* perhaps, in her case, because she considered most of the rest of humanity to be inferior in some way to her own little circle. Not that she was ever rude about it. Heaven forbid. Her response to this was to treat other people with a formal civility, a tacit sympathy for their social handicaps: lack of money, lack of pedigree, physical defects, unprestigious alma mater. When Terence had brought school friends home to visit, he always knew where each one stood in his mother's estimation by the scrupulous courtesy which she displayed toward those found wanting. "Your mother is so sweet," his public school friends from church would say, and Terence would writhe in silent mortification, knowing that he had seen the last of them.

"No, dear," she said at last. "I wouldn't know anybody down there. He never remarried, so there's only you for family, I suppose. I had met his parents, of course. Simple, earnest people but of course they died years ago."

Simple people. And I'll bet you bought them really expensive presents while you were their daughter-in-law, Terence was thinking. That was another velvet subtlety in Claudia Paxton Clark's rules for killing with kindness. If she really liked and respected you, she gave you jokey, trifling presents on Christmas or your birthday, because it was assumed that you could buy whatever you really needed or wanted. Only social inferiors received elegant, costly gifts. The fact that most of the recipients never saw her generosity as an insult in no way diminished her satisfaction in the gesture.

Terence knew she didn't want to go to the funeral. *Wouldn't* go. If he insisted, she would reluctantly agree to accompany him, but it wouldn't happen. The night before they were due to leave, something would come up to prevent her going. A virus, a domestic crisis, car trouble — anything vaguely plausible, though never, of course, true. Anyhow, he was in New York and she was in Washington, so they couldn't travel together, and she would be no help at all with "ordinary people," so why should he bother to insist on her coming? He would get a direct flight from LaGuardia to Charlotte, and rent a car there for the rest of the journey. Getting a few days off from the brokerage shouldn't be a problem. After all, you could only go to your father's funeral once — well, you could go any amount of times in these dysfunctional days, Terence corrected himself, but this was his *biological* father, and surely that funeral was a once-in-a-lifetime opportunity. Anyhow, Merrill Clark, his stepfather ever since he could remember, was such a fitness zealot that he would probably outlive everybody else in the family, so surely this paternal funeral was a rare occurrence in Terence's life. He did not mind going alone.

There was one way in which his mother might be helpful, though. "What should I wear?" he asked.

Again the delicate hesitation. "Well, I hardly think it matters, Terence. Heaven knows what the rest of the mourners will be wearing. Anything from kilts to bib overalls, I should imagine. I think you should wear what you'd wear to anybody's funeral. Don't dress down, of course."

"All right. My new black suit. The Armani."

"Perhaps. Or even something a little less . . . obtrusive. Anyhow, darling, I think it's very brave and martyr-ish of you to go to the funeral. You hardly ever take time off work for anything, poor you. I wish it could be a wedding — you know, something less dreary than this for your outing." She paused again, and Terence waited for the rest of it. "Actually, Merrill and I have a dinner party this weekend. You know, the congressman's wife has written a children's book and I've put together a little group of people she might like to meet. Published people."

Terence nodded to himself. This was the actual way that his mother gave gifts: by introducing people she liked to people who would be useful to them. Sometimes he thought of her as an elegant silk-clad spider, tweaking her web each time a new fly alighted. The mention of the dinner party had been intended as the broadest of intimations that she could not possibly attend this funeral, in case he had been too distracted to register her previous reluctance.

"You needn't go," said Terence. "After all, it's only strangers. I don't suppose it

159

matters to *him* anymore. I just think I ought to attend. Thanks for letting me know."

"Safe journey, darling," she said. "And, of course, Merrill and I will send along a sweet little wreath."

The most expensive one in the shop, thought Terence, replacing the phone.

On the red-eye flight the next morning, he tried to tell himself that he was not going out of vulgar curiosity — he hoped he wasn't — but he didn't suppose that one could sincerely mourn a total stranger, even if you shared half his DNA, and the truth was that he did wonder how his expensive and elegant mother could have come to marry the man she called "the hog farmer." If she mentioned him at all, which happened no more than half a dozen times that Terence could remember.

When he was twelve, he had pieced together some of the story from old photo albums in a trunk in the attic. In fading snapshots, he saw the progression of his mother's coming of age: the times they are a-changing, indeed. This impossibly young version of her was so strange to him that he found himself thinking of the girl in the snapshots as a Seventies Barbie doll. There were high school photos in which a laughing Claudia Paxton with a Jackie Kennedy hairstyle and a watermelon-pink sheath dress posed with her girlfriends beside a Corvette convertible. There she was, a few pictures later, in a white prom dress beside the obligatory crew-cut jock in a white sport coat. Graduation gown, cradling a bouquet of roses. And then came the college pictures. The hairstyle changed after that and so did her outfits. Gone were the preppy clothes and the Breck Girl good looks. The collegiate Claudia, decked out in army fatigues, hunched over a folk guitar, scowling at the camera through a curtain of lank hair. Counterculture Claudia, cigarette in hand, sprawled on the grass with a gaggle of equally scruffy companions. A young soldier began turning up in the pictures after that. Terence knew who he was because a version of that face looked back at him from the mirror. This was Tom Palmer, the soldier from Camp LeJeune, who met Claudia Paxton at a folk music concert, and three months later eloped with her to Dillon, South Carolina. It hadn't lasted long. The young sergeant from the hills of Carolina and the genteel belle from the Tidewater had been chalk and cheese, and when the passion cooled, there was nothing to keep them together.

161

Well, nothing except Terence himself, but apparently that hadn't been enough.

After a few months of playing house as the wife of an enlisted man, trying to live on his army pay while her stock dividends piled up in the bank, young Claudia had taken the baby and gone back to her parents' house. If her parents had wanted her back, they had used the perfect strategy: no hint of disapproval toward the déclassé groom with the high school education, but refusing to provide any financial assistance to the newlyweds. Terence didn't know if his father had followed his wife and son to the coast, or if he had ever made any effort to save the marriage. If so, it hadn't worked.

A divorce, handled by the family lawyer, had ended Claudia's "Adolescent Rebellion," and she had never strayed again. Her second marriage, when Terence was four, had been to Merrill, an investment banker and eminently respectable son of friends of her parents. He supposed that they were happy as a couple. He had no complaints about the courteous but distant Merrill as a stepfather, and if the man was dull, he was also reliable and prosperous. Perhaps Claudia had experienced enough drama in her year as a sergeant's wife to last her a lifetime.

★ ★ ★

Around him, the sonorous words of the funeral oration droned on.

Terence kept his head bowed in what he hoped was a respectful pose for a next-of-kin, but his mind would not focus on the service. He kept thinking a dozen other thoughts: that he could have worn his Armani after all and not looked out of place among the other mourners; that the minister did not look or sound like a television evangelist; that the flowers were all real; and that the apple-blossomed hillside looked like a nice place to spend eternity.

Now that he considered it, the decal on the coffin had not really surprised him. It was exactly the sort of thing he had been expecting at the funeral for the father he never knew. It was the only thing that had lived up — or down — to his expectations of the burial of the man his mother always spoke of as "the hog farmer." He hadn't seen any hogs, either, come to think of it, which was a pity, because Terence was fond of animals. He had never been allowed to have a pet when he was growing up, but lately he had been thinking of getting, perhaps, a cat. He didn't think he could manage a dog in a small Manhattan apartment.

"A pet is a lot of work," his secretary remarked when he'd mentioned the idea to her.

Not as much work as people, Terence thought.

At last the minister finished his homily and invited those present to share their reminiscences of the deceased. Terence felt a moment of panic, envisioning all eyes turning to him, but that had not happened.

Instead, Vance Howard stepped forward and nodded to the assembled mourners. "If Tom is listening to all this somewhere, then he'll probably laugh when I say how much I'm going to miss him. We're all going to miss him. He was an original."

When the services ended, most of the people lingered for a few more minutes in the spring sunshine, talking quietly among themselves. Then they shook hands with Terence and walked back down the hill to their cars. A few stragglers accompanied him back to the house. A few minutes earlier, Mrs. Nash had touched his arm and whispered that she was going back to the house to set out the food. Before he could whisper his thanks, she had hurried away.

The white frame farm house sat in a grove of old oak trees in the shelter of the hill. Two stories high with a pitched roof, its columns supported a square, covered porch above the front door. The sunny kitchen, a one-story addition at the back of the house, had obviously been added many years after the original structure had been built. Terence supposed that this was the Palmer family homestead, but he knew nothing about that half of his heritage.

On a starched linen tablecloth, Mrs. Nash had set out plates of fried chicken and bowls of potato salad, sliced tomatoes, deviled eggs, and a glass pitcher of iced tea. Now she was stacking plain dark earthenware plates at one end of the table next to a tray of silverware. Beside it was an assortment of glassware — none of it plastic, he noted.

"This is really kind of you," said Terence, nodding toward the laden table. "It looks lovely. Did you bring the plates and silver from home?"

Sarah Nash gave him an appraising look. "All this belonged to your father," she said. "So you can tell your mother he didn't eat off paper plates."

The shot hit home, for he had been thinking exactly that. "The others will be along soon, I guess," he told her. "They stopped to talk to that older gentleman in the black suit. Mr. Johnson. Who is he,

165

anyhow? A senator? Everyone else seemed awed by him, so I didn't like to ask."

Mrs. Nash smiled. "That was Junior Johnson," she said. "Now, why don't you look around a bit? He left everything to you, you know."

Terence nodded. He had been wondering what on earth to do with all of it. The furniture looked old, comfortable, and well-made, in keeping with the style of the house, but he could hardly turn his tiny Manhattan apartment into a set for *The Waltons*. But uppermost in his mind was what she had just said. "Junior Johnson? *The* Junior Johnson?"

Sarah Nash smiled. "That was him. I didn't think you'd know who he was."

"Of course I know who he is. He's in the lyrics of Bruce Springsteen's 'Cadillac Ranch,' for heaven's sake. *Junior Johnson* came to my father's funeral?"

Sarah Nash's expression did not change but there was a twinkle of pleasure in her eyes. "Well, he lives around here," she said.

"And I guess I expected him to look like Jeff Bridges. You know, the movie. *Last American Hero*. You forget how long ago that was. He's older now. Of course he is." He looked down musingly at the hand that had shaken the hand of Junior Johnson. "I love that film. Haven't seen it in years."

Sarah Nash was still studying him, as if she were trying to guess his thoughts. Finally she said, "Well, you own it now. There's a copy in the den. It was Tom's favorite movie, too. All of this is yours now."

He nodded. "I'm not sure what to do about that," he said.

"I don't think it matters what you do, as long as you do it intelligently."

"What do you mean?"

She considered it. "Would you know what a David Hockney painting looks like?"

"A Hockney?" Terence blinked. "I think so. Well, in a museum, I would. And if it had a swimming pool in the foreground. Maybe not if I found one unframed in an attic."

She gave him a tight smile, and went back to rearranging the covered dishes. "Well, don't worry about that. You won't find one here, nor a Rembrandt nor a Faberge egg. Your father was an art collector all the same, though, and some of his things are more valuable than you might suppose. I don't believe you'd recognize the sort of art he went in for, so I thought I'd mention it to you before you start giving museum pieces to Goodwill."

Terence looked around, seeing now not a shabby old farmhouse, but a carefully arranged set piece of American primitives. He thought the furniture must be Stickley. He had seen pieces in the apartments of some of his artsy colleagues. Of course! It was made in North Carolina. The old man must have bought it years ago, probably for a song. Terence wondered if his father had known how much the pieces would go for today. He probably did.

The pottery was more of a problem, though. He didn't recognize it at all. There was a display of ceramics in the china cabinet behind the table, but one shelf display in particular looked so amateurish that he might have supposed his father had taken beginning ceramics classes for a hobby. More importantly, he wondered if Mrs. Nash had assumed that he had only come for the pickings, rather than out of duty. Perhaps she was testing him.

"I have a trust fund," he said at last. "And a job on Wall Street."

The tight smile again. "Well, I didn't suppose you needed the proceeds from a yard sale, Terence, and I doubt if any of this is to your taste. I can't say much of it is to mine. I just think it would be a shame if you went away not understanding what

you saw. Like these." She nodded towa
the shelf of blue and green pottery decorated with white figures. At first glance he
had taken them for Wedgwood: he was familiar with the graceful white classical figures that decorated the English cameo
ware of Josiah Wedgwood and Company,
but these vases — and sugar bowls and tea
pots and coffee mugs — were different
both in theme and in execution. The ren-
dering of the puppet-like figures suggested
that the artisan had never mastered pro-
portion. Instead of the elegant Grecian
themes of Wedgwood landscapes, the
clumsy beings on this pottery inhabited a
world of log cabins, tepees, and covered
wagons. Had his father or one of his
friends been attempting to imitate Wedgwood in some American idiom?

"That's Pisgah Forest pottery," said Sarah
Nash. "Made near Asheville in the first half
of the twentieth century by a man named
W. B. Stephen. I wouldn't expect you to
know it, but piece for piece it sells for more
than Wedgwood, and rightly so, because
each piece is the work of just one man
instead of a mass-produced factory item."

Terence peered at a brown coffee mug
depicting an Indian on horseback in pursuit of a buffalo.

"I suppose you recognized the Stickley pieces. That desk over there is American chestnut, which was wiped out back in the Thirties, so the desk is irreplaceable. And those five-gallon jugs with jack o'lantern faces on them belong in a museum."

Terence looked at the leering faces and protruding ears on a row of brown pottery jugs — ceramic jack o'lanterns, he thought. Still wondering if the conversation had a subtext, he made a guess. "Would you like any of these pieces as a keepsake?"

She smiled. "That's kind of you, but they would wreak havoc with my Williamsburg decor. Your father liked American primitive, but I favor the cavalier-in-denial school of decorating — the furniture of the settlers who pretended they were still in London instead of on the eighteenth-century frontier."

"What would my father have wanted me to do with all this?" he asked.

Mrs. Nash shrugged. "Enjoy them if you can. If not, there's a good auction house in Asheville. Brunk's. Collectors prize these things. Or there are museums and universities that would be glad to have them."

"I was hoping to get some idea of what my father was like from seeing his things,

170

but this isn't telling me much, except maybe why he didn't stay married to my mother. She's a cavalier-in-denial type, too."

"Why didn't you ever come to see him?"

Terence hesitated. "Shyness, I guess. He never asked me and I was afraid to push it. I thought about going when I turned twenty-one, but I had so many other things to do. Job hunting, moving . . . I thought I'd like to have figured out who I'd grown up to be before I met him. I always thought I'd have time for him when the chaos subsided in my life."

"We always think that. I guess we'd go crazy if we didn't. Well, if knowing your father's interests will get you any closer to him, you might want to take a look in the den there." She nodded toward a closed door at one end of the kitchen. "That was Tom's study. Go look."

Terence turned the handle of the door, wondering if he were about to be inundated with more face jugs, quilts, and wood carvings, but the exhibits displayed in the paneled den suggested quite a different sort of museum.

The pine-paneled walls were covered with color photographs of men in coveralls

171

leaning against brightly painted race cars. A bookcase held volumes of coffee-table books on racing and a shelf of small die-cast cars. There were hats and clocks and calendars. Terence noticed that the white number 3 figured prominently in most of these displays, and the same familiar face — a chicken hawk of a man with dark shades and a caterpillar mustache looked back from most of the photos. Terence barely glanced at the leather sofa, the oak desk, or the big-screen television, after-thoughts in a room devoted to an obsession.

When Terence was nervous, he smiled and smiled, waiting for someone to come to his rescue before he said the wrong thing.

"Tom wanted to do this himself in his younger days," said Mrs. Nash from the doorway. "He told me he felt deprived because his family was too well-off to run moonshine, so he used to volunteer to make runs for some of the poor farmers hereabouts."

"*Last American Hero*," he murmured, glancing at the wall of racing pictures.

Sarah Nash nodded. "Nearly fifty years ago now. And it wasn't just Junior Johnson. That's how most of that first bunch learned to drive. Outrunning the law. Then there were the little races — Wilkesboro, Hickory, Darlington. Your father raced in those a few times — against Ralph Earnhardt, to hear him tell it. Some of them worked in the mills or the furniture factory to support themselves. Raced instead of sleeping, sometimes. He took pride in that."

"Did you know him back then?"

"No," she said. "My husband owned the factory. But that was a long time ago. By the time Tom tried to make a go of racing for a living, NASCAR had become big business and it took serious money sponsors and a team of mechanics to keep you in a ride. He said he missed his chance. Always regretted it, I think."

"But he still followed the sport, obviously."

"Yes. Especially Dale." She nodded toward the man with the number 3 car. "Sometimes I think Tom gave up fighting that cancer after Dale Earnhardt died at Daytona. Anyhow, the rest of the items in this house can wait until you've had time to decide what to do. The one thing you have to make up your mind about fairly quickly is this." She walked to the desk and picked up a travel agent's brochure. "Tom had already paid for this trip. And you need to decide what to do about that."

173

Terence took the brochure. A Dale Earnhardt Memorial Tour. He scanned the contents. Ten days, beginning in August . . . visit Winston Cup Speedways . . . see the races at Bristol and Darlington . . . "My father planned to do this?"

She nodded. "Almost enough to stay alive for, in spite of the pain."

He looked around the room, at all the familiar faces of NASCAR's heroes looking out at him from signed photographs. The Allisons. The Pettys. Cale Yarborough. At the artifacts of a pastime he had watched only from a distance. Familiar faces whose images had also been taped to his walls at home — much to the consternation of his mother. Funny thing about DNA, he thought. You spend your whole life assuming that your absent parent is a total stranger with whom you have nothing in common, and then one day you walk into a room and discover another version of yourself.

"I wish I had known him," said Terence.

"I wish you had, too. I think you two would have got along well."

He looked again at the travel brochure. "A ticket to Bristol!" he exclaimed. "They're impossible to come by."

Sarah Nash nodded. "That's exactly

what Tom said. There's two tickets there by the way. Tom gave me one for Christmas."

"Oh. You were an Earnhardt fan, too?"

"Not the way your father was," she said. "I respected him." She paused for a moment, as if searching for a diplomatic way of putting it. Then she smiled. "I thought he was a roughneck, if you want the truth. Tom used to enjoy teasing me about that. I'm partial to Bill Elliott myself. But Tom didn't want to go on the tour alone. Couldn't, maybe. He was pretty sick by then. So there's two places booked on the tour, if you'd like to take a friend with you."

If Terence had thought about it for even ten more seconds, his practicality would have overruled the impulse. He heard the back door open and then the sound of footsteps: the mourners were filing into the kitchen to pay their respects and the moment would be lost. "I want to go," he said quickly. He could do it. The tour was months away, and he had vacation time coming. "Will you come with me? It's the one thing I can find in common with my dad. We could talk about him along the way."

"A memorial tour to Tom Palmer as well

as to Dale Earnhardt?" Sarah Nash sighed. "Well, I did promise him that I'd go," she said. "Me. On a Dale Earnhardt memorial bus tour, God help me. Wherever Tom is, he must be laughing right now."

CHAPTER IX

May the Best Man Win

The Wedding at Bristol Motor Speedway

After the obligatory posing for photos of hat waving and three peace salutes against the backdrop of the giant Earnhardt face, the Number Three Pilgrims threaded their way toward the Speedway entrance through a solid mass of race day crowd: spectators, ticket hawkers, photographers, and souvenir vendors. As they walked, Harley pointed out a catwalk bridge shielded with red nylon strips of privacy covering. The elevated walkway snaked its way up from an enclosed area of the parking lot and led down to a private entrance to the building. "Anybody know what that is?" Harley asked, pointing up at it. "You don't have to raise your hand, Matthew. Lord knows this isn't school. Okay, then, what?"

Matthew's eyes grew round with awe as he contemplated the walkway above them. "That's where *they* walk," he whispered. "It leads to the drivers' entrance."

"That's right," said Harley, remembering the feeling of having several hundred people look up to you even if you're only five feet eight. You get used to that feeling. He had walked up there once. Up there with Elliott and Earnhardt and everybody. He was glad that there was nobody up there now to see him down here. "Well, come on, folks," he said to the group. "They're not here yet. Nothing to see here."

After a long climb up the stairs, Bekasu led the pack from the interior hallway and out into the sunlight in the Richard Petty section of the grandstand overlooking the center of the oval track. In design and construction, the building resembled a football stadium except that there was no grass on the field of play below. There had been years ago, when football had been played here, but now concrete lined the entire floor of the arena and the brightly painted tractor trailers that transported the race cars to the track were lined up in serried rows within the oval.

"I still say that it's a wedding no matter where they hold it, and we're not properly dressed, and — *They're going to race around that?*" Bekasu, pausing for breath, looked straight down for the first time. Haloed in sunshine on the top step of the grandstand, she squinted down into the half-mile oval track, dwarfed on all sides by canyons of concrete bleachers. It was like looking the wrong way through a megaphone.

Harley Claymore came up beside her and smiled down at the familiar scene. "Yeah, I told you it was confining. You should see what it's like when you look up from down there."

"It looks like the inside of a cement mixer," murmured Bekasu. "Do they really go 200 miles per hour in that?"

"Nah! 'Course not! — Ninety miles an hour is about average speed. There's more than forty cars competing, remember, so things get crowded out there, too. Slows things down."

"On *that* track?" Bekasu pointed a shaking finger at the narrow strip of concrete. "Impossible. You couldn't get more than three cars abreast on the width of that track."

"They don't race on the flat part of the track," said Justine. "Don't you ever listen when I explain things to you? The racing is done up there." She waved her hand, indicating the concrete embankment that encircled the track as a steep sloping wall.

"But it's nearly vertical. How could anybody drive on that?"

"Centrifugal force," said Terence Palmer softly. "I expect it feels like being in a blender."

Bekasu turned to stare at him. He hadn't said much so far on the tour, and she had wondered if he were a racing fan at all.

As if he'd heard her thoughts, he said, "I learned that in physics class, not on the SPEED Channel."

"Well, I can attest to the truth of it," said Harley. "The race is run there on the embankment, but no matter how crowded it gets, there's plenty of room for errors."

Harley, who had been checking their seat numbers, was pleased to find that they had been situated high up in the grandstands, which was good. Unlike most other sports, the high seats in the grandstands are better than the lower ones for stock car racing, because to really see the race, spectators need an overview of the entire course. So did the drivers themselves. Their vista was limited to the short stretch of road in front of them, which is why each team had a spotter, positioned sniper-like on the very top of the structure, relaying information to the crew and driver about the position of other cars and possible trouble on the track ahead. There were times when a driver's windshield was so clouded with dust or smoke that his visibility was zero, and the only way for him to keep going, even to get off the track, was to drive blind and rely on the spotter's directions.

"It's remarkably like the Coliseum," said Bill Knight, peering over Bekasu's shoulder. "That oval appears to be about the length of the Circus Maximus, which is where the Romans actually held their chariot race, though of course their track was flat. Ninety miles an hour, did you say? The Essedarii couldn't get up that much speed in chariots. Surely they can't drive *cars* up on those steep embankments?"

"Centrifugal force," said Harley, trying to look as if he had not just overheard the explanation.

"Just you wait," said Justine. "It's quite a sight."

"But surely it would be suicide!"

"No. Bristol's pretty safe," said Harley. "Those are thirty-six-degree angles on the turns, sixteen degrees on the straightaway. Makes it interesting. It's low speeds, like I said." He wished the tourists would stay together so that he wouldn't have to keep answering the same questions over and over.

"Low speeds?"

"Well, relatively speaking. They go about 180 at Daytona. And they have crash helmets and safety harnesses and all. It's exciting to watch, though. The short tracks call for more driving skills than the long flatter speedways. But it does get hot in there. Sometime back in the Seventies, twenty-five out of the thirty racers had to let relief drivers take over for them on account of the heat. That's probably why they schedule the summer race for the evening these days, but of course we'll be out in the brunt of the heat for this wedding. Everybody got sunblock?"

Justine smiled. "Already in my moisturizer," she said. "Anyhow I wouldn't need it for the race where I'll be sitting." She tugged at her sister's arm. "Right now, we've got to get down there and see the wedding." She beckoned for Bill Knight to follow. "A judge and a preacher — you two can compare notes about the ceremony!"

"Oh!" said Cayle, waving her digital camera. "Look! The Cale Yarborough section is right below us. My dad will be thrilled. Can somebody get my picture next to the sign as we go down?"

"What did she mean, she won't need sunblock where she's going?" asked Bill Knight nodding toward Justine.

Harley shrugged. "Maybe she's driving."

Although the race would not begin until evening, the Speedway was already a hive of activity. Spectators trickled into the grandstands or wandered about the infield. Pit crews busied themselves in preparation for the pre-race inspection and then the race itself and television crews set up for the late afternoon event. On the Speedway infield, a plain wooden podium had been placed before a white lattice garden trellis decked with summer flowers: the site of the morning nuptials. Some of the reporters had decided to cover the NASCAR weddings as a sidebar to the Bristol race story. Wearing summer-weight brown suits and smarmy smiles, they roamed among the odd assortment of brides and grooms, microphone in hand, with a photographer or video-cam operator in tow, seeking out the most stereotypical-looking couples to feature.

As the Number Three Pilgrims reached the bottom of the grandstand, they could make out brides and grooms in every stage of sartorial splendor, milling around or posing for snapshots against the Speedway backdrop.

"Oh, aren't they cute?" said Justine as

they reached track level. "There must be a dozen cloned Dales out there waiting to get hitched. Look at that one!" She pointed to a slender youth in black jeans, black tee shirt, and cowboy boots. "Or the one over there in the white Goodwrench firesuit and sunglasses."

"Striking resemblance," said Cayle. "I just wish it wasn't the bride."

"Dale Earnhardt got married in that outfit?" asked Bill Knight, peering over her shoulder.

"I seriously doubt it," said Justine, "though it's hard to be sure, 'cause he tied the knot three different times, which gives you a lot of options. But I can think of at least one Mrs. Earnhardt who wouldn't have let him get away with it. These guys today aren't worried about what Dale actually got married in, though. They're just dressing up in what they think of as the typical Dale outfit."

"And the brides let them dress like that for the wedding?"

"Well, I figure that any guy who can get his woman to marry him in the middle of a motor speedway on race day could probably get away with just about anything. Some of them went for a more formal look, though. See that guy over there in the tux?"

"There's certainly a range of styles here."

"Yeah, from Dale Earnhardt to Dale Evans."

"I don't know when I last saw a pastel tuxedo," said Cayle.

Bekasu spotted a television crew ambushing a young couple. "Vultures!" she muttered. "The thing is, those smug reporters down there are going to assume that none of these people know how silly they're going to look to a TV audience, but most of them *do* know."

"Really?" said Terence Palmer with raised eyebrows. "You detect postmodern irony?"

"Betcher ass we do," said Justine. She pointed to the wedding participants. "Now I'll bet this is a second or third marriage for some of those older couples, and they've done the whole white-gown-and-church bit before. So now they're going to do it their way and they don't give a damn what anybody thinks."

"She knows whereof she speaks," sighed Bekasu. "I was there for all three of Justine's nuptials. The first time was white satin in the Grace Episcopal Church, with a groom who had children our age. Then there was the time she married her boss in the medieval ceremony with velvet cloaks

185

and lute players in the Charlotte Renaissance Festival Village, when the groom wore a kilt."

"Oh, so that's when she didn't care what anybody thought —"

Justine laughed. "No, that would be the *third* time, when Sonny Watts and I tied the knot at sea and insisted that the captain marry us."

"Ah. Was that a Caribbean cruise?"

"The Ocracoke ferry," said Bekasu. "Which was just as well, all things considered, since it wasn't legally binding."

"Oh, just you wait," said Justine. "Old Sonny will clean up his act one of these days. This Speedway wedding looks like fun, though. I just wish they were having it at Darlington instead of here. Remember Toby Jankin? My escort for cotillion?"

Bekasu shuddered. "The one who wore Converse hi-tops and white socks with his tux?"

"I knew you'd remember! Well, Toby's a doctor in Florence, South Carolina, now, which is only about ten miles from Darlington. I'm hoping to get to see him when we get there. I'll bet he'd just love to get married at the track."

"I wonder what he'd wear," muttered Bekasu.

★ ★ ★

The brides presented the greatest range of costumes in the crowd. In defiance of the sweltering heat, some determined women wore traditional satin wedding dresses, complete with long sleeves, high lace collars, and trailing net bridal veils. Their bouquets of daisies and Sharpie marker pens (courtesy of the management) were already wilting in the relentless August sun. Others were making Dolly-Parton-is-my-bridesmaid statements in full-skirted square dance outfits and stiletto heels, or sporting the faux-western attire of fringe and turquoise once popularized by Dale Evans and now employed by country singers who want people to think that Alabama borders New Mexico. The smallest group of brides, in complete denial of their surroundings, wore rosebud corsages and pastel business suits appropriate for a ceremony at the registrar's office. The youngest and most slender brides had joined in the spirit of the raceway festivities, dressing in sync with their intended husbands: NASCAR firesuits; motorcycle chic; or black jeans, black tee shirts, and silver-studded cowboy boots. Sometimes it was hard to tell man from wife.

"I wonder if you could predict the length of the marriage from the wedding clothes?" mused Bekasu.

"I never could," said Bill Knight. He sighed, thinking perhaps of twenty-thousand-dollar church-and-country-club spectacles that came to naught. At least these couples would have a race to remember some day, even if they'd rather forget the ceremony that preceded it.

Near the wedding trellis, one of the black-garbed grooms was stamping his cowboy boot on the asphalt and refusing to listen to reason.

"But, Shane," Karen Soon-to-be-McKee's eyes welled up. If Shane kept carrying on, she thought, her tears would spill over her mascara and make her cheeks look like a car that had been passed on the last lap by Dale Earnhardt — black streaks all the way down the sides.

"He was supposed to be here. Everybody said so. I was counting on it."

"I know, but this will be just as nice, won't it? I mean, it's not like it would be *really* him."

"In the pictures it would be. In the pictures." Shane looked dangerously close to tears himself. "Who remembers their wedding? It's the pictures that are real."

For the twentieth time, Karen scanned the crowd, hoping to catch sight of a man in sunglasses, white Goodwrench coveralls, and a black-and-red cap. Or even for somebody who had the right height and body type who could be persuaded to don a hat and dark glasses for the occasion. She was hoping for a miracle, and wondering what would constitute one. Kerry Earnhardt, maybe. Everybody said he was the spitting image of his dad, but he wasn't driving in the Winston Cup series this year.

She put her hand on her bridegroom's arm and tried for a compromise. "Shane, wouldn't it be better to have a real, live NASCAR driver act as best man, instead of some guy in a costume? Look, there's Jerry Nadeau right over there. He seems really nice and all. Said he'd be best man or whatever if anybody wanted him to. And then you could have a real NASCAR driver in the wedding pictures."

Shane sneered. "Dude's from *Connecticut.*"

"Yeah, but he lives in Mooresville now. Just like Dale did."

"He ain't Dale."

"Well, no. But he's really *himself.* And doesn't he look nice in his racing gear? Are

189

you sure you don't want him?"

"Huh. As often as Nadeau wrecks, it'd probably be bad luck to have him stand up for people getting married."

Karen sighed. "You're just making excuses, Shane. He seems like a great guy. I can go ask him. That is, if you promise to be nice to him."

"Whaddaya mean, be nice to him?"

"Well, you know. In the '99 race here at Bristol, when they gave Jerry Nadeau that two-lap penalty for spinning out Dale Jarrett when he didn't even mean to, and then on the last lap of the same race Dale spun out poor Terry Labonte and won the race, and NASCAR acted like nothing had happened. And you said that Earnhardt ought to be able to do anything he wanted just because he was Earnhardt. You just better not throw that up in poor Mr. Nadeau's face and make him feel bad, that's all, Shane."

Shane weakened for a moment, glancing over at Jerry Nadeau who was smiling and chatting with an assortment of bridal couples, then his mulish frown returned, and he said, "No. I don't want anybody, then. Just an empty space. Dale can be beside me in spirit."

Karen nodded. "Yeah, hon. I'm sure he will be."

She scanned the crowd again, this time hoping for a glimpse of people she actually knew, but no one had turned up yet. She had left her mother and the Wiccan Friends of the Goddess contingent sleeping late in their tents back at the campground. They hadn't been able to find other accommodations, because on race weekend every motel for fifty miles around is booked solid months in advance, so they had spent an uncomfortable night in close quarters with sleeping bags, Mrs. Tickle's homemade wine, and multigenerational girl talk, to which Karen had contributed very little. Somehow, there didn't seem to be much you could say to a bunch of women who averaged 2.2 husbands apiece when you hadn't even managed to bag one yet officially, and she certainly didn't want to hear any advice from them on the subject of marriage. There was something deeply depressing about being lectured on grounds for divorce and alimony strategies the night before you were going to stand up and vow " 'til death do you part."

She wondered what they were going to wear to the wedding. Quite ordinary clothes, probably. Most of the Friends had nice jobs as librarians or professors or realtors, and they tended to clean up pretty well when they wanted to, so she doubted whether the rayon robes with sequin-and-glitter constellations would figure into their wardrobes for the ceremony. Of course, if they did wear them, she didn't suppose it would matter, what with all the square-dance outfits and racing gear in evidence. As long as they didn't come sky-clad. *Please, Lord . . . Please, Dale . . . don't let them come sky-clad,* she thought.

Karen thought she herself looked within hailing distance of normal, anyhow. She had steadfastly refused Shane's urging to wear the feminine version of the Dale man-in-black outfit, and instead had opted for a more traditional look, although not the white satin gown she'd yearned for. Even she had to admit that the Barbie bridal dress would be ludicrous in the center of a racetrack when the other half of the wedding party was dressed in boots and jeans. In the spirit of compromise that she felt should accompany any venture into marriage, she'd accepted the help of the Friends of the Goddess seamstresses, who had found a bolt of white washable silk at JoAnn Fabrics and fashioned her a Greek tunic with handkerchief hems and a silver cord belt. Lace-up Roman sandals completed the outfit that she felt was cool in both senses of the word. She resolved to purge from her memory Mrs. Tickle's laughing assessment of the couple: "Xena the Warrior Princess Marries Tim McGraw."

"Are you nervous?" One of the cowgirl brides asked her. "I sure am." Sweat poured down the woman's cheeks from damp red hair squashed under an aqua cowboy hat.

Karen nodded. "I just hope it goes okay. After all, you only do this once."

A passing square-dance bride overheard this remark and giggled. "Don't count on that, sugar!"

Karen tightened her grip on the Sharpie bouquet with the handkerchief and the little tube of sunblock tucked into its depths. "My intended is over there sulking because he wanted Dale Earnhardt to be his best man."

The cowgirl raised her carefully tweezed eyebrows. "Dale *Senior?* He's a little late for that, isn't he?"

"Well, not the *real* Dale Earnhardt. And not even Junior. But Shane was such a huge fan of the Intimidator that he wanted some reference to him in the wedding."

"I hear you," said the cowgirl. "My intended cries every time he watches a race these days, he's still so tore up about Dale."

"Shane hasn't even watched a race since Dale died at Daytona. This will be the first one he's seen since then. He says it hurts too much. In fact, this year I — well, never mind. But Shane heard there's an impersonator on the circuit who's the spitting image of Earnhardt, and he was hoping the fellow would show up today and stand in for Dale."

The woman laughed. "Well, that impersonator probably has to be careful about when and where he shows up, because if the folks at DEI catch him at it, I reckon they might arrange for him to actually *meet* Dale."

"Here's our girl!"

Karen stiffened at the sound of a bugling drawl from ten yards away. Moments later she was engulfed by a horde of Friends of the Goddess, redolent with perfume and sunblock and all talking at once while Miss Welchett circled the group snapping off shots with her digital camera. To Karen's immense relief none of the Friends had come sky-clad. They didn't even look like a unified group. Mrs. Tickle and Karen's mother wore straw hats and chintz-patterned summer dresses, while several of the other ladies had chosen pantsuits topped by gauzy chiffon big shirts or the sort of outfits they wore to class, and the rest were in muumuus that made them look like a succession of upturned ice cream cones.

"Have you got the four things, Karen?" asked her mother.

"Umm . . . four —" Karen's startled mind refused to come up with any list other than the Wiccan standby: earth, water, wind, and fire.

"You know!" prompted Miss Welchett, still clicking the shutter. "Something old, something new . . ."

"Oh." Karen shrugged. At least they were staying mainstream with their pagan superstitions. "Well, the dress is new, the underwear's old, and I borrowed Mom's earrings. I can't think of anything blue, though."

"Your aura," said her mother. "Your aura is blue today. So you'll be fine, dear. At least, I hope so."

" 'Course I will." Karen gave her mother a quick hug, and hurried away before she was made to listen to the usual speech about the uncertainty of human relationships and the unreliability of men and the Never Give Up Your Day Job maxim.

The rest of the morning went by for Karen like a slide show on fast forward, forever to be remembered as a series of still images following in rapid succession accompanied by the aroma of gasoline, drooping flowers, and by canned wedding music and hugs from well-wishers and strangers. Shane's dad hadn't bothered to show up, but he moved around a lot so they weren't even sure he'd received his invitation, but Shane's mother was there in a pink linen dress that would have made her look young enough to be a bride herself if she didn't look so tired and nervous. Shane's grandmother had come wearing her best navy blue church dress and a Dale Earnhardt hat to get into the spirit of the occasion.

Also present were their fellow travelers from the Earnhardt bus tour, who mostly looked too presentable to be mixed up in all this, and the dozen other wedding couples who somehow made Karen feel more alone than she would have walking down a church aisle by herself. And finally there was Shane, with that firing squad look of a man facing the unknown, stepping up to the podium all alone — except in his own mind, that is — and saying his "I do" in a clear steady voice in response to her own faltering vows. Then he looked up, past her to the nearly empty Junior Johnson grandstand, and broke into a beaming smile.

Suddenly Jerry Nadeau was shaking her hand and wishing her well. "Um, you, too," she said. "You know — for the race. May the best man win." She was proud of that little play on words. She'd been saving it up to say to him when she shook his hand, but before Jerry Nadeau could even kiss the bride, Shane had taken her by the arm and pulled her aside. "Karen, I saw him!" he hissed in her ear.

She turned back to look at the rows of still vacant seats. "Who?"

"Dale! He was right there! In his firesuit and his sunglasses, with his arms folded the way he always stood, and when I looked up at him, he nodded at me. I think he might'a smiled."

"Well, that's great, Shane . . ." Jerry Nadeau was gone now, swallowed up by the crowd of laughing newlyweds, hugging and shaking hands and posing for snapshots. "I'm real glad you saw the Impersonator after all."

Shane shook his head impatiently. "Look up at those stands, Karen. Do you see anybody there? No. 'Cause he's gone. And nobody could disappear that fast from the middle of the bleachers. That wasn't the Impersonator, Karen. That was the *Intimidator*."

The rest of the bus tour turned up for the combination tour lunch and wedding reception, and when the introductions, hugs, and picture-taking subsided, the newlyweds, the Number Three Pilgrims, and the Friends of the Goddess trooped off together to find some shade in which to eat the picnic lunch courtesy of Bailey Travel augmented with a selection of salads and vegetarian dishes brought along by the Friends. The two-tiered wedding cake, a little dented from its trip to the Speedway, featured red-and-black rosettes and garlands on white icing, a replica of Earnhardt's signature in black icing on the side, and a little die-cast number 3 Monte Carlo next to the traditional plastic bride and groom on the top of the cake.

"Well, I think the whole ceremony was sweet," Justine insisted.

Bill Knight sighed. "I just wish some of them had kissed each other before they kissed the start/finish line."

Shane's mother, a colorless waif of a

woman who looked like she hadn't had enough sleep in fifteen years, hovered uncertainly on the fringes of the crowd beside Shane's grandmother, until Justine discovered them and managed to get them involved in a discussion of wedding fashions and unusual ceremonies (beginning with her own), so that Mrs. McKee finally forgot her nervousness. By the time Shane's grandmother had begun to swap herbal remedies with the Wiccans, Justine had fetched Mrs. McKee a second glass of champagne, and introduced her to Jim and Arlene. The three of them started on a comparison of NASCAR craft items and Shane's mother had begun to feel that she was being amusing and clever after all. She even summoned up a grin for the family wedding picture.

The reception hummed along despite the heat of midday, while Shane, Harley, and Terence stood off to one side and talked about the strategy of the pit stop in racing, with particular emphasis on the genius of the Wood Brothers. Karen chewed her roast beef sandwich in thoughtful silence, summoning up a smile every time somebody congratulated her, which was about every third bite. Finally, after she and Shane had cut the cake and everyone else was lined up to receive a slice, and while Justine and the Friends of the Goddess were leading a lively discussion on the feng shui of the Speedway, Karen walked up to Mrs. Tickle and asked, "Do you believe in ghosts?"

"Oh, no!" said Mrs. Tickle. "Certainly not."

It was typical of the Friends of the Goddess that Mrs. Tickle did not ask why Karen would ask such a question. This was exactly the sort of thing they thought everybody wondered about all the time, but Karen had expected a less conventional answer. "Oh, okay," she said.

"No, indeed," said Mrs. Tickle waving her fork. "I believe in the lingering spiritual presence of departed souls."

"Well, do you think the departed soul of . . . um . . . Dale Earnhardt could come back to the NASCAR circuit?"

"Certainly not," said Mrs. Tickle.

"Oh. Good. Well —"

"Because he never left," said Mrs. Tickle.

CHAPTER X

Circus Maximus

The Sharpie 500

Harley had hoped that the long afternoon at the Speedway would have given him a couple of hours to ditch the tour and hunt up some of his old friends on the pit crews before the race. The stock car circuit was like a small town: everybody knew one another and many of the participants had grown up together. Bill Elliott's brothers had been his pit crew in the early days, and even now Dale Earnhardt Junior had one of his Eury cousins as crew chief. With the influx of new talent from California and the Midwest, this was not as true as it had been in the old days, but in many ways stock car racing was still a closed world where you felt that you could dial a wrong number and still talk.

To get back in, he needed to pick up the current gossip on the circuit: Who might need a relief driver sometime during the season? Who was looking to field another car? Which of his old friends was in a position to do him a favor? Unfortunately, his Number Three Pilgrims required more personal attention than he had anticipated. Between them they had a hundred questions about the Bristol track, about the drivers he'd raced against, the rules and strategies of stock car racing, and about the details of the bus tour. *And, no, Terry Labonte was indeed a kindly fellow, and he probably would recognize Harley on sight — well, he might, anyhow — but he would be far too busy to give anybody a ride around the track today. And, no, Harley could not arrange for the group to meet Dale Junior.* What with one thing and another, Harley didn't even have time to drink his lunch.

Finally, hoping to distract them, he led them out of the Speedway for a walking tour of the souvenir stalls in the outer parking lot and then in the camping area across Beaver Creek. The rows of vendor trailers, each dedicated to a different driver, distracted them for a good forty minutes, as they wandered from stall to stall examining caps and die-cast cars, tote bags and posters. The Earnhardt souvenir trailer was at the track, still doing a brisk business in coffee mugs and decals; there were some people who still wanted to be

Dale fans, even a year after his death. Heck, there were some people who had quit the sport cold turkey on the day he died — for them it was Dale or nothing. Harley thought Ray Reeve might be one of those.

The current custom of mourning was to write messages of remembrance on the side of the black trailer itself. *You'll always be my driver, Dale!* one fan had written in black marker across some white space. Another inscription read: *Number Three: The fastest angel in heaven.* One of the messages on the trailer had been written by Bobby Labonte himself. Everybody wanted to say good-bye. The messages were simple, but heartfelt, bearing an undertone of bewilderment that the universe would allow someone so rich and famous and beloved to be taken away.

The unofficial vendors across the highway from Speedway property were the group's favorites, because the homemade goods offered by the mom-and-pop sellers were more irreverent and whimsical than the officially licensed merchandise. Technically, some of it was illegal, too, since drivers' likenesses and car designs were trademarked by the companies they drove for. He wondered if corporate killjoys ever raided the little flea market in search of such violations. Many of the current offerings, tee shirts and bumper stickers with current in-jokes and catchphrases geared to true racing aficionados, elicited more questions from Harley's charges.

"Look at this!" said Jesse Franklin, laughing as he held up a white tee shirt with the hand-lettered slogan: *Don't Hit Me, Tony!* "I need one of these. I could wear it to the office."

"*Stay in the car Sterling?*" said Bekasu, reading aloud the slogan of another one. "What on earth does that mean?"

Harley was saved from having to devise a diplomatic explanation by a grinning Jim Powell, who was eager to share the joke. "That happened last February at the Daytona 500," he told her. "It was just half a dozen laps or so from the finish, and Marlin and Jeff Gordon tangled and spun out into the grass of the infield. Okay — long story short — the officials red-flagged the whole bunch of them there on the backstretch. So they're supposed to sit there and wait for the go-ahead, but Sterling Marlin got out of his Coors Dodge and started messing with the fender. It had been bent in one of the melees, and he must have thought it would cut his tire if he didn't see to it."

"Okay," said Bekasu, with an expression suggesting that Her Honor was trying to follow expert testimony. "Is that frowned upon?"

"They were under a red flag," said Jim. "NASCAR says nobody does anything under a red flag. A couple of other drivers reported him, but I reckon the officials had spotted it anyhow."

"So what's the penalty?'

"They send you to the back of the line at the restart, which means he lost a lot of ground. Never did catch up."

"Did he think he could get away with it?"

Sarah Nash who had been listening to this explanation with an expression of solemn disapproval, interrupted. "Sterling Marlin admitted that he had pulled the fender away from the tire to stop the rubbing, but don't forget what else he said."

"What was that?" asked Jim.

"He said that he had once seen Earnhardt do exactly the same thing at the race in Richmond, and that NASCAR had not penalized Dale for it." She gave him a sour smile. "Sterling said he supposed the rules must have changed since then. Of course, he didn't suppose anything of the kind. All the drivers will tell you that

Earnhardt got away with things that the rest of them would be slapped down for trying."

"Bekasu always says the same thing about me," said Justine. "I used to break curfew and every other rule Daddy handed down, and he just couldn't bear to punish me for it. I guess some people just get to go through life in the express lane."

"Poor old Sterling. He lost the Daytona 500. Think how he must feel," said Cayle.

"I know exactly how he feels," said Bekasu.

At the next vendor table Matthew, who knew all the facts and foibles of the NASCAR crowd, had happily explained to Bill Knight what Marlin and Stewart had done that season to become the butt of tee shirt jokes. Next year it would be somebody else's turn. Now he was naming the driver and make of car that went with each of the racing bumper stickers on display.

One of the vendors had NASCAR-related badges in the shape of race cars or drivers' numbers. Harley found the red and blue emblem of the Bristol Motor Speedway and held it up. "Y'all ought to get you one of these!" he called out over the din of the crowd. "You can get one pin for every speedway we go to." In the mad scramble that followed, Harley reflected that he ought to have asked the guy how many Bristol pins he had on hand, but fortunately the item was not in short supply and, by checking with other merchants in the same tent, they managed to round up a Bristol badge for each pilgrim.

"Should we put them on our hats?" asked Cayle.

Bill Knight smiled. *"On his hat seten Signes of Synay,"* he said.

"Was that a yes?" asked Justine.

"It works," he said. "I've always pinned mine to my hat. I have a cockle shell and a bell and a badge of keys."

If he had been hoping to use this remark as a springboard to discussing his retracing of medieval pilgrimages, the gambit did not succeed. With a collective shrug, his fellow travelers surged forth to the next table of goods — Earnhardt memorial tee shirts. The one that pictured a dove in a rainbow and the caption *Dale Got His Wings — Feb. 18, 2001* was much admired, but no one bought it.

Justine, yawning broadly, noted that the race would not start for another six hours, and she suggested that they all go to the bed-and-breakfast to rest before it began. Harley, spotting his chance to get off the leash, immediately offered to sprint back to the bus and ask Ratty to take them away.

"He'd be glad to do it!" he assured them with a straight face, hustling them back across the footbridge to the parking area.

Ratty had not been glad to do it in the least. Harley had found him curled up in the driver's seat, his Winged Three cap over his face, and the bus door closed to keep in the air conditioning. A few determined thumps on the window brought him back to consciousness, and he cranked open the door with a sleepy scowl. "What?"

"Can you take the folks over to the bed-and-breakfast?" said Harley. "They want to rest up until race time. It's been a long day already for some of them."

Ratty stared at him open-mouthed. "Have you seen this traffic?"

"Well, it's not far is it? It's not downtown. The place is on a country road according to my notes here."

"Might as well be Memphis, this traffic."

Harley assumed his most sympathetic expression. "Well, I told them that," he said. "But it's awful hot out here, and some of them are pretty well up in age. And there's the little sick boy, of course . . ."

tions were met with scorn. What needy child wouldn't be glad to have a fine new pair of shoes, she had told him. At last he had given up, since sassing teacher ladies was also on the list of activities forbidden to Moore children. Reluctantly he had given in, accepting the new brown oxford shoes in exchange for his scuffed and worn old pair. The younger ones followed suit and that afternoon they had all walked home, a little self-consciously, in their new footwear. The teachers and the charity folks must have congratulated themselves on a job well done. Every time he ever told this story, Willie Moore would say that he wished those school people had been there to see what happened when the children got home. The next day, all the children came back to school in worn-out shoes or barefoot, and some of them had to eat their lunch standing up.

You don't take charity. That lesson had been drummed into Harley six ways from Sunday. Where he came from, one way or the other, you learned that lesson. Later he had learned that it wasn't how the world worked at all, and that sucking up took some people further than talent took others, but that didn't make it any easier for him to attempt it.

Swallowing his shame, Harley walked up to the drivers' entrance. He didn't have a pass to get onto pit road, but the Cup circuit was like a small town where everybody knew one another and Harley had been around long enough to be acquainted with a lot of people. Not just drivers, but owners, haulers, mechanics, spotters. All he needed was for one of them to remember him and to be in a benevolent mood that afternoon. He just hoped that the old acquaintance would be somebody he genuinely liked, so that it wouldn't feel so much like begging when he had to ask for help.

Just in time he remembered to stuff the embarrassing Winged Three hat in his back pocket. He'd never live *that* down.

There was always a gaggle of people standing beyond the barrier, cameras in hand, pens and autograph pads at the ready, waiting for a celebrity to walk by. Harley eased his way into the crowd, close enough to the walkway to make himself heard without shouting, waiting for his chance. At least he had kept his license up to date — his NASCAR license, that is, the one that qualified him to drive in any NASCAR competition. Flashing that card ought to get him past the gatekeepers if somebody vouched for him. He tried to remember if he'd got in anybody's way in his last few races, because being snubbed by a driver holding a grudge was just about more than his pride would take cold sober.

It was still too early for most of the drivers to be going in, but some of them did opt to enter by mid afternoon, either from nerves or from an obsessive need to observe the team's last minute preparations. There were still some drivers who knew their way around an engine. Ryan Newman, for instance. Harley wiped his brow in the hot sun, and listened to the conversations around him while he waited for his chance.

"Which one is Ryan Newman?" asked a young girl nearby.

"The one that looks like Prince Andrew," said the older woman next to her.

Harley filed that remark away in case he needed to make small talk with Ryan Newman anytime soon. The woman went on to make other driver celebrity comparisons, some of them quite astute. She said that Ricky Rudd looked like former President Clinton, but Harley couldn't detect any resemblance there. His fans were the best dressed, though. Whatever that meant. Instead of the tee shirts worn by most other race fans, the Rudd supporters wore snazzy black sweaters, emblazoned with the word *Rudd* in red, and matching racing pants. But a resemblance to the former president? He couldn't see it. Kurt Busch and the Keebler Elf, though — now that one registered. He didn't plan on mentioning it, but Harley figured his chances of being able to talk Kurt Busch into getting him past the guards were even more remote than his chances of winning the race from the grandstand.

Finally, after half an hour of eavesdropping in the breathless heat, a rabbity young man in coveralls headed past. Harley recognized the guy as a former CART driver, who had given up the steering wheel for a job on the pit crew of a Winston Cup driver. Now what was the guy's name?

Tony Something. That was it. Harley edged up to the restraining rope, with very little resistance from the rest of the crowd. This guy wasn't a driver, and he wasn't famous, so no one wanted a picture with him and only the diehards and the anal-retentive would request his autograph. Everybody else had rushed to a spot farther back, because someone claimed to have spotted Rusty Wallace on his way in.

"Hey, Tony!" Harley stuck out his hand,

and tried to look casual about the encounter. Desperation wouldn't get you in. "Harley Claymore," he said, by way of reminder. "How you doing, man?"

"Can't complain," said Tony, glancing about nervously. "Guess I'd better get in there and work, though."

"How 'bout I come with you?" said Harley. "I'd like to say hello to the boys while I'm here."

Tony gave him a long appraising stare. "You got a hot pass, Harley?"

Harley's smile never wavered. "Not on me, Hoss. But you know me. I'm no tourist. I just need to talk to some people."

The mechanic hesitated, embarrassed by the exchange. Finally, he shrugged and said, "Come on in, then. But if Security throws you out, don't blame me." He nodded to the guard and jerked his thumb toward Harley. "Ex-driver," he said by way of explanation.

The guard, young enough to be just out of high school, looked doubtful, but Harley had already crawled under the plastic rope and was striding past the checkpoint, feigning a deep interest in what Tony had been up to for the past couple of years.

"So how are you feeling these days?" Tony asked him, when he had run out of team and family news of his own. "You wrecked pretty bad a while back, didn't you?"

"Oh, I'm a hundred per cent again now," said Harley. "Can't wait to get back in the game."

Tony looked at him for just two beats too long, the politest expression of disbelief. Finally he said, "Yeah, well . . . I reckon you know best, Harley, but, I gotta say, sometimes when a man gets hurt while he's racing, he loses that killer instinct that a driver has to have in order to win."

"I'm as good as I ever was. All I need is a chance to prove it."

"Well, good luck, man. Long as you're not after my job, I wish you the best." Tony hurried away then, ready to start his day's work in preparation for the evening race, and maybe anxious not to be seen with someone down on his luck. Nobody wants to be jinxed on race day. He remembered the story about a driver's lucky underpants — a winning streak lost because he left them behind in the truck after one race, and the Wood Brothers did the laundry.

The Wood Brothers . . . the legendary team owners out of Stuart, Virginia . . . Their list of drivers read like a *Who's Who* in NASCAR, and stretched all the way back to the Fifties. Harley wondered if it would be any use talking to them . . . He must take care to be nonchalant in his visiting this afternoon. Any whiff of desperation would doom his chances from the outset.

He began by strolling up and down pit road, making a mental note of who he saw that he knew, so when he had decided which one of them constituted his best ally in getting taken back into the charmed circle, he could work his way back along pit road and then make his pitch to the most sympathetic ear.

He wandered from one team to another, and although a few old acquaintances looked up and muttered hellos, they were busy getting ready for the evening race and nobody had the time or the inclination to socialize with an outsider. Harley kept walking.

"I 'member you!"

Harley turned, hoping to see a crew chief or an owner, but the stout fellow with the scraggly gray ponytail, the turquoise track suit, and the matching squash blossom necklaces was not part of anybody's race team. He was a fixture at the Speedway, though. Harley summoned a smile and stuck out his hand. "Hello,

Hector," he said. "Long time no see. How's it going? — And, by the way, that was just a standard greeting. I don't really want to know."

Hector Sanders, NASCAR fan and self-proclaimed Indian shaman, had appointed himself the prophet of the Bristol Motor Speedway. The consensus was that Hector was (a) harmless, and (b) probably not a powerful wizard, despite the fact that, during a Winston Cup race, it was his custom to stand in the infield or some other prominent spot and hex the drivers of his choice. He would strike a theatrical pose, make a series of hand signals, and chant as he spun round (although, this may have been an attempt to follow the progress of the race at a track in which a lap took fifteen seconds). Everybody in racing knew him and they put up with his antics because, in a profession in which you risked your life on a regular basis, it was nice to find somebody who made you look sane by comparison. (Besides, what if he really could put a curse on your tires?)

"You're not back driving tonight, are you, Harley?" Hector shut his eyes for a moment, as if he had the day's roster inscribed on a chalkboard in his head.

Harley stared. Hector was wearing a red

218

cap sporting a white number 9 and a Dodge emblem. Bill Elliott. He wondered if this was a good sign for Bill or an impending curse. Aloud he said, "No, Hector. I'm not driving in the race. I'm just here as a spectator, same as you are."

Hector struck a pose. "I am not a spectator. I channel the luck. I decide who gets blessed this evening."

Harley nodded. Hector played favorites. Some of the drivers humored him — gave him caps and signed photos. He repaid these favors with spells of protection or, perhaps, by hexing the competition. Nobody was sure what the rigmarole of chants and hand signals represented, but they looked impressive, and in a sport where dying was always an option, it didn't hurt to play it safe with purveyors of good fortune.

Hector fingered one of his turquoise necklaces and peered at Harley from beneath caterpillar eyebrows. "You're out here a-trying to get you another ride ain'tcha, boy?"

"Guess I wouldn't say no to one," Harley admitted. "Why? Have you heard anything?"

"I don't gossip," said Hector. "I know things."

"Anything about me?"

Hector closed his eyes again, reading his internal message board. A moment later he opened them wide. "Dale Earnhardt's going to help you out, Harley."

"Junior?"

"Did I *say* Junior?"

"Uh-huh. Well, it's great to see you again, Hector. Who are you zapping tonight?"

"Rusty Wallace. I'm partial to old Rusty."

Harley nodded. "Rusty's going to win, huh?"

Hector shrugged. "No. I can't let him win, but I'm going to protect him. He'll come through this race without a scratch on him."

"Well, I expect he'll appreciate that."

Hector nodded majestically, accepting his due as a maker of miracles. "And would you like me to speak to somebody about getting you hired on?"

Harley shook his head. That was all he needed, the local space cadet to champion his cause. With help like that, he'd be lucky to get the night shift in a car wash. "I think I'll just do it the hard way," he said, walking away.

Hector Sanders called after him, "Okay,

suit yourself. I'll give your good luck spell to Jeff Gordon, then."

Harley nodded. "Yeah, good idea," he said to himself. "Give Jeff Gordon a little more luck. He can't walk on water yet."

The rest of the hot and noisy afternoon went by in a succession of shouted conversations and sweaty handshakes. People promised to keep Harley in mind, but nobody came out with a firm offer. He scribbled his post office box address and a cell phone number on a succession of napkins and autograph cards, but nobody had made him any promises to get in touch. By five o'clock, Harley figured he had done all the networking his constitution could stand, so he left pit road in search of a cold drink and wet washcloth before it was time to meet the tour group for the race.

Half an hour before race time, he settled the tour members into their assigned seats, did a head count, and handed out the earplugs that would enable them to watch the race without suffering through the deafening roar of forty-three engines without mufflers reverberating in a giant concrete bowl.

"Oh, thanks, but I won't need those," said Justine, handing back the purple plastic capsule that contained the earplugs. "I'm going up there." She pointed to a glassed-in enclosure at the top of the grandstand.

"To a skybox?"

"Uh-huh," she said, rummaging in her purse for her pass. "A friend of mine owns a company that has one here at Bristol, and when I told her I was going to be here, she invited me to come up there and watch the race."

"Lucky you," said Harley, squinting up at the glass windows far above the Richard Petty seating section.

"Well, it'll be comfortable, and there's a bathroom and all, but for Bonnie the race is as much a business occasion as a sports event, so she's always letting VIPs into the suite to mix networking with pleasure. I'll probably have to make small talk with the governor or somebody, when I'd really rather be watching the track." She gave him a bright smile. "It'll be fun, though. I'll see you back here after the race. Don't y'all leave me!"

Harley promised to wait and, with a wave and a wink, she hurried up the steps to the skyboxes. Skyboxes were for the patrician spectators of the sport. Usually leased by corporations for their executives and business clients, the apartment-size rooms were furnished with kitchenettes and bathrooms, and offered a buffet spread to fortify the well-heeled guests. The media had its own skybox where the *Sports Illustrated* guy, the stringers for various newspaper syndicates, and other journalists from all over the world watched the race in air-conditioned comfort. Afterward, the winning driver was escorted up to that skybox so that he could be interviewed by the press corps without their even having to get up. Harley had been the driver of the moment in the press skybox one autumn Sunday in Martinsville, but he couldn't remember a single question that any reporter had asked him. That fifteen minutes of fame had been a blur of sore muscles, thirst, and an attempt to downshift his brain from 100 miles per hour.

He could remember only two things from the experience. The first was looking out the press box window at the panoramic view of the Martinsville Speedway and seeing a grandstand that wasn't there. There it was on the right side of the press box, an enormous upper tier, filled with cheering crowds, against a backdrop of dark hills similar to the ones that encircled the speedway at Bristol. But in Martinsville those distant mountains were cloud banks and the right upper tier of seats was equally ephemeral. By moving his head a little to alter the angle of reflection, Harley had satisfied himself that what he had actually seen was a mirror image of the grandstand on the left of the press box projected onto the skybox glass to create the mirage of a grandstand on the right where there was just sky and clouds. He never forgot that phantom grandstand at Martinsville and he sometimes wondered who might be sitting there to watch the race. Tim? Neil? Davey? Dale himself, now? The other thing he never forgot was the remark he had overheard as he walked to the podium in front of the press box picture window for his winner's interview: "Aw, I was hoping Earnhardt would win. Who wants to talk to *this* guy?"

Bill Knight had settled young Matthew on the seat beside him, making sure that he was fortified with his medication, a Diet Coke, and was wearing his earplugs. The boy seemed to tire easily, but his excitement had borne him up through the heat and noise of race day, and now he was bouncing up and down on his seat, trying to follow everything at once.

As a preliminary to the race, there was a drivers' parade: a patriotic convoy of pickup trucks, solid red, solid white, and solid blue, each one carrying a firesuited driver standing in the flatbed, waving to the roaring crowd for one turn around the track. Matthew stood up on the seat and waved his number 3 cap at the procession, and Bill Knight muttered something in Latin.

"You rooting for anybody?" Terence asked Ray Reeve, who was seated next to him.

"Not anymore," growled the old man, not taking his eyes off the track.

"Who do you want to win, Matthew?" asked Cayle.

Matthew shrugged. "I don't really care," he said. "I just wish I could have been here when Earnhardt was racing."

Bill Knight wondered why it would have mattered. The race would consist of a cluster of cars speeding past. Except for the numbers, how could anyone tell them apart, he thought. Still, he made an effort to get into the spirit of things. "At least they have an electronic scoreboard," he said. "So that we can tell what lap they're on."

"I wonder how the Romans kept track of

laps during chariot races?" asked Bekasu, already in need of distraction.

"Ah," said Knight. "I know that one. Eggs and dolphins."

"Dolphins?"

"Yes. Poseidon was considered one of the patron deities of the game. Because of the horses, I believe."

"Not *actual* dolphins?" said Cayle, who had been listening.

He laughed. "No. Stone ones. You see, inside the oval of the Circus Maximus was a wall called the Spina, and at the end of it were two columns, each topped by a crosspiece. One crosspiece held a row of marble eggs, and the other, a row of dolphin statues. Each time the chariots circled the course, the *erectores* ran out and removed an egg and a dolphin, so the crowd could keep track of how many laps were left."

"Did those guys ever get run over by chariots?" asked Matthew.

"Well . . . possibly," Bill Knight conceded. "I expect electronic scoreboards are an improvement." He wasn't so sure about the cars, though.

Sitting at the end of the row, Harley stuck in his earplugs because he didn't want to hear the voices of the Number Three Pilgrims asking him any more silly questions. He wanted to remember the other voices — the ones from the times he raced here. Stock car drivers wear headsets, so that even though they drive alone for five hundred laps in a monotonous circle, they have as much company in their heads as they do on the track: a Babel of voices, issuing instructions, assessing the car, cheering them on. High above the track, the team's spotter was positioned, relaying information about conditions on the track ahead — who had wrecked, where a bottleneck had developed, whether to go high or low as you passed. The mechanics chimed in from time to time, concerned about the condition of the car. Was it time to pit for new tires? More fuel? Or should they wait and hope for a yellow flag? The crew chief offered strategy, encouragement, and a sounding board for whatever ideas the driver might have. You might be alone in the car, but you didn't feel that way, with all those voices shouting in your head. And a goodly number of spectators owned receivers that tuned to the frequency of the radio communications between the drivers and crews. They would tune the set to the frequency of their favorite driver, and listen to his own private race — his comments, his voices.

There was nothing like having a couple of thousand people eavesdropping on your conversation to make you watch your language.

Harley missed it, though. Not just the racing, but the voices. It had been like being in a big, close family — not that he was an expert on that feeling, really. But the idea of having a dozen people rooting for you, ready to do whatever they could to help you — that was a rush. Okay, their salaries were inextricably linked to your performance, which gave them a good reason to wish for your success, but still the support was good. Sure it was conditional, but, hey, what wasn't? He wished just once he could have felt as sustained in life as he had on the track. In life or in his marriage. And most of all he wished he didn't have to be sitting here in the cheap seats wearing earplugs, with no voices in his head to guide him around the oval.

He felt a tap on his shoulder. It was Bill Knight, looking politely inquisitive. "I'm new to all this," he said. "What exactly should I look for?"

Harley thought about it, and decided that he wasn't annoyed at the question. At least the man knew that the sport did have its complexities, which made a nice change

228

from all the idiots who thought NASCAR stood for Non Athletic Sport Centered Around Rednecks. Why did women always say things like that? Well, yeah, he had told a local news anchor chick once at one of those wine and cheese do's. And modern art is just slapping paint on canvas. So what does that make simple — the art or you? It had felt good to say that — almost worth the drink in the face and going home alone.

"Okay," he said. "The human element here is that you've got two experienced drivers trying to put an end to very long losing streaks. One of them is Rusty Wallace, who has lost forty-nine races in a row. He always used to complain about Earnhardt getting away with murder, spinning him out to get past and all."

"Ah. So now he has a chance to see if he can succeed without Earnhardt to contend with."

"Well, technically, there *is* a Dale Earnhardt in the race. Little E. Dale Junior, that is. He'll be out there, going strong in the 8 car."

"Ah. Yes, of course."

"Rusty complains a lot. He got mad about a black flag call at the Hanes 500 in Martinsville a few years back, so during

229

the post-race interviews, he cut loose with some swear words. NASCAR takes a dim view of such behavior, and they fined his ass five thousand bucks. Know what he did?"

"What?"

"He paid it." Harley grinned. "Sent half a million pennies over to Bill France in an armored car."

"Ah. Well, sometimes rage can work wonders. I knew a fellow once who could only write sermons about things he was mad about. You mentioned another driver with a losing streak?"

"The other fellow trying to outrun his bad luck is Wonderboy. That's what Earnhardt called him anyhow. Jeff Gordon."

"Now I *have* heard of him. I think he's the one Justine called the California Ken doll."

"People do," said Harley. "He's in the 24 car. He's got the movie star face, all right. He started young, and he looks even younger, which is why he got tagged with that nickname, but he's a natural. Gordon's marriage to a beauty queen is falling apart, though, and people think it might be affecting his concentration or something." Harley shrugged. "I don't know. I never could think about women when I was driving, but I suppose it's possible."

"Have you picked the winner?"

"Hard to say," said Harley. "Too many variables. This race will take a couple of hours, and that's a lot of time to screw up in. Who's going to wreck? Who's going to have mechanical problems? People don't realize how much strategy is involved in motor sports. It isn't just who has the fastest car, because every time a team gets a faster car than the competition, NASCAR thinks up more rules to even things up again."

"So, if all the cars are about the same, what determines who wins?"

"I said. Strategy. Races have been won or lost on the decision to take two tires instead of four at a pit stop. Do you stop for gas and lose your lead or keep going and hope for a caution flag? Earnhardt lost at Daytona once because he ran out of gas."

Bill Knight digested this information. "Okay," he said. "But other things being equal, who would you expect to win today?"

Harley considered it. "If wanting was getting, then I'd put my money on Jeff Gordon, I think. He has gone thirty-one races without a win. That's got to be killing him."

"But I thought you said that Wallace had a longer losing streak than that?"

"Well, but Rusty's used to it," said Harley. "He's been around a while. But Gordon, now, he's the Tiger Woods of motor sports. A child prodigy. He was younger than Matthew there when he started winning championships in go-carts. He just kept moving up to bigger and faster rides. This losing streak must be hard to take after all that early success." *Whereas I'd give my eyeteeth to be Rusty Wallace,* he finished silently.

"So you want Jeff Gordon to win?"

Harley sighed. The new bland, non-Southern face of NASCAR, all vanilla all the time. "Let's just say that with my luck, Gordon is the one who will end up in Victory Lane."

Sitting next to Bill Knight had given Harley a new perspective on watching races. He looked out across the grandstands at the blur of spectators. One hundred and sixty thousand people, each one seeing a different race. He glanced at the old couple, Jim and Arlene, sitting there holding hands in their matching Dale

Earnhardt tee shirts and vests, and he thought, *Some people are even seeing cars that aren't running here tonight.*

The pregame show at Bristol was always a thrill to watch. First came the parachutist floating down out of the sky, hauling a gigantic American flag in his wake. Harley always waited for the skydiver to get blown off course and come down outside in the creek, but he never did. Smack on the track in front of the grandstand, same as always. And then, while all the pit crews in their bright matching jumpsuits stood on the track, a spectrum of respectful attention, the event began with a Bristol tradition: the National Anthem, sung by the children of the drivers: winsome blondes in pinafores and sturdy little boys waiting for their turn at the wheel.

At the end of the row Ray Reeve was the first one to his feet when the chords of the anthem were struck. He was *the old soldier salutes the colors,* straight out of Norman Rockwell, even to the trickle of a tear across his cheek.

Cayle Warrenby touched Harley's arm. "I don't see Dale Junior up there," she said, peering at the crowded grandstand.

Harley actually stood up to point out the position of the Number 8 car at the pit before he realized what she was getting at. *Drivers' kids.* "No," he said with a weak grin. "I reckon Junior won't be singing the National Anthem tonight. And neither will CooCoo Marlin's boy Sterling nor Kyle Petty."

"Voices changed," said Bekasu.

"Well, that, and the fact that they're driving in the race themselves tonight," said Cayle, who was never sure how much Bekasu knew and pretended not to.

The cars sped past, wobbling to warm up their tires, the green flag went down, and with a roar that shook the bleachers the race began: a blur of brightly colored cars spinning around a steep, tight circle like marbles in a blender. You'd have to be traveling at a high rate of speed just to stay up on that high-banked track — centrifugal force trumped gravity.

The third lap came within a minute after the start of the race, and when the scoreboard indicated that the cars were indeed on lap 3, many of the spectators stood up, one arm upraised, with three fingers held up in tribute to their fallen hero. Harley, remembering his current assignment and his promise to Mr. Bailey, got to his feet and made the sign of the three, though he could not escape the image of a trans-

234

parent man in sunglasses and a white Goodwrench firesuit pointing at him and laughing.

"It's the three-peace salute," he shouted to Bill Knight, before the question could be asked. He noticed, however, that young Matthew was already on his feet, making the sign on his own, so *he* knew.

"In memory of Dale Earnhardt?"

Before he could answer, the third lap was over. Harley was the first to sit down. "Yeah," he said. "All last year, everybody did it on the third lap. Even the sportscasters up in the box, they tell me."

"It seems such a solitary sport," said Bill, putting his lips close to Harley's ear to make himself heard over the noise of the race.

"We'll talk after the race!" Harley yelled back, replacing his earplug.

It wasn't a solitary sport, though. It might look that way to Bill Knight's untutored eye, but Harley knew better. It wasn't just the teamwork between crew and driver, it was the feeling of the fans as well. Talk to any dedicated race fan, ask him to describe his favorite driver's progress in the race, and chances are good that he'll use the pronoun "we." As in: "We had a little trouble with the left front tire after turn four . . ." or "We thought the car was a little loose on that last lap, so we decided to pit early . . ." We. As if the spectator were sitting in the passenger seat of the race car. If you knew enough about the sport, it felt that way. You tuned your scanner to your driver's frequency, and you heard his voice, every lap of the race, guiding you through the experience, as if you were riding along beside him. Maybe pro football was a spectator sport, but motor sports was a virtual ride-along. No other sports fans could get so close to the participants while the event was taking place.

For the rest of this race, though, Harley was the most solitary person in the Bristol Motor Speedway. Without a scanner he was cut off from the voices of the participants, and without a ride, he was shut out of the sport altogether. One part of his mind followed the intricacies of the race, but beneath that was the undercurrent of worry: replaying this afternoon's conversations with the owners and crew chiefs, wondering what he was going to do when the tour ended, if he didn't have a job lined up by then. And in his head, the musical accompaniment for the Sharpie 500 was an old James Taylor song, called "Carolina in My Mind." He wasn't sure why his mental soundtrack kept looping that song, until he focused on the words to the chorus, the line after the sunshine and the moonshine. The part about the friend who hits you from behind. Oh, yeah. That was Carolina, all right. If they ever did a music video of that tune, they ought to run footage of Earnhardt racing. Ain't it just like that old Carolina boy to hit you from behind?

The race went on, punctuated occasionally by caution flags, and sometimes by Speedway-sponsored diversions, like an air cannon shooting tee shirts into the stands to the scrambling spectators. Harley wondered if there had been an equivalent to that in ancient Rome, but it was too noisy in the stands to ask the reverend about it.

The laps mounted up while the song cycled around in his head. Yeah, ain't it just like a lot of those Tarheel boys to hit you from behind? In the course of the race Dale Junior smacked Ward Burton out of the way, parking him for the rest of the night. Of course, Carolina didn't have the monopoly on roughhousing. Jeremy Mayfield, a newcomer from the Waltrips' hometown of Owensboro, Kentucky, took Hut Stricklin out of the race, and Robby

Gordon drew a penalty for wrecking Jimmie Johnson, whose car then bumped Mark Martin's, so they were all about equally furious, he figured. Nothing out of the ordinary for a Bristol race, though. A series of wrecks punctuated by fast laps.

As he watched, Harley began to wish again that he had left the Bodines a message of encouragement on the graffiti walls, after all. Poor Todd, who had crashed early on, finished dead last. On the other hand, a last place finish paid $76,634, which is more than Harley would make in a year of leading speedway bus tours, so he couldn't feel too sorry for the Bodines.

At one point, Bekasu leaned over and tapped his arm. "This is a long event!" she shouted above the roar.

Pointless to try to converse, so he smiled and nodded. Even at 90 miles per hour it takes a while to go 500 laps. He wondered if the lady judge had prepared for the bus tour by renting a racing movie like *Days of Thunder.* If he remembered rightly, that film covered the whole Daytona 500 in five minutes of screen time. Anybody who expected motor sports to be run in horse-race time was in for a long evening of disillusionment.

Fifty laps to go.

Harley felt someone grab his arm. He turned to see a stricken Jesse Franklin, round-eyed with shock. Without a word he pointed toward the walkway at the bottom of the grandstand. Harley leaned forward, scanning the crowd, and suddenly he saw what had upset the man. Dale Earnhardt was standing there with his back to the fence. Sunglasses. White Goodwrench firesuit. He just stood there, waiting — but not for long. A woman in a black number 3 jacket approached him, waited until he nodded for her to come ahead, and then threw her arms around him and hugged him for dear life. People in the lower seats, those nearest where he stood, came forward a few at a time to shake his hand or to pose for pictures with him. They seemed to forget the race, and the fact that Dale Junior was out there trying to win. The Intimidator was back.

Sarah Nash had seen Mr. Franklin's reaction, and she leaned over and said above the roar of the engines, "It's the Impersonator. Dresses up like Earnhardt and goes to races."

He still looked blank, his gaze wavering from Sarah Nash to the familiar figure now walking toward an exit.

"An imposter," said Sarah, carefully

mouthing the word. "He's been to a number of races this year."

Harley nodded. He'd heard about the Impersonator. Funny how people seemed more interested in the pale imitation of Earnhardt than they did in the real drivers out there in an actual race. The imposter's resemblance to Dale was striking, but if DEI caught him, he'd be impersonating chopped liver.

Forty laps to go.

Forty-three drivers had started the Sharpie 500 and only thirty-six finished the race, par for the course at Bristol where the banking and the short track made collisions inevitable. Nobody got hurt, though. Harley was glad, partly because he wouldn't wish an injury on any of the drivers — not even if it meant a chance at their ride — and partly because he figured a wreck might upset some of the people on the bus.

The final "hit you from behind" came on the very last lap of the race, with Rusty Wallace in the lead, barreling for the finish line, when the colorful number 24 car — Jeff Gordon, the Wonderboy — smacked Rusty out of the way to win. Wallace managed to keep control of his car, and took second place, followed by the number 8 car, Dale Earnhardt, Jr., running third.

Bill Knight tapped Harley on the arm, and motioned for him to take out his earplugs.

"What?"

"You were right! You predicted the outcome of the race. You said Gordon and Wallace were the drivers who wanted to win the most, and that Jeff Gordon probably would win. And he *did*. So I guess there must be more than pure chance and speed involved in racing. Well done!"

Harley nodded. Gordon had won. Just his luck. He felt a little cheap taking the credit for the gift of prophecy, when all he had been doing was indulging in a little pessimism with his prediction. Who had he *not* wanted to win the most? Bingo!

The crowd was beginning to push its way out of the grandstands now, though why anybody bothered to hurry was more than Harley could fathom. Fifty-plus thousand cars all trying to leave an area at once to proceed on just two lanes of blacktop in each direction would result in a traffic jam of biblical proportions. (*Exodus*, to be exact.) You could live five miles from the Speedway and not make it home for two hours in that logjam of vehicles. He signaled for his group to stay put. "No hurry," he said. "We'll be here a while."

Justine must have left the corporate skybox the minute the race ended, because she fought against the tide of departing spectators, made it down the steps to their row, and rushed up to Harley, big-eyed with some new revelation. "Did you notice that Little E. finished third?" she said. "Get it? *Third* — like the number three. Do you think that means anything?"

Harley sighed. "Well, it means about $131,000 to Junior," he said. "And there's another three in that sum for you. I wouldn't read any more into it than that."

Justine rolled her eyes. "Well, I think it means something," she said. "All those threes."

He sighed again, but it was useless to argue with a mystic. Maybe he ought to introduce the group to Hector the Shaman. Come to think of it, Hector's prophecy had been right on the money. Harley was glad he hadn't asked the Speedway mystic about Earnhardt, though. He was afraid of what Hector might have said.

CHAPTER XI

Paycheck to Paycheck

April 1982

Three miles back on Bear Creek Road —
just about the only flat, straight stretch in the
whole county. At least one without oncoming cars to worry about. The perfect
Thirteen-Twenty: Just over a quarter mile of
straightaway, creek on one side, woods on
the other; a fine and private place. It was late
April, the first time since winter that the
narrow road was dry, and by now most of
the potholes would have been filled in with
gravel by the farmer who lived at the end of
the lane. Newly minted leaves ruffled in the
night breeze, and moonlight silvered the tree
branches, turning the dirt road into a white
river shadowed by the blackness of Bear
Creek rippling alongside it.

Harley Clay Moore had been the first to
arrive that night. He had skipped baseball
practice (which he wasn't much good at
anyway) to get home early and tinker with
the engine, and now it was as ready as it

would ever be. He had to leave before his dad got home, though. If the old man saw him working under the hood, he'd be bound to guess what was going on and then Harley wouldn't have had a cat's chance in hell of getting out that night. So he had taken a package of Twinkies for dinner and driven out to Bear Creek Road before it was even dark. He was too nervous to wait anywhere else, half afraid that if he delayed his arrival, he would chicken out and not show up at all. Taking advantage of the solitude before the others arrived, he had walked up and down the Thirteen-Twenty, the quarter-mile straightaway, checking for rough patches, noting where the edge of the road was clear of logs and boulders. In a drag race that lasted only a couple of heartbeats, there was no use trying to figure out the best place to make his move. There wasn't time for strategy in a drag race. Later on, though, if he was good enough, there'd be real races when tactics did matter. Finally he might reach the big leagues of NASCAR: three-hour campaigns that played out like battles, where supplies and strategy counted for as much as skill and courage.

As a last resort for killing time, he'd

brought his English book, more as a distraction than out of dedication. Harley was nobody's idea of a scholar. He passed the time until sunset trying to finish the reading assignment in the gathering twilight, but he found that he was reading the same sentence over and over. Too keyed up to focus on a page full of long, peculiar words. *Wann that aprille* . . . Well, it was April, all right. That's about all he could relate to in that moldy old story. He opened the glove compartment and took out a picture of his favorite NASCAR driver, Darrell Waltrip, last year's champion. He had torn the photo out of the sports page of the *Charlotte Observer* and he stashed it in the car for luck, like a St. Christopher's medal, but better.

He looked at his watch. Half an hour until the appointed time — still too early, but he'd have first choice of a starting position. Meanwhile, he would find ways to pass the time. Walk the course again. Maybe take another look at the engine. His driver's license was so new that the clothes he wore in the photo hadn't even been twice through the wash yet, but that didn't mean he was new to driving. He had been behind a steering wheel ever since his feet could touch the pedals. That was one of the advantages of living on a farm. There were plenty of places to drive without getting on a state road. But this was a far cry from mowing the hayfield with the tractor, and Daddy had never let him do much more than steer the race car out of the barn. He had spent most of his childhood washing wrenches and sweeping up the garage, waiting his turn in the driver's seat, but his father seemed to think that sixteen was about half the age you ought to be before he'd trust you with his race car, which was ridiculous. Why, the old man hadn't been much more than sixteen himself when he first started spending his weekends driving dirt track. He hadn't cared what his parents thought about the matter, but nowadays he seemed to think that inflation applied to age as well as to money. So Harley burned with impatience, knowing that he'd be a better driver than the old man if only he had half a chance to prove it.

He knew the theory. He understood the moves, the tactics. He'd watched racing scenarios play out in everything from toy cars to local dirt tracks, to the occasional race on television — Formula One stuff, mostly, but some of the techniques were the same. And he listened to the NASCAR races on the radio. Sometimes he could see those races better in his head than he could see the ones broadcast on television. He argued about them with his friends, guys like Mike Gibbs, who was so car-crazed that he didn't have car magazines on his bedside table, car magazines *were* his bedside table. And Connie Koeppen, another aspiring racer, who was a rabid fan of a surly young driver named Dale Earnhardt.

Connie had been teased mercilessly about his idol's fall from grace in the past season, '81. Earnhardt had started his career in a blaze of glory, being named Rookie of the Year and then winning the championship itself the next year, but in '81 Earnhardt had not won a single race. Connie would argue that he would have won at Charlotte if his ignition hadn't cut out, and he was looking like a contender in Atlanta, too, before engine failure took him out of the race.

Harley's favorite was Darrell Waltrip, who had won the championship last year and now was driving for the legendary Junior Johnson. Waltrip was brash and confident, earning himself the nickname "Jaws," but he had the skill to back up his bravado. Harley thought he wouldn't care what people called him as long as they respected him — or, even better, envied him.

A race. Finally, after an apprenticeship that had seemed to last his whole life, he was going to see if he really could measure up. Tonight he would be driving for real. A challenge. A taunt really, made by a couple of the school's older daredevils, ready to cut a new driver down to size.

Connie Koeppen and his buddy Lorne Lupton, a couple of car-crazed seniors, had heard about Harley's souped-up Trans-Am, and they dared him to pit it against their machine. "Paycheck to paycheck," Connie had said, thrusting his hatchet face close to Harley's nose. This wasn't strictly accurate, since Connie was a rich kid who had an allowance instead of a job, but Harley took his meaning and the challenge.

Koeppen and Lupton thought their joint effort was unbeatable, and they were itching to prove it. Ever since they had pooled their skills and their savings to put together the fastest car they could afford, they had been trying to test their creation against anybody else's set of wheels, but since they preferred to race for cash instead of bragging rights, nobody wanted to take them on. Until Harley, who had more guts than sense. He knew they would be tough competition. Connie claimed that he had even driven a few dirt track races at the local speedway — without his parents' knowledge, of course. Doctors' kids weren't supposed to be hanging out with the riffraff at the racetrack.

"Bear Creek Road tonight at seven," Connie had said in the hall after algebra. "Put up or shut up."

Midnight would have been better. More fitting somehow for such a momentous showdown, but, hey, it was a school night. Lupton and Koeppen might think they were kings of the road, but they had curfews, same as Harley did. So he would be racing against their best shot at a race car, just at dark, for a week's salary, winner take all.

Harley couldn't afford to lose. His wages from a weekend job at the sawmill didn't amount to much, a little less than fifty dollars after they took the taxes out, but it kept his gas tank filled, and sometimes when Daddy ended up a little short from needing a new part for the race car or when he didn't place in the money in the Saturday race, Harley's check might mean meat instead of beans for supper that week or paying the overdue light bill. He supposed that he was a fool to risk that money on one minute of hell-bent driving up the darkness of Bear Creek Road, but Daddy could hardly object, could he? Well, he would object, of course, if he knew. He'd raise Cain if he ever found out, but Harley figured that racing was in his blood, so Daddy had nobody to blame but himself.

Racing. Pouring money down a gas tank. Wasn't that what Daddy was doing at Hickory or Asheville or Wilkesboro most every weekend? It took a chunk of money to run a stock car, even if you did every lick of the mechanic work yourself. You still had to buy parts and gas and tires. Every week. You were lucky if a set of tires got you all the way through one race, which meant that for the next meet, you'd need enough cash to buy a whole new set. Whoever said polo was a rich man's game ought to try fielding a stock car.

So between the parts and the entry fees and all, a good bit of Daddy's factory salary went to feed his racing habit, and Harley had never begrudged him a cent of it, even when it meant going through the winter with holes in his shoes. Racing was important. He just wanted to be a part of it — not just cleaning up around the shop, but really in the middle of it, clashing fenders in a red-dirt arena in piedmont North Carolina. Daddy wasn't too keen on sharing that part of the experience, though. As far as he was concerned, Harley could jockey the wrenches and leave the driving to the old man.

Being the race car driver's apprentice was getting old now, though. At sixteen Harley thought it was time he found out if he had the knack for it. Even if he lost the race tonight, the run would be worth the money he'd lose just to find out if he could out-drag the brainchild of Lorne Lupton and Connie Koeppen. Maybe if he could hold his own out here, it would be time to ask Daddy if he could go along to the dirt track, too. Or figure out a way to get there on his own.

Lorne Lupton didn't come from a family with money, so he couldn't manage a car of his own, but Lorne was one of Nature's born mechanics. He could probably soup up a lawn mower. Knew his way around an engine blindfolded. That's where Connie came in. Constantine Koeppen — Connie for short — was no great shakes as a me-chanic but he was a daredevil, mad for fast cars and the thrill of a race. His dad was a surgeon at the county hospital, which meant that he could afford the basics of a good ride. Money buys speed — it was the first article of faith in the racing bible.

For his sixteenth birthday, Connie's dad had bought him a new red Camaro. Within three months he had blown up the Camaro's engine drag racing, and his cutthroat driving had left the car with more dents than a golf ball, but instead of asking his dad to get him a new ride from the dealership, Connie had gone into partnership with Lorne, who told him what he needed to make the car a contender, and what all of it would cost. After Connie ponied up the repair money, Lorne went to work, replacing the original engine with a 454 out of a wrecked '70 Impala wagon they'd found at the local junkyard. That heart transplant from Seventies iron made the Camaro faster than the Chevrolet people had intended for a street rod to go.

Their partnership had made for one formidable opponent. Lorne was the mechanic. Connie Koeppen did the driving. Besides his lust for speed, Connie had a mean streak that would do justice to a tusk hog, coupled with a complete absence of fear, which probably explained his devotion to Dale Earnhardt. Like Dale, Connie Koeppen would do flat-out anything to keep from coming in second. The Camaro had probably cost more than Harley made in a year, between the purchase price and the cost of the parts that Lorne used to soup it up, but Connie didn't seem to care if he wrecked it or not. He figured that as long as he was careful not to get any speeding tickets, he could always get his dad to finance a replacement. Besides, Connie Koeppen was crazy. Give him an inch, and he'd put you into the river. If you found yourself on a narrow lane, barely wide enough to hold two cars abreast, and if Connie Koeppen was driving the other car, he was bound to take his half of the road right out of the middle — even if he had to bash in his own car in the process — and leave you scrambling along on what was left.

Lorne, a quiet, methodical soul who probably pretended he was the engineer on the Starship *Enterprise*, had given the Camaro's engine a high-tech advantage, and Connie had the killer instinct to make the most of it. Harley wasn't sure what his own special gift was. Desperation, maybe. Nobody could have wanted to win more than he did.

It had taken Harley more than a year of sawmill wages and odd jobs to scrape up enough cash to make his own shopping trip to the junkyard. Before he went, he'd asked for advice from one of his dad's racing friends, a hurried conversation at the track while his dad was making a test run. The old fellow, a jackleg mechanic, had scribbled a wish list on the back of his pay envelope. After a few weeks of scratching around Harley had managed to locate most of the items he'd recommended.

First, Harley had used his savings and his little bit of Christmas money to buy an old Trans-Am. He'd paid a local farmer to tow the heap to his tobacco barn, where Harley had proceeded to rip out the motor, which he swapped back to the scrap yard for more small parts. In place of the regulation motor, he had installed the 455 out of a wrecked '70 Bonneville. Then he jazzed it up with a set of Holly four-barrels on an Edelbrock manifold so fine that the result was an uber-motor that could practically pass you in neutral. The old Pontiac was a lot faster than it looked, that was certain.

When he had finished the Trans-Am's transformation, Harley continued to keep it stashed in his neighbor's barn. One look under the hood and his old man would know exactly what he was up to, and then he'd be grounded until gasoline was ten bucks a gallon. He was careful not to let Lorne get too close a look at the car, either. On the outside, the Trans-Am still looked like a rusty bucket of bolts, but if all his little adjustments kicked in as planned, the thing should take off like a rocket. Sure, the car was older than the Lupton-Koeppen Camaro, but there was no disadvantage in that. Nobody in his right mind would race an actual Eighties car when there was Sixties iron to be had. Harley's dad always said that the new emission standards had done the same thing to American autos that neutering did to a bull.

It was dark now, but still warm from the heat of the day. Harley was sprawled in the driver's seat, almost relaxed enough to drop off to sleep when the distant shine of headlights announced the arrival of his opponent and a few carloads of spectators. So this wasn't to be a private heat between racers, but a public ritual, with half the senior class along for the ride. Just as well, thought Harley. With spectators there'd be some neutral person to hold the money, drop the rag, and witness the outcome. (*Or to go for help.* But Harley didn't think of that. He was sixteen and immortal in that first race, and the thought of anyone's needing assistance never crossed his mind. Maybe if you were a no-holds-barred racer, the thought of a wreck couldn't enter your head, or else you'd hold back. You'd choke and you'd lose.)

The crowd of hangers-on — mostly the guys who hung out at the smoking yard at school — had brought six-packs and a couple of fifths of bourbon. A couple of football players had also brought their female counterparts, girls of the big hair and raccoon eyeliner persuasion, to whom this event would have all the prestige of a prom. Connie would thrive on the attention of an adoring audience, with girls to cheer him on. Harley and Lorne, probing under the hoods of their respective cars, barely noticed that anyone else was there.

Connie was all swagger, strutting around in a Duke Blue Devils sweatshirt — his dad's alma mater. It remained to be seen if his grades would get him into the university as well, or even if he could be persuaded to go. He tapped Harley on the shoulder. "Did you bring your piggy bank?" he asked. "This race is gonna cost you all of it."

Lorne still had his nose stuck in the Camaro's engine, too focused on some mechanical adjustment to care about the theatrics of the occasion. He looked up only briefly, to say to no one in particular, "Get those other cars out the way. Park them up the road toward Akers Farm, behind the starting point."

When this was done and the preliminaries had been settled, the dark road was lined with shivering spectators, and Mike Gibbs was standing in the middle of the dark road between the two cars, holding a white handkerchief at shoulder height. Harley hunched over the steering wheel, keeping his eyes on Mike, waiting for the go sign. He had forgotten about the faces peering at him from the sidelines, so intent was he on revving his engine against the brake, with one foot on the accelerator and one on the brake to keep in check until the signal was given.

Harley knew Connie preferred another method of revving up: he aimed for the red line but kept his car in neutral. At the instant the handkerchief dropped, Connie would slam into gear and lunge forward into the darkness. That split-second gear shift would cost him an instant of precious time, but he must have figured that the Camaro had enough power to make up for it. Connie hadn't even insisted on a coin toss for who had to drive on the wrong side of the road. Since Harley had arrived first, he declared, he could keep the right-hand side. Besides, nobody drove up Bear Creek road after dark, so side-of-the-road was not a factor in the race.

Harley kept his eyes on Mike's handkerchief, shining in the pool of headlights. He felt a film of sweat on his upper lip and his hands felt so clammy that he had to wipe them on his jeans to make sure that they didn't slip on the steering wheel at the crucial moment, which was fast approaching. A heartbeat later the white handkerchief began to fall, and Harley slammed the gas pedal to the floor. Tires squealed and the Trans-Am hurtled forward, even with Connie's Camaro; then the two of them sped down the dirt road, heedless of the shouts from behind them.

A quarter mile farther on — a distance carefully paced out in daylight — Robbie Bradley was leaning against the big sycamore, flashlight in hand, to signal the end of the race. The contest would be over in fifteen seconds. A quarter of a mile in cars that could go from zero to sixty in one breath. Sixty miles an hour — that's 88 feet per second, then, steadily accelerating to who-knows-what for most of the next 1,320 feet. Fifteen blurred seconds. It was all reflexes. Stomp and go and steer and before you could blink you'd passed the tree and it was over.

Harley gripped the wheel and hung on, focused on the light that Robbie Bradley was waving from his post by the sycamore . . . Almost there . . . almost there when the deer burst out of the woods and stopped dead in the glare of the headlights. In the middle of the road.

That one second of realization seemed to stretch into timelessness. A tableau in which everyone was frozen forever in the places they'd held at that instant. Robbie, illuminated by the lambent glow from the Camaro's headlights, and the dirt road, a path hanging in dark nothingness, and in the middle of the road, as motionless as if it were already dead and taxidermic, stood a yearling doe, daintily poised on her little hoofs as if they were high heels. She stared into the lights, uncomprehending, perhaps, or else frozen with fear — not unlike Harley himself.

Trees on one side . . . creek on the other . . . deer straight ahead . . .

Later he'd tried to remember what exactly he had been thinking, so as to get a better grasp of his opinion of himself. Had he been thinking: *Here is a beautiful live*

creature; let me not kill it with my recklessness?
Or was he thinking: *Hitting a deer at sixty will put the damned thing through your windshield, maybe kill you, and turn your car into a damn museum courtyard sculpture, so for God's sake, don't run into it?* Maybe he was thinking both things at once. That second seemed long enough for any amount of surmising. But while his brain had switched into slow motion, the Trans-Am kept hurtling forward at 88 feet per second, heedless of any obstacles in its path.

It didn't matter really what conclusions his brain had reached in that leisurely instant in which it had weighed and considered all the many options — steer for the creek; slam on the brakes; swerve to the left; stay on course — because while his brain was making all those judicious evaluations of the situation at hand, his body had switched to automatic pilot and was already reacting to the situation. His foot had touched the brake — not enough to send him into a skid, not enough to make much of a difference really. Except that Connie had also reacted to the sight of the deer on the road.

He had speeded up.

Even as Harley was wondering why

Connie was pulling ahead instead of swerving or trying to stop, he had eased the Trans-Am in behind the Camaro, still tapping the brake, hoping to stop in time, and watching the red taillights streaking ahead. He braced himself for a collision that never came.

At the last second, the doe, resisting the spell of the headlights, had left the road in an arching leap. As Connie's car passed the sycamore that signaled the finish line, another bound took the deer over the creek and into the dark thicket beyond.

Harley felt like twisting the wheel and going after it. He had lost the race. Useless to protest extenuating circumstances. A bet was a bet. He took most of a mile to slow down, and then he drove slowly back to the starting line where the Camaro was parked, surrounded by the roaring crowd of Connie's friends.

Harley forced himself to get out of the car and plaster on a smile of congratulations.

Connie Koeppen had tried not to gloat too much as he watched Harley lean over the hood of the Trans-Am to endorse the paycheck. "Tough break, man," he said as he pocketed the money. "But you know what they say: No guts, no glory."

"Yeah," mumbled Harley. "But this

doesn't prove anything. There aren't any deer on race tracks."

Connie shrugged. "No. But there's other drivers. You can't hit a deer — what makes you think you could hit an Allison or a Bodine if the race demanded it?"

"Well, I didn't want to win bad enough to kill for it," said Harley.

Connie just looked at him, and walked away. No retort could be worse than what Harley himself had just said. He'd remembered those words all these years, wondering if that was why he had lost his ride. You have to be willing to kill to win — and he wasn't willing. Did that make him crazy — or sane?

Years later Harley would sometimes see people from the old high school at NASCAR events, and sooner or later somebody would mention Lorne Lupton and Connie Koeppen. *Funny to think of you being the one to make it to the big time, Harley,* they used to say. *We always thought it would be Lorne or Connie out there racing against Bill Elliott.* Or sometimes one of the more cautious types — usually female — would say, "How can you make a career of racing after what happened to Lorne and Connie?"

And Harley would shrug and say, "What I'm doing now isn't what we were doing back then."

And it wasn't. Maybe Lorne and Connie would have made it, but he didn't think so. Maybe if they'd channeled their skills and their love of the race, but that drag race on Bear Creek Road had told Harley that wasn't going to happen. Maybe you have to have the killer instinct to be a champion, but you also have to have enough common sense to live to get there.

Lorne and Connie didn't live to see him make it to the big leagues. Late one night, the summer after graduation, they'd managed to get hold of a second car for Lorne to drive and they took their private drag race to a paved straightaway southwest of town, just the two of them. It wasn't a quarter-mile sprint this time, but two, three miles, maybe, and not a straight road either. Maybe the twists and turns were part of the challenge. Anyhow, they'd been neck-and-neck, running wide open on the blacktop, when they rounded a curve at the end of the woods and saw the dark mass of a freight train blocking the road ahead.

There was no stopping. Not at that speed.

The next day, most of the guys in town went out to look at the site of the crash. The wreckage had been cleared away by then, and the bodies were in the funeral home, being prepared for two closed-casket funerals.

Harley had parked on the side of the road and walked the last quarter mile to the tracks, studying the road, trying to picture those last frozen seconds. All you had to do was look at the road to see it happen.

Two cars, one in each lane, side by side, streaking toward the implacable steel wall of a freight car. And one set of skid marks.

There was no surviving that collision. Surely both of them knew that. No way to avoid it, either, not at that speed.

So one of them . . . one of them . . . had slammed on the brakes, maybe a reflex, maybe a grab at one last split second of life.

And the other one had mashed the accelerator, hurling himself even faster into the side of that freight car. Accept the inevitable and get it over with. Courage or despair?

Harley never forgot the look of that quarter mile of asphalt, although from time to time he still puzzled over what it meant. Because the car that didn't brake going into the train was the one driven by Lorne Lupton.

CHAPTER XII

Martinsville

Grandfather of NASCAR Tracks

Jim Powell stood at the window of the country chintz bedroom at Possum Hollow, looking out at the sunny morning, already as bright as noon. In the distance beyond a rose garden at the back of the house lay green folds of Tennessee mountains showing not a trace of human habitation. You'd think you were out in the middle of nowhere. Strange to think that last night after the race there had been so many cars on Volunteer Parkway that it had taken the bus a couple of hours to go three miles. He wondered where all those people were now. The drivers had taken their helicopters back to Tri-Cities to their waiting jets, of course, but that still left nearly a hundred thousand spectators earthbound in a mostly rural area. Surely there weren't enough hotel rooms and B&Bs in the vicinity of Bristol to hold all of them. He supposed that many of them were in yet another snails' procession of traffic on I-81 heading for more distant highways to take them home. Soon the bus tour would be joining the line of cars in the eastbound lane, because the next stop on the tour was the speedway at Martinsville, just under two hundred miles to the east.

Jim had been awake for more than an hour, lying wide-eyed in the darkness because he hadn't wanted to disturb Arlene by turning on the bedside light. At daybreak he took his magazine over to the desk chair, and angled it so that the sun illuminated the pages, glad that the sun came up well before seven in August, because he could never sleep for more than six hours anymore. His wakefulness was partly a factor of age and partly because he needed to be a light sleeper now in order to keep an eye on Arlene. Her illness made her restless. Sometimes at night she would get out of bed and begin to wander — he wasn't even sure she was fully conscious at those times — but she would slip out from beneath the covers and begin to walk around in the dark. Jim was always afraid that she would fall or, worse, manage to open an outside door and wander off into the night. He had read newspaper accounts of old people getting lost like that, straying off into the woods, their remains found weeks or months later by hikers or a party of hunters.

It didn't happen every night. The new medication seemed to help some. Arlene could go for days or even weeks seeming almost like her old self and then, without warning, the erratic behavior would begin again. Being in a strange place could cause it; he'd noticed that. Any change in routine seemed to upset the precarious balance of her reason and send her tumbling into confusion once more, but he was there to protect her. He wanted to keep her in the world as long as he could, because he didn't want to live without her.

She had slept well last night, perhaps tired out by the plane ride and the excitement of the race. The trip had exhausted him as well, so he was thankful to have had an easy night with her.

"We're leaving bright and early!" the bus driver had announced.

Jim looked at his watch and sighed. *Early. Nine o'clock — early?* Why, by that time back home in Ohio he'd have had breakfast, read the paper, and done half a day's work. Well, at least the late departure would give Arlene a chance to catch up on her rest. He glanced over at the other double bed to make sure that she was still sleeping. Yes. The lump under the blankets stirred a little in sleep, but there was no sound from her. He smiled as he watched her sleep. He supposed that other people looking at Arlene would see a vague and frail old woman, but he just saw — Arlene. Most of the time he didn't register the changes that time had wrought in the pretty golden-haired girl he'd married back in 1955. When you live with someone every day the changes of age come so gradually that you scarcely notice them unless you happen to come across an old photo album, and then the shock is so great that you wonder how it slipped your mind. *Slipped your mind.* Everything was slipping Arlene's mind, and that he could no longer ignore. It was the same with the mental changes, too, at first. Even now it was hard to separate ordinary carelessness from the earliest symptoms of the disease. The time she'd burned her hand getting the cornbread out of the oven? Was that the first sign or not?

Martinsville. That brought back memories. He wished that when the bus headed off up I-81 that the road would roll up behind them, erasing all the years between this room, this day, and the last time they had been together at Martinsville.

Arlene had been so excited to be at the race. Her hair was still more honey-colored than gray back then, and her eyes had sparkled with delight as they walked together through the campground, greeting old friends and looking at all the banners and handicrafts celebrating the fans' favorite drivers. Arlene was wearing her Earnhardt vest, the one she had quilted together into a patchwork composed of threes, black Monte Carlos, and checkered flags. It had been much admired by passersby as they strolled hand-in-hand past the rows of campers, and Jim remembered how proud he had been, how happy.

The word among the longtime fans was that Dale Earnhardt was going to be available for twenty minutes that afternoon to sign autographs at a sponsor's booth behind the Speedway, and he had suggested that they go early before the line got too long. But Arlene just shook her head and looked up at Jim with a smile tinged with mischief. "Let's go back to the camper instead, Jim," she said. "I believe I'd rather spend the afternoon with you."

"But why are you taking mother on this bus tour?" his oldest daughter had asked. Jean lived in Seattle, was married to some software baron, and she was always after her parents to come out and visit with her. Jim suspected that she saw their visits as a grown-up form of Show-and-Tell, an opportunity for her to display her tasteful gray Escalade, her angular modern house with its geometric furnishings of steel and glass. Jean seemed to think that good taste meant emaciation in all things. They would go out and visit her, perhaps for Christmas if Arlene was feeling up to it, but a trip to Seattle wasn't what he wanted for their anniversary journey.

"I understand your wanting to travel with her while she's still able, Dad, but surely there are things she'd rather do? She's always wanted to go to Ireland."

Jean hadn't spent much time around her parents in the past decade. Jim realized that her image of her mother was frozen in some past era, perhaps when Jean had been in high school. No matter how many times he talked about Arlene's deteriorating mental condition, it didn't quite register with Jean. Perhaps denial was in itself an incurable form of dementia.

Ireland. Arlene couldn't even recognize their own home some of the time. He'd explained to Jean that going to a foreign country would be a little more difficult than he could manage. Suppose Arlene became ill while they were abroad. Would they be able to get medical treatment? He didn't want to risk it.

"Or you could come out and see us," Jean had said. "It's lovely here in Seattle in August."

He thought, but did not say, that Jean was unprepared for a visit from them, given her roseate picture of her mother. Let her keep her memories intact, at least. Or perhaps he was being selfish. Visiting grown children was not the holiday he had in mind. He loved his daughter, but he wasn't altogether sure that he *liked* her anymore. These days she seemed to talk like one of those upscale lifestyle magazines. When she and her husband were building their house, it seemed like every other sentence out of her mouth was *our architect* says this and *our architect* says that, as if he were a priest of Yuppiedom issuing commandments.

Besides, seeing their little Jean, now an exercise-trim matron with reading glasses perpetually perched on top of her head, would only remind him how old they were and how little time was left. He wanted to escape the narrowing present. To go back to a happier time.

"But — a Dale Earnhardt tour, Dad?" Jean had said in tones of icy condescension. "I thought racing was *your* thing. Did mother even care about auto racing?" Jean wasn't worried about her mother's interests. She never could see the world from any point of view except her own, and now she was thinking *How will this affect me?* He suspected that she was a little embarrassed by her parents' interest in motor sports. Jean had been on the West Coast nearly a decade now, and she had managed to get rid of any lingering trace of a Southern accent. He imagined her making slighting references to her friends about her down-home parents, but he doubted that she would mention the NASCAR tour to anyone she knew. She would think that she could never live that down. Useless for him to point out that there are more NASCAR drivers from California than from anywhere else. He had ignored Jean's self-serving concern for her mother's interests, and had promised to send her a copy of the itinerary with the telephone numbers of the hotels in case she needed to reach them. That would satisfy Jean's sense of duty. She wouldn't call, but she'd be able to tell herself that she was "on top of things," one of her pet phrases. Jim resolved to send her a postcard of a speedway or a stock car from somewhere along the way, just for the pleasure it would afford him to picture her dismay at receiving it.

Jim looked again at Arlene. Soon it would be time to wake her up and find out if this would be a good day or a bad day. The people on the tour had been nice about it, though. He was glad of that. The other ladies all took turns making sure that Arlene did all right at the rest areas, and they'd talk to her over meals — better still, they listened, no matter how much she rambled or got tangled up trying to tell them something. He was glad that they'd come. Whether she remembered or not, Arlene had come to say good-bye to Dale, but he had come to say good-bye to Arlene.

"So," said Harley, "next stop Martinsville, right?"

Ratty nodded. "I-81 east to Roanoke and then south on 220. All four-lane. With this bus, I'd say maybe five hours, not counting lunch."

"Let's eat fast food for lunch along the way," said Harley. "For dinner we can go to Clarence's Steak House near the

273

Speedway. It's a landmark. All the drivers used to eat there, and it can't be too far from where we're staying. Where are we staying, by the way?'

"Days Inn on 220, a mile or two from the track," said Ratty. "Since we've got the place to ourselves, there's no problem. We can eat anywhere you want."

"Good," said Harley. "This will be an easy day. We ought to be done by four o'clock."

"Enjoy it while you can," said Ratty. " 'Cause once we get south of Charlotte, there's so many miles between tracks that you'll get saddle sores from riding on this bus two-three hundred miles a day."

"I know," said Harley. "Atlanta to Daytona takes forever."

Too drowsy to bother with talking or even to play his Game Boy, Matthew Hinshaw pressed his cheek against the cool glass of the window to watch the gray pavement of the Interstate slide past. The bus was traveling east on a broad highway called I-81, and he thought they might already have crossed into Virginia, but he wasn't sure. He might have closed his eyes for a few moments and missed the road sign. The land looked the same as it had in

274

Tennessee — a wide green valley bordered on either side by darker green mountains. He had never been in either state before, and he had hoped for some dramatic changes in the scenery to mark the boundary. The silver expanse of a tractor trailer pulled alongside the bus for a moment, obscuring his view, and for an instant he thought it was his father's rig keeping pace with their journey, and that any moment now the bus would pull level with the cab of the truck and he would find himself looking into his father's dead eyes.

He blinked a few times to clear the smoke from his thoughts, careful not to let any tears fall on his cheeks. All he had to do was turn around and start talking to Mr. Knight or to any of the other passengers, and the spell would be broken, but he remembered something the counselors had said in one of their sessions: that he would not be able to move on until he faced what was bothering him. So he held his peace.

Maybe his father had driven this highway before, but he wasn't here now. His 18-wheeler, its cab so high that Matthew had to stand on a stool to get in, had ended up on I-93 north of Concord, like a giant metal frog in a puddle of oil and broken glass. The image was clear in his mind, but he realized now that he probably had never seen it. In the hospital, they had told him over and over that he had been unconscious when the rescue squad pulled him out through the window of the cab. The doctors thought that Matthew would stop remembering it if they could convince him that he had not actually seen it, but it hadn't worked that way. His imagination, fed on a lifetime of TV car chases and movie collisions, was more than equal to the task of fashioning an image of the wreck. He dreamed it every night for weeks after the accident, but the nurses never knew it, because he neither screamed nor cried when the images jolted him awake.

His father was dead. Okay. And his mother — might as well be. She wasn't going to wake up. They hadn't wanted to tell him that for a long time, but finally they took him to see her, and a tall man in a white coat had explained it all very carefully. The man kept looking around nervously, as if he wanted somebody to come quickly in case Matthew started to scream, but he hadn't. The first time he saw his mother lying in that hospital bed, white and shrunken amidst all the tubes, he had been so numb that he couldn't have made a noise if they'd asked him to.

He just kept staring at the wax doll that had been his mother, while the man in the white coat showed him a chart and explained that his mother wasn't going to die, but that she wasn't going to wake up, either.

"But who's going to stay with me?" he had finally asked.

At that, the hospital people had brightened as if he'd just answered a particularly hard question. You tell us, they'd more or less said. Who else have you got?

He had explained to them that he didn't even belong in New Hampshire. Not really. His dad was a long-haul trucker, so he hadn't been around much, but this one time he had got some days off in July, and he'd been taking Matthew and his mom to the New Hampshire Speedway to see the July race. They hadn't made it, though. They were riding over from upstate New York (*As near as dammit to Canada,* his dad always said), and Matthew had been dozing off in the back of the cab, so he couldn't say for sure what had happened on I-93. Somebody said that maybe a car had tried to pass and cut it too close, and that Matthew's dad turned the truck over trying to avoid a wreck. By the time Matthew was aware again, he was in an ambulance, and a guy was asking him if he was all right, and trying to make him hold a teddy bear. It wasn't his, though. Later he'd learned that cops keep toy bears in their patrol cars, in case they meet any little kid whose life has just gone down the tubes, which his certainly had.

And there wasn't anybody else. Dad was an orphan, and his mother's mother had just died of a heart attack the winter before. Maybe there were distant relatives, but nobody he knew. Nobody who wanted him.

They explained that New Hampshire would take care of him, since the wreck happened there. So he was never going to get to go home, back to his school and his friends. His dad had turned the stupid truck over — maybe he had been arguing with Mom and not watching the road. That wouldn't be anything new. It was all his dad's fault for having the wreck, but Matthew and his mom were the ones being punished for it. She wasn't going to see or hear anything ever again, and Matthew was now a prisoner in New Hampshire.

It turns out that they didn't have orphanages anymore. Not like the kind you see in old movies around Christmastime. Nowadays, kids without parents went to group homes for a few months while the state scurried around trying to find them a new set of parents. He didn't have any say in the matter. Whoever wanted him could have him — like the dog pound, he thought.

They kept him for a couple of weeks in the hospital, because he'd had some broken bones and various injuries from the wreck. Later, he had to spend a couple of hours a week talking to a marshmallow of a woman who was forever dabbing at her own moist nose with the tissues meant for her patients. "How does that make you feel?" she would ask him, leaning toward him until her black plastic glasses almost touched his nose.

He didn't feel anything, but he knew that was the wrong answer. If he said that, he might have to come even more times a week to see the marshmallow woman. He tried to work out what she wanted him to say. "Sad," he said at last. "I feel sad."

Most of the time he sat through the counseling sessions playing Eminem in his head. "Cleaning Out My Closet." That said it all. Matthew thought they should have played that at his father's funeral.

Every time he thought he might cry in counseling, he'd crank up Eminem's voice in his mind until the numbness came back. The marshmallow woman didn't try too hard to get him to open up, though. It hadn't taken him long to figure out that in Child Services, if you were quiet and did what they told you to, they forgot about you. There were too many kids with problems on the outside; the kids with problems on the inside were easy to overlook.

I feel sad.

His bruises from the accident had nearly faded away before he figured out what it was he really did feel, which was that "I feel sad" had been the truth, but the rest of the sentence would be, ". . . sad that Dad wasn't alone in the truck when he wrecked it, but not sad that he's dead, because he was never around much anyhow."

He had breezed in from one of his long hauls with speedway tickets, and announced that they were going to have a family outing. He had a short run in the truck that weekend in the vicinity of Concord, so they'd ride along with him, and go on to the track after he made the delivery. Matthew's mother had been doubtful about the idea. Would he get into trouble taking them along as passengers on his run? Matthew knew that she'd have been just as happy to watch the race on television. She didn't like the noise and the crowds of the speedway itself, and she was always worried that things cost too much. But she had allowed herself to be persuaded to go along. After all, Matthew didn't get to spend a lot of time with his dad, and both of them were so excited at the prospect of going. They never made it to the race, though. The wreck happened on the Interstate just a few miles from Loudon. The last lap, Matthew thought to himself. Just like Earnhardt — almost home free, but not quite. He had never cried for his father, but sometimes even now he would bury his face in the fur of the teddy bear that the highway patrolman had brought him in the hospital, and he would cry for Dale.

The Martinsville Speedway was almost within sight of Highway 220, less than a minute's diversion on a sunny weekday afternoon with no Winston Cup race scheduled until October, but try it on a race day, and you'd better have a full tank of gas to compensate for the time you'd spend idling in bumper-to-bumper traffic.

They had stopped for lunch a few miles

up the road at the McDonald's in the village of Rocky Mount. To the pilgrims' great delight, the place was decorated with a NASCAR theme. Between bites of French fries they studied the stock car wallpaper and took turns identifying the cars featured in the design. Earnhardt was there, of course, in the black number 3. Harley was summoned to identify the red and yellow number 17 car with the Tide detergent logo. Darrell Waltrip, of course, from days gone by.

"That bronze-looking job — the number 6 — that's Mark Martin. The Viagra car," said Ray Reeve.

Jesse Franklin chuckled. "That Viagra car runs great all right, but they have trouble keeping the hood down."

"That last car, the bright yellow number 4 car. I believe that's Ernie Irvan," said Jim Powell. "His dad builds big old monster toolboxes for race teams. Nice folks."

The identification complete, they took turns posing for group snapshots with the wallpaper as a backdrop, and finally Ratty had to announce that they were welcome to stay as long as they liked, but he and the bus would be departing in five minutes.

"This is both the oldest and the smallest

of the tracks in the NASCAR Winston Cup circuit," said Harley, a few miles down the road. "In fact, Martinsville is even older than NASCAR. It was founded by Mr. Clay Earles back in 1947. The track is a point-five-two-six oval — but the banking isn't steep like Bristol. The odd thing about this track is the paving."

"Two drag strips connected by U-turns!" said Jim Powell. "We love this track. Short track racing is the best!"

"I guess I ought to translate Mr. Powell's comment," said Harley. "What he means is that the track here at Martinsville is paved with asphalt on the straightaways and concrete in the turns. It makes for a tricky racing surface — takes some getting used to. Power steering was first used in Winston Cup racing here in Martinsville in 1981. Anybody know who the driver was?"

Obviously they didn't, because they guessed Petty, Waltrip, Yarborough, Allison, and Earnhardt.

"Geoff Bodine," said Harley.

"That some pretty deep trivia, Harley," said Justine. "Can't you ask us something easier?"

"Okay. Who holds the record for the most wins at Martinsville?"

"Earnhardt!" cried a chorus of voices.

"Richard Petty," said Sarah Nash.

Harley nodded. "How'd you know?" he asked her.

"Stands to reason," she said. "Petty has more wins overall."

"Well, you're right. It was indeed King Richard. We'll be dropping in on him tomorrow morning, in a manner of speaking."

The Martinsville Speedway was not perched on the summit of a hill, posing, like the Bristol Motor Speedway. In Martinsville, unless you knew to slow down on the four-lane and look to the south, you might only catch sight of the structure as you were driving past, too late to make the turn. Ratty, who had been well-briefed on the routes for his driving assignment, was going slow enough to make the turn, so that the passengers first saw the track as a backdrop for a neighborhood of small, neat brick homes.

"It must be a nightmare to live there on race weekends," said Bekasu with a little shudder.

"Don't you believe it," Jesse Franklin called out. "Those folks can make good money renting out parking spots!"

"There's a railroad track that runs right

behind the Speedway," said Harley. "Sometimes during a race you can watch the train go by."

"It must seem strange to you to see all these parking lots so empty," said Cayle.

"Well, we'd come for practice runs a few days before the race," said Harley. "The place wasn't always crowded then, but, yeah, it does look unnaturally peaceful right now."

"That's why it's going to take us two minutes to get there instead of two hours," said Ratty without turning around.

Justine waved a heavily braceleted arm. "Hey, Harley! I got another trivia question for y'all!"

"Fire away, Justine," he said, deciding that with two minutes until arrival he could afford to be generous.

"Okay, everybody. What piece of furniture do Richard Petty, Dale Earnhardt, Darrell Waltrip, and Bobby Allison all definitely own?"

Jim Powell laughed. "Well, I'm sure they all own a sofa, a bed, a table — but I believe the answer you're looking for, Justine, is a grandfather clock. Right?"

"Trick question," said Harley to a collection of bewildered expressions. "When you win the race at Martinsville, they don't give you a trophy. They give you a grandfather clock, which seems fitting since it's the oldest NASCAR track, but it's a tough one."

Ratty parked the bus next to the little house that served as the offices for the Speedway, and Harley led the Number Three Pilgrims out into the parking lot. He motioned for them to crowd around, so that he could speak his piece before they wandered off to use up more rolls of film.

"I have a favorite story about this track," said Harley. "It dates from the time when I was racing. I'll bet the North Carolinians in the group remember Hurricane Hugo." He saw a few solemn nods — Sarah Nash, Jim Powell, Bekasu and Cayle. "It was the fall of 1989. Every twenty years or so, it seems like North Carolina gets broadsided by a monster hurricane. My folks used to talk about Hurricane Hazel in the early Fifties, and then there was Camille. The one I remember best is Hurricane Hugo. It cut inland through the piedmont North Carolina, and even made it up into the Virginia Blue Ridge, ripping out oak trees as if they were staples. It finally blew itself out and ended up a soggy tropical storm, but it left millions of dollars' worth of damage in its wake. And the bad weather played havoc with everybody's travel schedules.

"Well, the next race after the hurricane was here in Martinsville. In fact, the day of the qualifying in Martinsville, the Charlotte area, where a lot of the teams and drivers are based, was digging out from under all the damage left by Hugo. A lot of people assumed that Martinsville would postpone the qualifying trials on account of the hurricane, but they didn't. By the time Sunday rolled around for the race itself, the weather would be sunny and warm as if nothing had ever happened, but the drivers had to be here well before then, for the qualifying.

"Dale Earnhardt's farm had been hit hard by Hugo and he wanted to be on hand to supervise the cleanup. His people called the Speedway up here and said that Dale would be able to come up for the race, but that he couldn't make it to Martinsville to qualify. Dale was driving a Chevy Lumina back in '89, and the crew could get the car there, no problem. But not the driver."

"Can you have pinch hitters in racing?" asked Terence.

"Sure, you can," said Justine. "Besides, it was *Dale*. You think the Speedway would let a hurricane cost them a chance to have him in the race?"

"It's legal to have someone else qualify for you," said Harley, sidestepping the rest of Justine's remark. "If you can let go of being a control freak long enough to accept whatever spot the assigned driver manages to get for you, you can use a substitute. The problem that time was finding somebody capable of doing the qualifying who would be able to make it to Martinsville in time. They got Jimmy Hensley, a Grand National driver, who lives up here near the Speedway, and who knew the track as well as anybody. So when Richard Childress calls and asks him to drive Earnhardt's Chevy in qualifying, Hensley is ready, willing, and able."

"How did it turn out?" asked Ratty.

Harley smiled. "Hensley put Dale's car in the pole position," he said. "He topped out at 91.9 miles an hour. How about that? The poor guy ran the fastest time in qualifying and then he personally has to sit out the race. Has to give the car back to its rightful driver. Sounds like *my* luck."

"So did Earnhardt win the race?"

"Nope," said Harley. "He had a good shot at it, of course, starting on the pole. That was important, because on a short track like this one, there's not a lot of room to pass, so you might not have much of a chance to make your way up to the front of the pack during the race. But, no, Earnhardt didn't win. Not even his luck was that good. The car had an off day — I don't remember what the problem was, if I ever knew. Anyhow, it was all Dale could do to keep up with Darrell Waltrip and Rusty Wallace. On the final laps, Wallace was in the lead and Dale was trying to get around him, which at a little track like this one means there's going to be some bashing and banging in the bargain. 'Rubbin' is racin',' he always said.

"Well, Earnhardt and Wallace, concentrating on this high speed duel of theirs, started drifting high toward the wall on Turn Two. Darrell Waltrip, who was running right behind them, figured that was his chance. All he had to do was snake past the two of them on the inside while they were concentrating on each other, and then hope that his Chevy had enough power to slip by them before they slid back down in his path. Waltrip said later he figured when he made his move that he'd have either a heck of a pass or a heck of a mess."

"And Waltrip won?" asked Cayle.

"He sure did," said Harley. "The big surprise is that Rusty came in fourth and Dale ninth. Their duel hadn't done either one of them any good. They were really contending for points toward winning the championship that year, so that last-ditch battle really cost them."

"Be careful what you wish for," said Cayle.

"What do you mean?" asked Bill from across the aisle.

"Well, I was thinking that maybe Rusty wished to keep Earnhardt from getting past him, thinking that would be synonymous with winning the race, but it wasn't."

"I did that once," said Bill.

She looked at him as if to say *Did what?* But this wasn't the time to talk about it.

"Where should we leave the wreath?"

"The Infield Gate," said Harley. "It leads directly onto the track. But Ratty will need some time to get the wreath out of the luggage compartment, so let's get the feel of the place first. I think it would be all right if we went in and walked around it. You get a different perspective on the race from the track level than you do from watching it on television, or even sitting in the stands. Come on — you'll see what I mean."

"Those front row seats are really close," said Karen. "If you were going 60 miles an hour coming out of a turn, it would look like you were going to plow straight into the seats. Can the drivers actually see the spectators at that speed?"

"Oh, they can," said Harley. "If somebody is cheering you on or giving you the finger every time you loop past his seat, it can really affect your mood. Tony Stewart swears he won a race here one time just to spite a guy on the front row who pissed him off."

"This looks very different from Bristol," said Bekasu.

"Drives different, too," said Harley.

When they got back to the Infield Gate, Ratty was waiting for them, dwarfed by a giant horseshoe of yellow silk roses. The black satin ribbon stretched across it said *In Memory of The Intimidator*" in white stick-on letters.

"Photo opportunity," said Bekasu without noticeable enthusiasm.

"We ought to take pictures of the laying of the wreath as well," said Cayle. "Who's going to do the honors this time?"

Jesse Franklin stepped forward with his customary cherubic smile. "Well, this might be a good time," he said. "I don't

291

want to have a lot of hard acts to follow in the eloquence department. Ray, what do you say we team up on this?"

The older man's scowl did not waver, but he said, "Suits me," as he took the wreath from Ratty. He knelt down and leaned the wreath against the metal gate. "Do I say something now?" he asked. "Okay. Well . . . I hereby lay this wreath to honor the memory of the greatest driver NASCAR ever had. Dale Earnhardt, the Intimidator. Gone but not forgotten."

"Not all that gone," muttered Justine, who was immediately shushed by her sister.

"Racing's not the same without you, Dale. Back in Nebraska, I plowed my alfalfa field with a giant number 3 last season. That was my farewell to you. I still root for the Big Red in football, but I just don't give a damn who wins in NASCAR anymore," Ray Reeve went on. "I'm done. Your turn, Jesse."

Jesse Franklin spent a few moments looking out at the bare track, the rows of empty bleachers, and then down at the horseshoe of yellow roses. He summoned a tremulous smile. "I've come a long way to see these places," he said. "Saw him race one time at our speedway in Michigan. It was the 1999 IROC. The time he raced against Dale Junior, the two of them beating and banging their way toward the finish line, and then Dale edging past his boy at the end by a whisker. Oh, that was a heart-stopper, that race.

"But you know, I thought about him more during the week than I did on race days. I work for the county, you know. Auditor. That may sound pretty impressive if you don't know any better, but I'll tell you it can be frustrating as all get-out sometimes. Local politics: being nice to idiots who hold a higher job rank than you do. You don't know how many times I've watched the qualifying races and wished we could do that in real life: reshuffle everybody's ranking every single week. But, no! My supervisor is always my supervisor — he outranks me every darned week, and I have to smile when he yells, and laugh when he calls me Doofus, and just take everything he dishes out. You may think they can't fire a government employee, but there's ways to get it done. Layoffs. Reassignment. Job restructuring. Oh, they can do anything they want, and you could take them to court, but you'd never prove it. And I'm not too many years from retirement — too old to start over, too young to quit working. I need this job, and the pension that comes with it. So I'm determined to be agreeable if it kills me, and I put up with whatever those fool bureaucrats dish out.

"But, you know, Dale didn't have to do that. When he raced he was in that car all by himself — no supervisor, no coordinator, no committees. And if somebody was going too slow, or got in his way — *bam!* He just tapped them aside and kept on going. Lord, it was better than tranquilizers, watching him race. I just wish you could be like that in real life. Do it your way, and tell people to like it or lump it. Thump them if they won't step aside. And that *was* his real life. I don't suppose I could be like that, even on the track and certainly not in the courthouse, but, oh, my! It did my heart good just to watch him work."

"Amen," said Ray Reeve.

After a few moments of uncomfortable silence, which Harley feared would be broken by a disapproving Rev. Knight, Ratty Laine said, "Well, it's hot enough out here to poach golf balls. Why don't you hit the souvenir shop for your Martinsville pins, and then we'll get back into the air-conditioned bus. We're putting up in the

Days Inn down the road tonight."

The awkwardness was broken, and the group surged back toward the parking lot, all talking at once. Bill Knight caught up with Harley. "What an odd speech," he murmured. "Were you surprised?"

Harley shook his head. "That old boy is practically a poster child of an Earnhardt fan. He was loved by the roughnecks, people who have trouble with authority, or else folks who were slumming." He nodded toward Terence as he said that last word.

CHAPTER XIII

The Garage Mahal

The Richard Petty Museum and DEI

"North Carolina loved Dale Earnhardt so much they even named a county after him." Harley Claymore had been saving up this joke for more than three hundred miles. "And here we are — in *Our Dale* County."

The sign at the side of the highway welcomed travelers to Iredell County, but given Harley's accent, there was a good chance he'd have pronounced it "our dale" even if it wasn't a play on words. Bekasu looked up sharply, and Harley could see her gearing up to explain to her fellow passengers that, in fact, the county had been named after some prominent North Carolina family in colonial times, but Justine must have also anticipated that speech, because she elbowed her sister in the ribs, all the while smiling sweet encouragement for Harley to go on.

"It's odd, isn't it, that two of the most legendary drivers in motor sports are commemorated less than forty miles apart? We visited Richard Petty's museum this morning in Randleman, and now we're headed southwest to Mooresville, headquarters of DEI, and shrine to the man himself. Anybody know what they call Earnhardt's building?"

In a burble of laughter, Jesse Franklin called out — "The Garage Mahal!" — but most of the other passengers had said it softly in unison with him.

"Why do they call it that?" asked Bill Knight, whose voice had been conspicuously absent in the reply.

Harley sighed. "Wait'll you see it."

After a pancake breakfast that morning in Martinsville, Virginia, they had set off, taking highway 220 past Greensboro, and into the heart of Carolina racing country. As they'd headed south toward the North Carolina border, the mountains fell away behind them, dwindling to foothills, and finally to the rolling country of the North Carolina piedmont with its red clay and pine forests. This was the land of textile mills and furniture factories, of tobacco fields and hog farms — and race tracks. Before Bill France had organized the informal beach races of Daytona into an empire back in the Forties, North Carolina had been the home of fast cars and daredevil drivers. But at the very beginning, it wasn't a sport. It was a living.

Up on the mountain farms that straddled the high peaks of the Smokies west of Morganton, economic necessity coupled with inclination inspired the making of moonshine. The tradition and the recipes for whiskey-making had come over from Scotland and Ireland in the eighteenth century with the settlers who homesteaded Carolina's wild mountain region. In the twentieth century, the pioneers' descendants found themselves on the losing end of an agricultural equation, in which steep mountain land couldn't produce enough crops to support the farm family — at least the crops in their traditional form weren't profitable. But if you took a few acres of corn, dirt cheap by the bushel, and distilled it through copper tubing, turning it into high-proof whiskey sold by the gallon, then the corn would yield the farmer a living wage. Such subsistence innovation was illegal, of course. The country had passed a whiskey tax in 1792, and bootleggers, who didn't feel like letting the government siphon off their profits, had been dodging the law ever since. Faced with a choice between accepting charity in order to survive and breaking the federal tax law to take care of themselves, they chose the latter without a qualm.

Fast driving came into the picture when it became necessary to get mountain-made moonshine to the big city markets in the Carolina piedmont — to Charlotte, Raleigh, Fayetteville, Durham — without getting stopped by the law and having the cargo confiscated. Those routes and their east Tennessee counterparts were the original Thunder Road, and a generation of drivers in the early days got their start on back country roads instead of at race tracks, when outrunning another car meant more than just a trophy and a kiss from a beauty queen: it meant food on the table, and not going to jail.

By the time Richard Petty took the wheel in the late Fifties, those days were over, but the love of fast driving in a motorized battle of wits had seized the Tarheel imagination, and dirt tracks were built to cater to that obsession: Rockingham, Wilkesboro, Hickory, Asheville. Only Rockingham retained its place on the NASCAR circuit these days, but all those tracks loomed large in the history of Carolina motor sports.

There wasn't time to crisscross the piedmont to visit all those legendary tracks, so as far as the tour was concerned the Monday afternoon trip to Rockingham would have to represent all the early days of the sport. First, though, the bus would stop in Randleman and Mooresville so that the group could pay its respects to the only two seven-time champions in the history of the sport: both sons of the North Carolina piedmont.

As the bus rolled down the highway from Martinsville, Harley consulted his notes while most of the passengers read or dozed, sleeping off the effects of the pancake breakfast.

"Two seven-time champions — both Tarheels," he said into the microphone. "Petty and Earnhardt. They're alike in a lot of ways, and totally different in almost as many others. So let's compare these two NASCAR legends. First of all they were both sons of well-known race car drivers on the circuit — that would be Lee Petty and Ralph Earnhardt. But Richard Petty won 200 races in his career, while Dale only won a total of 76."

"Apples and oranges," said Sarah Nash, looking up from her newspaper. "They raced in different eras. Things were a lot more competitive by the time Earnhardt came along — and the NASCAR rules on modifications were stricter, too."

"No argument there," said Harley. "I'm just spouting numbers, is all."

Karen McKee sighed and leaned back in her seat with her eyes closed, but she wasn't asleep. The wedding had gone off as planned — at least as Shane had planned — and now that the milestone was passed, she had an empty feeling as if someone had forgotten to write The End across the sky. *Mrs. Shane McKee.* That phrase, which had seemed so complete in itself in all the months leading up to the ceremony, was unfailingly followed by *"Now what?"* in the unending conversation she had with herself inside her head.

Because there would have to be a Now What. Maybe in Karen's grandmother's time, a woman could get married and that was it — a permanent job with long hours and no pay, maybe, but still an identity and a profession entirely unto itself. But those days were past praying for, and even if you did marry somebody who could afford to support you (which she hadn't), there was no guarantee that you'd stay married to him forever, so you'd better not risk your future on his account. Karen had derailed that topic of conversation every time her mother or one of the Friends of the Goddess had tried to bring it up, but that didn't mean she hadn't heard them.

Shane had his headphones on, listening to his new Linkin Park CD — she made a mental note to get more batteries out of her suitcase when they stopped for the night. First wifely duty: Keeper of the Batteries. Karen wasn't sleepy, and she'd finished the magazine Cayle had passed on to her. Across the aisle, Terence Palmer was also awake and restless. Karen watched him for a few minutes. She'd never seen anybody as young as he was who actually looked comfortable in a necktie. He looked like he forgot he had it on, while Shane, who could seldom be persuaded to wear one, even for church, would pull constantly at his collar, wriggling like a chained-up dog. "He looks like you had to throw him on his back to get his shoes on," one of the Friends of the Goddess had remarked once, but she hadn't said it to be mean. The Friends were all in favor of flouting conventional social customs.

There was no use trying to get Shane to look like a preppy, though, because even if you got him in a necktie and a tailored suit, Shane would still lack that carved-in-marble look that Terence Palmer was born with: a small, straight nose and light brown hair like a cap of loose curls that made you think that's what Michelangelo had been trying to depict when he carved the head of David. Karen thought he put her in mind of that poem she'd read in senior English, the one about Richard Cory: "He glittered when he walked."

She felt shy around him, and she realized that she had been carefully avoiding him, sitting at a different table at each meal stop, and keeping her distance when they had walked around the track at Martinsville. She told herself that she was being overly sensitive. It was a NASCAR tour, for heaven's sake — if Terence Palmer was such a prince, what was he doing here?

She was still looking at him, thinking all this, when he turned back from the monotonous sweep of pines, and met her gaze. Flustered, she said the first thing that came to mind.

"I bet Dale Earnhardt himself would be surprised to see you on this bus."

He looked puzzled for a moment, maybe trying to decide if she'd meant to be insulting, but then he said, "I don't believe he would have been surprised. Not by the end of his career, anyhow."

Karen nodded. He was probably right about that. Maybe in the beginning, when he was still a raw high school dropout from a mill town, maybe then Earnhardt would have been surprised to have fans among the wine-and-cheese people. But not later. President Reagan was in the stands when he won the Daytona 500. And the year Earnhardt died, he was on a list of the country's richest people. Compared to that level of success, Terence Palmer, for all his airs and graces, was a shoeshine boy.

"So, how come you're here then?" she said.

He was silent for a few moments. Karen thought that maybe they didn't ask personal questions in his crowd. At last though, he said, "My dad died."

"Oh. I'm sorry."

"Well, I am, too, but only because I missed the chance to know him. My folks split up when I was a baby."

Karen nodded. There was a lot of that going around. Then she smiled. "For a second there, I thought maybe you were Kerry Earnhardt."

Terence considered it. "No," he said. "He looks a lot like his dad — at least in the photos. I think I'm probably taller. My dad bought tickets for this tour, and I came in his place."

"I guess you want to know why I'm here," said Karen.

He studied her for a moment, and Karen squirmed, wishing she had worn something dressier than jeans. "Not really," he said. "You got married at the Speedway. I figure this is your thing."

Something in the way he said it made Karen want to deny all interest in motor sports, but she thought that doing so might be disloyal to Shane, who hadn't a trace of irony in his soul, and who had been so proud and happy to make this pilgrimage. "Yes," she said. "Our thing. I guess it is. I'm just trying to figure out what comes next."

Again, the silence. Terence was looking over at Shane, who was sleeping with his mouth open and his head thrown back against the seat. *Fifty years of tuna casserole,* he seemed to be thinking.

Karen squirmed in her seat. "Don't sell us short," she said. "We may be young, and we didn't get a fancy education, either one of us, but neither did Dale, and he did all right." But Dale knew where he was going, she thought. And she didn't.

Dale Earnhardt, Incorporated was on

the schedule for the early afternoon, but the first stop of the day would be a location farther north than Mooresville: the museum of North Carolina's other seven-time champion, Richard Petty.

Highway 220 south of Greensboro was a four-lane corridor cut through forests of longleaf pines. Once they crossed into Randolph County, official state highway signs directed motorists to Exit 113, which led to the small town of Randleman, home of the Richard Petty Museum, a newly constructed one-story brick building fronted by a white arched portico. The place looked as if it had been designed by a firm of architects who specialized in branch banks. It sat back from Academy Street behind a bank-sized visitor parking lot with only a decorous sign to identify the building as a museum.

Terence Palmer peered out the window, studying the scene with a puzzled frown. "Odd," he said to Sarah Nash. "It looks so dignified. I was expecting an outside display of cars, checkered flags, neon displays, sort of a circus atmosphere."

She sighed. "That's Manhattan talking," she said. "I don't know a single driver in NASCAR who wouldn't crawl under his car and not come out if you tried to show him off in the outlandish way you imagined. They're not showy people. Mostly not, anyhow."

Justine, camera in hand, was the first one off the bus. "Anybody who wants to pose outside the Richard Petty Museum, put your caps on, and bunch up over by the door," she said, waving the other passengers into place, while Ratty parked the bus, and Harley headed inside to arrange admittance for the bus tour.

Cayle obligingly joined the posing group under the white covered porch at the glass-fronted doors of the building. It was an unassuming place, she thought, considering that the museum was dedicated to a man whose nickname was "The King." It looked like a museum that had come into being by popular demand; not to make money — admission was a nominal five bucks — but to accommodate the kindness of strangers. Cayle imagined a steady stream of Richard Petty fans over the years, arriving in the little North Carolina village in search of their idol, because after years of watching him race, they felt like family. They would be wanting to see something in commemoration of the legendary driver, and hoping to leave with a picture of the 43 car, a tee shirt, a postcard, or Richard Petty's name scrawled on a napkin. Anything. They would have wanted to pose for pictures of themselves with the most famous face in racing: Richard Petty, whippet-thin, with his big cowboy hat and boots, his palm-sized belt buckle, and the sunglasses obscuring that hawk-billed face. And always a smile like winter sunshine. Cayle pictured an endless procession of shy, but determined race fans. *Just one more picture, Mr. Petty! It's for Grandad who couldn't come with us. Can you sign this napkin?*

So, finally, a kind but busy man with an empire to run had despaired of getting any work done with the endless stream of visitors, and he arranged for the fans to have a place to go. He converted an old furniture store into a showroom to house some stuff he thought visitors would like to see — like seven championship trophies, Chrysler Hemi engines, a selection of his race cars from over the years, and pictures of the man himself, posing with movie stars and presidents. He hired some local people to run it. Five bucks to get in — that ought to cover the light bill and the clerks' wages, and whatnot. Then The King went back to all the other million things that clamored for his time.

The Number Three Pilgrims filed into the museum, which on a weekday morning wasn't crowded, and Cayle's impression of a homey and unassuming visitor center was confirmed. Here, she thought, was the museum equivalent of making your mashed potatoes and pork chops stretch to feed a crowd of unexpected dinner guests. A line of race cars, each surrounded by a knee-high picket fence led the visitor down memory lane, a reminder that Richard Petty was truly a king in the dynastic sense: that is, he was just one cog in a long succession. Four generations of Pettys had driven the NASCAR circuit, an amazing achievement in a sport just over fifty years old.

Bekasu studied the framed photographs that lined the walls. "Here's a picture of Lee Petty, when he was racing back in the Fifties," she remarked to Harley, who was reading over her shoulder. "Having a father in the business must have helped young Richard get started."

"I guess it did," said Harley. "It's just —" He shook his head and started to walk away.

"Just what?" said Bekasu, hurrying to keep up with him. "Nobody else is listening. What were you going to say?"

Harley turned back to study Lee Petty's old race car from the Fifties — truly a stock car, one that its owner could have driven to the race track, on the race track, and then to the grocery store afterward. Not like today's seven-hundred-horsepower monsters with the paste-on headlights, the treadless tires and glassless windows, and the doors permanently welded shut. Seeing that old car reminded Harley of his own father's obsession with racing. The self-made man back in the early days before engineers and wind tunnels and product placement — those old-time drivers had done it all, and all the money they'd spent on those cars wouldn't buy you a fist-sized decal's worth of advertisement on the last-place driver's trunk in today's sport.

"Racing was almost a one-man operation in the old days," he told her. "Lee Petty would have worked on this car himself. Modified it. Tested it. Driven it in races in whatever time he could steal from a day job and a wife and kids. And Lee Petty won the first *ever* Daytona 500, you know. *Daytona.* Can you imagine the incredible force of will it would have taken to succeed under those circumstances? How much you would have to want to win?"

"Oh, men always want to win," said Bekasu, still looking at the genial face of Lee Petty. The determination must have been buried beneath that affable exterior. "Men can't even lose jurisdiction over the remote control for the television. I don't see why racing should be any more cut-throat than, say, a law practice, which is my family's profession."

"Well, maybe it isn't," said Harley. "We don't have any lawyers in my family and I try to avoid them, myself. But I do know about fathers and sons in the racing business. It would put you in mind of a deer herd. The young buck may have been sired by the old stag, but that doesn't mean the father is going to step down to his successor without a fight. I'll tell you a story about the young Richard Petty. When he was first starting out, summer of 1958 that would have been, he drove up to Canada to compete in his first Grand National race. So there's Richard, a few pounds heavier back then, but short on experience, whizzing around the track but a lap back from the front runners, when all of a sudden two cars come up on him — Cotton Owens is driving one, and Lee Petty is driving the other. Slam! Two old pros battling it out, and young Richard can't get out of their way fast enough, so he gets knocked aside as they go past, and he goes into the wall. Guess who put him there?"

"Not his father?"

"None other. The old man won the championship that year, and flat nobody was going to stand in his way."

"But that's terrible! — Maybe he didn't realize it was his son that he hit."

Harley shrugged. "I'd have an easier time believing that if there wasn't an even better story about them. Richard Petty's first NASCAR win came the next summer, 1959, at the old Lakewood Speedway in Atlanta. But the victory was taken away from him when one of the other drivers, upset about some infraction or other, protested the outcome of the race. Guess who cost Richard his first win."

Bekasu stared. "His *father?*"

Harley nodded.

"Well . . . maybe there was a good reason for it," she said. She couldn't think of one. "Maybe he wanted Richard to learn racing the hard way."

"Maybe old Lee hoped that Richard would quit and go to law school." Harley laughed. "No, that's not true. Racing was always the family business. I don't think

Richard Petty considered any other career for more'n five minutes."

"I still bet Lee Petty was sorry about putting Richard into the wall when he realized the other driver was his son."

"That's for sure. Lee was the car owner. Every dent he put in the car that Richard was driving would have to be fixed with money coming out of his own pocket."

Bekasu shook her head. "Poor Richard Petty." She had begun to picture The King as a sooty waif in a Dickens novel.

"Richard Petty wouldn't see it that way," Harley said. "There's a saying on the track: 'Rubbin' is racin'.' Dale Earnhardt lived by that motto. You've heard it?"

"Yes," said Bekasu. "But what on earth does it mean?"

"It means that there's more to competing than just driving a car at high speeds around an oval. There's conflict with your opponents — that's the rubbing. Bashing somebody out of your way so that you can win."

"Your stag metaphor again, huh? Locking horns."

"Right. It's all part of the deal. Richard Petty knew that, and if he couldn't handle the roughness back then, he'd have had no business in the sport." Harley turned to look at the line of trophy cases, glinting gold in the fluorescent lighting. "But he turned out all right, didn't he?"

Cayle and Justine had wandered to the back of the museum, where case after case of belt buckles were on display, and behind that was a room full of floor-to-ceiling glass shelves, housing The King's gazillion pocketknives and the doll collection of Mrs. Richard Petty.

"I used to have that one!" Justine declared, pointing to a round-faced Madame Alexander storybook doll. "Got it for Christmas when I was nine."

"I'll bet this freed up a lot of space for them at home," murmured Cayle, surveying the size of the two collections.

"I'll bet their fans just eat this up," said Justine. "Richard Petty's *stuff*. It's like getting to go upstairs and peek in your hosts' bedrooms. These exhibits are good for the wives and kids, too. I mean, if somebody in your family is bored spitless by racing, but on the vacation they get dragged to this shrine for Richard Petty, why, the non-race fan can come back here and look at the pretty dolls and the fancy belt buckles, while the menfolk are drooling over the race car exhibits."

"Speaking of stuff," said Cayle. "I just had a cute idea for the newlyweds. I think we ought to get them a wedding present. So what if we all take turns buying them a coffee mug from every museum and speedway we visit? I bought a mug in Martinsville, so I can give them that."

Justine considered it. "You think she'd like NASCAR mugs better than Royal Doulton?"

"I don't think they're mutually exclusive, Justine. Shall we do it?"

"Sure. I'll pass the word," said Justine. "Oh, look! A Prince Charles and Princess Diana! Aren't they adorable?"

Cayle sighed. "I wonder if Princess Diana has a Richard Petty doll in *her* museum at Althorp," she muttered.

"Nope," said Justine. "I went there last summer. It's just dresses and old pictures — stuff like that. This is much more interesting."

Terence Palmer and Sarah Nash stood at the knee-high picket fence surrounding Adam Petty's tricycle, which was parked beside Adam Petty's multi-colored race car. Terence thought that the 45 car, a Chevrolet Monte Carlo, looked quite appropriate parked beside a tricycle, because its flamboyant paint scheme suggested that it had been designed by a kindergartener with crayons. The car's roof and doors were shamrock green, its hood a royal blue, and the bumpers bright red. Various sponsor decals in yellow and white lettering and the 45 on the sides and roof in buttercup yellow gave the car a festive air, as if it ought to have been a parade float instead of a race car. It seemed strange to think that someone so young, driving such an exuberantly colored car, should have died.

"The tricycle is a nice touch," said Sarah Nash. "It reminds you that the drivers are just ordinary people, not superheroes in firesuits."

"Seeing his car here in his grandfather's museum makes me feel that I missed something," said Terence. "Not family exactly. My childhood was fine. I know people hate it when privileged people complain, and honestly, I'm not. I think what I'm lacking is a sense of continuity. Look at Adam here: the fourth generation in the same family business. It seems to me that he could share much more with his father and grandfather than most people."

"It's rare, though, that kind of closeness." Sarah Nash gave him an appraising stare.

"You're not about to tell me you wish you'd gone into farming with your father instead of being a tycoon in New York?"

"Hardly a tycoon," Terence said quickly. "More like one cog in a big machine. And after all the education and training I've had, it would be a waste to walk away from that. No, I don't think I'd have any aptitude for farming — or for stock car racing," he added, nodding toward the car. "I just think it would be nice to feel like a part of something that started before you were born and will continue after you're gone. Do you think my dad felt that way about his farm?"

"It's hard to tell," said Sarah Nash. "We never talked about it. I know that he enjoyed living there. It could have been no more than that. He wouldn't want you to feel obligated to do anything you didn't want to do, just out of some misguided sense of family tradition. And if you threw away a high-paying job to go broke farming in Wilkes County, he'd have called you a fool."

"I used to wonder why he didn't come and see me when I was a kid," said Terence. "Why he didn't try to forge a relationship with me. Do you know why he stayed away?"

"I think so," said Sarah Nash. "During his last illness, there were days when he was in quite a lot of pain, and I'd go and sit with him. Once I said that I'd be tempted to take an overdose of the painkiller just to get the suffering over with, but you know what Tom said? He smiled at me — as much as he could smile, hurting as bad as he did — and he said, 'I can't do that, Sarah. I've got too much mountain blood in me to kill myself. Mountain people never go where they haven't been invited.'"

Terence nodded, and they walked on to the next exhibit. No, Tom Palmer had certainly not been invited to visit his son. He was sure that had he turned up on the doorstep, his mother would have been gracious about it, but Terence knew that without so much as a harsh word or a raised eyebrow, she could make people feel profoundly out of place, so that they took the first opportunity to flee and never come back. He wasn't sure how she managed it, and his two old girlfriends from his high school days who had been thus exiled would never explain to him exactly what had happened.

The truth was, he hadn't made any effort to contact his father, either, but he told himself that he'd had no way of knowing whether his father had wanted to see him or not. Terence had always preferred to do without rather than to risk rejection.

Bill Knight had wandered up, reading the label on each exhibit, as if he were going to be tested on the material. "I really must get some postcards to send back to Canterbury," he told them. "So many folks up there would love to come and see this. Well, this is a colorful car — practically a Christmas tree on wheels."

"It was Adam's," said Terence, indicating the sign.

Bill Knight's smile faded. "Oh, my," he said. "*Adam Petty*. It's odd, but I feel as if I knew him. My church is near the speedway where he was killed. I wish I could tell him how many people cried for him up there when it happened."

"I'd like to think he knows that," said Sarah Nash.

An hour later, and a few miles down the road, Shane McKee stood in a dimly lit entry foyer, beside the roped-off black number 3 car. He gazed down the dark and cavernous hallway, illuminated only by the faint glow of picture lights above each exhibit, and then he began to walk away from the sunshine of the entryway, and down the long dark hall of memories.

The place looked more like church than church, he thought. The visitors were acting like it was church, too. Singly or in pairs, the visitors wandered down the hall with its cathedral ceilings and its glass-encased Earnhardt trophy collections. If they spoke at all, it was in whispers.

"This isn't much like the Petty Museum, is it?" said Karen, looking around her. "Mr. Petty's museum looks like a branch bank in Mayberry. But this place feels like the Lincoln Memorial."

"Richard Petty isn't dead," said Shane with a catch in his voice. When they first arrived he had stood in the foyer, staring at the black number 3 car on display, and wiping his eyes with the back of his hand. Karen had pretended not to notice.

"Well, no, Mr. Petty isn't dead, Shane, but Adam Petty is, and yet they had his car out there on display with that little knee-high picket fence around it, right alongside the cars of his father and grandfather. With his tricycle parked next to it. I got the feeling there that they remembered Adam fondly, but that they weren't wallowing in their grief."

Shane turned on his bride with glistening eyes. *"Wallowing?"* he said. "Wallowing?

320

Dale was a seven-time Winston Cup champion. He deserves all this respect and more!"

"Richard Petty was champion seven times, too," Karen said softly as her new husband stalked away. Maybe she ought to run after him and tell him she was sorry, but she couldn't figure out what she ought to be sorry for, except telling the truth when he didn't want to hear it. Maybe it was a good thing she hadn't made a habit of that.

She watched him for a few moments. Better give him time to get over it, she thought. Shane always took things to heart. Instead of following him down the hallway, she wandered over to the back of the foyer where Sarah Nash and Terence Palmer were standing in front of a floor-to-ceiling glass wall at least twenty feet high.

The room behind the glass wall, the size of a school gymnasium in an electric twilight, contained an exhibit of several incarnations of Dale Earnhardt's rides — the black number 3, each emblazoned with sponsor stickers, all set many yards back from the glass, so that the cars were too far away for sight-seers to tell much about them.

"We're not allowed up close to the cars?"

Karen asked, still thinking of the knee-high picket fences at Richard Petty's cheery public attic.

Terence shrugged. "Can't even photograph them through the glass. I suppose it's a security thing."

"Like Princess Diana being buried on that island at Althorp," said Sarah Nash in that expressionless drawl that made it hard to tell when she was being sarcastic. Karen thought she probably was.

A new thought struck her. "Where *is* Dale Earnhardt buried? He's not here, is he?" She looked down the long, dimly lit nave as if she expected to see a marble sepulchre at the end of it, past the glass cases that housed rows of Winston Cup trophies and the guitars presented to Dale by Brooks and Dunn and Alabama.

Terence Palmer shook his head. "I checked that out online before I came. They're careful never to say. I suppose it's not inconceivable that some distraught racing fan would try to practice suttee on the grave site."

The three of them paused to watch Shane McKee wandering alone down the hall, barely glancing at the exhibits. After a moment of silence, Karen said, "I guess you can tell that Shane's mad at me. I said this place reminded me of the Lincoln Memorial, and that Richard Petty's was homier, and now Shane's furious. Was Dale Earnhardt really that much more famous than Richard Petty?"

Sarah Nash smiled. "Part of being a legend is knowing how and when to die," she said. "That's the difference. If Richard Petty had been killed in the last lap of the Daytona 500 instead of retiring into a peaceful and revered old age, I expect his face would be the back of the North Carolina state quarter."

"I wish I could tell Shane that, but it wouldn't improve his mood any," said Karen. "He was complaining that we went to Mr. Petty's place at all. Said it was disrespectful of Earnhardt. I'm trying not to upset him any further."

"You've been married, what? Three days? I'd say the sooner he learns to handle a disagreement without making a federal case out of it, the better off you're both going to be."

Terence Palmer, who was beginning to look uneasy at the prospect of being trapped in a "relationship" conversation between two women, strolled away, willing himself not to hurry, in search of a less embarrassing discussion. He saw Harley Claymore heading toward the gift shop, and he walked faster to catch up with him.

"Surely you're not buying souvenirs?" he said.

"No. Just looking at this pot of gold," said Harley. "You going to get another badge while we're here?"

Terence grinned and touched the Bristol and Martinsville pins on his hat. "Can't stop now. When I get back to Manhattan, this is how I'm going to find out who the cool people are. The ones who recognize the logos. Screen my dates."

The DEI gift shop was an Aladdin's cave of NASCAR related merchandise, devoted not only to Dale Earnhardt, but also to the current drivers for DEI, Inc., including Dale Earnhardt, Jr. and Mike Waltrip, but the majority of the items offered were mementos of the Intimidator. Racks of Dale Earnhardt shirts and jackets lined the wall, and his face glared out at passersby from calendars, posters, playing cards, coffee mugs, mouse pads, and keychains. The image of the black Monte Carlo frozen in acceleration zoomed across a hundred different items within the shop. Visitors, who had toured the memorial hallway in respectful silence, regained their voices in the gift area. In small groups they stopped at each display, examining the exhibits and checking price tags against whatever their budget allowed for the acquisition of souvenirs.

Terence examined a metal coffee mug emblazoned with a replica of Earnhardt's signature and the number 3. "I wonder if I should get my mother something from here," he mused.

"You think she'd like that?" asked Harley.

"No. It would drive her up the wall. But it would be worth — how much is this thing? — Twenty bucks — to see her face on Christmas morning."

"So NASCAR doesn't run in the family?"

"Well, not on that side of my family," said Terence. "My dad was an Earnhardt man, though. Funny, that's almost all I know about him."

"Well, it might tell you more than you think. Different drivers attract different types of fans. The Earnhardt anthem would be 'I did it my way.' Mark Martin is big with older, serious guys who don't like flashiness. The Labontes are family-friendly. The characters on *Friends* would root for Jeff Gordon, if NASCAR was on their radar screen at all. Find out which driver a person supports, and you learn a lot about him."

"Who do you root for, Harley?"

"Back in the day, I was a Darrell Waltrip fan."

"And what does that say about you?"

"Damned if I know," said Harley.

Bill Knight wondered if anyone ever forgot and genuflected in this dimly lit shrine. He had never seen anything like it. Well, he *had* — shrines were his hobby — but nothing that wasn't consecrated by some theological authority. A strange and powerful place.

"What do you think of it?" asked Cayle, who had appeared at his elbow.

"Why, I feel right at home," he said. *"Opus DEI."*

"Oh — church, you mean. Yes, I guess it is rather somber. People still miss him so much. They come every year, you know, on his birthday. Justine and I drove over this past April. It was amazing. There were tough-looking guys out there in the parking lot — looked like they ought to shave with a hacksaw — and they were crying. Just bawling. I'll bet Dale is embarrassed — well, I almost said *embarrassed to death* — seeing his old supporters still carrying on like that."

Bill Knight gave her a puzzled look.

"Embarrassed? So, you think Earnhardt is up in heaven looking out for his old supporters?"

Cayle shook her head. "No, I guess I don't," she said.

"Ah. Well, I suppose that most of the people who do think —"

"I mean, I don't think he's away in heaven, because I met him on that road out there. The one that runs right by this place."

"Really? You knew him?"

"Not exactly." Cayle looked around to make sure that no one else was close enough to overhear them. "Listen — I met him this past spring — the year *after* he died. I was driving alone one night coming back from Virginia, and I took a wrong turn trying to find Justine's shortcut. My car broke down on a country road, and I was stranded with a dead cell phone. Then suddenly out of nowhere this black Monte Carlo pulls up behind me, and *he* gets out, and he fixes my car. Good thing I drive a bow-tie."

"A what?"

"Chevy. They call them bow-ties because of the Chevrolet emblem."

He stared at her, waiting for the punch line to her story, but she still looked perfectly serious. "Dale Earnhardt? A ghost, you mean?"

Cayle shrugged. "He wasn't transparent or anything. He was just acting . . . well, ordinary. Fixed my car, told me how to get back to the Interstate, and left."

"You said it was late at night and you'd had a long drive."

"I didn't dream it, Bill. He fixed my car."

"Have you told any of the other passengers about this? Or Harley?" He almost smiled, picturing Harley's reaction to the further sanctification of his racing colleague. Harley Claymore would be horrified.

"No, I don't talk about it much," said Cayle. "Justine and Bekasu know, of course, but I don't talk about it. I don't want to end up in a tabloid."

"Yes, I expect a supermarket newspaper would salivate over a story like that. I'm surprised they didn't invent it themselves."

"Well, I didn't invent it," said Cayle. "But I can see how people might think I had, which is why I don't talk about it. I certainly don't want any publicity. I just wondered what you'd think about it, being a minister and all. Give me the benefit of the doubt. Trust me that it happened. So — what *do* you make of it?"

Bill Knight hesitated, searching for a diplomatic answer, partly as a kindness to Cayle, and partly because he felt it would be rude to ridicule her story while standing in the shrine of the man himself. A breach of hospitality — like making atheistic remarks on a tour of Notre Dame — bad taste. "Well," he said at last, "if I had been alive in the fifteenth century, and Joan of Arc had told me that some angels had ordered her to go and save France, I might well have thought her mad. The English certainly did. So it's a bit hard for me to respond. If amazing things were easy to believe, they wouldn't require faith."

"I guess you're right. I can't prove it, but it did happen."

He smiled. "Well, somebody once said that in a world where Jewish carpenters come back from the dead, anything is possible."

"I was surprised to see him, you know. I didn't really expect him to come back or anything. He was a Lutheran."

Bill nodded. "Yes, one feels that Martin Luther would not approve."

Cayle headed back toward the gift shop to buy a badge for her collection, and Bill continued his walk to the end of the long hall. He was standing with a group of silent visitors, studying an enlargement of a black-and-white photo of soldiers in Desert Storm, posing beside the plane they had decorated in imitation of Dale Earnhardt's "Black Number 3" when Shane came up beside him. "Awesome, isn't it?"

"He touched a lot of lives," said Bill, still thinking of Cayle's story.

"It's hard to believe he's gone."

Bill nodded, but he was thinking, *It's not hard to believe he's gone when you're standing in this place. It's a mausoleum.*

"You're a minister. Do you believe in saints and miracles and stuff?"

Again? Bill Knight studied the boy's earnest face. "Well, that's a pretty general question," he said, stalling for time. Modern clergy didn't really deal in miracles. They were more into homeless shelters and social justice issues, but old traditions die hard. Two supernatural confessions in one day was almost more than he could manage. What next? An exorcism? "I suppose it would depend on the miracle," he said carefully. "Did you have some sort of supernatural experience concerning Dale Earnhardt?"

Shane's eyes widened. "Me personally?

Of course not. But there is something sort of . . . cosmic . . . about Dale. Karen doesn't believe me. Well, she knows it's all true. She just doesn't think it adds up to a miracle, I reckon. Thought maybe I'd ask you about it."

Bill Knight looked around for Matthew. The boy was walking with Bekasu Holifield, examining the trophy cases in the center of the hall. He seemed to be explaining the significance of each one to her, and, bless her heart, the judge was allowing herself to be instructed with the meekness of an apprentice. He ought to be all right for the next ten minutes or so. Bill glanced at the worried face of the young man beside him. "All right," he said. "Why don't you tell me about it?"

"Okay. Dale was a seven-time champion, right? Same as Richard Petty. But Richard Petty won the Daytona 500 seven times as well, and Dale couldn't seem to win that race for love or money. It was like a curse, you know?"

"Perhaps he found that particular track difficult?"

"No," said Shane. "Dale was great on restrictor plate tracks. The master. He won lots of races at Daytona. Thirty-four of them, in fact. They'd have a week's worth

331

of races before the big one on Sunday, and some years Dale would win every single one of the preliminary races, and still he would lose the one that really counted."

"Why?"

Shane shook his head. "That's just it. It didn't make sense. He was never out-driven, and most of the time he had as good a car as anybody on the track. Some-times it just seemed like the finger of God would come and push down on the hood to keep him from winning." He paused, perhaps waiting for a theological quibble, but Bill merely nodded for him to go on. "One time he hit a *seagull*. That was in '91. Another time he ran out of gas. Or he'd hit a piece of debris and go into the wall. And it wasn't on just any old lap, either. Most of the time he'd be leading the race and he'd be on the very last lap of that 500-mile race — I mean just *seconds* from the end of it — and then when it looked like he couldn't possibly lose, disaster would strike."

"How many times did that happen?"

"He lost that race nineteen times in a row. People used to say that if it was the Daytona 499 instead of the Daytona 500, he would have won it every year."

Bill Knight considered it. "A kind of

negative miracle, you mean?"

"No. Let me finish. He lost nineteen times in a row, right at the end for stupid, trivial reasons, all right? So in 1998, on the day before the race, a six-year-old girl in a wheelchair is brought to visit the track. She's a big Dale fan, and so they take her to meet him, and he talks to her for a while, and then she says to him, 'You're gonna win this year.' He must have thought, 'Yeah, that'll happen,' because he *never* won that race. But this little girl insisted. Then she held out a penny, and she made him take it. Said it was a lucky penny and that if he would take it, he would finally win that race."

Bill Knight raised his eyebrows, thinking *urban legend.* "This is a true story, Shane?"

"Sure, it is. Ask anybody." He waved a hand at the gaggle of tourists walking along the hallway. "Everybody knows this story."

"So, Dale Earnhardt took the penny given by the sick child?"

Shane nodded. "He did. I guess he figured *What the heck?* He took that penny back to the garage and glued it to the dashboard of the race car."

"Don't tell me he won that race?"

"He did. Old Number 3 finally broke the

jinx. That was February 15, 1998. That's important. That date."

"Why?"

"Because — you know when and where he died?"

"Of course. He died in the Daytona 500. Last year. 2001."

"He died eleven seconds from the end of the race. The last lap, as always. February 18, 2001," said Shane, emphasizing each word. "Reverend, that is exactly *three years and three days* after he won the race."

"I see," said Bill, who thought that dying seemed a high price to pay for winning a race, even a race that was the crown jewel of your sport.

"That's not all there is to it, though," said Shane. *"Since he died, he hasn't lost the Daytona 500."*

"How do you mean, Shane? Obviously if he's dead he can't compete —"

"No, he *can*. He was an owner. Earnhardt himself drove for RCR — Richard Childress Racing — but a few years back he formed his own company —"

"Ah. DEI." He remembered Justine's story about the castle in heaven with the name on the drawbridge.

"Right. So in the race in which he died, the winner was Mike Waltrip."

"The announcer's brother? Yes, I saw that one."

"The announcer? Oh, you mean D.W. Yeah, Mike is Darrell Waltrip's little brother, but my point is that he drove for DEI. And then this past year, Junior won it. Dale Earnhardt, Junior — *also driving for DEI*." People were beginning to walk toward them now. Perhaps it was time to leave. Shane leaned closer, and said in a low, urgent voice, "If one of the DEI drivers wins again next February that'll be *three* wins in a row for DEI, ending in the year two thousand and *three*. You see what I'm talking about?"

Bill Knight nodded. "Yes, Shane, it's a striking set of coincidences. Or facts, if you will. But it's numbers. And the third win isn't even a sure thing yet. You can make numbers do anything. I wouldn't call that —"

Shane shook his head impatiently. "Don't you see? Death transformed him. He reached a higher power."

For one stricken moment Bill Knight thought Shane was going to compare this transcendent state to the transfiguration of Christ after the resurrection, but before he could object Shane rushed on, "It's like *Stars Wars*, you know? When Obe Wan Kenobe is killed, he becomes even more

335

powerful. Or Gandalf the Grey becoming Gandalf the White. A higher power."

"Oh," said Bill, willing himself not to smile. He thought of pointing out that Obe Wan Kenobe and Tolkien's Gandalf were fictional characters, but he didn't see what good it would do to bring that up. He'd met people who expected Jesus to look like Kevin Sorbo, and there was no arguing with faith like that. "Well," he said at last, "I don't suppose there's any harm in thinking that. I'm sure that people in a dangerous sport like racing could use a guardian angel looking out for them. Though I'm not convinced that celestial beings are allowed to influence the outcome of sporting events." A hundred arguments to the contrary spiraled through his mind like a Hail Mary pass, but he ignored them.

"And you know about the goat, right?" said Shane. "Born in Florida. White number 3 on its side."

"Well, you can't have reincarnation *and* transfiguration," Bill pointed out. "They cancel each other out, you know. You're either *here* or you're *there*."

Shane groaned. "It's just a sign. A sign that he hasn't left us. Like — like the rainbow."

"Well . . . I don't think Christian doctrine subscribes to the idea of people hanging around after they've died. I think they're supposed to have gone on to heaven. Isn't that what you were told in church?"

Shane waved away a millennium of theology. "But I've seen him," he said. "At Bristol before the race. I *saw* him!" Shane walked away before Sarah Nash and Harley could catch up with them.

Bill Knight stared after the boy. He considered going after him, but he saw that Karen had taken the young man's arm, and they seemed to be heading for the gift shop. Before he could make up his mind to follow them, someone touched his arm, and he looked up into the worried face of a stranger: a dark-eyed young man with a thick crew cut, who was dressed in the uniform of an army enlisted man. "Excuse me, sir," he said. "I didn't mean to eavesdrop on your friend there, but I couldn't help overhearing what he said about Dale and the miracles and all."

"He's — he's given it a lot of thought," said Bill, searching for a remark that was both courteous and truthful.

"Yes sir, I could see that he had," said the soldier. "Interesting stuff. Just one problem with it, though."

Just one? thought Bill.

"Yes, sir. Ward Burton."

"Well, it's nice to meet you, Ward."

The soldier heaved a sigh and rolled his eyes. Civilians. "No, sir. I'm not Ward Burton. Name's Alvarez. What I meant was that Little E. didn't win the Daytona 500 this spring. Ward Burton did."

"I know nothing about racing," said Bill, "but are you sure? Shane seems quite knowledgeable."

Private Alvarez shrugged. "Ask anybody, sir. Heck, ask *Junior*. He sure knows he hasn't won the big one yet. Your friend was right about Mike Waltrip winning in '01, and everything else sounded right, too, but not this year's Daytona. 2002: Ward Burton."

"But it's such an important thing. Why would he get it wrong?"

"I don't know, sir. I wondered that myself. You take care now." With a wave that was just short of being a salute, the soldier walked away.

"Isn't this place amazing?" said Sarah Nash. "Look what I bought in the gift shop!" She handed Bill a large, expensive-looking bottle tinted sapphire blue. He examined the label, expecting to see the word Chardonnay or Chablis, but instead the elegant script proclaimed the bottle's contents to be *Dale Earnhardt Spring Water.*

He saw the twinkle in her eye, and he smiled back. "You know, Sarah," he said softly, "if Dale had lived, he would have turned that into wine for you." Then he thought again of Shane McKee and the legend he'd fashioned out of his grief. *Lord of the Rings — and Pistons?* "I shouldn't joke about it," he said. "People are genuinely mourning this man — even after more than a year. I had no idea that the feelings ran this deep."

"Well, if it'll make you feel better," said Sarah Nash, "I think Dale himself would have thought that remark about the water was a hoot."

CHAPTER XIV

The Rock

North Carolina Motor Speedway

"The Rock deserves more than the tail end of an afternoon," said Harley, "but from here on out the distance between the speedways becomes so great that we have to make sacrifices in order to fit them all in." He was sitting at the head of two pushed-together tables at a North Carolina barbecue. The other passengers, between trips to the salad bar, listened while they ate with varying degrees of attentiveness.

Either by luck or because the decor was inevitable in a restaurant in that area, the place was a shrine to Dale Earnhardt. There were the usual barbecue restaurant ornaments: cartoon pig statues on shelves, and signed publicity stills of celebrity patrons, mostly of Nashville singers passing through on the way to gigs in Charlotte, but besides this standard fare, the pine-paneled walls were dedicated to the Intimidator.

From official Earnhardt posters in narrow chrome frames, the Intimidator stared down at the restaurant's patrons, stern-faced in his black-and-white Goodwrench firesuit, his eyes obscured by the usual dark sunglasses. A glass-fronted curio cabinet from the Hickory Furniture Market displayed die-cast replicas of the number 3 Monte Carlo and its predecessors, along with a collection of Earnhardt caps, coffee mugs, statuettes, framed 8x10 photos, and black-framed posters of the car and its driver at different race tracks or in posed publicity stills. The two most interesting posters were a departure from the standard fare. One from the *Dukes of Hazzard* era showed a young, shaggy-haired Earnhardt in jeans and boots, holding a cowboy hat, and perched atop the rail fence of a shady pasture. A western saddle was balanced on top of the rail beside him; just past it, a bay horse poked its head over the fence as if to inspect the blue-and-yellow race car parked on the grass verge of the country road.

"That was in the old days," Ray Reeve remarked to no one in particular. "Back when he was sponsored by Wrangler, when he won his first championship in 1980. Boy, he looks young. I'd forgotten." He

341

pointed at the framed poster beside it. "That there's his last championship, I do believe."

His friend Jesse nodded happily. "I'd say it was, Ray. I surely would."

Bill Knight, who had been staring in dismay at the latter image, said, "What an odd poster. What can they mean by it?" Repressing a shudder, he looked to Harley for an explanation.

Harley shrugged. "Coincidence." He picked up a menu and began to study it as if there'd be a quiz.

No firesuit or sunglasses in this last championship poster. Instead, an older, debonair Dale Earnhardt, tuxedo-clad and confident, stood in a full-length photo scaled larger-than-life and superimposed at the far left of a nightscape of the New York skyline. Looming just past the Intimidator's shoulder stood the glittering shapes of the Twin Towers, bright peaks against a blue twilight. In the composite photo, Earnhardt stood taller than the towers. At the other end of the poster, the traditional image of Earnhardt in racing mode was superimposed on an enormous moon image set in a slate blue sky above the cityscape. This black-and-white image wore sunglasses, and sported the

Goodwrench logo on his white helmet: the man in the moon, waiting for the green flag. At bottom right, where the Hudson River ought to be, sat the black number 3, scaled to dwarf the skyscrapers in the background.

"What do you think they're trying to say in that poster?" Bill Knight asked Harley, tapping the menu. "That Earnhardt's death was more significant than 9/11?"

"They're not trying to say anything," said Jesse Franklin, looking distressed at the misunderstanding. "Ray told you: that poster dates from 1994 — the year of his seventh championship. The NASCAR awards banquet is held in New York City. That's all it means."

Justine, who had come over to examine the poster as well, said, "Yes, but isn't it odd that they would pose Earnhardt beside the Twin Towers, and that we lost them in the same year?"

Bill smiled, partly in relief that his hasty conclusion had been wrong. "It's easy to spot omens after the fact," he told her. "Anybody can be Nostradamus on those terms. But Monday-morning prophets are as useless as Monday-morning quarterbacks. If you had looked at that poster back in 1994 and foreseen the disaster, then you'd have my attention."

"But, look," said Shane. "That year was his seventh championship. His *seventh*. In 1994. And it was *seven* years later that the Towers fell." He did a quick calculation on his fingers. "He died in February, 2001. February to September. *Seven* months after he died."

Ray Reeve shook his head. "You've lost me there, son," he said. "Maybe if those towers had been in Charlotte, I could see Earnhardt being a thread in a doomsday prophecy, but Manhattan was not his turf. I just can't see it as any more than a coincidence."

"And you can stop humming that *Twilight Zone* music, Bekasu," said Justine, turning around to glare at her sister. "We're trying to make sense of two tragedies here."

"It's a poster, Justine."

Justine sniffed. "You wouldn't recognize a miracle if it stepped on your foot. I know they say that seeing is believing, but maybe it works the other way, too. Maybe *believing* is *seeing*."

"Well, I think you all ought to stop talking about it," hissed Cayle, glancing around nervously. "Terence lives in Manhattan, you know. We might upset him with all this talk about 9/11."

Terence and Sarah Nash were already seated at the table with Matthew, helping him decipher the menu, seemingly oblivious to the discussion taking place at the Seventh Championship poster. Sarah Nash had discovered that neither of her table partners knew what hush puppies were or why they were called that, so she had embarked upon the tale.

The others took a last look at the poster, and walked back to their seats. Harley and Ratty had pushed two large tables together so that those who were not hard-of-hearing could converse with anyone else in the group, but there still wasn't room enough for everyone, so Bill Knight and Bekasu Holifield volunteered to sit at a smaller table nearby. They had tried to make this offer seem like a sacrifice, but their feigned reluctance to leave the group convinced no one.

Bill Knight studied the menu (*what was red slaw?*), still thinking about the concept of hindsight prophecy, and wondering how he should phrase his thoughts on the matter when he recorded it in his little notebook. He had set the notebook beside his fork in hopes that something would occur to him before the end of lunch. The motion of the bus tended to make his handwriting illegible. Hindsight prophecy: He supposed that it was human nature to look for omens in connection with significant events. Portents would be a sign that there is order in the universe: that things are predestined and foreseeable. The idea of a chaotic, random universe in which events have no meaning was more than some people could bear. He didn't much like the thought of it himself. Perhaps that was what drew him to the ministry: God was a promise of order in a world of chaos.

Bekasu, who had sat down next to him, noticed his look of preoccupation. "I love my sister," she said, "but sometimes I need a break from Planet Justine."

"She's an original," said Bill, smiling politely.

"About that Manhattan poster," said Bekasu, talking behind her upraised menu so the others wouldn't overhear. "They really don't mean to be blasphemous."

"No, no," said Bill. "I wasn't offended, and I don't think Terence Palmer even noticed. They're so obviously sincere. Misguided, perhaps, but sincere. Perhaps they are postmodernists."

Beksau smiled. "If you accused Cayle or Justine of being one, they'd say they were Presbyterian, but I take your point. The theory that people try to make a connection between random events in order to give the universe a semblance of meaning. Justine, searching for the mystical significance of all the threes, or a connection between two tragedies that some of them probably *do* see as equal."

"Yes. If it's only a set of coincidences that they are trying to impose order on, we needn't consider it, but some of the things I've heard are a bit puzzling, I admit."

Bekasu looked uneasy. "Well, Cayle for one may have good reason to think there's a supernatural connection with Earnhardt."

"Yes, she told me about her encounter on the road to Mooresville."

Bekasu twiddled her spoon. "She swears it really happened. I don't know what to make of it. I've known her forever, and she's not a flake. Now if it were Justine, I'd know exactly what to think. Justine is capable of finding the Holy Grail in a Coke machine. But Cayle . . . I guess as a minister you must be used to it."

He shook his head. Marriage counseling and fund-raising for charity were more in his line. Beans-and-rice suppers for Latin American political causes, yes; divine revelations, no. "You don't expect to hear things like that these days," he said. "Not outside of a supermarket tabloid, anyway. I suppose that if Cayle had told me that she'd met Mother Teresa, I might have been skeptical, but at least I'd have been more —"

"Respectful?" said Bekasu, smiling. "Well, I don't know if I believe it, either, but I'm enough of a contrarian not to want anybody's elitists electing our saints. I don't think we should doubt her because of *who* she saw. Besides, I think there's more than one kind of saint."

Bill Knight stared for a moment at a forkful of barbecue. "Okay," he said. "Angels — like St. Michael. Prophets and mystics — St. John the Baptist, Joan of Arc. Humanitarians — Mother Cabrini."

"Don't forget the political saints," said Bekasu. "People who become saints because canonizing them was one in the eye to the enemies of the church."

"Thomas More," said Bill. "Well, I'm an Episcopalian, so obviously we don't claim him, but Rome does."

"Exactly. And have you considered the people's saints? I mean the ones who got in by popular demand. Thomas Becket was one of those."

"Surely he was also a political choice? Archbishop of Canterbury — defending the church against secular law?"

"Yes — canonizing him was a papal rap on the knuckles for Henry II, but don't you think he was also a grassroots favorite?"

"Becket? Well, he became powerful despite the fact that he was a Saxon in Norman England, so by definition a member of the lower orders."

"In other words, a redneck," said Bekasu.

Bill stared at her. "Yes, but of course he transcended his humble beginnings."

"Well, then I'd say that's something he and Earnhardt had in common." She nodded toward the image of the man in the tuxedo against the backdrop of Manhattan. "And I'll tell you another resemblance. Neither one of them got above their raising, as we say down here. Remember Becket giving away the archbishop's fine clothing to the poor and wearing a hair shirt? And here's Earnhardt — fortieth richest person in America — and where does he live? Iredell County, where he started. Not Palm Beach. Not Palm Springs. Not New York or L.A. Mooresville. Ordinary people loved him for it."

"Well, I grant you the similarity, but of

course it doesn't make him a saint." Bill had begun to shred his paper napkin. "A Roman historian named Priscus said pretty much the same thing about Attila the Hun. How modest and well-spoken he was, I mean. Drank out of a wooden goblet, but served his guests in gold ones. Nobody ever mistook Attila for a saint. Or Earnhardt. Not that I'm comparing them," he hastened to add.

Bekasu laughed. "He'd probably consider it a compliment. Okay, Dale and Attila weren't saints by the church's standards, no. But the clergy may not have the last word anymore. Not culturally, anyhow. I think in the twentieth century, the people started choosing the saints. Elvis. Princess Diana. Speaking of the princess, a few weeks before she was killed, she auctioned off her formal gowns at Sotheby's and gave the money to charity. Does that sound familiar?"

"Becket's robes . . ." murmured Bill. "Shortly before he was killed, he gave away his archbishop's clothing to the poor."

"Right." She waved a hush puppy for emphasis. "They were *of* the people, and *for* the people. Scorned by the aristocracy. Becket was an uppity Saxon redneck. Elvis wasn't 'serious' music. Diana wouldn't toe the line with the royal family; and Dale was just a race car driver, which elitists don't even consider a sport. All of them died in their prime, and all of them elicited the same public reaction: people felt rage as much as grief — that someone they loved had been taken from them."

Bill stared at her. "I thought you hated stock car racing."

Bekasu shrugged. "I'm a lawyer. I can argue both ends against the middle. I don't particularly enjoy watching racing as a sport — not the way Justine does. But it annoys me when cultural snobs belittle it. Fighting for the underdog is in my blood, I suppose. A judge I clerked for once called me a Jacksonian Democrat, and I suppose I am."

"But do you think Earnhardt — I mean, all those supernatural things?"

She shrugged. "I'm keeping an open mind, I guess. I've known Cayle all her life and she isn't a liar, so I'll take it as real that she saw *something*. But I'm reserving judgment on the rest. Mystical symbols in the posters. He touched a lot of lives much more deeply than anybody ever thought he would. I don't know what it means."

"Fair enough," said Bill.

"But isn't he an unlikely saint?" Bekasu

nodded toward the Earnhardt-Twin Towers poster. "I grew up in North Carolina. I'm about the same age as Dale. And I keep thinking that I knew him. Oh, not *him*. But I went to school with a lot of Dales way back when . . . Sullen little chicken hawk guys with shaggy hair and long sideburns. They lived in the same small town that we did, but in another world. I grew up fettered with rules and expectations. Thou shalt not wear white shoes after Labor Day. Go to church. Make the honor roll. Don't make waves in thought, word or deed. Respect your elders. Don't get serious about a boyfriend in high school, because you've got to get through college and grad school unencumbered."

"Sounds familiar," said Bill.

"Yes, but not everybody had to follow those rules. My dad was a lawyer, and my friends were the doctors' kids and the other lawyers' kids, and the rest of the adolescents in our leafy upper middle class neighborhood. We all went to the nice new junior high school in the suburbs. But across town was the other junior high school — the old one — on the other side of the tracks in the working class part of town." She sighed. "I used to envy them so much."

"I know," said Bill. "They didn't have to be home by ten or do volunteer work with the church youth on weekends."

"The girls could wear raccoon-eye makeup and tight skirts, and they could drink beer and go steady in ninth grade."

"And you wanted to be like them?"

Bekasu took a deep breath. "Well, okay. You're right. I probably wouldn't have gone through with it. Justine was the family wild child. I had to be the responsible one. The honor student. But those kids from the other side of town seemed so free. So unencumbered by expectations. I was the rough beast, slouching toward graduate school since before I could even spell it."

Bill smiled. "Same here. And you're saying that Dale Earnhardt was from the other side of the tracks?"

"Of course he was! He dropped out of school in junior high! If I'd done that, my parents would have sent me off to a nunnery. And we were Presbyterian. He was a dropout, got married at sixteen or so, and worked in a mill or a garage or something. I knew a slew of guys from that world. They turned up in tenth grade, when both junior high school classes got dumped into the same city high school. But the two groups mostly stayed separate even then. It's as if we knew even as adolescents that we were headed in different directions."

"It must have been a big surprise for some of Earnhardt's classmates to reach the pinnacle of society and find Dale way ahead of them."

"Yes," said Bekasu. "Some of those wine-and-cheese conversations were probably quite strained, but I don't think Earnhardt's success would have changed their fundamental outlook on life. You don't cancel your electrical connection just because lightning strikes once."

Harley Claymore stood up, and tapped his spoon against his iced tea glass. Since the glass was plastic, this did not have much effect, but the conversation subsided anyhow. "It looks like we're on the last lap of lunch, so I thought I'd get back to talking about The Rock, before we drive on over there." His note cards were propped against the bottle of hot sauce, but when he was standing up, he was too far away to be able to read them. He didn't think he'd miss much, though. "Some housekeeping notes first, though. We'll be spending tonight in the Greater Charlotte area — that's — how far are we, Ratty?"

Rattly Laine paused with his coffee mug inches from his lips. He had been in the middle of a story about taking Mick Jagger to Graceland, a tale that was no less entertaining for being implausible. "Charlotte?" he said. "Seventy-five miles west of here. An hour and a half, barring rush hour. But, of course, we're not going to Charlotte proper, are we?"

"Oh, right. We're staying tonight at Exit 49 off Interstate 85." In the early days Lowe's Motor Speedway had been called the Charlotte Motor Speedway, but the track had always been located in Concord, a little town northeast of Charlotte. If they had been traveling in strict geographical order, the tour would have visited Lowe's before Rockingham, but Bailey Travel's research indicated (rightly) that there would be more accommodations around Concord than there would be in Rockingham. Besides, the Charlotte Interstate corridor was the route they'd be taking the next afternoon to reach Talladega.

Harley winced. It was past two o'clock now. There was no way they could miss Charlotte's rush hour, unless they dithered in Rockingham until after five o'clock, and that didn't seem likely. On a weekday with no Cup race scheduled there for months, the Speedway would be deserted. A walk around, a few minutes to lay the wreath — he thought they'd be out of there by four. Anyhow traffic was Ratty's problem, not his. He half expected one of the wealthier passengers to ask why they weren't staying in Pinehurst instead of closer to Charlotte. Rockingham bordered North Carolina's golf resort country, and he hadn't wanted to have to tell them that the Bailey Travel budget would not stretch to such luxuries. He'd already had to tell Sarah Nash that time did not permit them to visit the famous Seagrove potteries while they were in Randolph County visiting the Petty Museum. No one had mentioned the golfing opportunities, though. Perhaps they could only concentrate on one sport at a time.

He cleared his throat and began again. "Rockingham. Technically, it is the North Carolina Motor Speedway, but you'll hear Sting called 'Gordon' oftener than you'll hear the Rock called by that long-winded title. It dates back to the 1960's, and is located in Rockingham — hence the nickname. They host the second race of the NASCAR season. This is the place for drivers to find out if they've corrected whatever problems they had in the race at Daytona. The second Cup race is held in

October. The track is ninety feet over a mile long, and it's hell on tires. The banking is slightly higher in turns three and four than it is in the first two. Well, you'll see. Shall we head on over there?"

"I wish my father could have made this trip," said Terence, settling back into his seat on the bus. "I'm having a good time, but he would have really loved it, wouldn't he?"

"Well, he had visited most of these places before," said Sarah Nash. "Rockingham and Charlotte were day trips for him. He only signed up on this tour as a lark, and maybe to relive some good memories of the old days. I think he'd be glad to see you enjoying yourself. If he'd have any regrets, it would be not getting to share this experience with you, so that you could hear his stories as well as the official NASCAR tales."

Terence hesitated. "I know he was planning on making this trip with you, and so I've been wondering were you and he — ?"

"An item?" She gave him a wry smile. "No. I told you. We were neighbors. And old friends. Besides, I have a husband, technically speaking."

"You — ?"

"There's a quaint old term people used when I was a girl. Grass widow. You know it?"

"I think so. Someone whose husband isn't dead, but has abandoned her?"

"Close enough. Richard didn't abandon me, though. We just — came to a parting of the ways."

Terence grunted. "Everybody does, in my experience."

"Well, Richard and I stuck it out for thirty-five years. We built Nash Furniture together. Heard of it?"

"Is it expensive? My mother probably has."

She smiled. "Reproduction colonial furniture in native cherry and walnut. Largely handmade by local craftsmen. Yes, it would set you back a thousand or so for an end table. Anyhow, about five years ago Richard wanted to sell the company and retire, which was fine with me — until he told me what he wanted to do with his newfound freedom."

"What was that?"

"Move to Florida. Buy a condo or a McMansion in one of those million-dollar stalag communities, and play golf with the wine-and-cheese people in perpetuity." She sighed. "I told him that if it was a choice between that and the back of Dr. Kevorkian's van, I'd just take the van, thanks all the same."

"He went without you?"

"He did. There were no hard feelings. We didn't get a divorce — neither one of us wanted a feeding frenzy amongst the lawyers. Richard just took his half of the money and went south, and I stayed in our house near Wilkesboro, with my horses and my volunteer work."

"So you and my dad really were just friends?"

"Sometimes it's nice to have somebody to talk to over dinner. Tom used to like to watch NASCAR on television with me so that we could argue about it. He was a nice man. I miss him."

"What would he have thought of all this?" said Terence.

"The tour?" Sarah Nash considered it. "Well, above all, Tom Palmer was a sensible man, but a reticent one. High as he was on Dale Earnhardt, I can't quite see Tom making a speech over a wreath on some speedway. I think he might have made a few caustic remarks about all this, but he would have done it in private. I know that if people had carried on this way over Tom's death, he'd have been mortified." She smiled. "That may have been a pun. Mortified. I think Dale would have felt the same way; they were a lot alike."

"And I never got to meet either of them," said Terence.

"I think the question is: how are you enjoying this trip?"

"Uh — fine." He honestly hadn't considered it. "My mother always stressed that a true gentleman was at home in any company, and I try, but sometimes I feel that I'm just equally ill-at-ease in any company. Mother never had any patience with people who wouldn't try the food in a foreign country, wouldn't learn to speak the language. She called them barbarians. So I never waste time wishing I were somewhere else, or comparing one place to another. I'm along for the ride. But it's great to see all the Southern speedways up close. It gives you a new perspective on the sport."

"And on your father's world."

"Well, I suppose," said Terence. "But it makes me wonder if I would have had anything to talk to him about besides racing."

"Well, if you want to find out, maybe you ought to try to talk some more to some of your fellow passengers."

Terence looked over at the rest of the

group and shrugged. "And say what?"

The Number Three Pilgrims stood in the parking lot gazing up at the deserted Speedway. "It seems fitting to see the place empty," said Ray Reeve gruffly. "More of a memorial, I guess."

"You got that right," said Shane McKee. "If you ask me, even when they're racing here, the place is empty."

Lord, here we go again, thought Harley. They'd end up passing around the handkerchief yet. To derail the wake, he held up his hand for silence. *Think of something to say about Rockingham.* "This place has changed some since I last drove it," he said. "Four years ago, when they took the word 'motor' out of the speedway name, they added a new high-rise grandstand over there between turns 2 and 3. I guess that's why they expanded the parking area. To me, though, the biggest change was in pit road. The Rock used to have pits on both sides of the track, but when they remodeled in '99 they put all forty-five pit stalls on the front stretch. It's a nice little track. Hell on tires, though."

"I kind of miss the mountains surrounding the Bristol Speedway," said Cayle. "It was such a pretty setting."

"Well, you may see those mountains again in a day or so," said Harley.

Justine seized the Rockingham memorial wreath before Ratty could get it completely out of the luggage compartment. "This is the best one!" she cried, holding it aloft. Smaller than the two previous tributes, the wreath was fashioned in the shape of a heart, using white silk dogwood flowers, a symbol of North Carolina, as Justine had informed them. Earnhardt's trademarked number 3 was picked out in the center of the heart in smaller flowers dyed black.

"Cayle, you ought to do this one," she said. "Since it's the next stop after Mooresville."

"I wouldn't know what to say," said Cayle. "I tried to tell him I was sorry it happened when — you know. But I'm no good at making speeches. You could help me. And we could get Matthew to carry it for us." Justine handed the wreath to the boy, and the trio wandered off in search of a suitable place to leave it, while the rest of the pilgrims trailed behind at a respectful distance.

Bekasu caught up with Bill Knight again. "I've been thinking about that sainthood business," she said. "You know, people have been trying to make Elvis into one for years."

"I know. I have a clip file on Elvis phenomena. The people who claim to see his face in cracks in the ceiling plaster, or to get advice from him in dreams. There's even a story claiming that there were strange lights in the sky the night he was born."

"UFOs," said Bekasu, and they laughed. "But, seriously, I wonder if there's anything like that about Earnhardt?"

Bill Knight hesitated. It had been on the tip of his tongue to say that it was too soon for the legends to spring up. He wanted to tell her that the gospel of St. Luke — the only one of the four to mention angels and the Star of Bethlehem — had not been written until a hundred years after the crucifixion. That was the sort of remark you had to be careful making if you were a minister, though. Even people who didn't believe expected childlike faith from the clergy. Instead he told her, "It's early days yet. Remember that Elvis died in '77, so there has been more time for the legends and myths to take root. Just wait a couple of years. There'll be sightings."

"Well, we've had that already," murmured Bekasu, looking around for Cayle.

"I just wish I knew what to make of it."

"You know the options as well as I do," said Bill. "Either it was real or it wasn't. If it wasn't real, then it could have been a dream. It was late at night on a dark road. Cayle may have drifted off to sleep without realizing it. Or it could have been a hallucination induced by the panic of being stranded on a lonely road. If it was real, then it could have been someone dressed up as Earnhardt for — I don't know — a costume party or a promotional gimmick. And then there's that last possibility that we come to with great reluctance. That she really did see him that night, and that it really was him, somehow. A ghost, perhaps? Such sightings are not that uncommon, after all. Ultimately, though, it doesn't matter. All through history there have been odd little events from time to time that no one could really explain, but they didn't change the fabric of civilization. Sooner or later, people just shrugged and went back to business as usual."

"But you don't believe she saw him?"

Bill Knight shook his head. "Of course I don't."

Justine put her hand on Matthew's shoulder. "How are you doing, hon," she said. "We need to buy you sunglasses at the gift shop here. It's real bright in this sunshine, and it's going to get brighter as we head south. I don't want you getting sick."

"I'm okay," said Matthew. "Just kind of tired."

The two of them had walked a little ahead of the others, still looking for a likely place to lay the wreath, which Matthew insisted on carrying.

"You're sick, aren't you?" said Justine, lifting up her sunglasses to give him a searching stare.

"Yeah," said Matthew. "That's how come they let me come on this tour." As they walked he told her about his father wrecking the truck, and how he ended up a ward of New Hampshire, and about getting taken to the doctor a couple of weeks ago when he kept saying he was tired all the time.

Justine frowned. "I can imagine the kind of medical care orphans get," she said. "Have you been to a specialist?"

Matthew scuffed a pebble on the track with his shoe. "I don't think so. Maybe when I get back."

"Well, what kind of treatment — oh, never mind. I'll see if your reverend friend knows any details. Listen, the next gift shop we hit, you just pick out anything you want and come find me. My treat. But make sure you get sunglasses, too, you hear?"

Matthew nodded. "Will they still have Dale Earnhardt stuff at Daytona?"

Justine smiled. "Honey, when you're as old as I am, they'll still have Earnhardt stuff at Daytona."

The group had assembled now to the left of the North Grandstand, where a tunnel led into the track area at turn 4. Solemnly, Matthew placed the number 3 heart next to the passageway and stepped back.

Cayle twisted her hands and looked uncomfortable. She motioned for Harley and whispered, "I don't know what to say. See, my car broke down outside Mooresville six months ago, and Dale came along and fixed it for me."

Harley was silent for a moment, while he digested this. He knew there'd be nuts on this tour; he just hadn't pegged the little blonde to be one of them. He whispered back, "Well, it was nice of Dale to fix your car for you. It sounds like something he'd do. Just don't tell DEI about it. They'll send you a bill for road service."

366

She was on her own. Justine motioned for her to go first, and after another pause to collect her thoughts, Cayle said, "Hello, sir. I have to say I wasn't a big fan of yours when you were alive. I was always a sucker for the cute ones. Rusty. Ricky. But seeing how many people were devastated when you died has really touched me. And of course, I want to thank you for what you did for me. A lot of people love you. I just hope you know that. And if there's some reason that I was the one to see you, I wish you'd let me know what it was. Well — bye."

Several of the listeners exchanged puzzled looks, but Cayle stepped back without any indication that she would enlighten them.

Justine had been standing very still beside the wreath, her eyes closed and her hands clasped in front of her. When Cayle finished speaking, she knelt down and spoke directly to the wreath, as if it were a celestial speaker system.

"Hey, Dale!" she said. "I don't know if I can explain this so it'll make sense, but I'm going to try. People I've known have died. My grandmother. A girl in sixth grade. People in car wrecks, and girlfriends from breast cancer. And I was always very sorry when they passed away. I felt bad for their families, and I was sad that they missed

367

out on more of life, and sometimes I regretted something I'd said or done or not done, or I'd wish I could see them again. So I thought I knew about how it feels when somebody dies. But, Dale, when you died, it didn't feel like that a bit.

"It's not like that sweet sorrow you feel when an acquaintance passes on. It felt — well, this sounds stupid, but it felt just the way it did when my house in Myers Park got robbed. Like a fist in my chest. They stole my grandmother's Gorham Buttercup silver tea set, and I knew I'd never get it back, and I was so angry I couldn't see straight. I thought my throat would close up when I tried to talk into the phone to report it.

"And that's just what it felt like when you died. Like somebody had taken something that belonged to *me*. It was my loss. My pain. I didn't have to reach inside myself to feel sympathy for you or for other people. I couldn't. I was too busy feeling sorry for myself. So I hope you're in heaven, and that it's everything you wanted it to be, and that your loved ones have found the strength to go on. But I'm still mad about losing you. You were *my* driver, my champion, and it's personal. And heaven or no heaven, if I could make them send you back I would. Amen."

CHAPTER XV

The Pass in the Grass

Lowe's Motor Speedway
Concord, NC

Harley Claymore looked at his watch. Eight forty-five. So far, so good, in terms of the timing for the tour. Harley had been worried about the distances and times allotted between destinations. He knew that Bailey Travel had never done this itinerary before and, as a novice in the guiding business, he had no faith in his own ability to keep them on schedule. But by some miracle — he winced at the word, thinking who Justine would thank — they had managed to make all the stops in a reasonable approximation of the appointed times.

Ratty's take-no-prisoners driving style and his knowledge of the back roads had enabled them to complete the trip from Rockingham to Concord in less than two hours. (He said that he had once been the governor's chauffeur.) Another hour had gone to getting them settled in the hotel within sight of Interstate 85, and just across from a megaoutlet mall called Concord Mills. This was the heart of racing country. Most of the teams had their headquarters within a few miles of here, and although Harley was stranded without a car, he thought there was an outside chance that a couple of phone calls might bring forth someone to talk business with. Besides the two race venues, this was the place to use his connections, if he still had any. For that reason, Harley had hoped to skip the communal dinner by directing the passengers to the many restaurants within walking distance of their lodgings. But Cayle and Justine, locals who knew the mall by heart, had insisted that they make a pilgrimage to the mall itself to see the life-size bronze statue of the Intimidator in his racing gear which stood on a pedestal near the walkway in silent benediction. The patron saint of local commerce and interstate tourism, Harley figured. He had nearly worn out his smile posing for half an hour with various combinations of the Number Three Pilgrims against the backdrop of that solemn statue.

Laugh, Ironhead, he silently told the bronze effigy. *Wait 'til the angels put you to work answering prayers in some celestial version of QVC.*

Harley had skipped dinner, but he let it be known that there was a place nearby that served mixed drinks. If anybody wanted to meet up with him there, he planned to show up around nine, he told them. Then he'd gone to his hotel room with a fist full of tattered business cards and numbers scribbled on beer mats, and started making phone calls.

"Hello, who is this? Justin? No kidding! How ya doin'? You sound a lot like your dad. I haven't seen you since before your feet could touch the accelerator. Hey, this is Harley. *Harley.* Harley Claymore. I used to drive for — well, it's been a while. Listen, is your dad there? Oh. Oh, right. Of course he is. Well, I'm headed to Darlington myself, end of the week. No. No message. I'll catch up to him down the road. Good to talk to you again."

That conversation multiplied by ten constituted his evening's worth of free time, an exercise in frustration and futility. He should have tried to set up some meetings before the tour started. Twenty-twenty hindsight, as usual.

Finally, at quarter to nine, he gave up and headed out to the bar where about half the party had taken over a large table in the corner. The Powells weren't there,

371

which didn't surprise him. Neither Sarah Nash, nor Terence, nor Ray Reeve were there, but Jesse Franklin was, and the newlyweds had come up for air. The Charlotte Three were in full force, and Bill Knight was present, though Matthew was not. He wondered what Ratty Laine did with his evenings.

"Where's the rookie?" Harley asked Bill Knight.

"Matthew? He said he was tired, so I told him he could stay in the room. Sarah Nash is looking in on him to make sure he's all right."

They had all finished dinner, except Shane, who was still toying with a basket of onion rings. (*Shame to let 'em go to waste.*) The others had ordered drinks, and they immediately hailed Harley with an offer to stand him a round. He accepted all offers, thinking as far as optimism and cheerfulness went, he was about a quart low.

Jesse Franklin took a sip of his drink and made a face. "This iced tea is sweet," he said. "I'm sure I ordered unsweetened."

"Send it back," said Shane.

He shook his head. "No. It's no big deal. I'll just drink it. I hate to make a fuss."

"We were just saying how much we're

enjoying the tour, Harley," said Cayle. "You're doing a great job."

Harley's bourbon arrived and he took a fortifying gulp. "I appreciate that," he said. "Hope you all are having a good time."

"Well, it has been enlightening," said Bekasu. "At least now I'll be able to decipher some of the hats and jackets that people wear into my courtroom. I used to think all those 8 and 24 tattoos were gang symbols."

Justine gasped. "Somebody has a *24* tattoo — in *Charlotte?* What were they in court for? Shoplifting at the health food store?"

Harley wasn't about to step into that one. He focused his attention on his drink while the conversation ebbed and flowed around him. They drifted away from talking racing after a while, because all these people had other lives, other interests. Cayle talked about her garden ornament craft projects, and Justine passed around pictures of her two dogs, which, surprisingly enough, were not yappy lap pooches, but a couple of sad-eyed blue tick hounds who looked like they ought to be living under a sagging porch instead of in a big stone-and-glass house in a toney Charlotte neighborhood. Their names were

Holly and Edelbrock, a reference that had to be explained to Bill Knight, the only one who did not smile when he heard it. Even Shane managed to almost get off the subject of racing. He talked about his job back home, working as a mechanic, and getting to put in some time on an ARCA car. Harley tried to think of something to say that didn't involve a steering wheel, but nothing came to mind.

"So you're working on a race car?" he said to Shane.

Shane nodded. "Not a Cup car, though. Maybe someday."

Harley nodded over his drink. He knew about *somedays*.

"How did you break into the big time?" asked Shane.

"That was a different era." Harley didn't believe in telling long stories in roadhouses. "That was before rookie drivers had engineering degrees from Purdue. If you're looking to get the family together and build a race car in your garage in Dawsonville, Georgia, or Stuart, Virginia, you are tough out of luck, son, because those days will not come again."

"I know that. I just don't know how to break in."

"Told you. Engineering degree."

Shane shook his head. "That's not happening."

"Grades?"

"Money."

Karen, who had been listening to this conversation, leaned across and touched Shane's arm. "Tell him about that program you started, Shane. Driving for Dale."

"Oh, he doesn't want to hear about that."

Which was true, but Karen told him anyway, and even pulled a well-creased newspaper clipping out of her purse and insisted that Harley hang on to it until he had time to read the whole thing.

Back in his hotel room, Matthew was glad of a little time to himself away from the grown-ups. He was often more tired than he let on — or at least, he would gallop through the day, fueled by the novelty and excitement of the excursion, and then after dinner, when the excitement wore off, he would tumble into bed with hardly any interval between lights off and sleep. Now he could make an early night of it, perhaps write a few postcards to some of his friends back in Canterbury. He had flipped through the channels on the television. He would have loved to see *Fast and*

Furious on a hotel movie channel, but it wasn't offered. Child services children were only allowed to see movies rated "G" or "PG," so all of them longed to see forbidden films, especially car chases and horror films.

Since there weren't any interesting movies offered on the hotel television, Matthew searched for some version of *Star Trek* to watch. He had briefly considered watching the SPEED Channel instead, but they weren't showing Cup racing just now, so he decided to hang out with old friends instead: that is, the characters on the U.S.S. *Enterprise*. Maybe if they were still filming *Star Trek: The Next Generation*, he'd have considered asking to visit there for his trip, but probably not, because the crew of the *Enterprise* were only acting, but Dale Earnhardt was real.

To boldly go where no one has gone before. Those actors hadn't done that. But Dale had.

"Why you wanna go on an Earnhardt tour, man?" asked Nick, who was one of his roommates, twelve going on forty. "Earnhardt is dead, dude. You're not gonna meet him."

But that was just it.

Maybe he was.

Matthew didn't talk about it, because mentioning death upset grown-ups. Nobody had come right out and said that he was going to die, but being a kid without parents taught you to pay close attention to the adults who had control of your life: whether or not they smiled or looked you in the eye; what they didn't say, and whether they were suddenly nice to you for no reason. So, he knew. Back in the winter he had been feeling tired and weak, falling asleep in school and going to bed before lights out, and finally somebody noticed and took him to the clinic for tests. Nobody told him what he had, but the staff member who took him to the doctor had insisted on stopping for ice cream on the way back to the Children's Home. That was a bad sign, he thought. He didn't ask any questions, though. The thing about being a kid is that you have no control over anything, anyhow. If the grown-ups say you're going to die, that's the way it is. He watched the word about his condition spread through the staff of the home: one by one the counselors and the office workers started acting funny around him, giving him pitying smiles and extra helpings at dinner. He contrived not to notice, because he didn't want to talk about it, but he had started thinking about it. Dying.

He didn't think it was going to hurt. Hospitals nowadays had all sorts of medicines to keep you from feeling anything, so the only thing to worry about was what came after. He thought that if dying just meant going to sleep and never waking up, then there was nothing to worry about. He wasn't looking forward to it, but at least he wouldn't have to deal with it.

If there was an afterlife, though, he didn't want to walk into it by himself. He'd barely known his grandmother, and he wasn't entirely sure that he could count on his dad even making it to heaven. His mom was sleeping on life support back in a white room in New Hampshire. But Dale Earnhardt was in heaven. Everybody said so. Just after the wreck, Mike Waltrip himself had said that in the twinkling of an eye Dale went into the presence of the Lord.

Matthew thought that if he stayed faithful to Dale as a fan, then Dale would stick up for him in heaven. One of his fantasies was of stepping out onto a cloud in front of the pearly gates, where the bearded old angel sat at a desk with a roll book. And there in front of the gates stood Dale Earnhardt in his dark shades and his white Goodwrench firesuit, holding up a

378

cardboard sign that said "Matthew Hinshaw." Then he'd be safe.

At the Concord restaurant the evening wore on, but no one left. Harley's sense of self-preservation kicked in and he switched from bourbon to beer.

Bill Knight looked thoughtfully at his shotglass full of Jack Daniels. "I'm a scotch drinker, myself," he remarked to no one in particular. "Still, I suppose that except for the change of grain from corn to barley, the recipe is basically the same as Glenfiddich. Hmm . . . I wonder if they make bourbon in Scotland? Surely they have corn over there. I wonder what you would call a Scottish bourbon?"

"Glen Campbell," said Bekasu.

"What's your room number, Cayle?" asked Justine. "I need to get my nail polish remover back from you tonight."

Cayle looked nervously around the bar, and then she leaned forward and said in conspiratorial tones, "Rusty Wallace and Mike Waltrip."

"Must be crowded in there," said the waitress, who was removing the empty glasses. She smiled to show that she was teasing, and then she pointed to the full-length Dale Earnhardt poster on the far wall.

"It's a code," Justine said, mouthing the words so that no one could overhear.

The waitress nodded, unsurprised. "Yeah, I figured," she said. "Room two-fifteen. Y'all might want to come up with a more obscure code to use around these parts. Driver numbers are no secret here. Darrell Waltrip swears he used to open his prayers by saying, 'Hello, God, this is number 17.' "

"She's right," said Karen. "That's how I taught the numbers to the little boy I babysat: with die-cast race cars. One, Rusty, Dale, Robby Gordon, T. Labonte, Mark Martin, Rusty's Little Brother, Little E, Awesome Bill, Ten."

"If you want to change codes, you might try using Bible verses," said Bill Knight. "Oh, wait, they'd probably catch on to that here in Concord, too."

"Bible verses?" said Harley.

He laughed. "Yes. I used to use that code to leave messages for people back in college. We had hall phones in those days, and you couldn't be sure that whoever answered the communal phone would pass along a message, so the trick was to make it a memorable one."

"Like what?"

"Well, the one I used most often was Job

13, verse 22." He waited with an expectant smile for someone to shout out the verse, but after a few moments of respectful silence, he gave it to them. " 'Call thou, and I will answer.' It worked every time."

Justine giggled. "I think Terence would enjoy hearing about the NASCAR number code," she said. "Bet you anything that nobody in Manhattan would get it."

"Some of them would," said Harley. "There used to be a NASCAR speedway in Trenton, and I hear they're looking to build another one somewhere closer to New York City."

"The Hoboken 500," said Bekasu with inebriated solemnity.

Bill Knight said, "I wonder if they use that code up where I live."

"Don't you know?" asked Justine.

"It would have gone right over my head," said Bill.

"Gotta trivia question for you," said Harley, downing the last of his most recent beer. "In 1986, when Geoff Bodine won the Daytona 500, what driver sold souvenirs in the nearby Kmart parking lot that afternoon after the race?"

"Umm . . ." Justine considered it. "Must have been one of the young drivers who was a kid back then . . . not Jeff Gordon, surely. He was probably in Indiana by then. Maybe Jimmie Johnson? Kurt Busch?"

"Or maybe one of the second generation drivers, who was there in Daytona because his dad or his older brother was racing that year?" said Karen. "How old is Dale Jarrett? Or the younger Wallaces?"

"How about Sterling Marlin?" said Shane.

"Not Dale Junior?" said Cayle.

The other drinkers nodded, exuding beer fumes and solidarity. "Could be him."

Harley shook his head sadly. "Naw," he said, blowing his nose on a cocktail napkin. "None of them. The answer is . . . *Geoff Bodine*."

Everybody froze as the name sank in. Then Bill Knight said, "Harley, that can't be right. You just said he won the race that day."

"S'true, though," said Harley. "He did win. That was the year Earnhardt ran out of gas nearing the finish line and Bodine won it. But in the Eighties the 500 wasn't the big old hype monster it is these days. No flying off in your private jet to the Letterman show. Back then you just did your victory lap, talked to a few sports writers, and went on home. So Geoff Bodine's parents . . .

s'parents . . . were selling souvenirs from a little old stand in the Kmart parking lot down the street and he went over . . ." his voice broke. "And he *helped* them." He dabbed at his eyes with his sleeve.

There was a shocked silence in the bar, and then Cayle began to sniffle too. "Pore old Bodine," she said.

There were rumbles of agreement.

"Well, that's not fair," said Shane. "Everybody these days gets a gazillion dollars and their picture on magazine covers, and on the day of his greatest victory Geoff Bodine has to sell keychains! That's not right."

"And now he can't even keep a sponsor," said Jesse Franklin, thumping the table. "Even that old Indian casino in Florida has dumped him . . ."

"Poor old Bodine," whispered Harley, wiping away a tear. "Sometimes I think I must have been a Bodine brother that got stolen away by the gypsies or something, because I sure do have the family curse — you work hard enough for two people, and you've got the talent to make it big, but you never, never get a break. And now no ride."

But nobody was listening to Harley's lament.

Bill Knight shook his head sadly. "The race is not always to the swift . . ."

"What number is that?" asked Bekasu.

"I forget. Ecclesiastes somewhere."

"Well, what are we gonna do about it?" Justine demanded. She opened her purse and fished out a twenty. "Let's pass the hat! Gimme that cap, Jesse!" She snatched off his Winged Three hat and waved it over her head. "Let's see some greenbacks, y'all. Come on. Toss 'em in there. You can spare it. Anybody got an address for Geoff Bodine?"

"I'm not usually expected to add to the collection plate," said Bill Knight, smiling as he tossed in a five-dollar bill.

"You're going to send him cash through the mail?" said Karen. "That's not safe."

"We could write him a check," said Cayle.

"Not anonymous enough," said Justine. "We don't want to hurt his feelings. This isn't charity. It's restitution."

"I doubt if a few dollars will be much consolation to him," murmured Bekasu.

Justine sniffed. "Okay, Miss High-and-Mighty. You call Letterman and Larry King and get Bodine on their shows, but until that great day, I say we make the gesture. Shaking our fists at the fates and all."

"Maybe you could buy a money order at a gas station," said Jesse Franklin, adding a pocketful of crumpled, tobacco-flecked dollar bills to the pot.

Harley looked at the hat full of fives and ones nestled alongside Justine's twenty-dollar bill. He was picturing Geoff Bodine's dismay if he should ever find out about this. Better try to set them straight before the disaster went any further.

"Okay, maybe he didn't get all the laurels that he deserved," said Harley, backpedaling for all he was worth. "But Old Geoff is not down and out. He was rookie of the year in '82. He's on the list of the 50 greatest drivers ever." *And he will kill me if he finds out I had anything to do with this,* he finished silently. "And — and — let's see — Okay, did you know that Geoff Bodine invented the bobsled used by the U.S. Olympic team? The Bo-Dyn bobsled. Famous for it. The man's a genius. And he's been racing a long time. Heck, just this year, old as he is, he was right up there with Ward Burton at the finish of the Daytona 500."

"With Ward Burton?" said Shane. "Well, what difference does *that* make?"

Harley blinked. He was about to point out that since Ward Burton had actually won the Daytona 500, it made quite a bit of difference, but before he could voice this thought, Karen tapped Shane on the arm to ask him a question, and Justine, who had been canvassing other tables, appeared at Harley's elbow with the hat full of money.

"I know he's rich," she said. "Or at least not missing any meals. I just felt like we ought to make the gesture, that's all. I hate it when people don't get a fair deal in life."

"That must keep you awful busy," said Harley.

She gave him a playful tap on the arm. "Oh, you know what I mean! I just naturally root for the underdog, that's all. I just never know what to do about it. Most of the time I just write a check and hope it helps."

Harley remembered a cartoon he'd seen once in one of his dad's *Saturday Evening Posts*. It showed a fellow in the water, obviously drowning, and a man in an overcoat on the dock was saying, "I can't swim. Would twenty dollars help?"

"Now, Harley, do you reckon we can get this hat full of cash turned into a money order or something?"

He groaned. "If you are hell-bent on doing this, I think there's an all-night gas station down the road. They'll probably sell money orders. But where are you going to send it?"

"Don't you know? I thought all you race drivers were buddies."

"Yeah, well, I don't have my Christmas card list on me." He'd be damned if he was going to tell her about the pile of business cards on the nightstand back in his room. In fact, if Bodine found out about it, he would *definitely* be damned.

"Oh, come off it. You know where to find him."

Harley sighed, thinking that Justine Holifield must go through life the way Dale Earnhardt went around a race track. "He lives in Cornelius," he said at last. "And Cornelius is about the size of that pool table, so I reckon that if you just wrote 'Geoffrey Bodine, Cornelius NC' on the envelope, it would find him sooner or later." He hoped she didn't know where Cornelius was; that is, only about seven miles west of where they were sitting. Harley was gearing up to explain to her that during racing season home is the one place you could be sure that a driver would not be, but Justine didn't press it further.

With her sweetest smile she said, "Cornelius. Thank you, Harley."

"Just don't mention my name anywhere on that letter." Another thought occurred to him. "You're not about to go walking up the road in the dark, are you?"

"Harley, it's Concord, not Beirut. Besides, Dale wouldn't let anything happen to me in his own backyard, so to speak."

Harley tilted his chair so far back that he nearly toppled over, which is when he caught sight of the Earnhardt poster tacked to the wall behind him, staring a hole through his back. With a sigh of resignation, he straightened up in the chair. "Naw, I guess Ol' Dale wouldn't let anything happen to you around here," he said. "In fact, he just told me to walk you to the damn gas station."

The next morning, Harley retrieved the wreath for Lowe's Motor Speedway before helping Ratty stow the luggage back in the bus. "Short trip this morning," he remarked to the driver.

"Enjoy it while you can," said Ratty. "It's a long way to Talladega."

Unfortunately the Number Three Pilgrims had overheard this remark, and apparently some of them were old enough to know World War I songs, because on the drive to the Speedway, they improvised a spontaneous version of "It's a long way to Talladega." When they got to the last line and, in a burst of exuberance, Bill Knight sang out, "But Earnhardt's still there!" They all fell silent for a moment, and then everybody began to talk at once.

Harley's head hurt too much for him to bother with his note cards, but if there was one speedway where he didn't need them, this was it. Home turf. He'd have to use the microphone, though, and even the sound of his own voice was grating on his nerves, but at least if he talked, they wouldn't sing anymore.

"Lowe's Motor Speedway," he began. "Short trip, folks. We're getting off the Interstate at exit 49, so don't try to get in a nap on the way, because we'll be there before you know it."

Cayle waved her hand. "Okay, Harley, but how come we're not going to Atlanta after this? It's right on the way."

From the driver's seat, Ratty spoke up. "We're staying on the outskirts tonight, but we have to go by there again to get down to Daytona, and the Atlanta Speedway is south of the city in Hampton, so it makes more sense to hit Alabama first."

"We'll get there," Harley said. "But we have one more stop in Carolina before we head south, and we'll be there real soon. Lowe's Motor Speedway. The house that Humpy Wheeler built. The place is about forty years old now, but like a lot of beautiful forty-year-olds, it's had a lot of work done to stay looking good."

"Don't look at me when you say that," said Justine.

Harley refused to be drawn. "This is a one-and-a-half-mile track," he said. "Used to be called the Charlotte Motor Speedway until 1999. Note that while it is big, it is technically not a super speedway. These days only Daytona and Talladega are considered super speedways — they're both high-banked, at least two and a half miles long, and requiring restrictor plates. This place looks big after Martinsville, though, doesn't it?"

A few of them nodded and went back to taking pictures.

"This was the first speedway to feature night racing, and — I'll take their word for this — they claim to be the first sports facility ever to sell full-time residences."

"Residences?" said Bekasu. *"Residences?"*

"They built condominiums above turn one," said Jim Powell. "I hear they're real nice."

"And you can stop looking like you were

weaned on a pickle, Bekasu," said Justine. "Because before you make some sneering remark, I would remind you that the baseball stadium in Toronto has a hotel built in it, too, and there's picture windows overlooking the playing field."

Jesse Franklin called out, "I hear this was the first track to sell its name for corporate money."

Ray Reeve's customary scowl deepened. "Kind of makes you wonder why they interrupt a televised race with commercials, doesn't it? Seems redundant to me. Advertising on the cars, advertising around the track walls, logos on the drivers' helmets . . . The whole damn race is a commercial. Wasn't like that in the old days." No one pointed out that he was wearing a University of Nebraska sweatshirt today.

"The Speedway seats 167,000 spectators," said Harley, raising his voice to regain control. "And you could get another third as many folks in the infield area, where they allow campers."

"You know, you probably don't need to give us all those statistics," said Bill Knight. "Most of your passengers know an approximation of them already, and the rest of us won't remember."

"I know that," said Harley. "But my cor-

391

porate masters want me to be thorough, so bear with me. Now there's a lot of reasons for drivers to like this Charlotte track. Anybody know of one?"

Terence Palmer looked up from his hotel copy of *USA Today*. "Since the banking in the straightaways is only five degrees or so, drivers can get up a good speed here, and they can pass, so I suppose it's not as frustrating as some of the other tracks."

"True enough," said Harley.

"Besides," said Justine, "it's within commuting distance of Lake Norman. Could Dale have slept at home when the race was being held here?"

"Him and half of his competitors," said Harley. "Lake Norman is the Beverly Hills of NASCAR. And before you ask: no. I did not live there."

"Dale did," said Shane. "Before he bought his farm."

"Most of the racing shops are close by, too," said Harley. "The Hendricks drivers could walk to the track from their garages. Of course, you know — most of you know — that all the Winston All-Star events except one have been held here, and that the Memorial Day race now gives the Indianapolis 500 a run for its money."

"Speaking of money," said Ratty. "What

are those humongous buildings over on the right?"

"Condominiums," said Sarah Nash. "They have a country club here, too."

"Don't get me started," said Harley.

"If this tour is going to be a true tribute to Dale, I guess we ought to tell some of the good stories," said Justine. "And this being Charlotte, you all know what that story is. Except you, Reverend. I know this is all news to you, but that's good, because there's nothing more fun than telling a great story to a brand-new listener."

Sarah Nash frowned and edged closer to Terence. "Here it comes," she murmured. "The pass in the grass. I suppose it was too much to ask that we get through this week without somebody telling that story."

"I remember thinking that it was wonderful," said Terence. "I was in eighth grade when it happened, but we talked about it on my hall for days. Why do you — Oh. That's right. You're partial to Bill Elliott."

"Let me tell the story, Harley!" said Justine, waving frantically. "I was here that day."

"You mean May 17, 1987?" asked Harley, who didn't even have to glance at his note cards. He had been there, too. Not driving. It was an all-star event. Harley had been just watching, open-mouthed, like everybody else. Justine was nodding eagerly at the mention of the date. He sighed. If he didn't let her tell it, she'd be chiming in every five seconds anyhow. "Go ahead, then," he said. "If you think you can manage to put in some facts and figures instead of just gushing."

Justine nodded, assuming the serious look of the sportscaster historian. "It was the Winston All-Star competition that Humpy Wheeler set up in mid-season, like an all-star game," she said, pausing for breath. This first bit was directed at Bill Knight, who had no idea what they were talking about. "It's a special three-segment race. They call it the shoot-out. And that was the third year they'd held it. Hey . . . *threes*. Do you think that means anything?"

"It means you're digressing," said Harley. "Get on with it." He waved his note cards as a warning.

"Okay, Bill Elliott won the first two, so he thought he was a shoo-in. But the last of the three races was only ten laps, and the prize —" she glanced doubtfully at Harley. "I don't remember, but a lot —"

"Two hundred thousand dollars," said Harley. "And remember that the rules said the whole ten laps had to be run under the green flag. Caution laps didn't count as part of the ten."

She rolled her eyes. "I *know* that. Okay — so Bill Elliott was the man to beat. He had won the first two segments, which was no surprise. Remember, back in the late Eighties, Awesome Bill was qualifying at over 200 miles an hour. And he was on the pole for that last race."

"What was he driving?" asked Matthew.

Sarah Nash spoke up. "A red-and-white Ford Thunderbird, sponsored by Coors."

"Next came your buddy, Justine, the one-and-only Geoff Bodine, who was yellow number 5, the Levi Garrett car," said Harley. "And then Kyle Petty. Before you ask — Earnhardt was in fourth position. He wasn't the Man in Black yet. He was still the blue boy, sponsored by Wrangler in those days, so —" The look of exasperation on Justine's face silenced him.

"Are you done?" she demanded.

"Go on, then. You remember the whole race, do you? Who was where? Who drove what? Blow by blow?"

"Blow by blow is right," she said. "They were driving like it was bumper cars in the amusement park. On the very first turn — *bam!* Elliott hits Bodine. Or maybe the other way around. Anyhow, the two of them collided and spun out, and Earnhardt, who was right on their tails, went low to get around them. He had the lead."

"Earnhardt caused that wreck," said Sarah Nash. "He was behind them at the start of the race. I always thought he tapped them with his bumper."

"Oh, he did not!" said Justine. "But Bill Elliott must have thought so, too, because instead of being furious with Bodine, he went gunning for Dale."

"How did he do that?" asked Matthew, whose expression suggested that he had taken the term too literally. 1987 was, after all, the Olden Days, as far as he was concerned.

Justine smiled. "Elliot wanted to get even for the bump, so he caught up with Earnhardt on the backstretch and bumped him right back."

"*Right back!*" echoed Sarah Nash.

"Well, he thought it was payback," Justine corrected herself. "Anyhow, when they were coming off the fourth turn on the track, Elliott ran Earnhardt off the track altogether. Dale's car ended up in the stretch of grass that separates the track from pit road."

"He did this on purpose?" Bill Knight was aghast.

Justine shrugged. "Rubbing is racing," she said. "I never heard that Earnhardt complained about it. Anyhow, it didn't have the intended effect, because Dale just kept on driving."

"At 150 miles an hour," muttered Harley. It sounded easy enough to say, but Harley knew different. Two miles a minute. Reaction time: a blink. And grass was the worst surface to drive on, especially on racing tires which had no tread at all. They didn't call them "racing slicks" for nothing. Not one person in a million would have done what Earnhardt did that day. You've left the track, going at a blinding speed, and your impulse would be to brake, at least to let up on the accelerator, or to put the car into a slide, maybe end up against the wall, just to have some control over where you ended up. But he did none of that.

"It was the most amazing thing you have ever seen!" said Justine. "I was jumping up and down in my seat and screaming for Dale like a banshee. There he was on the grass, where he ought to be slip-sliding all over the place and crashing into Lord-knows-what, and instead he just kept right on going full throttle in a straight line like

397

it was nothing out of the ordinary, and a few seconds later — zoom! He comes out back on the asphalt — and he's still ahead of Awesome Bill. 'Course, now Earnhardt is pissed, because he was run off the track by Bill Elliott. There's no getting around that." She paused to see if Sarah Nash had any rebuttal, but not even an Elliott fan could deny the facts.

"So never mind the rest of the field," Justine went on. "Earnhardt has got a score to settle with Elliott. They're racing side by side on the backstretch, and Earnhardt just starts easing over to the right and forcing Elliott close to the wall. Bumped him, too. I know he did it that time. He was getting even. Anyhow, Elliott ended up with a cut tire and finished four-teen, and Earnhardt won the race. And *that* was the Pass in the Grass, the greatest move in the history of motor sports bar none — and I saw it happen!"

"Your father has the poster they made of the drivers who competed in that race," Sarah Nash told Terence. "They look like such kids to me now. Earnhardt was kneeling in the center of the photo in his royal blue Wrangler suit, almost smiling, and right beside him is a baby-faced Terry Labonte, looking like Potsy on *Happy*

398

Days, and then next to him Neil Bonnett with his Siamese cat blue eyes. On the other side of Dale is Bill Elliott, in his red Coors firesuit, kneeling alongside Richard Petty, who could still cast a shadow in those days, though he was still pretty thin."

"I love that picture," said Jim Powell. "Bill Elliott looked like the country boy he was. You'd think he'd take half an hour to ask you to pass the salt — and then you think of him going 212 miles an hour without batting an eye. Imagine!"

"Speaking of Mr. Elliott," said Harley. "Anybody remember what happened after the race?"

Justine nodded. "You'd better tell that, though," she said with a glance at Sarah Nash. "I don't want to make anybody mad."

The Elliott fan dismissed this concern with a wave. "Go right ahead and tell it," she said. "I said Bill was an extraordinary driver. Didn't claim he was a plaster saint."

"Well," said Harley, by way of apology for the man who once gave him a ride in his helicopter, "remember that it takes a special killer instinct to make a fearless driver. If these guys took losing philosophically, they wouldn't be champions. Okay, that said, Earnhardt's worthy opponents were more than a little perturbed about how the race had played out, and the fact that the checkered flag had ended the race did not mean that they had turned off their tempers. The drivers were taking the post-race cool-down lap, and Bill Elliott went after Earnhardt. Coming out of the first turn, he rammed the number 3 car in the rear. They kept on going and then, in the backstretch, Awesome Bill cut toward Earnhardt, so that he'd have to slam on his brakes. I saw smoke coming off those tires, he braked so hard. Bodine went after him, too. It looked to me like they were going to use the Intimidator's car as a punching bag with him in it. Elliott was playing cat and mouse with Earnhardt: he cut him off when he tried to enter pit road, and then at the entrance to the garage area, he cut him off again. That was about it, though. Nobody got hurt. The season went on after that, and Earnhardt ended up winning his third championship."

"That three again!" Justine called out.

Harley rolled his eyes. "I wish we could get Bill Elliott out here to go after *you*," he said. "Try telling *him* that Earnhardt's a saint now."

"Well, he's getting a wreath, anyhow," said Justine. "I don't think Bill would begrudge him that. Whose turn is it?"

Jim Powell spoke up. "Do you folks mind if Arlene does it? She set a store by Ol' Dale, and this was our home track, so to speak. Before we moved to Ohio."

Jim Powell and Jesse Franklin had trotted back to the bus to retrieve the wreath, leaving Arlene standing next to Harley, smiling her tremulous smile. He hoped it was one of her good days. Harley smiled back at her. "Well, Arlene," he said, "do you know where you want to put this wreath?"

She shook her head. "You choose."

"We'll find a place for it," he said.

"And I'll take your picture with it and send you a copy," said Justine.

When Jim Powell and Jesse Franklin came back with the wreath, they were escorted by the two Earnhardt mourners from Bristol — Cannon, the racing-scrap dealer and his friend the weasel.

"Told you we might catch up with you again!" said the smaller man. "Old Cannon was mighty touched by this whole idea. Wanted to see it again."

Jesse Franklin edged up close enough to Harley to whisper. "They were waiting by the bus," he said. "And when they asked us if they could come along, I just didn't know how to turn them away."

"It's all right," said Harley. "They won't hurt anything. That wouldn't be respectful to Dale."

Cannon and his associate had come dressed for a solemn occasion, having traded their customary black leather and denim for shiny dark suits, royal blue shirts, and skinny ties. They stood next to the Number Three Pilgrims in respectful silence while Jim Powell stepped forward with the wreath.

"In memory of Dale Earnhardt, the Intimidator," he said. "Arlene?"

Arlene nodded. "Yes," she said. "I remember Dale. People thought he was mean, but he wasn't. He was always nice to people off the track. I think he was doing what he wanted to do, and he'd have done it whether anybody else cared or not. Maybe he was surprised that people did care so much. But he was an ordinary feller from Carolina, like my Jim." She smiled up at her husband. "But there wasn't nothing he couldn't do. And he never got above his raising about it, either." She began to smile, as if she'd forgotten they were there.

They waited a few moments, but Arlene's tribute was finished.

As they started to walk back, the weasel caught up with Terence. "Say, my buddy Cannon's got some pieces of Dale's wrecked car out there in the van. Made 'em into key chains. Y'all want to buy some?"

Terence stopped walking and stared at the little man. "Nobody has pieces of that car," he said.

"Yeah, we do," said the weasel, turning to speak to the others as they walked past. "Pieces of Dale's car for sale!"

Shane McKee stepped up beside Terence. "You carry a cell phone, don't you, man? I've got a brochure here with DEI's phone number on it. I think they should hear about this. You call them while I get the license number off their van."

He began to run after the hastily retreating hucksters. But by the time they reached the parking lot Cannon and the weasel were gone.

"Good move," said Terence to Shane. "Those guys were scum."

"Wish I'd a caught 'em," said Shane.

They exchanged satisfied smiles.

CHAPTER XVI

Talladega Ghosts

Talladega Super Speedway

"You know what they say about Talladega, don't you?" asked Harley. He was swaying a little, trying to stand up as the bus roared down I-20 through the green sweep of eastern Alabama. He thought they must be about half an hour out of Talladega, and now, having taken a surreptitious peek at his notes, he quizzed the passengers with the expectant look of a teacher addressing a class. He pointed to Matthew. The boy had slept most of the way out of Atlanta, but a few miles west of the Alabama state line he'd perked up again, and now his hand was waving in the air. "Okay, sport," said Harley. "Stop with the imaginary checkered flag. Lay it on us."

"This is where Dale Earnhardt won his last race," said Matthew solemnly.

Harley nodded, trying to look as if he'd remembered that. Might be in his notes somewhere. "Okay, Matthew. Good call. That was in —"

"October, 2000," said Cayle. "The fall race at Talladega."

Harley waited a couple of seconds to see if anybody was going to dispute her, but several heads nodded, so she must be correct. He smiled. "Right again. Anything else?"

"I'd almost call it a miracle, that race," said Jim Powell. "Remember it? I saw it on television. Dale was running in eighteenth place that day. It didn't look like he had a cat's chance of winning. Then all of a sudden toward the end of the race, he moved from eighteenth place all the way up to first in only five laps. Then he went on to win it. Most incredible thing you ever saw."

Arlene spoke up. It was one of her good days. "You didn't see it, Jim," she said. "You went to the bathroom, thinking Earnhardt was out of the running, and when you came back, I was jumping up and down screaming for Dale just as he took the lead."

Jim looked pleased to be corrected. "Why, that's right, hon," he said, patting her hand. "I guess it's never wise to give up on somebody, is it?"

Bill Knight, who had been looking out his window, admiring the green hills in the distance, said wonderingly, "You never think of Alabama having mountains. It looks like New Hampshire out there."

Sarah Nash leaned forward and touched his arm. "They're the same mountains," she said. "The Appalachian chain begins here in north Alabama and ends up in New Brunswick, Canada. So the Bodines from upstate New York and the Allisons from north Alabama may have more in common than one might think."

Harley laughed. "Well," he said, "that's one thing I sure never heard anybody say in connection with Talladega. Anything else?"

"That track cost $4 million to build back in '69," said Jesse Franklin. "Some of the speedways they built in the late Nineties cost around 200 million to construct. Being an auditor, I keep up with monetary things like that."

"Okay, that's more than I knew, folks," said Harley, making a silent vow to dig his guidebooks back out of his suitcase to-night. "I was waiting for somebody to say that it's a super speedway, and one of the restrictor plate tracks. The *reason* for restrictor plates, some folks say."

Justine heaved a sigh of exasperation. "Harley, *everybody* knows that," she said.

"But what everybody *really* says about Talladega is that it's haunted."

"Justine!" Bekasu turned back from the window and tried to shush her sister.

Justine shrugged. "Well, *somebody* had to say it," she said. "I bet you were all thinking it. Well, maybe not Reverend Knight, 'cause he doesn't know Neil Bonnett from Robin Hood, but the rest of y'all know what I'm talking about. And it's not just the fact that Davey died here, either."

"I've never heard anything about this," said Terence, glancing at Sarah Nash. "Haunted?"

She gave a little shrug and then nodded. "So they say."

Harley knew exactly what Justine was referring to, but it wasn't the kind of thing drivers talk about, not even when they're paid to be tour guides. He glanced down at Ratty to see if he had any reaction to Justine's announcement, but Ratty was keeping his eyes on his lane of I-20, seemingly oblivious to the chatter behind him.

"You might as well tell them now, Justine," said Cayle. "You'll end up telling everybody one at a time at the next rest stop anyhow."

Harley nodded. "You opened this can of

worms," he said. "You might as well spill it."

"Okay," said Justine. "Microphone?" She swayed up the aisle to stand next to Harley. "This used to be Cherokee land, you know. These hills. Now, Talladega — which means 'border town' in Cherokee — some people say that the place was built on an old Indian burial ground, or something, and that there's a curse on it because of that." She was solemn now, and round-eyed with the enormity of the tale.

Bill Knight frowned at this unexpected lurch in subject matter. He glanced down at Matthew, but the boy didn't even seem surprised, much less disturbed, by this announcement. He supposed that between the zombie video games and the slasher movies, it would take more than a ghost story told in broad daylight to frighten a modern child.

"What kind of curse?" Terence called out. He had glanced around to see if anybody was laughing, but they weren't.

"Okay, here's the story," said Justine, leaning into the microphone and assuming the hushed tone of the campfire storyteller. "Remember Bobby Isaac? He was the Winston Cup champion in — well, when I was a kid —"

Jim Powell spoke up. "Nineteen and seventy," he said. "Year Arlene and I moved into our house in Shelby."

"Right," said Justine. "I knew it was B.D. Before Dale. Anyhow, Bobby Isaac was a successful, dedicated driver, okay? He was well paid and well known. So, in 1973 Bobby Isaac was racing in the Talladega 500 —"

"As a matter of fact he was in the lead at the time," said Ray Reeve, who knew where this story was headed.

"Wow. I'd forgotten that," said Justine. "Okay, so he's on the front stretch when all of a sudden he pulled into the pit without any caution flag, and without being told to by his crew chief. Just ups and parks the car. The crew all came running up to him. 'What's the matter?' 'What's wrong with the car?' 'Are you sick?' And you know what he said?" She looked to Harley for confirmation.

He sighed. "Go on," he said. "Tell them."

"Okay, when they asked Bobby Isaac why he pulled out of the race, he said that *something told him to get out of the car and walk away.*" And he did. Cross my heart, it's the truth. He didn't finish that race — we're talking about thousands of dollars at stake here, y'all. And he may have raced a time or two after that, but basically he was done right then and there. Now can you imagine somebody in his salary range — a surgeon or a trial lawyer, maybe — just walking away from his chosen profession just because a supernatural voice ordered him to?" She looked back at Terence. "Would *you*?"

Terence coughed and looked embarrassed. "I don't know," he stammered. "Maybe. If I'd really heard the voice."

"Wasn't there more to the story?" asked Shane. "I thought I heard that they checked over Bobby Isaac's car after he parked it, and they found some problem with it that would have put him into the wall if he hadn't got out."

They all looked up at Harley for confirmation. "I don't know," he said. "It was before my time, and it's not the kind of thing drivers want to talk about. How about if we gripe about restrictor plates instead?"

"Well, that's just another wreck story," Ray Reeve pointed out. "I mean, if you're talking about why they implemented them in the first place. Bobby Allison."

"Restrictor plates!" said Shane, in the tone people usually reserve for words like "maggots."

"I know," said Justine. "But if you don't want Bobby Allison in your lap, you'd better put up with them."

"Or Bill Elliott," said Sarah Nash. "Bill Elliott is the one who did 212 miles per hour at Daytona. Not that I'd mind having him in my —" Her voice trailed off and she snatched up her magazine, holding it a bit too close to her face to actually be reading it.

Bill waved his hand to attract Harley's attention. "What's this about having Bobby Allison in your lap?"

Harley smiled with relief at the prospect of getting the tour discussion back on track. This he knew. "Now that's the story you ought to tell, coming into Talladega," he said. "The 1987 Winston 500. Dodging the bullet. Everybody knew it was going to be a fast race that year. Talladega is a super speedway — a long straightaway to build up speed on. Bill Elliott took the pole in qualifying with a speed of 212.8 miles an hour. That's more than three miles a minute, folks. I can't even tell you what that feels like. That was before restrictor plates — in other words, back when there was no limit on speed except the capabilities of the engine and the driver."

"What was Bobby Allison's qualifying

speed?" asked Matthew.

"His Buick topped out at 211, putting him second to Elliott. And, before you ask, Earnhardt was fourth. So that race was shaping up to be a whirlwind, and they got 22 laps into it — what's that, about seven minutes? — when Bobby Allison's Buick ran over some debris that wasn't supposed to be on the track, and cut his tire. The car went airborne."

He paused for effect, hoping his listeners were picturing a Buick lifting off like a *Star Trek* shuttlecraft and launching itself missile-like at a grandstand packed with people.

"The good news is that Allison was going so fast when he took off that he managed to clear the five-foot concrete wall between the track and the spectators. Maybe it's even better news that although the car was airborne, it did *not* manage to clear the wire fence on the top of that concrete wall. The car ripped up a 150-foot section of fence, sent stuff flying everywhere. Then the car wobbled for an instant and rolled back onto the track. It put me in mind of a basketball hovering on the rim of the basket and then falling away again."

There was a little silence while most of the bus waited to see if it would be Bill or Bekasu

412

who asked, "How badly was he injured?"

Bekasu got the question out first, and everybody was laughing before she finished it.

"Not a scratch on him," said Harley cheerfully. "Those drivers' safety harnesses do work most of the time. It scared the hell out of Davey Allison, though, seeing his dad go into the wall like that. He must have said a prayer or two just then."

"He recovered well," said Ray Reeve. "Davey won that race, as I recall."

"And none of the spectators were hurt?"

"Maybe a cut or a bruise. Nothing major that I ever heard about," said Harley.

Shane McKee was scowling. "Yeah, the only casualty that day was the sport itself."

Harley nodded and tried to look sympathetic. He wasn't sure he agreed, having been a driver himself, but he could see how fans would feel resentful about the hobbling of their sport. "NASCAR saw that wreck as a red light on their dashboard," he said. "The officials knew that at those speeds on super speedways, sooner or later there would have been a tragedy. If Allison's car had cleared the wire fence, there's no telling how many people he could have killed. So they came up with a new piece of equipment designed to prevent that."

413

"Restrictor plates." Shane spat out the word.

Harley sighed. If you ever wanted to stop a bar fight, just say the words "restrictor plates," and you'll see instant unification take place. Everybody hated them. Maybe it would have been different if the tragedy had been allowed to happen, but it hadn't. Earnhardt used to get wistful about how much he missed barreling around Talladega and Daytona at 200-plus miles an hour, but common sense told him and everybody else in the sport that the thrill wasn't worth risking the lives of innocent bystanders. That was what people forgot: the restrictor plate wasn't put on to protect the driver; it was there to protect the fans.

"It's a device attached to the carburetor to limit the speed of the car to less than 200 miles an hour," said Harley, in case anyone was still confused. He figured that women could be race fans without necessarily knowing the mechanical aspects of the sport, but if he had to guess among this particular group of passengers, he'd bet that Terence Palmer and Bill Knight were the ones who didn't know. Well, Arlene, maybe. Whatever she had known was falling away, but she didn't seem to mind. Just looked out the window or at Jim with a vague smile, like a stranger at a birthday party.

Ray Reeve laughed. "Does anybody remember what Earnhardt used to call the restrictor plate decision?"

Jesse Franklin clapped his hands with a whoop of joy. "I had forgotten that! *The Waltrip Rule!* He claimed the high speeds made ol' Darrell nervous."

"They were always saying stuff like that about one another," said Harley, unable to resist the urge to defend his boyhood hero. "The real reason that Earnhardt objected to restrictor plates is because restrictor plates did more than slow down the cars. They also softened the throttle response. Knowing how to use that throttle had been a skill that separated the Earnhardts and the Elliotts from the run-of-the-mill drivers. Now, with restrictor plates, the cars mellowed out on the corners. That's what Dale called it: mellowing out. He meant that there was no longer a surge of power in reserve when you took the corners. Earnhardt said that he and Elliott and Bodine had the skills to run their cars wide open on the corners while lesser drivers would get loose trying to make the turn, so they'd get left behind. When restrictor plates became mandatory on the super speedways, that no longer happened, and the big dogs lost their advantage. Now everybody could keep up with them, which meant more bunching up in the race. And sometimes more wrecks."

"I always thought there was another factor, too," said Ray Reeve.

Mr. Reeve hadn't said much on the tour except for an occasional grumble, but Harley thought a chance to spout off might improve his mood, so he held out the microphone and motioned for the old man to come forward. Ray Reeve had to grasp the backs of the seats to keep from falling, but finally he made his way up to the front, looking a bit disconcerted to be facing rows of listeners.

"Well," he said, blinking at his fellow passengers, "all I was going to say was that there's another reason Dale didn't like restrictor plates. At least I think so. When nobody had the advantage of extra bursts of speed, the field was evened out so much that the only way to win a race like Daytona was to get a drafting buddy. And, you know, Dale would rather work alone, which I can certainly relate to. If I can't do it alone, I won't do it at all." He looked doubtfully at Harley. "Do I have to explain drafting?"

Ratty Laine spoke up from the driver's seat. "Anybody wants a demonstration of drafting, just look out the window into the other lane!"

Harley smiled. In the left hand lane an 18-wheeler was in the process of passing their bus, and scooting along behind the big rig was a white Ford Taurus, pulled along in the wake of the truck.

"Does anybody know who came up with the concept of drafting in stock car racing?"

Sarah Nash spoke up. "Junior Johnson."

"Right. Well, Mr. Reeve, why don't I go ahead and explain drafting." Harley looked at the bewildered faces of Bill Knight and Bekasu. He would have to explain drafting, preferably in words of one syllable. He took back the microphone and waited while the old man threaded his way back to his seat.

"Okay, folks: drafting. Ratty was right about that Taurus in the other lane traveling in the wake of the truck. The Taurus is getting pulled along, but if it tried to pass that truck, it might swerve a little because the air displaced by the body of the truck would hit the passing car, catching the Taurus in its turbulence. With me so far?"

"I have passed a truck on an Interstate, yes," said Bekasu without noticeable enthusiasm.

"Okay, well, on a race track this principle can be an important factor. You're whizzing along on one of the big tracks, and you ease up behind another car and stay on his bumper so that he's cutting through the air for both of you. You'll both go faster that way. Okay, Matthew, I see your hand, so let me say right now: don't anybody ask me why you'll both go faster one-behind-the-other, you just do. Ryan Newman has the engineering degree. Take it up with him. But I can tell you from experience that if a car gets out of the line of cars in single file, he's in trouble, because he can't go as fast alone as the rest of them can by teaming up. The ideal strategy is to save your gas by drafting behind somebody right up until the end of the race, and then as you approach the finish line, you slingshot around the leader in the last few seconds to win. Of course, when the driver veers to the inside to make that move, he needs a drafting buddy to give him the power to pull it off."

Jim Powell spoke up. "Darrell Waltrip said one time that trying to pass at Daytona without a drafting partner was like running into a brick wall."

"He's right," said Harley. "Sometimes teammates will help you out, or your old buddies. I've seen drivers help an old running buddy make that move just because they didn't like the kid who was otherwise going to win the race."

"Earnhardt could see the air," said Shane. "That's why he was so good on super speedways. He could *see* the air flow."

"Well, everybody says that," said Harley, "but nobody's ever been able to explain to me how he managed it."

"One other thing you ought to make clear," Ray Reeve called out from the back. "Restrictor plates aren't used on the short tracks, like Bristol and Martinsville, and so on. Just on the super speedways where there's enough of a straightaway to build up the higher speeds."

"Never mind all that technical stuff," said Justine. "I still say this place is haunted. I mean, look where Bobby Allison's wreck happened. *Talladega,* which is Bobby Allison's *home turf* — he's from Hueytown, just on the other side of Birmingham. And who won the race that day? Bobby's son. And nobody got hurt. It's like the spirits were protecting him, but they were also giving a *warning*. Kind of a cosmic slap on the wrist. Just like the one Bobby Isaac got back in '73. I'm telling you, this place is *haunted*."

A few silent minutes later, Bill Knight glanced back at the newlyweds. Sure enough, Shane McKee met his look with an unsmiling gaze and a slight nod, as if to say *See? I told you so. Miracles. First numbers and now voices on a racetrack telling Bobby Isaac to park it.* Bill managed a reassuring smile in return, but he hoped that Shane wouldn't want to continue their earlier discussion of miracles in motor sports. He didn't want to destroy the young man's faith — even if it wasn't a faith he personally subscribed to — but he could not in good conscience encourage such unorthodox beliefs. He sighed. He used to worry what to tell High Church–inclined believers about Lourdes and Joan of Arc, and now — this! Angels in the driver's seat. He hoped he wouldn't be called upon to voice any opinions in the matter.

"Speedway exit coming up!" Ratty sang out from the driver's seat.

Bill Knight looked out the window expecting to see a suburban sprawl of hotels and fast food joints but the intersection of

420

state road and Interstate was much less cluttered than he expected. It was odd that so many race tracks were set out among green fields in unspoiled countryside. Oh, the place would be a zoo on race day, he was sure of that. Eighty thousand cars and twice that many people would turn this bucolic country road into a nightmare of ozone and noise, but since the next big race was weeks away — at the end of September, the great empty Speedway and its pastoral surroundings lay as empty and silent as Pompeii.

It was a beautiful setting. The Speedway, encircled by low wooded hills in the distance, was painted bright red and blue like a child's toy, and its sheer size invoked awe in the beholder. The longest grandstand in the world, Harley had told them earlier, reading from a printed card. Bill had forgotten all the specifications — how many spectators the place would hold, how long the track was — somewhere around two miles long, he knew — and all the other bits of numerical trivia. Staring at it in the distance he was reminded of a twentieth-century Stonehenge or Machu Picchu, some monument to human ingenuity, obscure of purpose, but magnificent in scale and ambition. A great steel temple that

421

had been built in the wilderness and then left to the elements. It was an automotive cathedral, and while he did not entirely endorse the purpose for its existence, he did acknowledge that it was an impressive architectural achievement.

The broad entryway that led into the Speedway was lined with lampposts, topped by lights in a swirling metalwork design that seemed quite artistic for so prosaic a place as a racetrack, he thought. The place was built in 1969 — Jesse Franklin had mentioned that — but it seemed to be well maintained and state-of-the-art. Well, they could afford it, of course. A hundred thousand people or so, times at least a hundred dollars a ticket, that ought to pay for as many gallons of paint as you'd need to keep the structure looking new.

Were they going to get out and walk the track, Knight wondered. On an afternoon in late August, the Alabama sun would be too intense for old Mrs. Powell, and perhaps too much for Matthew as well, though the boy was game for anything. He would probably enjoy himself immensely.

Harley thought it was a shame that such a nice kid was so ill. After so many days of sitting still, cooped up in the bus, over hundreds of miles of Interstate, it would be good for all of them to spend an hour or so stretching their legs.

Harley reached for the microphone. "Those who want to walk around the track for a bit and take some pictures are welcome to do it. That building over there houses the gift shop and the International Motorsports Hall of Fame." He looked at his watch. "Couple of hours do you, and then lunch at one-thirty?"

"Shall I get out the wreath?" asked Ratty.

Harley looked at the great canyon of a Speedway, empty and silent in its cradle of hills. "No," he said. "If it's all right with everybody, I'd like to make a small change of plans here, and put the wreath in a somewhat more intimate place a few miles down the road. More fitting, I think."

The Talladega Texaco Walk of Fame and the Davey Allison Memorial was a small park set one street back from the main street of the small town of Talladega, maybe ten miles south of the Speedway itself. It was a pretty little Southern town, with a red brick courthouse, and an old-fashioned main street lined with storefronts that could have been a movie set for a heartwarming film. Bill Knight, who had been admiring the scenery, hadn't noticed any signs directing visitors to the park, but perhaps the people who would come here knew where to find it: turn left on the little street beside Braswell's Furniture Store. The memorial park was on the street between Talladega's main drag and the hill on which the police station sat. Facing the side street stood a fieldstone marker, inset with a granite tablet, inscribed with three lines of tombstone lettering:

Talladega Texaco Walk of Fame
Davey Allison Memorial
Talladega, Alabama

Harley noted that the Number Three Pilgrims had turned solemn at the prospect of visiting this shrine. Even Justine was more subdued that usual, and he was pleased that they were approaching the memorial in the proper spirit. Sure, he was skeptical about the veneration of the Intimidator, but the idea of a memorial park for fallen heroes of motor sports appealed to him. He had pretty much given up the idea of being there himself one day, but he was glad to see the great ones remembered: Fireball Roberts, Neil Bonnett, Tim Flock.

"You know why it's here, don't you?" he

said softly into the microphone. He didn't need his notes for this part of the tour. This was his era in racing, and he knew it like a family story. Most of the passengers did know why the park was in Talladega, but for form's sake he had to tell them anyway, because he was the guide, and guides never assumed that everybody knew anything. "Well, for one thing he was from around here. Davey was one of the Hueytown gang, like his father and uncle — The Allisons. Hueytown is a little place over there west of Birmingham. So Davey was a native son, and one of the best drivers ever.

"But the reason for this park. The reason it's here. It's because he died at Talladega. Oh, not on the track. It was a freak accident. I never heard anybody explain exactly how it happened so that it made sense. But what happened was, they were having practice runs that day on the track, and Davey decided to fly his new helicopter over to watch the action, and also to check up on Neil Bonnett, another one of the Alabama Gang. Neil had sustained a head injury at a race the week before, and Davey wanted to check on him, make sure he was feeling okay to race."

"I thought he was going to see David

425

Bonnett," said Ray Reeve. "Neil's son."

"Well," said Harley, "I wasn't there, so I can't dispute that with any certainty, sir. But we agree that he was flying over to watch a friend doing practice runs, all right? Anyhow, Davey Allison and another driver in the Alabama Gang, Red Farmer, flew over to the track in Davey's new helicopter, and they were just about to touch down — a foot from the ground, people say. Close enough to step out, except, of course, you wouldn't. You'd wait for the touchdown, for the engine to be turned off . . ." Harley's voice trailed off then. He was replaying an image that had come to him many times over the years: a smiling, dark-haired young man, jumps out of the hovering helicopter and sprints away. But he hadn't. Of course, he hadn't. The thing must have cost most of a hundred thousand dollars, serious money even if you're Davey Allison. He would have landed it properly. Apparently the voices at Talladega weren't warning people that day.

Bekasu didn't know this story, but she saw the somber faces of the others and Harley's stricken look as he remembered. "What happened?" she asked.

"I can tell you *what*. But not *why*. The helicopter shot up into the air — thirty feet

426

or so, I heard. And then it just slammed back down to earth on its side, with Davey and his passenger inside. Like someone spiking a football. And Neil Bonnett — the driver he had flown over to check on — Neil was the one who pulled him out."

"He didn't make it, did he?"

Justine touched her sister's arm. "No," she said. "They got him to the hospital, but he died a few days later."

"The race the next week was at Pocono," said Jim Powell softly. "And Dale Earnhardt won it. So when it was time to take his victory lap after the race, Earnhardt drove to the start-finish line on the track and it looked like he and his pit crew were saying a prayer. Then somebody handed him a Number 28 flag — that was Davey's number — and Earnhardt drove a Polish victory lap — backwards, the way Alan Kulwicki used to do it — and a-waving that 28 flag out the window, to honor the both of them. Alan had died back in April and Davey only a week before."

"It's no wonder that Talladega is haunted," said Bekasu. "The wonder is that all the tracks aren't."

The memorial to Davey Allison was a

circular park of green lawn and young hardwood trees bisected by a brick path, and encircled by a walkway. Two white marble walls flanking the brick walkway on the circular path displayed information about Davey Allison and his racing career. In front of the wall, a slanted checkerboard platform symbolized a winner's circle, and in its center was the Texaco star, acknowledging the oil company that had sponsored Davey Allison and now honored his memory with this park. It was so green and peaceful that to Bill Knight it seemed at first to be the very antithesis of a speedway, but then he considered the shape of the park, and realized that its configuration was indeed that of a racetrack. Perhaps it was an Elysian field of a track, someone's idea of racing with the angels.

At intervals around the encircling paved walkway, set on poles at reading height for visitors, were rectangular bronze plaques, each bearing the bas-relief bronze likeness of a legend of motor sports, and a few sentences describing the man's achievements. The first plaque to the left of the entrance to the circle bore the name of Donnie Allison, the uncle of the young driver to whom the park was dedicated. According to the plaque, Donnie Allison was the first

NASCAR driver to complete a lap around the Talladega track. Bill Knight read that plaque, and the one after it — Dale Earnhardt. As he moved away to the next one, several of his fellow travelers were grouped around the Earnhardt plaque posing for a group photo.

Fireball Roberts . . . Dale Jarrett . . . Ned Jarrett . . . To Bill, the exercise of reading these commemorative plaques felt a bit like reading someone else's hometown newspaper: the facts were still there, but devoid of any emotional content for the casual stranger.

Many of the other names were unfamiliar to him, so he contented himself with a glance at each bronze plaque and stopped trying to take in all the new information. This was, after all, a memorial, not a trivia contest. He admired the beauty and the restraint of the landscaping. Here there were no angel statues or topiary race cars, only a cozy little park of well-tended lawn, dotted with young oak trees, and bisected by a simple rose-colored brick path cutting across the middle. Slender trees with branches like upraised arms lined the path, an arboreal honor guard. A few feet back from the entrance a flagpole had been set in a wrought iron semicircle in the walkway; from it a new American flag rippled in the slight breeze.

Bill noted that Matthew was posing for a group photo with Harley and the McKees. Shane was holding Matthew up so that he could read the bronze plaque, and Ratty, camera in hand, was waving directions for them to pose. Pleased to have a few moments of solitude, Bill walked alone, keeping to the outer path, glad of the sunshine and the chance to stretch his legs. He decided that when he reached the midpoint of the outer walkway, he would enter the brick walk on the back side of the park and follow it to the beginning. A quarter of the way along the path, he sat down on the Valley Electric Co-op bench, nestled in the shade of a large tree. He settled in to study the scene, while the other passengers continued to make their way around the park, reading the plaques and taking turns photographing the scene and posing for more snapshots. As he watched, a bobtailed ginger tom cat emerged from the shrubbery and jumped on the bench beside him. The cat bumped his arm with its head, intent on having its ears scratched by anyone who would sit still long enough. Obligingly, Bill scratched its head, and was rewarded with a rasping purr.

Justine motioned for him to come and join in the photo session, but he smiled and waved her way, pointing to the cat, and mouthing *"Later."* Perhaps, though, he ought to ask one of the others to take a photograph of the park for him. It would make an interesting slide to accompany his lectures about pilgrimages, for surely this was a modern-day shrine to the faithful. He was pleased to see that there were no souvenir stands, no hawkers of postcards or commemorative badges — quite unlike some of the European shrines he had visited, in fact. For some reason, he found himself thinking of a little shrine in Cornwall that he'd visited on a walking tour during his student days. The place was a holy well, consecrated to a saint, of course, but really a remnant of the old Celtic beliefs that had been in place before the Romans arrived. After all these years, he had forgotten when he'd visited it and exactly where it was, but the image of the path to the well was still clear in his mind. It was a narrow winding track that led from a roadside field through a dense thicket of trees and shrubs into the woods to the clearing where the well was. Impossible to miss the path, though, for at shoulder height, the branches bloomed with a rainbow of colored rags and ribbons, tied among the leaves by pilgrims on their way to the sacred water. Some of the bits of cloth were tattered and faded from the winter rains and the glare of long summer days, others were as bright and crisp as if they had just been left that morning. Did people bring these scraps of red and blue and yellow with them when they came, or did they, seeing the profusion of ribbons lining the path, tear a strip off a sleeve or a scarf to add to the offerings. Those bright bits of cloth — were they tangible prayers, left behind by hopeful believers or were they simply a custom like saying "bless you" when someone sneezes, a shadow of an old belief, shriveled now to a hollow ritual, its significance long forgotten.

Two ideas slotted together in his mind. There was another ritual associated with holy wells. The "pattern." You had to say prayers the requisite number of times — usually a multiple of three, of course — and you had to walk in a circle around the site of the holy well, also for a designated number of times. Sun-wise. You had to walk your laps in the sun-wise direction, because if you went around the other way, it would negate your prayers, even bring down bad luck upon you.

What was it Jim Powell had been saying about Alan Kulwicki going the wrong way around the track? The Polish victory lap, he'd called it. And then Earnhardt had duplicated the maneuver in memory of Kulwicki at the race following Kulwicki's fatal plane crash. Two drivers going the wrong way around in the ritual — both died violent deaths.

Bill Knight sighed. He must not voice that ridiculous thought to anyone on this tour. Surely there were many other drivers who had driven the Polish victory lap over the years without fatal consequences. He was being fanciful.

There were no tokens of faith in this memorial park — no ribbons on shrubs or beads draped over statues. There were the inscribed bricks, of course. He had noticed that the center walkway was studded with personalized bricks inscribed with messages from people who still mourned Davey Allison or from those who wanted to express love or luck to someone else. Tangible prayers.

Bill smiled. In some ways people changed very little over the centuries. In Roman times in Britain, they had thrown small objects into pools as offerings to the gods, small incentives that prayers should be granted, and the impulse to reach out to the hereafter had not gone away. It had only taken a new form. What prayer would he write on a sacred brick, he asked himself. Asking for material goods — a new car, perhaps — seemed at best childish to him, and those beauty pageant wishes, like "world peace," seemed to reduce complexity to a platitude and he would have felt foolish expressing such a wish. Perhaps the greatest gift one could hope for was the ability to believe that there was someone out there who cared that you wished for anything at all.

The ginger tom interrupted his reverie with a butt of its head against his arm. Obligingly he stroked the cat's head, as it arched its back in contentment. It seemed well fed, so it wasn't a stray, but why would it hang around a public park dedicated to motor sports. "So, Cat, who are you the reincarnation of?" he mused, glancing up to see whose plaque was stationed opposite the bench.

Cayle, who had been walking by at that moment, smiled at the pair of them on the bench, and she stooped to scratch the ginger tom's ears. "I didn't think Episcopalians believed in reincarnation," she said.

"No. No, they don't. I was just being whimsical. He seems so proprietary of this place, as if he belongs here. Probably lives across the street."

She nodded. "I suppose he does. Somehow I can't imagine any of the people on these plaques being reincarnated as a house cat. A cheetah, maybe — for speed."

Bill detached the cat gently from his lap, and stood up to walk with Cayle. He gave it a final stroking along its arched back. "Well, he isn't the Exxon tiger. That checkered wall over there was donated by Texaco."

"It's peaceful here," said Cayle.

"Yes. Something beautiful that came about because of a tragedy. There may be a sermon in that, but I've resolved to be off duty for this trip. I would like a photo of the brick walkway, though, for my pilgrimage lecture."

"Consider it done," said Cayle.

He scanned the park again for Matthew, who had scampered off the bus ahead of him. The boy was standing beside Justine near the flagpole on the brick walkway, and the two of them seemed to be studying a piece of paper, perhaps a map.

"The children are all right," said Cayle, following his gaze. "At least if they get into mischief, they're together."

"She's very good with him," said Bill. "Does she have any children of her own?"

Cayle nodded. "One son from her first marriage. He's grown and gone, though, so we don't hear much about him. He's a professor somewhere, and I gather he doesn't approve of her."

"Why not?"

Cayle shrugged. "Well, she's impulsive and funny, but she's not anybody's idea of a sedate parental authority. I think Scott took after his father. Or maybe he would have preferred to be the flamboyant one, and for that he'd need a calm center, but Justine would never be that. I think she's meant to be a comet, not a sun."

"There are some children who'd find fault with their parents no matter who they were," said Bill.

"That's Scott. If he had Mr. Rogers and Mother Teresa, he'd complain that they weren't Clint Eastwood and Madonna — and vice-versa. It's mostly that, I think. Or else he's still mad about a divorce that happened twenty-something years ago. She doesn't talk about him much."

"She's a law unto herself obviously, but she seems like a very easy person to get along with."

"Yes," said Cayle. "But maybe not an easy person to compete with."

They reached the midpoint along the outer path and started up the brick walkway that led through the center of the park and joined the encircling path on the other side. Matthew was kneeling on the bricks, tracing the inscriptions with his finger.

"Look," he said, pointing to the path. "Some of these bricks have messages written on them."

"Yes, Matthew, I see that. Interesting, isn't it?"

The boy wandered up the path to examine more of the bricks. Bill knelt down to read some of the tributes that fans and well-wishers had left. Many of the messages were in honor of Davey Allison himself — "True #28 Fans, Bernie and Denise" — but some of the bricks bore inscriptions addressed to Earnhardt as well. "In Memory of Dale Earnhardt," one said. A couple named Pat and Mike wished good luck to Dale Junior on their brick. Others commemorated fans' wedding dates or honored the memory of a friend or family member.

"I'm glad to see some bricks in honor of Earnhardt as well as Davey," said Cayle.

"It's good for people to have a place to say good-bye."

"It's odd that so many people seem to see Earnhardt as a saint," mused Bill.

Cayle stared. "As a *saint?* The Intimidator? Surely not."

"Well, the outward trappings of beatification, anyhow." Bill smiled. "I'm being technical here. The winged threes on cars. Threes in Christmas lights on the roofs of houses. Tee shirts with slogans like 'God Needed A Driver.' Bekasu and I were saying that it reminded us of the way people reacted when Thomas Becket was martyred. A sudden recognition of the loss of an extraordinary presence."

"That connection would never occur to his fans," said Cayle.

"No. I think it's instinctive. The object changes over the years, but human responses stay the same. Perhaps we have a fundamental need for reverence."

"How strange."

"It is strange. For instance, Shane —"

Before he could finish telling her, Matthew came running up waving a brochure. "Did you know you can buy a brick for the walkway here? And they'll write whatever you want on it, and put it right here on the path."

Bill Knight glanced down at the litany of tributes. "I gathered as much," he said.

"The brochure says it costs sixty bucks for three lines of a message, and Justine said she'd buy me a brick and send in the form for me. — Is that okay?"

"It's very kind of her," said Bill.

"I just told him he has to promise to come back some day and visit his brick," said Justine.

"So we're gonna sit down over there and work on what we want it to say," said Matthew. "You have to count every letter."

Bill Knight had thought of asking Cayle to elaborate on her experience of seeing the late Dale Earnhardt, but she had walked away. He didn't believe her, of course. He wondered if he would have believed someone who had claimed to see Thomas Becket in Canterbury in, say, 1171.

It had been a long time since he'd had the kind of faith that kindles saints. He had to think all the way back to childhood to find that reserve of belief. Of sitting beside his mother in church — so small that his feet didn't even touch the floor yet — and while all the congregation had their heads bowed in prayer, Bill would try to peek out of the slits of his eyelids, hoping — but

439

also dreading — to catch a glimpse of an angel on the sill under the big stained glass window of Jesus in Gethsemane. He had really believed that the angel hovered there during services, but he knew that the sight would be a terrible one. No sappy Valentine cherubs for him. Bill's dad had been a minister, too, so he knew his theology, even as a kid. Angels were soldiers. They had kicked the devil's butt out of heaven, so they were not to be trifled with. As a kid, you didn't know what might be true and what wasn't. There were rules for everything. Would stepping on a crack break your mother's back? What if you sneezed and nobody said bless you? What if you died without saying your prayers? There was a belief that was more terror than faith, and he was glad to have outgrown it. How much of the belief in the hereafter was just the fear of letting go or the fear of nothingness?

Before he could consider the implications of selective faith, he saw that Harley was coming toward him, carrying the wreath box. "I thought this would be the best place to leave the Talladega wreath," he said. "And maybe since this is a memorial park, you ought to be the one to say a few words over it."

"Of course." Bill Knight had been dreading this moment, wondering what he could say that would satisfy his traveling companions without trespassing on their beliefs. He took a deep breath and tried to compose his thoughts while the others gathered on the outer path around the bronze plaque dedicated to Dale Earnhardt. *What did I say to that congregation of weeping women when Princess Diana died?* he wondered.

The wreath this time was a hubcap-sized circle of white silk lilies and eucalyptus. By this time, thought Bill, the florist must have been getting giddy from doing a succession of tribute wreaths to Dale Earnhardt. A black ribbon stretched diagonally across the lilies said in white letters, *"#3: Forever In Our Hearts."*

Bill looked out at the peaceful expanse of green lawn with its red brick walkway bright in the afternoon sun. "We'd like to think heaven is like this," he began, letting the place speak to him. "A familiar place filled with the colors and shapes with which we feel most comfortable. Blue sky. Grass. Trees. A companionable cat." He smiled a little as he nodded toward the ginger tom, still sprawled on the bench in hopes of more attention from the visitors.

"Every now and then somebody will even write a hymn about a heaven for country singers or movie stars. There may be a song like that about NASCAR, for all I know."

"*Tracks of Gold*," murmured several voices in unison.

Bill sighed. It figured. "I don't know what heaven will be like," he went on. "The Bible offers a number of images, which, since we are human, may be beyond our comprehension. I do know that the idea of having an eternal place for heroes is a very old tradition throughout human civilization. The Greeks thought that ordinary people crossed the river Lethe and forgot about their earthly existence, but that heroes went on to the Elysian fields with their earthly personalities intact. The Norsemen envisioned the Valkyries swooping down to the battlefield to take fallen heroes back to Valhalla for an eternity of mead and feasting with their comrades. I'm not sure what kind of afterlife I can envision for race car drivers. To me it seems a contradictory proposition at best: trying to accommodate many different people's dreams of heaven when some of those ideas conflict with others. I think of all the fans who yearn to shake Dale

Earnhardt's hand when they get to heaven, but I'm pretty sure it wouldn't be much of a heaven to Earnhardt himself if he had to stand around all the time glad-handing strangers. I suppose that if God has set aside a part of His kingdom for heroes, it will be a wonderful place. What that place would be like — well, I'll leave that to God, because He's wiser than we are, and I'm sure He'll manage to sort out all the contradictions. The one thing I am sure of is that if there is a place up there reserved for heroes, Dale Earnhardt is bound to be in it. Let us thank God for the gift of him, and rejoice in his translation to . . ." *What was the phrase they'd used?* ". . . to Tracks of Gold."

After the visit to the memorial garden in Talladega, Ratty backtracked the ten miles or so to the Interstate, and deposited the pilgrims in a hotel at the Oxford exit on I-20 just east of the Speedway turnoff. In the waning hours of daylight about half the group had gathered at the hotel's tiny outdoor pool, although only Shane and Matthew were swimming.

Terence Palmer sat at a white metal table some distance from the rest of the group, talking into his cell phone. "No, Mother,

I'm fine, really. Lovely weather. A bit warm, but that's only to be expected this far south. You sent me a package? No, it didn't reach me before I left New York. What was it? Oh, a book about an Irish princess. Ah, your book group loved it. Well, I don't have much time for reading this week anyhow. No, Mother, no one in the group chews tobacco or wears overalls. By the way, have you ever heard of Nash Furniture? Really? On a waiting list for a china cabinet? Really? Oh, no reason. Well, I have to go, Mother. Love to Merrill. Bye."

He closed the cell phone with a sigh.

CHAPTER XVII

The Changing of the Guard

Atlanta Motor Speedway

The journey from Talladega to the Atlanta Motor Speedway would take only a couple of hours, mostly backtracking I-20 to Atlanta and then south on I-75 to Henry County. Since they had passed this way the day before, there was a monotony to the landscape now, and Karen McKee took the paperback out of her purse, because she felt like reading another chapter in the novel about the princess in ancient Ireland. *I am reading a book on my honeymoon,* she thought. How weird is that. If anybody had told her six months ago that a few days after the wedding she would want to read a book or write a postcard to her mother instead of hanging on Shane's every word, or holding his hand hour after hour, she would have laughed in disbelief. But it was true. It wasn't that she loved Shane any less. She couldn't imagine life without him. It was just that having got the wedding out of the way, there were new

445

things to worry about, and reading was a good way to keep from worrying about them for a while, as long as she ignored the fact that her bookmark was an acceptance letter from East Tennessee State University.

Well, at least they'd be in Florida tomorrow. People actually did go to Florida on honeymoons. Maybe there'd be time to spend a couple of hours on the beach. She wished she could talk Shane out of visiting Daytona — skip the Speedway and come to the beach instead. That wasn't going to happen, though. Shane had come to pay his respects to Dale, and in his view the holy of holies was the track where he'd died. There was no getting away from it. Maybe it would be all right. So far Harley and the other passengers had been telling stories about races that happened ages ago. They'd hardly said a word about NASCAR-A.D. After Dale. Maybe it wouldn't come up. She knew she should sit Shane down and talk to him about it. Time he knew. What kind of a world was it when you had to choose between lying to somebody you loved or breaking their heart? Dale had been dead eighteen months now. Time to move on. Start watching racing again, instead of watching old videos of Dale's old races when the new season was on television. Why couldn't he just pick a new driver to root for — Matt Kenseth maybe, or Jamie McMurray, who looked like Hollywood's idea of a really nice guy. She had a feeling that they would never get to the future until Shane let go of the past.

So far, so good, Harley Claymore was thinking. He had managed to get through this much of the tour without losing any passengers to heatstroke, making any egregious mistakes in his racing trivia, or pissing anybody off by voicing his opinions on the new face of NASCAR. He had been trying to decide what to say about the Atlanta Motor Speedway — beyond remarking on the obvious — that it wasn't actually in Atlanta, but about thirty miles south of the city in Hampton, Georgia. Of course, at the rate Atlanta was spreading — like architectural kudzu — it wouldn't be long before the city sprawl engulfed the rural areas between city and Speedway, so that it would indeed be in the suburbs. He noticed that a new development — something called "Liberty Square Park" was going up across the road from the Speedway.

The track was located on Tara Road. Harley had thought up half a dozen sardonic remarks to make about that, but discarded them all not only for the sake of harmony but also because he realized that the old NASCAR with its strictly Southern tracks and its mostly Southern drivers had been a low-rent sport, forcing its competitors to work day jobs just to stay in the game. He had to admit: if he ever got a ride again, he'd be grateful enough for the new NASCAR glory days and the chance to make a million dollars in one season.

"Okay, folks," he said, seeing the S&S Food Mart across from the Speedway — his cue to begin his spiel. "We're here. Sorry, Bill, but I have this note card that says I have to spout a few stats at you."

Justine rolled her eyes. "This is like when the stewardess goes through the safety rigmarole. Let us do it. Size of track, somebody!"

"Mile and a half!" said Jim Powell and Ray Reeve in unison.

"Banking? Anybody?"

"Ummm . . . Almost flat on the straightaways, maybe 25 degrees in the turns," said Shane McKee. "They can go really fast on this track. They repaved it about five years ago, and the new surface really helped speeds."

"Anybody want to guess who holds the

track qualifying record?" asked Harley.

"Petty!" said Cayle and Sarah Nash.

"Earnhardt!" said a chorus of male voices.

"Geoff Bodine!" said Bekasu.

Harley stared at her. "I thought you didn't know anything about racing."

"No, I've been observing you," she said. "And you're partial to Geoff Bodine."

Harley sighed. "He is my brother in adversity," he said. "All work and no damn breaks."

They turned in at the house-shaped Atlanta Motor Speedway sign, which bore an enormous Coca-Cola sign on its right side — a fitting display, as Justine noted, because Coca-Cola was headquartered in Atlanta.

"This is another speedway with condos," said Harley, pointing to a soaring modern building that put him in mind of *Star Wars*. "Tara Place Condos. So if you have a couple of hundred thousand dollars to spare, you can watch the Georgia 500 in style, come October. Some serious money here, I don't have to tell you."

The bus came to a stop in the parking lot, and Harley raised a hand to stop his stampeding troops. "Okay, we're going to be a little rushed on this stop, just because it's so damn far to Daytona from here. Wreath first. Then tour. Then gift shop. Got it?"

They nodded.

"Whose turn is it?" asked Cayle.

"For the wreath? I'm not keeping track," said Harley. "Ever who wants to, far as I'm concerned." He remembered that the newlyweds had not yet had a turn, and he smiled at Shane, inviting him to volunteer.

Shane McKee shook his head. "Daytona," he said.

"Okay. Ratty. Where is he?"

"Opening the baggage compartment," said Cayle.

They turned and watched the little man scramble headfirst into the storage area beneath the bus. A moment later, he wriggled out again, like a terrier with a rat, and handed off the cardboard wreath box to Bill Knight, who happened to be standing closest to the bus.

The group gathered around while Bill Knight lifted the lid. White silk lilies, red rosebuds, and a black ribbon which bore the message, *"Gone to Race in a Better Place"* in white lettering.

"I'll do it," said Terence.

"I know just the place," said Justine. "There's a wonderful statue of Richard

Petty on a pedestal erected over near the condo. I'm sure he wouldn't mind if we put a wreath to Dale at the base of that."

Betcha he would, thought Harley, but since Mr. Petty was unlikely to find out about this bit of memorial favoritism — or at least not to catch him in the middle of it — he voiced no objection to Justine's plan.

The little procession marched toward the track, with Terence carrying the wreath as if there were a fuse attached.

Harley, shepherding his troops along the road, got back into gear as a tour guide. "Fancy place, isn't it?" he said, waving a hand toward the sumptuous condominium and the state-of-the-art grandstand and skybox complex. "But never mind the trappings here. When you're talking about the Atlanta Speedway, there's one race that stands out above all the rest," he said.

"Oh, God," said Bekasu. "Who got killed at this one?"

"No. That's not what I'm getting at."

Jim Powell turned to Ray Reeve. "Which race did Dale win here?"

"Well, he didn't win the one I'm talking about," said Harley. "But he was in it. And it was a landmark race. The Hooters 500 in 1992."

"You drove in it, right?" said Justine

451

quickly, before Bekasu could make any scathing remarks on the subject of Hooters Restaurants' dress code for waitresses.

"I didn't win it, either," said Harley, as if that didn't go without saying.

"Atlanta 1992." Sarah Nash turned the idea over in her mind. "That would be about the time Richard Petty retired."

"You nailed it. The Hooters 500 was his last race. Maybe that's why the statue is here. And it was the very first Cup race for somebody else."

Ray Reeve's expression suggested that he had stepped in something. "Not *Wonderboy?*"

"It sure was," said Harley. "Very symbolic, don't you think? The end of the old era of Southern good old boys in a regional sport, and the beginning of the new world of NASCAR as a national pastime with media-savvy golden boys at the wheel."

"Should'a called that race the Armageddon 500," said Ray Reeve.

"Well, I agree with Harley about the Hooters 500 being a landmark," said Jim Powell. He was leading Arlene along by the hand, slowing his steps so that she could keep up. "But not just because of Petty and Gordon. That race decided the championship that year, too, didn't it?"

452

"It was a three-way tie going into the race," said Harley. "Davey Allison was the front-runner, thirty points ahead of Alan Kulwicki and forty points ahead of Awesome Bill."

"My God," murmured Bekasu. "I know who all of them are."

Justine beamed and patted her sister's arm. "See? I told you this tour would be educational!"

"Well, at least it will give me something to talk about when I get my car serviced," she muttered.

Justine sneered. "It'll give you something to talk about to the governor."

"Did Davey crash in that race?" asked Jesse Franklin, trying to remember a competition that had ended a decade before.

Harley nodded. "With Ernie Irvan. Wasn't serious. Just took him out of the running."

"So Kulwicki must have won," said Matthew, "because I know he was the defending champ in '93 when his plane crashed at Bristol."

"He won the championship, but he lost that race," said Harley. "Elliott finished first, with Kulwicki right behind him. This is where it gets complicated." He turned to Bill Knight and Bekasu. "You two might want to tune out here. Kulwicki's second-place finish left him five ahead in overall points. So the championship came down to who led for the most laps, *not* to who won the race. Elliott led for 102 laps during the race, and Kulwicki led for 103. If it had been the other way around, they would have been tied for points for the championship, because the person who leads the most laps in the race gets five bonus points."

"Then what? Toss a coin?"

"Nope. Then Elliott would have been declared the champion. Rule says in case of a tie, you look to number of races won during the season. Bill had five victories, while Alan Kulwicki had only two. So although Bill won the race, he lost the 1992 championship by one lap."

"Oh, poor Bill!" said Justine. "To be so close and still lose. I'll bet he took it hard."

Harley clenched his teeth. "I am not going to the S&S Food Mart to buy a money order for Bill Elliott," he said.

"No," said Justine. "I'm sure he's okay with it, and I think even he'd say now that it was for the best. Alan won the championship, and three months later he died in that plane crash at Bristol. But at least he had the championship. Bill is too much of a gentleman to begrudge him that."

So here I am, thought Terence Palmer, *walking along the path to a speedway holding a memorial wreath for someone that most of my friends have never heard of.* He had joked that most of the people at the office thought that Dale Earnhardt was the chancellor of Germany. Of course, he didn't have to tell anybody about this when he got back to Manhattan. He had actually been enjoying himself, as one can if one knows that the experience is simply a vacation from real life. Barbecue. Speedways. People who shopped at Wal-Mart. What an adventure. Maybe it would even give him some insight into how certain companies would do in the future, if he knew what middle America ate and wore. *Pork rinds or beef jerky futures?* He had actually enjoyed talking racing with Shane McKee, and Jesse Franklin had proved quite knowledgeable about the stock market.

It occurred to Terence that this might have been his life for real if his father had ever wanted to fight for custody of him and if by some miracle Tom Palmer had won. He wondered who he would have turned out to be. He wouldn't have a diploma from Yale. His clothes would be less elegant, his tastes less refined. He wondered if there could be an upside to that different self. If he could have been someone who did not watch himself making every move, who never spoke without gauging what the other person needed to hear. Someone who could make friends instead of contacts, socialize instead of network, accept a friendship without wondering what it would ultimately cost him. Someone who did not hear an endless loop of ironic commentary running inside his head in the voice of his mother. Would he rather be Shane McKee? No. But he doubted if Shane would be so foolish as to envy him, either.

They stopped in the paved area beside the Tara Condos where a bronze Richard Petty stood on his pedestal, in his customary garb of cowboy hat and boots, smiling in perpetual benevolence at a young fan, as he signed an autograph for her.

"Doesn't he look like himself?" said Justine admiringly, raising the camera to capture the scene.

"It's funny to see pictures of Richard Petty from the old days, though," said Cayle. "Remember how he used to look back in the Fifties before he got so thin?

Kind of like Harrison Ford in *American Graffiti*."

"Well, if he ever writes a diet book, put me down for the first copy," said Bekasu, gazing up at the human heron immortalized in bronze.

"Is this where you want the wreath?" asked Terence, setting the circle of flowers at the base of the pedestal. He turned around to see the circle of his fellow passengers closing in around him and decided that he'd rather face the effigy of Richard Petty than a group of live people. Now he wished he had spent some of the walk over here thinking out what he was going to say. There was some comfort in knowing that he didn't have to worry about making an impression. He could experience the novel sensation of telling the truth without any agenda at all. Now if he could only work out what the truth was.

He had listened to the speeches of the others, and while he might have shared some of the same emotions as his fellow passengers, it was for different reasons. Some of the others saw Earnhardt as the embodiment of possibility — proof that a poor boy without education or connections could rise to greatness, but since Terence had taken care to cultivate precisely the education and connections that Earnhardt had lacked, he found no inspiration in that. Jesse Franklin seemed to revere the Intimidator for being — well, intimidating — for riding roughshod over his opponents without caring what anyone thought or said about it, but again Terence could not even aspire to such a code of behavior. His world was a spider web of obligation and cooperation, and he could not behave otherwise and remain in it. Why antagonize authority figures when you aspired someday to replace them? And yet as far back as he could remember he had rooted for Dale Earnhardt. He had never asked himself why.

He looked up at the smiling bronze face of Richard Petty, larger than life on his pedestal, and seeming to invite the solace of confession. NASCAR's authority figure: The King himself. Terence could talk to him.

"I never knew my dad. About all I ever heard about him was a passing reference in my mother's carefully muted tones of disapproval. I knew my dad was a Southerner — from somewhere near Charlotte, North Carolina, more or less . . . He'd been in the army, but he was only an enlisted man. *Only.* She always put it like that. And I tried to imagine what my dad would be like, without having very much to go on. Every now and then I watched movies about the South — *Deliverance* and *The Beverly Hillbillies*, that sort of thing — and I didn't want my dad to be that. I guess I wanted an image that fit the description of him without being demeaning. Not for the sake of my mother — I never intended to discuss it with her, and I never did. But just because I needed an image to carry around in my head, somebody I wasn't ashamed of, because after all, half my DNA came from my father, I wanted something to represent him, I suppose.

"I've been trying to remember when and how I first heard about Dale Earnhardt. I think I was about ten years old — it was the year of one of his early championships anyhow. A guy I knew at church was a racing fan, and I got to go to the Richmond Speedway once with him and his folks. I think we must have told my mother that it was a horse race. She'd never have let me go if she'd known it was stock car racing, but, anyhow, we went, and like most boys that age, I loved cars and danger and speed — anything to freak out the parents. So I was hooked. And Earnhardt was really hot that year — not just winning, but being outrageous. He was the Indiana Jones of sports. So I guess I started out by hoping my real dad was like that, until finally that image just took root in my mind so that I didn't care if it was true or not. It worked for me. And then last spring when my dad died, and I found out that he had been an Earnhardt fan, too, it just seemed to seal the bond. So I guess I'm here to say thanks." He stepped back.

Justine touched his arm. "Terence, aren't you going to say anything? You've just been standing there staring at that wreath for ages."

He hadn't said any of it. Terence looked around at the circle of politely puzzled faces. At last he mumbled, "I leave this wreath in memory of Dale Earnhardt, Sr., a great man."

"Well put," said Harley Claymore. Then he glanced at his watch and clapped for the attention of the group. "Take an hour or so to examine the track and raid the gift shop for Speedway pins, folks. And don't forget to go to the bathroom. In fact, flush twice. It's a long way to Florida."

CHAPTER XVIII

The Mother Church of American Racing

Daytona International Speedway

Matthew lay back in the seat and closed his eyes. He was tired of the Game Boy, and the south Georgia scenery was monotonous. There were no palm trees, just plain old pines, and long flat fields full of some kind of crop, tobacco or peanuts, or something. It was a couple of hundred miles from the Atlanta Motor Speedway to Daytona, and as far as he could tell, there was nothing much worth paying attention to in between. He was tired, anyhow. He didn't feel like reading or talking, either. The motion of the bus started him thinking about little Madison Laprade, back at the children's home, and what a weird experience it was to ride with her. She wasn't really a friend or anything. She was only four, but she had big space alien eyes and limp blonde hair, and she never, ever smiled. A few months back, he and Madison had been taken for their dental

461

appointments on the same morning. Madison hardly ever spoke to anybody. Nick said that she'd been taken away from her folks, because they did terrible things to her, so it wasn't surprising that she was a little strange. So Miss Salten started driving them into town, and after a minute or so, Madison, sitting beside him in the backseat, said, "Bump." Very softly. Just one word. *Bump.* He turned to ask her what she meant, but before he could pose the question, the car went over the railroad tracks. "Bump." Sure enough, all the way into town, Madison would whisper an announcement of every turn, every curve, every rough spot in the road. She never missed. Matthew thought about it, and he decided that she'd memorized the road because she didn't like surprises of any kind. She watched everything all the time, remembered everything, because she'd always had to watch all around her for danger, and try to figure out who was going to hurt her and when. Now the danger had been taken away, but she couldn't stop watching. Matthew felt sorry for the kid, and he thought about sending her a postcard, but she'd only have to get somebody to read it to her, and then she'd have to memorize it. He didn't want to put her to the trouble. He wondered if being on his own was going to turn him funny, too. He could already feel himself beginning to watch grown-ups with clinical interest, to see who felt like talking and who didn't feel uncomfortable around kids. Perhaps it wouldn't be long before he was sizing people up to see who might buy him a candy bar or a toy in the gift shop. Nick said that sooner or later everybody learned what they had to in order to get by. *Bump.*

It had been Justine's idea for everyone to change seats, because as she explained, "If Bekasu has to listen to me for much longer, she'll probably strangle me. And you two —" She pointed to Shane and Karen. "You have the rest of your lives to be together, so why don't you take some time off for a couple of hours? And Mr. Reeve — you and Mr. Franklin need to stop sitting together before folks start thinking *y'all* are a couple."

With no apparent logic, she proceeded to play musical chairs with the passengers — "It's just like a dinner party!" — pairing Cayle with Mr. Reeve, Bekasu with Jim Powell, Sarah Nash with Shane, Karen McKee with Terence Palmer, Jesse Franklin with Arlene Powell, Bill Knight with herself, and she sent Matthew up to the front to talk racing with Harley.

If anyone objected to these assignments, they decided that putting up with the change was easier than arguing with Justine.

Shane McKee looked doubtfully at the elegant older woman, thinking that if he had to sit beside her, he was glad it was at a time when which fork to use would not be an issue.

But Sarah Nash's decades of wine-and-cheese parties had served her well. Somehow, she seemed to ask the questions that Shane knew the answers to, and then she told him about the flock of ducks on her farm — the Fonty Flock, she called them, and each one was named after a NASCAR driver. "Unfortunately Todd Bodine turned out to be a lady duck," she said. "So now I call her Mary Todd Bodine."

Shane laughed. "Do you know about the goat with the number three marking on its side? I was hoping to see it, but the tour isn't going there."

"Yes, I've heard of it. It's not too far from my husband's place." Seeing his wary look, she added, "Long story, which I don't propose to go into."

Shane was still thinking about the Fonty

Flock. "Aren't you worried about foxes or coyotes getting your ducks out there at the pond?"

"Well, we pen them up at night. And I've got a great big, loud goose, at least twice the size of the ducks, to act as their bodyguard."

Shane smiled. "What's his name?"

Sarah Nash glanced around to make sure that Harley wasn't listening. Then she leaned over and whispered, *"Darrell."*

He laughed. "I'd like to see him."

"Well, you and Karen are welcome to come over sometime. You live over in east Tennessee, don't you?"

"Near Johnson City," said Shane. "I work as a mechanic there."

"Well, that'll come in handy," said Sarah. "All I know about car repair is how much everything costs to fix. How about Karen? What does she do?"

"She's been waitressing while we were going to school, but she didn't like it much. I don't know what she wants to do now."

"And what do you want to do? Your goal in life, I suppose I mean."

Shane didn't have to think about it. "The show," he said. "Get a job with a NASCAR team, but it isn't easy."

"No. The old way would be to have kin-folks in the business. The Elliotts, the Earnhardts, and the Pettys all went racing with relatives in their pit crews. The new way is to get an automotive degree." She smiled. "I guess it's too late for you to marry a Shelmerdine."

"Getting an engineering degree wouldn't be any harder."

Sarah Nash considered it. "Well, Shane, my husband Richard is on the board of directors at a place that might interest you. Maybe what you need is a pass in the grass."

Cayle Warrenby gave Ray Reeve a bright smile, and cast about for some topic other than Dale Earnhardt. "I was checking my e-mail last night, and one of the engineers from my company had sent me one of those redneck quizzes. They know I hate those things."

Ray Reeve grunted. "In Nebraska we get pretty sick of hearing about the heartland, too," he said. "The Flyover Zone crap."

"But the quiz did have one interesting question, I thought," said Cayle. " 'Which of these cars will rust out the quickest when placed on blocks in your front yard? A '65 Ford Fairlane, a '69 Chevrolet

Chevelle, or a '64 Pontiac GTO.' I'm an environmental engineer, so of course I wondered if there's a way to determine the answer."

Ray Reeve considered it. "Don't bet on the Fairlane," he said. "They're duller than ditchwater to look at, but they didn't call them Sixties iron for nothing."

Jim Powell, who had overheard this exchange, said, "What year's Fairlane? '65? Okay. Wasn't that the fourth year they used that same structure?"

"Different sheet metal from the roof down, though," said Ray Reeve. "But I take your point. The Ford folks must have got the hang of making 'em by then."

"I never did see many of them rusting in junkyards," said Jim Powell. "And it's not like anybody would bother to rescue one."

"So not the Fairlane," said Cayle. "Okay, y'all agree on that?"

They nodded.

"Me, too. So that leaves the '64 GTO and the '69 Chevelle." She considered it. "Both GM A-bodies."

"Yeah, but not the same," said Ray Reeve. "Remember they designed a new from-the-ground-up A-body in 1968 for all GM intermediates, which included the Chevelle."

"And the Skylark, the Olds Cutlass, and the Pontiac Tempest," said Cayle, nodding. "We had a burgundy Cutlass when I was a kid. Well, my dad had it, but the rest of us got to ride to church in it."

"That's an awful lot of makes and models," said Jim Powell. "And then the government started throwing all those safety regulations and pollution controls at the manufacturers, so maybe things began to slip a little at the factory."

"So which rusts first? The Chevelle?"

Jim Powell and Ray Reeve looked at each other and nodded. "In a junkyard? Chevy first," said Ray Reeve. "I can see it. There'd be some rust at the base of the back window. It's a steeper angle, so the water would collect there, and after the water took hold in there, more water coming in would rust the rocker panels and the lower rear fenders."

Jim Powell gave him a thumbs-up. "The GTO would be the next to rust out. In a junkyard." He smiled. "Unless —"

"Unless a car buff chances upon them and decides to rescue one," said Cayle, grinning. "And he sure wouldn't pick the Fairlane. He'd save the GTO, I think."

"Would, if he had any sense," said Ray Reeve.

After a moment's silence Jim Powell said, "Didn't know you knew so much about cars."

Cayle laughed. "Doesn't my name tell you?" she said. "I was daddy's 'boy.' I used to toddle around the garage after him and my uncles, learning car talk. Can't fix 'em, though."

Jim Powell sighed. "I couldn't even teach our Jean how to drive a stick shift."

"Cayle," said Ray Reeve thoughtfully. "Cale Yarborough. He was all right. If he was still around I might root for him. But he's not Dale."

"I know how you feel," said Jim. "Nobody was hit any harder than we were when Dale was taken, and Arlene spent last season crying through damn near every race, but you know, like I told her, I don't think he'd want you to give up the sport for him. He wasn't into giving up, was he?"

"I wonder which one of those cars Ralph Earnhardt would have salvaged?" said Cayle.

The three of them spent another hundred miles rehashing memories of Sixties iron, and when Cayle drifted off to sleep Jesse Franklin was telling Ray Reeve a war story about a soldier's wife named Dora

Jean who was afraid her husband's ship would sink in the harbor when it came home to port, so she had an affair with the captain of the minesweeper.

"How are you liking the tour?" said Terence politely to his new seatmate.

Karen sighed. "I wanted to go to the beach," she said. But she was too worried to make small talk. With a tentative smile she said in her smallest voice, "I need to ask you a question. I mean, since you're a guy. I need some advice. Before we get to Daytona."

Terence Palmer closed his magazine with no apparent enthusiasm. "I hope it's about your stock portfolio," he murmured.

"No." She glanced around to make sure that no one was listening. "But it is kind of an ethical question."

Terence blinked with alarm. "Why ask me then? There's a minister on board."

Karen wrinkled her nose. "He's nice, but he has to be older than Mark Martin. You're the only guy on this bus who's anywhere near Shane's age."

Terence turned away, rattling his magazine. "I can't help you."

"Well, you could listen," said Karen. "You don't have anything better to do.

470

Maybe it would help me just to talk about it."

Terence closed his eyes and sighed deeply, which was what his family did instead of shouting and throwing plates, but meant the same thing. "All right," he said. "Talk about it."

"Okay, suppose you tell somebody a lie because you love them and you don't want them to feel bad, but now you think they might find out the truth and be mad at you for keeping it from them."

"Okay," said Terence.

"Oh, good, so you think it's all right?"

"No. I thought you just wanted to think out loud. Now you're asking me to say what I think?" His eyes drifted back to the open magazine.

Karen snatched his copy of *Fortune* and stuffed it into the seat pocket.

Terence reached for the magazine, but he succeeded only in pulling out the letter that had been the bookmark in Karen's book about the Irish princess. He opened it before she could snatch it back.

"I'd appreciate it if you wouldn't mention that to anybody," she said. "Especially Shane."

"Why would I?"

"Well, you might not realize it was a secret. He doesn't know. Listen, I need some help here. I've only been married six days, and I'm afraid I've ruined things already. Or I will have, when Shane finds out."

"About the letter?"

She shook her head. "Something else."

"Something *else?* What — No — don't tell me. Doesn't matter. You sound like my mother."

"Your *mother?*"

"It's the sort of thing she'd do. One year — I think I was nine or ten — they sent me off to camp for two weeks, and I had a pet hamster. I wasn't allowed to have a *messy cat or a smelly dog.*" He did a passable imitation of his mother's Tidewater Brahmin accent. "The only reason I had the hamster was that we'd had it in the classroom at school, and the teacher asked for a volunteer to take it home over the summer. So every day from camp I called home to ask about Chip, the hamster, and Mother always said he was fine. Was she feeding him? I'd ask. Giving him a little lettuce or a peanut? Oh, yes, all taken care of. So — two weeks later I get home from camp —"

"And the hamster is dead?"

"Gone, anyway," said Terence. "I don't know if she let it go, gave it away, or forgot to feed it. Anyhow, it was gone. The cage

472

was gone. Like it had never happened. And when I started to cry, she said, '*I did it for your own good, dear. You really didn't need any bad news to make you sad while you were at camp.*'" He shrugged. "You know how that made me feel?"

Karen shook her head.

"Enraged, of course. But insulted, too. Who was she to decide what I was capable of handling? Who was she to lie to me and then expect me to be grateful?"

She studied him for a moment. This was the longest speech she'd ever heard Terence make. His voice shook with anger. "You're still mad about that hamster after all these years, aren't you?" she said.

He shrugged. "I don't think about it."

"But you wish she'd told you the truth, even if it hurt you at the time?"

"Look, don't try to solve your problem based on a dead hamster. I don't know what you did or how upset Shane would be about it, so my advice would be useless."

Karen leaned over and whispered a few words into his ear.

Terence's eyes widened. "You told him *what*? You'd never get away with that."

"If he ever heard any different, it didn't sink in. It's what he wanted to hear."

"Well, if it matters that much to him, I

hope I'm not around when he finds out," said Terence.

Karen, looking shaken, went back to her novel about the princess of Ireland. She didn't notice Terence staring at the book cover, lost in thought.

Harley thought there was something a little depressing about entering Florida via the Interstate. Maybe it was all the tourist-trap exits, luring motorists to buy fresh oranges or come and see the real fifteen-foot alligator (deceased and leathery, displayed on a ledge surrounded by knickknacks and more oranges). It made him want to get away from there as fast as he could. He could forgive some drivers for hoping that the "95" signs posted along the way meant the speed limit.

Daytona International Speedway was within sight of I-95, at least from the overpass at the U.S. 92 exit. International Speedway Boulevard was as urban a setting as you could imagine for a noisy, traffic-spawning speedway. A Holiday Inn and a Hilton stood across the road, and the sprawling Volusia Mall took up much of the next block. Harley had a spiel written out on yellow index cards: the Daytona 500 is the Superbowl of

NASCAR, the first Cup race of the season; the highest paying win and the event that makes you a celebrity. (*In these days of* David Letterman *and* Good Morning, America, *anyhow,* he reminded himself. *Sorry, Bodine.*) A 2.5 mile super speedway, restrictor-plate track . . . Daytona is where NASCAR began, back in the Forties when drivers raced along the hard-packed sandy beaches, racing tide as well as time. Harley nearly had the hang of this lecture business now, and he thought he could do a good twenty minutes of Daytona stories without too many slipups, but nobody wanted to hear it. Not the folks on this bus.

Oh, maybe Bill Knight would have been all courteous attention, because he would be anyway, even if the lecture was on Sanskrit . . . *in* Sanskrit. But the folks who really cared about Daytona probably knew the note card trivia as well as he did and, judging from their expressions at the moment, they didn't give a damn about any of it.

Maybe someday the excitement would return, and the thrill of Speed Week would matter again, but right now, row upon row of somber faces said it all. This was where he died. Just now, for Earnhardt's supporters, a visit to Daytona evoked not the excitement of seeing, say, Yankee Stadium, but the somber reflection one might feel at the USS *Arizona* Memorial at Pearl Harbor.

"Park anywhere in the front lot, Ratty," said Harley. "You know where we're going first."

As he turned into the parking lot, Ratty looked over the facade of the Speedway with its adjoining museums, and then he saw what Harley was talking about. "Right," he said. "I'll get as close as I can."

The solemn little group assembled on the sidewalk a few yards from the entrance to the building labeled "Daytona USA." Beside the white building was a raised flower bed encircled by a knee-high white cement wall. In the center of the circular garden stood Dale Earnhardt on a bronze pedestal, trophy in one hand, and the other arm upraised in a gesture of triumph.

There he was. So many hundred miles they'd come, all the way from Bristol, where he'd won his first race back in '79, to here, where it all ended twenty-two years later. But the moment frozen in time in that bronze statue was a happier one: February 15, 1998, the day he finally won the big one.

"That's the Harley Earl Trophy," said Harley. "My dad had high hopes, I guess, naming me that. Anyhow, that's what you get when you win the Daytona 500."

"It was the only race he won that year," said Jim Powell, nodding to the man in bronze.

"I'll bet he didn't care," said Sarah Nash with a fond smile. "It took him so long to finally win this race, I'll bet he felt like getting dipped in bronze right on the spot, so that he'd never have to put that trophy down."

"This is where we ought to put the wreath," said Cayle.

"That's what we decided," said Harley. "But I thought we'd look around first. We're taking the tour of the Speedway here. They put you on a little tram and drive you around the track. There's so much history connected with this place we couldn't cover it in a week. Who won the first Daytona 500?"

"Petty!" said Cayle.

"*Lee* Petty," Jim Powell corrected her. "That was a good ten years before young Richard started racing."

"Okay, that was a hard one. Now for the younger crowd," said Harley, putting a hand on Matthew's shoulder. "Who won

477

the last Daytona 500, back in February?"

"Ward Burton," said Matthew.

Shane shook his head. "Sorry, Matthew," he said. "It was Little E. Last year Mike Waltrip, and this year Dale Junior." He looked around for confirmation, but no one met his eyes, except Karen whose stricken look puzzled him. "What?"

"Sorry, Shane," said Harley, sounding puzzled. "Matthew's right. Little E. won the July race here in 2001. I expect that's the race you were thinking of, but Ward Burton did win the 2002 Daytona 500."

"No! He couldn't have!" Shane reddened at the looks of pity and confusion on the faces of the others. Were they teasing him? It wasn't funny. "Junior won," he said again. "It's part of the miracle."

Bill Knight patted Karen's arm. As soon as he'd heard the name "Ward Burton," he had remembered his conversation with Pvt. Alvarez back at DEI and he had known what was coming.

"What miracle?" said Jim Powell.

"Overcoming the curse. You know how the Intimidator tried twenty times to win this race and lost from '79 to '97, right?"

Nods from the Number Three Pilgrims.

"Ran out of gas. Cut a tire. Hit a seagull, for God's sake. And then the little girl in the wheelchair gave him the lucky penny in '98 and he won the race."

"And he lived three years and three days after that," said Bill. "We know, Shane."

"Okay, but since he died he hasn't lost the Daytona 500. Because the drivers of his company DEI have won every year. And they'll win next year, too. *Three* times. That's the miracle."

A bewildered Jesse Franklin stared at Shane for a moment, as if waiting for a punch line or for someone else to speak up. When no one did, he said, "But, hold on there, son. Ward Burton doesn't drive for DEI."

"Ward Burton didn't win!" Shane said it so loudly that passersby turned to stare at them.

The others looked at him in awkward silence.

Then Justine said gently, "You didn't see the race, did you?"

He blinked. "Of course, I . . . well . . . I . . ."

Karen was shaking her head. "You made it through the first couple of laps, I think, Shane. Until they showed Kevin Harvick's car up close, anyhow. The Goodwrench logo. Remember? And then you walked out of the den, saying you couldn't stand to watch it. You went off to the garage and you spent the rest of the afternoon tuning up my mom's car, which it did not need. And later you made me tell you who won."

"That's right. And you said Junior won it."

"I know, Shane," she murmured. "I know I said it. It just wasn't true, that's all. But you were so sure that the miracle was going to happen . . ." Her voice quavered. "I couldn't tell you any different. I'll bet half a dozen times since then people have mentioned that Ward Burton won. We even saw a program on television where they said it, but it seemed like it just went right over your head. You didn't want to be wrong, Shane."

He stood there, fists clenched, taking heaving breaths, while the other passengers stood in embarrassed silence, contriving to look elsewhere. Karen looked as if she might burst into tears at any second.

The seconds ticked by while they glanced at each other, wondering whether to try to comfort the young man or to pretend it hadn't happened.

"You got the wrong miracle, man," Terence Palmer said at last. He stepped up beside Harley, concerned but not distressed by the public scene playing out before him. He managed a reassuring smile at Shane. "The first miracle *was* Kevin Harvick."

Distracted now, Shane simply stared at him. "Huh?"

Terence nodded, and went on in the earnest voice he might have used to discuss mutual funds. "Look, after the Intimidator was killed in the 2001 Daytona 500, his Goodwrench car went to Kevin Harvick, right? And it was Harvick who won the 3rd race after Daytona that year. There's your number three, Shane. The third race A.D. That made it the fourth race of the season. What's Harvick's number, Shane?"

"Twenty-nine."

"Right. Okay, in that race at Hampton, Harvick started in the fifth position. But he came in first. Fourth race. Twenty-nine car. Starts fifth, finishes first."

"So?" Shane was no longer angry, just confused.

"What was Earnhardt's birthday, Shane?"

"April 29, 1951," said Shane without a second's hesitation. Then it hit him. *"Four. Twenty-nine. Five-one."*

"Right. There's your sign." Terence glanced up at the bronze features of Dale Earnhardt, forever in victory. "But as for

Junior winning Daytona this year, *he'd* never stand for that."

"What do you mean?"

"The Intimidator. Well, think about it. Dale Senior tried twenty times to win that race, and got jinxed every time. You said so yourself. So do you think he's going to let Little E. win the big one the third time the kid ever tries? At the age of twenty-seven?" Terence gave Shane a pitying smile. "Oh, please."

Shane nodded, not happy yet, but on the verge of being handed back his dream. No one else moved, for fear of breaking the spell.

Terence pulled a checkbook out of his hip pocket, and looked at the three-year calendar on the back of the deposit record. "Okay," he said. "I'll bet you want to know when Junior *is* going to win it, don't you?"

Wordlessly, everyone nodded.

"When did Dale Earnhardt win the 500, Shane? The date."

"February 15."

"Right." Terence tapped the checkbook calendar. "And the next time the race will fall on that date is in 2004. The sixth anniversary of the win. Two times three, Shane. Two drivers — Dale and Junior — times the magic number three. And 2004 is *three* years after he died. By then Junior will be twenty-nine. Harvick's number again."

Shane was nodding eagerly now. "Right. But it's also the age Dale was when he won his first championship."

Terence closed the checkbook with a snap. "That's when Little E. will win it," he said.

Everybody nodded solemnly, and Justine started to clap, but Cayle and Bekasu each grabbed a hand, glaring at her until she stood still.

Shane still looked shaken, but he was nodding now and his eyes shone with the newly kindled light of belief. Karen took his arm and they walked away.

"I'll buy that," said Harley to the group. "How about you, Reverend?"

Bill Knight smiled. "No devil's advocate here," he said. "There are saints who have been given shrines for less. I suppose we'll all find out in February, 2004."

"Now, how about we check out this Speedway tour," said Harley, motioning them forward. "We can talk more over lunch."

As the group began to file into the museum and gift shop building, Sarah Nash caught up with Terence. "That was a fine thing you did there," she said. "Was it all true?"

He nodded. "Sure, it was. I'm a numbers geek. I just try not to let it show. This morning on the bus Karen warned me that she'd lied to Shane, so I had some time to think about it. Miracles. I want one, too."

"Well, you helped out that young couple. I didn't think you'd get involved."

Terence smiled. "Rubbin' is racin'," he said. "I guess that's as true in life as it is on the track."

Sarah Nash chuckled. "The gospel according to St. Dale. Never thought I'd see the day. But they're nice kids. She's the brains of the pair, but he's got a good heart. She could do worse."

Terence didn't answer at first. They had entered the building now and followed the rest of the group into the gift shop — an unauthorized detour that Harley had been powerless to prevent. Finally he said, "I've just realized who they remind me of. It's my *parents*. That's what they must have been like. A smart, ambitious girl who marries a nice guy who'll be content to drift through life, and maybe she doesn't even know why she married him. She's using a college acceptance letter for a bookmark. She never told him about that, either. She'll leave him one of these days, when she gets tired of him holding her back."

"Maybe not, Terence. Sometimes an anchor keeping you grounded is a good thing. Not all women want to be outranked by their husbands these days."

"But do you think I'm right about them resembling my parents?"

"Now that you mention it? Of course I do. I just hope they don't end up the same way." Sarah Nash looked thoughtful. "Maybe what they need is a drafting partner. May I borrow your cell phone?"

"What are you going to do?"

"I'm going to call my husband and ask for a favor. Northeast State Community College in Blountville offers an industrial technology program in automotive service. That's near enough to where Shane lives that he could take courses there, if we can get him in. Richard is on their board, so I think he can put in a good word for Shane."

"So Shane can learn how to be a NASCAR mechanic?"

"It's a start. While he's studying at Northeast, he could do an internship at the Bristol Motor Speedway, which is about two exits away. Richard can probably arrange that, too. If Shane does well, maybe he can get financial aid and go on to a more specialized program, like the one in Mooresville specifically designed for NASCAR."

Terence handed over his cell phone, still looking bewildered. "But how do you know about all this?" he asked.

She hesitated. "Well, Terence, your father told me about those programs. I think he had hoped that you might want to do that someday. Of course, he'd be very happy about the way things did turn out for you, I'm sure."

While Sarah Nash placed her call, Terence walked into the gift shop, so lost in thought that he barely noticed the brightly colored displays of drivers' emblems. One featured item did penetrate his reverie. You could get a dog or cat collar that said "The Intimidator," marked with the red-outlined Earnhardt number three. He smiled, picturing his mother's surly Bichon Frise in a Dale Earnhardt dog collar, but his thoughts were mostly elsewhere. He was still considering the purchase when a smiling Sarah Nash reappeared and returned his phone.

"Richard was there," she said. "I'd forgotten how much I missed the old bear.

Watching the Powells this past week has made me think about my husband more than I ever thought I would. And he sounded right glad to hear from me. I think Florida may not be as riveting as Richard thought it would be."

"You asked him about Shane?"

"Yes. He wants to meet the newlyweds and talk to Shane about maybe going to Northeast State. He was so pleased to hear from me that he even promised to take us all out to see Li'l Dale the sacred goat, and said that if Shane and Karen want to stay at his place for the rest of their honeymoon, they're welcome. His place is on the beach. I thought Karen would love that. I just spoke to them and they want to go."

Terence blinked. "Stay with your husband?"

She blushed. "Well, Richard won't be there. He said he might like to come back to North Carolina for a while. So we're going to take on the McKees as a project, I suppose."

Terence nodded. "I've been thinking about them, too. And about my dad. You know you asked me what I wanted to do with all the art pottery in my father's house? Well, I think I'd like to send it to that auction house in Asheville, and put the money in a trust for the McKees. That way my dad would get to send someone on to NASCAR, even if it isn't me. I think he'd have liked that."

"I think so, too. I think Tom would be proud. Do you want to come with us?"

"With you?"

"We're going to leave the tour. Shane wants to see that goat, bless his heart, and Karen wants to spend part of her honeymoon at the beach."

"But how will you get home?"

"Didn't I mention it? Richard has his own plane."

"At all the other tracks we've reminisced about Dale's past races," said Harley. "And I know that now that we've reached Daytona there's one tragic race that looms large in your minds. His last one: 2001. But I just want to remember another race that Dale drove here. You know he tried from 1979 to 1997 to win the Daytona 500 and never made it. But he loved racing. Somebody — I think it was Rusty — said one time that if NASCAR had ever announced that they were going to hold a race, but no crowds were going to turn up, no prizes would be given, and they were going to charge five bucks for drivers to run on an empty speedway, Dale Earnhardt would be the only fellow to show up. He just flat loved driving, win or lose.

"That's why the story I'd pick to tell here is not the 1998 Daytona 500, which he finally won, but the one before that — 1997."

"Wonderboy won that year!" said a scowling Ray Reeve. "Why do you want to talk about that?"

"You're right, Ray. Jeff Gordon did win in '97, but that isn't my point. See, that was the year that Earnhardt had his bad luck a little earlier than usual. Most of the time he managed to have his disaster on the very last lap of the 500-mile ordeal — within spitting distance of the finish line if possible. I swear, it was like God's thumb — well, anyhow, in '97 the curse hit a little early. He barrel rolled the black number three on the back straightaway, which ended his chances of a win that year. He wasn't hurt, though. Shaken up, of course, but he crawled out of the car and walked to the ambulance under his own steam. They were supposed to take him to the track clinic to get looked at, but while he was sitting there in the back of the ambulance, Dale got to thinking about his car, and he decided that it was upright and therefore still able to be driven."

Bekasu's eyes widened. "He didn't!"

"Oh, he did. He climbed out of the ambulance, went back to the Monte Carlo, and took off again. Didn't have a hope of a win, of course, but he came in thirty-first. He loved being here. He loved it."

The tram tour began with the recorded voice of Bill France, Jr., the head of NASCAR, welcoming visitors to the Speedway. The little caravan of trams began on the top of the 480-acre Speedway with its view of the airport next door and the Hilton across the street, trundled through one of the tunnels leading to the infield, and began its circuit of the two-and-a-half-mile track, while the Speedway guide told anecdotes about Daytona, not unlike Harley's performance on the Earnhardt Memorial Tour. He pointed out the 44-acre Lake Lloyd in the Speedway infield, where the Intimidator had won a fishing tournament with a 10.8-pound bass. Around the track they went, staying off the 31-degree banking where the racers actually drove, past the orange balls on poles which were actually observation towers for the spotters to crouch in. Past turn 4. That was where it happened. But the guide didn't say so. When he mentioned Dale, it was the win, the fishing tournaments, the happy memories.

"I guess I can understand them not referring to Earnhardt's death on the tour," said Ray Reeve, when the Number Three Pilgrims had assembled again in the parking lot, with yet another speedway pin affixed to hats and tote bags. "But they didn't talk about Neil, either."

"I guess we ought to talk about Neil," said Harley.

Bill Knight saw the somber faces of the others. "Neil?"

"Yeah," said Cayle softly. "Dale Earnhardt's best friend. The other guy who died on turn 4."

Harley thought this was a sadder story than Dale, but you couldn't stand there at Daytona talking about grief and loss and not mention Neil. So he told them. Neil Bonnett had been a pipefitter back in Alabama, before he decided to become a race car driver. He was part of the Alabama Gang with the Allisons. If there were any ghosts in the voices at Talladega, they should have been telling Neil to slow down and be careful. Not that he'd have listened. Neil and Earnhardt were the Butch and

Sundance of motor sports, for what? Fifteen years or more? They competed on the track. They tried to catch the biggest fish or shoot the biggest buck in the woods. They were either the most macho pair who ever lived or else neither one of them could spell death, because they went at everything full tilt. They both went into the wall more than their share of times, but Earnhardt got away with it. Neil didn't. He'd come out of the wrecks with broken bones, injuries that would sideline him for weeks. One multicar crash at Darlington in 1990 gave him a head injury that wiped out his memory for months. So he retired. Became a TV announcer. But life in the slow lane didn't suit him, and he was itching to get back in the show. So Earnhardt helped him out. Got him a job test driving the Monte Carlos that would replace Earnhardt's Lumina beginning in 1994. So Neil started driving again, and if he was driving, he might as well be racing. A farewell tour for a 46-year-old daredevil who already had enough money to stop taking risks. Five races in the 1994 season, just to go out in style. But in a butt-ugly car: a garish pink and yellow Country Time Lemonade Lumina. Car owned by Earnhardt. The farewell tour would begin, of course, with the first race of the season: the Daytona 500.

Only he never made it to the race. On February 8, 1994, in a practice run, Neil Bonnett crashed in turn 4 and died. Some people say Earnhardt never got over it, but he drove in that year's Daytona 500, and he came in seventh.

Seven years and seven days later, he would also die at turn 4 at Daytona.

Harley's voice trailed away. He didn't trust himself to say anything else. He had known Neil.

Nobody said anything. Not even Justine, who wiped a tear away with the back of her hand, but did not speak. The others looked at the ground, doubly solemn now.

"Okay," said Harley. "Anybody have anything they want to say?"

Nobody did.

"Then let's say our good-byes. Speaking of good-byes, four of our group are getting off here. The newlyweds and Terence and Sarah have had a change of plans, so make sure you take time to wish them well at dinner tonight before they head off down a different road."

Shane stood there holding the wreath, trying to think of something to say. He was excited about the prospect of a new future that might someday bring him back here, but saddened, too, at the memory of the loss of his hero.

"This place is so . . . what's that thing Lincoln said in the Gettysburg address? So consecrated, that what we say here has to be special. I didn't write a speech or anything, but I can't just say any old thing. Not here. I thought about a poem that Karen put on a quilt for me last year, but then I remembered something even better. Hey, Karen, what's that thing your mother's club says sometimes? The 'bright flame' thing they say?"

Karen blinked. "Well, it's an old Gaelic prayer, Shane. I don't remember all the Gaelic. Besides, it's a prayer. Well, not a prayer, I guess. I think it's actually addressed to a guardian angel, but still."

"To an angel. That's it. But it says what I want to say. You know it in English. Just say it in English. Please."

Karen glanced doubtfully at Rev. Knight, as if she expected him to pronounce it blasphemous to utter a prayer at a speedway, but he simply smiled and looked eager for her to begin. There was nothing for it, then. She hoped she wouldn't get so nervous she'd forget the words. Probably not. She'd told Shane about the college letter, and now that he had the chance to go somewhere, too, he was okay with that. They were finally checking out — which is what NASCAR drivers say when they're making a burst of speed to leave the rest of the field back in the dust.

She nodded for Shane to place the wreath at the foot of the Earnhardt statue, and then she said:

"Be thou a bright flame before me,
Be thou a guiding star above me,
Be thou a smooth path below me,
And be ever a kindly shepherd beside me,
Today, tomorrow, and forever."

"For Dale," said Shane, touching the wreath.

"And for Neil," whispered Harley.

CHAPTER XIX

The Lady in Black

Darlington Raceway

"Are we there yet?"

Nobody said "Shut up, Justine," for a change, because they had all been thinking more or less the same thing for many a mile. Harley supposed that putting together a ten-day bus tour that would encompass two NASCAR races was quite a feat, and that you could not in good conscience skip Daytona on a tour devoted to Dale Earnhardt, or on any NASCAR tour for that matter, but the distances involved were still brutal. It was one thing to drive 500 miles around an oval track in an afternoon at 180 miles per hour, and quite another to dodder along I-95 at considerably lower speeds for the nearly 400 miles between Daytona Beach, Florida, and Darlington, South Carolina. Rest stops. Food stops. Stretch-your-legs breaks. Four hundred-plus miles from the Atlanta Speedway to Daytona, and then turn right around and go almost that far again to get to Darlington.

At least they'd had two days for the last leg of the journey. They visited Daytona on Friday, and they'd had until Sunday to reach Darlington. So they'd stayed Friday night in Daytona, and taken their time on Saturday heading north again to Darlington. Harley thought that he would have been less tired if he could have made the trip in a Monte Carlo alone, nonstop, but coddling a group of strangers over more than a thousand miles in a week made him feel like he'd walked the whole distance in wet boots.

He thought about all the fools who considered racing monotonous. Had they ever driven I-95?

The bus was quiet now, not only because four of the Number Three Pilgrims had gone their own way in Florida. Harley didn't take it personally. It had been a long trip, and the itinerary could use a little work. The remaining passengers were feeling the effects of the long haul, which meant there was much less banter than usual. Everyone read or slept, just wishing for the traveling to be over. They were subdued by the visit to Daytona, too, of course. Someday maybe — a few races down the road — the Speedway would again be just another place to race, but right now it was still haunted by the image of the Intimidator's last race, and it had saddened them all to be there. Despite the punishing distance of this last leg of the journey, Harley was glad that the tour had not ended in the sadness of Daytona, but with the pageantry and excitement of a race day in Darlington. Of course, they might someday look back on that race with regret and nostalgia if the fools in charge of NASCAR ever made good on the threat to take the Labor Day race away from Darlington, but for now it was an exciting time in a happier place, and for all their sakes he was glad.

"The Darlington Motor Speedway is called the Lady in Black. Everybody knows that." Harley began his spiel by stating the obvious, but then he noticed Bill Knight's smile of disbelief. "Okay, maybe not *everybody* knows it, but certainly anybody who follows motor sports. Would one of you like to tell the reverend how Darlington got its nickname?"

"It was the first track to be paved," said Jim Powell.

"The Lady in Black," said Arlene with her vacant smile. She rested her head on Jim's shoulder, and he smiled back and patted her hand.

"Are you going to spout all those numbers at us now?" asked Justine wearily.

"Nope," said Harley. "You're going to be sitting through a race there, so I guess you can work it out for yourselves. The information will be in the program, I expect. But I have driven here, so I might have some useful points to make."

"Fire away, Harley," said Matthew, who was sporting a new Earnhardt windbreaker bought for him at the Daytona gift shop by Bekasu.

"They also call Darlington 'the track too tough to tame,' which means that a lot of drivers can't handle it. Earnhardt himself said something to the effect that every so often the Lady in Black slaps you down if you get too fresh with her. Anybody know the top three drivers having the most wins of the Southern 500? Wanna guess, Cayle?"

"Is that a hint?" She smiled. "One of them must be my namesake."

"That's right. Cale Yarborough has five wins. David Pearson has the most, and then Earnhardt. By the way, the last Winston Cup race Pearson ever won was on this track — the 1980 Rebel 500. Darlington can be tricky, because it's lopsided on account of the ponds."

"Ponds? It has ponds?" said Bekasu.

"Well, no. Not like Lake Lloyd at Daytona. People don't wear life jackets to race here."

"Do they at Daytona?" asked Bill.

Harley smiled. "Well, Tom Pistone used to. He worried about going in the water. What I mean about ponds here is that when Harold Brasington was trying to build this track back in 1950, the farmer who owned the adjoining land wouldn't sell him the portion that his pond was on, so Mr. Brasington had to work around that obstacle to build his speedway, and he ended up with a track shaped like an egg. Wider on one side than the other. Because of that, it has tighter, steeper turns on one end. Keeps you on your toes. If you're not mindful of which turn you're going into, you end up going into the wall. Ever heard of the Darlington Stripe?"

"Paint mark along the side of your car that you get from scraping against the wall as you race," said Jim Powell. "Badge of honor."

"Are we going to the Stock Car Hall of Fame?" asked Justine. "It's right there in front of the Speedway."

"No," said Harley. "Not with the crowds we'd have to fight to get in there on race day."

"Speaking of the race," said Jesse Franklin, "are we going to bet on the winner again? Dibs on Mark Martin, and five bucks says he wins. Unless one of the rest of you folks want him."

Cayle waved away Mark Martin. "Bill Elliott," she said. "I promised Sarah Nash I'd cheer him on."

"Well, I'll take Dale Junior," said Justine. "He's better on the super speedways, and he's never even made the top ten here, but it just wouldn't feel right to root for anybody except an Earnhardt. Here's my five bucks."

"What about you, Harley?" asked Jim Powell, who had taken off his hat to collect the wager money. "I was thinking of taking Rusty Wallace, just because I want him to break that losing streak, but if you were going to pick him, I'll plump for Dale Jarrett. This track calls for old-style racing, and he's good at that."

"Jeff Gordon," said Harley. "I'll stick with Jeff Gordon — masochist's choice."

"Didn't he just win on Sunday at Bristol?" said Bekasu.

"Yeah," said Harley. "Well, with my luck he'll win every race I ever attend for the rest of my life just to depress me."

"Harley's being a gentleman," Cayle told

them. "He's picking the least likely driver to win. Gordon's been on a thirty-one-race losing streak before Bristol. Take Matt Kenseth, Bekasu. You have sweaters older than he is, but he's got real promise. And he's from Wisconsin, just like Alan Kulwicki."

"Whatever," said Bekasu, going back to her book.

In the back of the bus, Ray Reeve cleared his throat. "I'd like to get into the pool," he said.

The others turned and stared at him.

"Well, sure, Ray," said Jesse Franklin. "Anybody you like, but I thought you stopped caring who won after Dale passed away."

"I know, and I've been agonizing about it. I thought about what Earnhardt did after Neil Bonnett died. He went back to the track and practiced an hour after Neil crashed. So I thought he'd think I was soft if I didn't move on. Well, last night in the hotel room, I took that Gideon Bible out of the nightstand, and I Bible-cracked."

"But you're from Nebraska," said Justine. "I thought Bible-cracking was a Southern thing."

"I expect they do some form of it every-where," said Bill Knight.

502

"So you opened the Bible and pointed at random to a verse, and now you want to get into the betting pool?" said Bekasu in cross-examining mode.

Ray Reeve reddened. "Well, the thing is I got Matthew seventeen, verse five. Knew exactly what it meant. Justine already picked him, but I'd like to go half with her."

"Glad to have you!" said Justine. "I hope we split the pot!"

Jim Powell smiled. "Okay, then. Ray is backing Little E. in the Southern 500."

"You know, Ray, Dale Junior isn't all that good on short tracks," said Harley. "He's a restrictor-plate racer."

"Don't care if he wins or not," said Junior's new supporter. "I just decided to root for him. I can cheer him on. He's Dale's boy."

The Darlington traffic was just as bad as it had been in Bristol — both races took place in small towns overwhelmed by an extra fifty thousand people for the weekend. Harley thought it was just his luck that the tour finale occurred at a track that wasn't out in the middle of nowhere. Because it had been built in the early days before NASCAR became a major attraction, the Darlington Motor Speedway wasn't a rural Pompeii, set amidst acres of empty fields that turned into parking lots a few days a year. This track filled a Wal-Mart-sized hole on a commercial road, with rows of small stores and houses all up and down the road around it. It wasn't even a four-lane thoroughfare. *No wonder people keep spreading rumors that NASCAR was going to move the Labor Day race to California,* Harley thought. Now that racing was a billion-dollar enterprise, this track, with no fancy skyboxes or modern amenities, must look pretty poky to the corporate moguls, but he for one hoped the relocation wouldn't happen. Darlington was a tradition that went all the way back to the days when Petty and Earnhardt meant Lee and Ralph, not Richard and Dale. He'd hate to lose that just for glitz.

His greatest concern at the moment was not the traffic but the weather. A misting rain fell out of a sky the color of pewter. That could spoil everything. You could play football in the rain, but motor sports was different. Driving out there was dangerous enough without factoring in a slick track from a mix of oil and rainwater. If it started raining, they'd stop the race. Sometimes drivers sat for hours waiting for the go-ahead to resume. Harley filled a few more miles with chatter by explaining that if more than half the designated laps of a race were completed during the afternoon, the winner would be whoever was ahead when the weather finally forced them to cancel it.

"Okay, the race is at one o'clock," he said into the microphone. "So we don't have time to go somewhere for lunch. Actually, Columbia would be favorite, because anyplace closer than that is going to be wall-to-wall people. We're going straight to the track, and those of you who are young enough or brave enough can try the Darlington culinary specialty: hamburger steak smothered with onions. Take each other's pictures in front of the palm tree there at the entrance."

"It's raining," Cayle pointed out.

"I know," said Harley. "I hope it quits, because if it doesn't, there won't be a race."

By a stroke of luck, which despite Justine's insistence, Harley refused to chalk up as a miracle to St. Dale, the rain stopped, the track was dried off, and the 53rd Mountain Dew Southern 500 roared to life.

"There are still so many terms I don't understand," said Bekasu plaintively. "What is a Biffle?"

Justine groaned. "In your case, Bekasu, it is a cross between baffled and bewildered."

The green flag went down, and Bill Elliott's number 9 Dodge took the early lead. When he still had it forty-three laps later, Harley was thinking that Sarah Nash would be sorry she missed this one, but after that Sterling Marlin led the pack, and Harley began to feel like a kid at a window watching a party he hadn't been invited to. He had fully intended to worm his way onto pit road again before this race, still trying to make connections, but then he'd made the mistake of talking about Neil Bonnett at Daytona, and the memories wouldn't leave him alone. Now common sense, a rare but unwelcome visitor, had dropped by to urge him to reconsider.

Darlington was the track that gave you fair warning to call it quits, but nobody ever listened. In 1997, Earnhardt had passed out here in the first lap of the race, and he had ended up in the hospital with a million people scared to death over his condition, but within days he was back in the driver's seat as if nothing had ever happened. A few years earlier the Black Lady was also the scene of Neil Bonnett's first serious crash — the one that left him with amnesia for many months. He had gone headfirst into the wall — a warning from Fate perhaps, but if so it had gone unheeded. Like Neil, Harley was forty-something and out of the sport after a wreck that any sane person would take as a divine message to call it quits. But also like Neil, he couldn't walk away. What else was there in life that compared to this? He didn't want to be a car dealer or a sportscaster while *the show* roared on without him. His thoughts seemed to go around in laps, too, always ending up back where they began: got to get back out there.

Nobody tried to talk to him during the race, or if they did he was oblivious to the interruption. He stared at the track with the glazed look of someone who was filtering this race through a dozen past ones. Halfway through the afternoon, a tap on his arm broke his reverie. It was Jim Powell, whose anguished expression said that he wasn't thinking about the race.

"I think Arlene is sick."

Harley hated hospitals. He'd been in too many emergency rooms after one wreck or another, and even worse was having to go there as a visitor, when some other driver had pushed his luck too far. He sat alone in the hallway now, staring at a pamphlet on heart disease, reading the same line over and over without absorbing a word of it, and cursing the sadists who had outlawed smoking in here.

It was a good thing that the race was still going on, so that traffic had not become a nightmare, because the ambulance had to go from Darlington to Florence.

"Aren't you going to Wilson on Cashua Ferry Road?" Harley had asked the ambulance guy. He'd remembered the place from his racing days.

"No ER, buddy. Have to take her to McLeod in Florence. You gonna come in your car?"

Harley nodded. Most of the Number Three Pilgrims had insisted on leaving the race to accompany the Powells. Reverend Knight was going to ride in the ambulance with Jim and Arlene, while Harley, whose car was parked at Darlington in preparation for the end of the tour, had agreed to bring Matthew, Jesse Franklin, Justine, Cayle, and Bekasu. It was all the car would hold, but the one remaining passenger, Ray Reeve, hadn't really wanted to go anyhow. He hated hospitals as much as

Harley did, and besides, he didn't want to leave in case Little E. won the race. He took Cayle's cell phone so that they could call him from the hospital and tell him how Arlene was doing and how to find them. Meanwhile, he would stay by himself and finish watching the race. When it was over, he'd go back to the bus, find Ratty, and direct him to the hospital.

The ambulance attendant had looked doubtful at Harley's proposal to follow them. "Well," he said, "you can try, but we'll be burning rubber — lights, siren and all. Doubt you could keep up."

Harley Claymore smiled and smiled.

"Oh, good. You're still here." Bill Knight had come around the corner, looking tired but composed. He was in professional mode now, Harley supposed.

"Of course I'm still here," said Harley. "How is she?"

"Well, she's in and out of consciousness. We don't really know anything yet. Except that it was a heart attack, of course."

"Knew that before we got here."

"Yes. At her age, it can go either way. At least we got her to a hospital in good time."

"Where's everybody else?"

"Well, Jim wanted Bekasu and me to stay with him, and with Arlene when we're allowed to see her. We've sent Matthew off with Justine."

Harley nodded. "That's good. Get the children out of the way."

"Er — something like that. Cayle has gone to call the Powells' daughter in Seattle, and then she's calling the airline about their flight tomorrow, and so on. And Jesse Franklin is wrangling over Medicare forms or some such red tape with a hospital administrator."

"Jesse? I thought he wouldn't say boo to a goose."

"Well, when it counts, he can assert with the best of them. He said he asked himself 'What would Dale do?' and there's been no stopping him since then. You should have heard him giving orders to the doctors. There is one more thing that needs to be done, though. Harley, the thing is . . . Arlene is asking for Dale."

"She what?"

Bill Knight sighed. "I think she's forgotten that he's dead. She's a bit agitated. I don't know. Anyhow, she keeps saying she wants to see Dale Earnhardt. And we thought — that is, Jim suggested that if we were to bring in that fellow who impersonates Earnhardt, she wouldn't know any different, and it might calm her."

"Okay."

"Oh, good. We'd really appreciate it."

"What do you — you mean you want *me* to go find him? Go back to Darlington *now?*"

"Jim said that maybe the race isn't over yet, and the Impersonator might be around. He usually shows up near the end of the race, doesn't he?"

Harley stared. "So you want me to drive back to the Speedway — do you have any idea what post-race traffic is like?"

"Well, yes," said Bill. "Bristol was only last Saturday. Seems longer, doesn't it?"

"And you expect me to find that — that imposter, and bring him back here? You think I can do that? What if he didn't show up at this race?"

Bill Knight smiled. "Oh, I think he will. By now I'm beginning to believe that Dale will help us out with a miracle."

He hauled himself to his feet. "Don't you start."

"And Harley, get this done quickly, if you can. Drive quickly."

Harley sighed as he got to his feet. "Oh, I can drive quickly," he said. "I can do that."

★ ★ ★

Justine held Matthew's hand as they walked down the corridor of the hospital. "I thought about taking you to the cafeteria," she said. "I'll bet the food is pretty good. I had a boyfriend one time who was so cheap he used to take me to dinner there."

"Was he a doctor?"

"No. That's just it. He was an electrician, but he'd found that hospital food is the cheapest meal around, and it's always pretty good food, so he'd just go there and eat. Nobody ever asked him why he was there."

"So what happened to him?" asked Matthew.

"I don't know," said Justine. "I dumped him. Maybe he found some girl who admired his thriftiness. Or else a nurse."

"Where are we going then?"

Justine stopped at a nurse's station. "Good evening," she said to the woman behind the counter. "Could you please page Dr. Toby Jankin for me? Tell him it's Justine. He's expecting me, but he didn't know I'd have a patient for him. Matthew, honey, if you'll sit over there on that bench for a minute while I talk to old Toby, I promise we'll hit the cafeteria before we're done."

When the Impersonator turned up near the end of the race, Ray Reeve was glad of the distraction. By this time Jeff Gordon had begun to dominate the race, and Ray had a feeling of dread that told him Wonderboy was going to win. Two races in a row? He wondered if Gordon was having extraordinarily good luck or if Harley was cursed. He wished this could have been Junior's day, a sign perhaps that he was right to transfer his allegiance from father to son. He stopped watching the blur of cars whipping around the mile-and-a-third track and rested his gaze on the man in the white firesuit at the base of the Colvin Grandstand, accepting hugs and solemnly posing for photos with Earnhardt fans. Funny how the sight of the red-outlined number three or even the Goodwrench logo whizzing past on Kevin Harvick's car could bring a lump to the throat. He could understand why people didn't want to let go. He was tempted to go down there himself and shake the man's hand, just for the hell of it. A gesture of goodwill, perhaps.

Every so often the Impersonator would surreptitiously glance around, on the lookout for track security or maybe DEI people — whoever was after him. Ray wondered whether the problem was copyright infringement or trespassing or what. He didn't think the guy was any worse than an Elvis impersonator. Or all the people on Halloween who dress up as ex-presidents. But he could see how it might upset Little E. to think that people would rather watch an imitation of his dad than see him out there trying to win an actual race. *We can't forget him,* he said silently to Junior, *no more than you can, but we'll all move forward, because he'd expect us to.* Out of the corner of his eye, he saw men in suits striding toward the Impersonator, and with a few more handshakes, the man in the white firesuit had eased through the crowd, picking up speed as he went, heading for an exit.

Ray Reeve turned his attention back to the race, but much to his chagrin the rainbow-colored 24 car was still out in front.

Cayle found Bill Knight and Bekasu in plastic chairs in the waiting room, leafing through old copies of health magazines. "Any word yet?" she asked.

Bill shook his head. "Not that we've heard. Did you get in touch with the Powells' daughter in Seattle?"

"Yeah. Jean. She's very concerned about

her mother, of course. Wants her dad to call as soon as he can leave the bedside. She wants to apologize, she said." Cayle smiled, remembering the conversation. "Apparently she gave her dad a hard time about going on a NASCAR tour. You know the type." She studiously avoided looking at Bekasu as she said this. "Well, it turns out that she mentioned it as a joke to some of her snooty wine-and-cheese friends and got told in no uncertain terms that Greg Biffle was the pride of Washington State. He was last year's Busch Series Rookie of the Year, Bekasu — before you ask. He's from Vancouver, Washington, and apparently he has a bit of a following out there. Now I think Jean is hoping to sweet-talk her dad into getting her a tote bag from Darlington so she can impress her *architect*."

Bill Knight nodded. "I'm not surprised. I had a similar experience in New Hampshire with a lawyer of my acquaintance, I'm ashamed to say. Cultural stereotyping was never kind. These days it is also most unwise."

"You didn't see Justine while you were wandering around, did you?" asked Bekasu.

"No. She's still with Matthew, isn't she?

I expect he'll keep her out of trouble."

"It would take a straitjacket to do that."

Ratty Laine had tired quickly of the noise and fumes of the racetrack, and especially of the humid heat of South Carolina, which might be all right at the beach, but in street clothes he much preferred the cool sanctuary of his air-conditioned bus. Races lasted about three and a half hours, Harley had told him, and then he had to get his charges back to their hotel for the last night of the tour, before tomorrow's drive to Charlotte. He was studying the map, just to make sure he knew where they were going. The tour was more interesting than he'd thought it would be, although he doubted he'd remember much of it after a couple of weeks. There was a Civil War battlefield tour coming up, and then Lee would again mean "Robert E." rather than "Richard Petty's dad." Maybe he ought to make some notes in case Bailey Travel decided to offer this tour again, though. He just wished that bus drivers got as much respect and pay as stock car drivers.

A sudden tapping on the glass pane in the door made him look up, and the bundle of maps slid to the floor as Ratty found himself looking into the face of Dale Earnhardt.

Dr. Toby Jankin's initial delight at seeing an old girlfriend had given way to the Justine-shaped headache that he now remembered as an integral part of the relationship. He tried again. "Justine, you are not this boy's guardian. I cannot run medical tests on a minor without permission from his parents. Well, not his parents," he hastened to add, forestalling her objections. "You said he's a ward of the state. His social worker, then. Somebody has been appointed his legal custodian, and I can't treat him without their permission."

Justine's mulish expression did not change. "I'm not asking you to do brain surgery, Toby. I just want you to take a look at him. You can do that, can't you? I can pay you whatever it costs."

He sighed. Trust her to act as if money were the problem and blithely ignore national laws about the treatment of minors. Justine never asked for much. Just her own way 24/7. People usually found that it saved time just to give in at once. But there was a limit to the number of rules he could break without exchanging his medical practice for a ferret farm. He was on her side, really. She meant well, and for all he knew she might even be right, but there were laws that had to be observed — or at least nodded at.

He tried again. "Look, Justine. Let's go talk to the boy. He probably has his social worker's card with him in case of emergency. If you call her and get her to fax an authorization, I'll run some tests. But it's Sunday, so I doubt you'll be able to locate her."

It had been a silly thing to say, really, he thought as she swept from the room calling for Matthew. Of course Justine could locate a social worker on Sunday afternoon. It would only mean that she might have to inconvenience a few more people on the path to getting her own way; that would be only a minor obstacle, an hour's delay at most. He might as well find a treatment room and get the instruments ready. She-Who-Must-Be-Obeyed was back in his life.

Eight miles back to Darlington, racing the race itself, because if Harley didn't get back to the parking lot before the checkered flag, he would find himself in a two-lane blacktop parking lot that stretched for miles. Why was he even doing it? Any sane person would drive around Florence for an hour, maybe get a burger, and then report back that he had been unable to locate the elusive Impersonator. Maybe it was because Bill Knight was a minister, and Harley's Bible-belt upbringing had left a residual fear of lying to clergymen. He felt that such treachery might jinx his already tenuous chances of getting a miracle of his own — that is, a ride. Besides, he might as well tell Ratty where the medical center was, in case Ray Reeve had forgotten the name of the place.

Harley glanced at his watch. He had maybe half an hour before the Black Lady would declare a new champion in the Southern 500. At least he was heading in the opposite direction from the departing cars, so there wasn't much traffic to hinder his reaching the track. Nobody in Darlington ventured out grocery shopping or Sunday sight-seeing on race day. Now if he could just get in and out before the stampede started.

The bus was parked across the road from the Speedway, directly opposite the Stock Car Museum with its portraits of Dale Earnhardt and Richard Petty painted near the entrance. Harley pulled in next to the bus, as close as he could get to the parking lot exit. He didn't want to end up trapped here. He saw that the bus motor was idling. Ratty and his air conditioning. He'd better tell the driver what had happened before he began the exercise in futility.

Harley tapped on the window, waited while Ratty cranked open the door, and then bounded up the steps so as not to let out all the cool air. The radio was on, and Ratty was listening to the broadcast of the race, probably as a warning of departure rather than because he cared who would win.

"Hey, Ratty," he said. "We got a situation."

"You're telling me," grunted the driver.

"Oh, you know? Ray told you about Arlene? Where *is* Ray?"

Ratty shrugged. "Still watching the race. I haven't seen him. What do you mean 'where's Ray?' What about the rest of the flock?"

Harley explained about Arlene's heart attack and how everyone but Ray had gone along to the medical center to be there with Jim. "McLeod Medical Center," he said. "It's in Florence. I wrote down the directions for you."

Ratty glanced at the hastily scribbled notes on a paper bag. "You drove all the way back here to give me that?"

"No. The reverend sent me on a damn fool errand. Poor Arlene's mind is AWOL again, and she's asking to see Dale, so they got the bright idea to send me back here to try to find the Impersonator, and take him to the hospital to ease her mind. In this crowd. And him dodging security left and right. It would take a damn miracle to find him!"

Ratty nodded. "I guess it would at that," he said. "A miracle. Fortunately, Dale seems to be ready to oblige you with one." He nodded toward the back of the bus.

In the very back row, a scruffy little man with a ragged moustache and black sunglasses waggled his fingers at Harley.

Up close the spell was broken. The resemblance was good enough, thanks to the moustache and the shades, but the little man lacked the presence of the Intimidator. About forty million dollars short on confidence, Harley thought. That was how the fellow had ended up on the bus in the first place. In a voice that sounded more like Georgia than Kannapolis, the Impersonator told Harley how he had just managed to get out of the Speedway with the security people hustling through the crowd in hot pursuit. He'd hidden behind a car and seen the posse heading off toward the area where his own Chevy was parked. Not wanting to risk going that way and getting caught, he had set off in the opposite direction where he'd run straight into a bus with the words "#3 Pilgrimage" emblazoned on the side. He figured if anybody would help him, it would be these folks, so he'd knocked and, sure enough, the driver let him in.

He had been planning to hide out in the back of the bus until the coast was clear, but then Harley had showed up in need of a good deed for a gravely ill Earnhardt fan, and the Impersonator thought it was his duty to obey the summons.

He wouldn't tell Harley his real name. You couldn't be too careful, not with DEI after your hide and lawyered to the gills. He told Harley to call him R.D. — for Ralph Dale, Earnhardt's given name.

All this was explained on the drive back to Florence. The race was in its last ten laps when Harley had discovered him, so they wasted no time getting back into Harley's car and peeling out of the parking lot, with Ratty wishing them Godspeed and promising to follow as soon as Ray Reeve turned up. When they were well clear of the Speedway, Harley turned on the radio in time to hear Jeff Gordon proclaimed the winner of the 2002 Southern 500. He didn't feel much like talking after that.

"Where have you been?"

Justine faced the circle of anxious faces with her usual cheerful obliviousness. "Hey!" she said. "Matthew and I had some business to take care of. How's Arlene?"

After an awkward silence, Bill Knight said, "We've all been praying. But, as poor Jim said, it's hard to know what to pray for. Arlene has Alzheimer's, you know, and it might be merciful if she were allowed to go now in peace."

"We're still waiting," said Bekasu. "It's getting dark. I guess the race is over, and Ratty will turn up eventually and take us on to the hotel."

"Well, I would ask Toby to give us a ride, but he's on duty tonight, and besides I've already imposed on him enough."

Bekasu looked up at her sister. "Toby Jankin? You've been bothering doctors, Justine?"

She nodded. "Good thing I did. I got him to examine Matthew here, 'cause I figured medical care for orphans must be pretty dismal. Anyhow, guess what?"

"Wait," said Bill Knight. "Aren't there regulations about treating minors?"

Justine waved away his objections. "Taken care of. Called New Hampshire.

523

Told her I was you, Bekasu. It's amazing what judges can get people to do." She smiled at her stricken audience. "Well? Don't y'all want to know what he found?"

Still bereft of speech, they nodded.

"Well, Matthew's sick all right. Guess what he's got, though? *Mononucleosis.* A little time, a few pills, and he'll be good as new. Toby says it's not unusual at all for doctors to misdiagnose mono as leukemia in kids. Similar symptoms, I guess. Or maybe it's all those three-day shifts they make the residents pull. Scrambles their brains, I think. It's a wonder anybody ever gets out of one of these places alive —"

"Shut up, Justine."

She subsided. "Well," she said, sitting down and helping herself from an open bag of Skittles. "That's half of Matthew's problem solved. Wish I could do something about his mom, but that's not happening. So Matthew is going back to Canterbury with you, Bill, and if he doesn't find a family he likes in six months, he's going to call me and I'll spring him from the Children's Home. Right, Matthew? 'Cause in the human race, buddy, I'm your drafting partner."

Matthew, who had been sitting next to the muted television playing with his

Game Boy, looked up at Justine and nodded wordlessly. If Terence Palmer had been present, he would have recognized the hunted look of a young man cowed by the Mother Goddess.

Harley Claymore hated hospitals. He'd had about all he could take of this one. He had managed to make it back with the Impersonator by dusk and escorted the fellow upstairs to where the Number Three Pilgrims had taken over the waiting room. But after a few cups of coffee that tasted like battery acid, he had come out to the parking lot to smoke cigarettes and commune with the darkness. The building and the cars were just shapes against the night sky. He could be anywhere.

He supposed the bus would be along whenever Ratty managed to fight his way through the traffic. He was glad to be out of that waiting room with its smell of disinfectant and stale doughnuts. And the pervasive air of grief. They didn't think Arlene was going to make it. He was sorry about that, but at least she'd get to see her hero before she went. Maybe it was a blessing to be so addled that you could have illusions at the end of life. Harley had a feeling that he would go out someday, cold sober and knowing just how alone he was.

He studied the red glow of the cigarette in the darkness, glad to be alone again, relieved at the prospect of turning the Number Three Pilgrims loose tomorrow. He had nowhere to go, but at least after tomorrow he didn't have to worry about anybody but himself.

"Evenin,' Harley," said a soft voice in the darkness.

He jumped at the sound of his name. A man in a white Goodwrench firesuit and opaque sunglasses stood a few feet away from him, leaning against the hood of a car. In the darkness he was little more than a shadow, except for that white suit.

"Hello," said Harley. "That was a great thing you did in there, man."

A shrug. "Well, I owed a kid a miracle."

"Huh? Oh, they must have told you about young Matthew. That's about the only good news, though. 'Owed a kid a miracle.' " Harley smiled. "Good one. Dale's lucky penny, cemented to the dashboard of his car."

"S'right."

"But bringing some comfort to poor Arlene was a good deed, man."

"Well, one of the ladies up there said it best, I think. *Believing is seeing.* But, hey, blessed are they who don't believe and yet still see."

Harley was too tired to work out that one. Bad coffee and too many cigarettes were making his head hurt. "You want me to take you back to the Speedway for your car?"

"Somebody's picking me up."

Something in the quiet voice caught Harley's attention. He didn't hear the Georgia accent anymore. He heard pure Iredell County, soft vowels over stainless steel. "Are you the Impersonator?" he blurted out before he could feel foolish for asking.

In the darkness, a chuckle. "Oh, son, I always was. I dropped out of school in the ninth grade, and a million people were wearing my face on tee shirts. I always felt like *he* was somebody I played in public. *I* did the driving. *He* did the handshakes and the autographs. The driving was the best part, though. The rest just happened along the way."

"And then one day you're a legend, and people are putting wreaths on speedways to commemorate you."

"Well, to commemorate something. They didn't know me from Adam."

Harley smiled. "They're leaving wreaths for Adam, too, man."

"I don't know what they wanted. I just wanted to drive."

"Yeah," said Harley. "Me, too. You know I wrecked a while back. But I want to get back in the show."

There was a pause so long that Harley decided he didn't want to hear the answer, but then there was a sigh, and the man in the blackness said, "Sooner or later, you gotta move on."

"You're one to talk," said Harley.

"Just don't be writing checks that your body can't cash."

Harley nodded. Giving that advice was easier than taking it. "Listen," he said. "About Mrs. Powell. Is the old lady going to make it out alive?"

The man shook his head. "None of us makes it out alive, son. The trick is knowing when to die." He raised a hand in farewell. "Well, I gotta go. My ride's here."

Harley turned to see an old beat-up car waiting near the entrance to the parking lot. He didn't know why he'd expected to see a black Monte Carlo, Goodwrench logo and all, but the old clunker idling under the light was an early Nineties Lumina, two tone. Yellow and some darker color that he couldn't quite make out in the dim light.

"That's your car?"

The reply was a grunt. And then: "I own it. I don't drive it. You take it easy, Harley. See you down the road."

The man turned and walked toward the idling car. He climbed in the passenger seat, and the Chevy took off with a roar and a squeal of tires. They were out of sight in seconds, and it was only then that Harley realized what the second color of that old '94 Lumina must have been.

Butt-ugly, lemonade pink.

CHAPTER XX

Checking Out

Harley's umpteenth cigarette had burned low. He was enjoying the warm solitude of the parking lot. He just wished the clouds would roll on by so that he could see the stars. He probably ought to go back to the stuffy little waiting room, but there were hardly enough chairs to go around, and now that Ratty and Ray Reeve had joined the throng, there would be even less room than before. He'd exchanged a few words with Ratty there in the parking lot, and he'd remembered to get him to unlock the luggage compartment so that Harley could transfer his gear to the trunk of his car.

He tossed the butt of the spent cigarette onto the asphalt and ground it in with his heel. Maybe he ought to see about his luggage now. They could be coming out any time. He lifted the metal door to the luggage compartment and began pushing suitcases aside in search of his belongings.

He found his firesuit and driving boots. How could he have been stupid enough to bring those? What did he think? That Tony Stewart was going to get sick before the race and they'd ask Harley to take the wheel? With a sigh of disgust at his own folly, he slung the gear into the open trunk of his car, and felt around in the hold for his duffel bag.

Instead his hand closed on the end of a narrow cardboard box. There beside his duffel bag was one last wreath box, the final Earnhardt memorial. He slid part of the way in and emerged holding the wreath box, which he set on the pavement beside the bus. In all the excitement of the afternoon race and then Arlene's heart attack, no one had remembered the wreath ceremony for Darlington.

He pushed the knob to illuminate his watch face. Nearly ten o'clock. The Number Three Pilgrims were inside the hospital now, keeping Jim company and waiting for word on Arlene. Even without the hospital vigil, it would have been a long day, and they'd be wanting to get back to the hotel soon. Tomorrow Ratty would rout them out early to take them back to the Charlotte airport to pick up their cars or to catch flights for home. He didn't suppose any of them would want to drive back to the deserted Speedway to leave Dale Earnhardt a wreath, even if he'd earned it.

"They've forgotten all about it," said a voice in the darkness.

Harley had to clutch at the wreath to keep from falling over. He turned to see Bekasu Holifield standing there in her sensible suit and her high heels, but now with the Winged Three cap mashed down over her dark hair.

He nodded toward the hospital entrance. "Are they coming?"

"Not yet. They're going to turn off Arlene's life support in a little while, and nobody wanted to leave Jim alone. Even he thinks it's for the best, but of course it isn't easy. Then I suddenly remembered that we hadn't left the wreath so I came to find you."

"Don't worry," said Harley. "I'll take it myself. I reckon it's my turn."

"I think it's mine, too," said Bekasu. "May I come with you?"

He looked at her for one bewildered moment, but then, shrugging, he jerked open the passenger door and nodded for her to get in.

"How come you're wanting to go?" he asked as they eased out into the road.

She sighed. "I can't explain it, really. I suppose I must feel a little like that Roman G.I. who, halfway through a routine execution, suddenly *got* it, and probably spent the rest of his life muttering, 'Oh, shit.' Or *cloaca maxima,* or whatever they'd say in Latin. I guess it's Matthew's being all right that really got to me. I just want to thank somebody." She laughed. "Mind you, by tomorrow, in the clear light of day, I'll be arguing coincidence louder than anybody, but right now . . . in the dark of night . . . I'm willing to give him credit for the win. Hey — an artificial wreath. As trophies go, it isn't much, is it?"

Harley smiled. "Well, he already has a grandfather clock," he said.

They drove the rest of the way back to Darlington in a companionable silence. Harley was glad that Bekasu was not one of those nervous women who feel like they have to fill every breath with inconsequential chatter. He was too tired to rout out his inner receptionist, that hail-fellow persona he dredged up for social occasions.

Finally, though, he asked how things had been in the waiting room.

"Subdued," said Bekasu. "Reverend Bill was working up some kind of a lecture. I don't think it was a sermon. Anyhow, he's making notes comparing Dale Earnhardt and Neil Bonnett to Gilgamesh and Enkidu — never mind, Harley, it's rather obscure — I think he's planning a whole segment on NASCAR in his shrine collection. And Cayle is now convinced that R.D. is the person who fixed her car for her outside Mooresville. She's so relieved not to be the Joan of Arc of motor sports. I think they may have to drop him off in the bus when they're ready to leave."

Harley felt a chill at the back of his neck. "Didn't somebody already come by and pick him up?" he asked, willing himself to sound indifferent.

"He was still up there in the waiting room when I left," said Bekasu.

Harley said nothing, but he fumbled in his pocket for another cigarette, and found there wasn't one. He decided that he was never going to say anything about that incident in the parking lot. For one thing, people might think he hadn't got over that concussion from the wreck, and for another, it wasn't such a big deal. Not compared to the *other* miracle: the one where the average-looking kid with no formal education and no money conquered the world and made a million people cry when he died.

"And Matthew was asleep on the sofa beside Justine, who was trying to top his score on the Game Boy," Bekasu was saying. "Everybody else was watching a racing show on television. By the way, Jeff Gordon won today."

"I know," said Harley. "Apparently we had reached our bag limit on miracles."

"Well, you get the betting pool."

"Yeah. I'd rather have Jeff's ride."

Enough time had passed since the end of the race to evaporate the traffic jams, so when they reached the Speedway the Lady in Black was living up to her name — a dark shape in a starless night.

There were still a few cars in the parking lot, but Harley didn't see anybody around. He pulled up in front of the white building in front of the Speedway, where a black banner bore portraits of Earnhardt (in a panama hat with "Darlington" written on the band) and Richard Petty (in his customary black Stetson) staring out through their respective dark glasses as the world drove by. "How about under his picture?" said Harley, getting out and popping the trunk lid. He was thinking, *If I'd remembered it twenty minutes earlier, he could have taken it with him.*

At his side Bekasu nodded. "I think so.

What does this one say?"

He lifted the wreath out of its cardboard box. It was made of holly. *Holly?* thought Harley, wondering if the florist had tossed in a leftover Christmas wreath, or if this was a play on Holly & Edelbrock, which Justine would have appreciated. He didn't feel like explaining carburetors to Bekasu, though. Across the wreath's white banner red letters spelled out: *Rubbin' is Racin'*. He nodded to himself. It was good.

"Holly," said Bekasu, touching the wreath. "Bill Knight would have loved the symbolism of this one. Holly doesn't die in the winter when the rest of the leaves fall and the flowers wither away. So it's one of the symbols of life everlasting. Or of not taking no for an answer, I guess — not even from Mother Nature."

Together they propped the wreath up against the wall, beneath the portrait of a smiling Intimidator. "I'm glad nobody else is around," said Bekasu, edging closer to Harley. "I'd feel silly." Then she straightened up and touched the painted face on the wall. "I feel like I know you now," she said. "I'm finally beginning to see what people were going on about all these years. And I'll bet you'd probably think we were very silly, if not downright impertinent, to

536

be leaving flowers for you at a succession of speedways, but I guess you'll never know about it."

Don't bet on that, thought Harley.

"And maybe the love and grief we feel for someone who has gone isn't supposed to go out to them anyway. Maybe it's supposed to evoke something within ourselves. And so if we all came together because of this man, and if good things came out of it — friendships and help for those who needed it, and kindness — then we thank you for being the inspiration for those good deeds. That is miracle enough." She turned away and ended with a muttered, "No matter what my sister Justine says."

Harley wiped his eyes with the back of his hand. He wondered if there was anybody listening to what they were saying, other than themselves. But he supposed it didn't matter. He was going to speak respectfully — why risk getting run down in the parking lot by a phantom 1994 hot pink Chevy Lumina? "Well, you changed the sport and you changed the world, man," he said to the face on the wall. "You're a lap ahead now, but then you always were. You don't need us to tell you that. But if you've got any luck lying around that you don't have a use for where

537

you are, I could do with some right now. Thanks for the ride, Dale." He gave the three-peace salute and turned away.

They were silent for a few moments. The tour was over. The last wreath placed. Now what?

"You did good," Harley told Bekasu. "You listened, and you took part, and you didn't make everybody miserable. That's good."

"Thanks," she said. "I'll make you a promise. Next time I hear one of my friends make some condescending remark about racing, I'll call them on it. I will."

Harley nodded. He didn't much care what smug, dumb yuppies thought, but he knew that the gesture was kindly meant. "Do you want me to take you back now?" he asked her.

"Not especially," she said. "It's not very late. That is, if you have nothing better to do."

Harley shook his head. "Nowhere to go," he said. "Why?"

She shrugged. "There's one thing Dale Earnhardt has made me realize. I've been on a short leash all my life, Harley. I was the honor student in high school, too up-tight to run with the fast crowd, but always wondering what I missed out on while I was home studying. All this has made me face the fact that life doesn't go on forever."

"Well, life's too short for restrictor plates, anyhow," said Harley.

"I feel like I want more out of this trip than sitting in a bus or watching a couple of races."

"Uh-huh." Harley was beginning to detect the family resemblance between Bekasu and Justine. The family madness was simply better camouflaged in the judge. And it took you longer to realize that she was pretty, while Justine practically hit you over the head with pheromones.

Bekasu was taking deep breaths of the moist summer air and shaking her head like a horse getting ready to bolt. "Can we do some laps out there on the track?" she said. "I want to see what it feels like to go that fast."

"Uh — I can go ask the guard. If he's an old-timer here, he'll remember me."

"Good. Can we do a yard?"

" 'Scuse me?"

"That's what the gang kids say sometimes in traffic cases. It means to go a hundred miles an hour. Doing a yard."

"I think I can manage that. And then

would you like to go get some dinner?"

Bekasu was on a roll. "How about we find a beer joint somewhere? Live music and sawdust on the floor!"

"One lap at a time," said Harley.

She smiled. "You remind me of this I guy I knew back in high school. I was always scared of him, because he was so remote. Like he was encased in ice, and the rest of us were beneath his notice. I always wondered what he did when he wasn't slouched in the back row of class, reading *Popular Mechanics*."

"What ever happened to him?"

"God knows," said Bekasu. "But *nothing* ever happened to me. So let's fix that."

Well, it would be a hell of a week, thought Harley, but sooner or later she'd start talking about getting an associates degree in automotive whatever, and then he'd start checking out. Or maybe not. She was right about one thing: if you don't start, you can't win.

Bekasu pulled out her cell phone. "You go ask if we can use the track. I just have to tell Justine not to wait up." She walked out toward the road, punching the number pad as she went.

Harley started to walk toward the guard's hut to the right of Gate Six, hoping that whoever was on duty tonight was old enough to remember when "Junior" meant "Johnson." He had his NASCAR license on him, though, and that ought to count for something.

"That was a nice thing you did back there."

Harley spun around wondering who the hell else had decided to turn up tonight. Louis Chevrolet, for God's sake? Harley Earl? But the man in the straw hat who had fallen into step with him was very much alive, and more powerful than a 1988 Elliott engine. He was somebody Harley had wanted very much to talk to — just not in a deserted parking lot with a runaway judge on his hands.

"Saw you all leaving some flowers back there under Dale's picture," the man said. "Some kind of memorial?"

"That's right," said Harley. "Wanted to say good-bye. Wish him well."

The man nodded. "That's a nice thing you did. I like that."

"Well," said Harley, "he's sorely missed."

The straw hat bobbed in agreement. "I was in the museum there with some of the guys. They let us look around after the race. Couple of cars in there for sale. I was thinking about getting one to put on display back at the shop, you know? That's how I happened to notice you outside. Good to see you around again, Harley. You back to speed after that crash you had?"

"Right as rain."

They walked on a few more paces, with Harley almost afraid to breathe for fear of jinxing himself. Then the man, who was so rich and powerful that his ordinary middle-aged appearance was practically a secret identity, said, "Speaking of the shop . . . you know, I could use a test driver. If you feel like you're up to it, why don't you come see me when you get back?"

Harley nodded. "I'll do that, sir," he said. "I'd be honored." Suddenly he remembered a scrap of newspaper that had been riding around in his wallet since the night in the bar in Concord. He fished it out and handed it to the man in the hat. "Speaking of Dale, sir, this article's about a young man who started a program called *Driving for Dale* to help senior citizens get to doctors' appointments and so on. The fellow is going to take automotive courses at Northeast State in Tennessee, and since he's a newlywed, I think he might need a little financial aid or an internship at Bristol. Can you see that the right people get to see this write-up?"

"I'll do that," said the man, pocketing the clipping. "And I'll see you at the shop — when?"

Harley hesitated. "Would Wednesday be okay? I have something to finish up."

Well, she worked in Charlotte. If she didn't start screaming at a hundred miles an hour, and if she didn't order anything with fruit in it at the roadhouse, and if she hadn't said anything about a community college by Wednesday, then . . . then they'd have to see.

"Hope to see you down the road," said Harley as the man walked away. But he was talking to the sky.

AUTHOR'S NOTE

Dale Earnhardt deserved a book not just for his excellence on the speedway, but also for the extraordinary effect he had on thousands of people he never even met — the people who mourned him by leaving flowers at the nearest speedway that February night, or by writing memorial poems in his honor and posting them on the Web, or by displaying the number 3 with sentiments like "God needed a driver." I'm sure that Dale would be the first to tell you he wasn't a saint, but I think the outpouring of grief that followed his death would have moved him.

For years, I have been fascinated by the idea of secular sainthood. When I was in graduate school, I cornered Dr. Charles Kennedy, who was then chair of the religion department at Virginia Tech, and asked him why Elvis had become the new saint, rather than, say, John Lennon, who seemed much more spiritual to me. Dr.

Kennedy said that perhaps Lennon was too avant-garde for the general population, but that Elvis, who had served his country, loved his momma, and given away Cadillacs, exemplified a level of righteousness that ordinary people could grasp. We talked about the qualities in the twelfth-century saint Thomas Becket that we could recognize in his twentieth-century counterparts: a rise from humble beginnings to a position of wealth and influence; a pattern of remaining true to one's roots and not losing touch with the common man; an untimely death that dashed the hopes of admirers who lived vicariously through the hero's exploits.

I wanted to do a book on the canonization of a secular figure — a *Canterbury Tales* with a modern saint — but I lacked the proper inspiration to do justice to the idea.

Then on February 18, 2001 a new saint entered the pantheon.

Dale Earnhardt, who was from my home state and my generation, was deeply mourned, even by people who had not been his supporters in life. When the memorial number 3s began appearing everywhere I looked (even in Christmas lights on a neighbor's roof), I thought I could

understand the substance and the under-
lying sorrow of his loss, and that I could at
last write about this theme. Perhaps because my dad was a football coach, I had
not grown up as a fan of motor sports, but
I knew the time and place of Dale's story.
So I began to study racing, and now I get
it.

Since this is a novel, I have taken small
liberties with chronology, most notably:
the Earnhardt Tower was completed at the
Bristol Motor Speedway a few days after
the 2002 Sharpie 500; the Richard Petty
Museum moved to its present quarters on
Academy Street a few months after the
Number Three Pilgrims's visit in the fall of
2002; and Route 136 in Iredell County became Route 3 six months after Cayle's car
trouble. In each case, since the time dis-
crepancy involved was only a matter of
days or months, I have described the place
as you will find it now if you visit.

My friend Jane Hicks, a published poet
with two master's degrees, has been a lifelong fan of stock car racing, so in the early
days of my research — back when I
thought that Kurt Busch was the governor
of Florida — she took me in hand and introduced me to the world of NASCAR. I
could not have done it without her. Now

she has to put up with e-mails from me raging over the points standings or the outcome of the last race.

Michaela Hamilton, my wise and fearless editor, took on this project when more timid souls at other publishing houses assured us that no one would buy a novel about stock car racing. Her encouragement and willingness to back this book has been a miracle in itself.

My thanks to Junior Johnson and to Leonard Wood of Wood Brothers Racing for their wisdom and patience; to East Tennessee State University and Bristol Motor Speedway for offering the NASCAR Experience course, which I took, and to Mark Martin, whose book *NASCAR for Dummies* was my starting point; step one of a long journey.

I'm grateful to the Junior League of Bristol for their help and encouragement. Mike Smith of the Martinsville Speedway let me observe two races from the press box, and he very kindly shared his reminiscences with me on the Earnhardt Era of racing. Thanks, too, to Dean and Teresa Mayer, Henry Knight, Kyle McCurry, JoAnn Reeves, Cal Royall, Amelia Townsend, Tresha Lafon, Chrissie Anderson Peters, Linda Wilson, Gale

Whigam, Kathy Calaway, and Laree Hinshelwood for their help and enthusiasm on various facets of this project.

Jerry Bledsoe, the greatest expert on stock car racing that I knew, heard me out at the very beginning ("You're doing what?") and was an inspiration and a great critic. Jerry's Down Home Press also published an early biography of Dale Earnhardt by Frank Vehorn that was most helpful in documenting races that happened decades ago.

Tom Deitz, who knows more about cars than a medievalist and fantasy novelist has any right to, kept me straight on mechanical details and the fine points of drag racing.

And thanks to you who are reading this, for being willing to read a novel set in the world of NASCAR — that makes you part of the miracle.

Sharyn McCrumb

About the Author

SHARYN MCCRUMB is an award-winning writer whose novels have been both *New York Times* Bestsellers and Notable Books. McCrumb's honors include: the 2003 Wilma Dykeman Award for Literature given by the East Tennessee Historical Society; AWA Outstanding Contribution to Appalachian Literature Award; Chaffin Award for Achievement in Southern Literature; Plattner Award for Short Story; Best Appalachian Novel. Her books have been translated into more than ten languages, and she was the first writer-in-residence at King College in Tennessee. In 2001 she served as fiction writer-in-residence at the WICE Conference in Paris. Sharyn McCrumb has lectured on her work at Oxford University, the Smithsonian Institution, the University of Bonn, Germany, and at universities and libraries throughout the country. She lives and writes in the Virginia Blue Ridge. You can visit her Web site at www.sharynmccrumb.com.

The employees of Thorndike Press hope you have enjoyed this Large Print book. All our Thorndike and Wheeler Large Print titles are designed for easy reading, and all our books are made to last. Other Thorndike Press Large Print books are available at your library, through selected bookstores, or directly from us.

For information about titles, please call:

(800) 223-1244

or visit our Web site at:

www.gale.com/thorndike
www.gale.com/wheeler

To share your comments, please write:

Publisher
Thorndike Press
295 Kennedy Memorial Drive
Waterville, ME   04901